Arroyo Coyote

Hooper's Junction
Book Two

KK Crews

01111623

Also by KK Crews

Hooper's Junction Series

Hooper's Junction
Arroyo Coyote
Moths to the Flame
Threshold

This book is dedicated to all the readers and writers of books, who find joy in surrendering to worlds that are just a little more magical and a little more supernatural than the real world. To the ones who choose to take that unorthodox sabbatical into the fantastical.

Contents

Sunny With a Chance of Rain

I

There are many reasons why people uproot themselves from their cozy homes and move into the unknown. I have two. The first is to help out a friend who is a sometimes-client. She is temporarily leaving the country to bestow her highly desirable financial and technological wizardry onto an international banking company in Dubai. Never mind that she is a quirky, obsessive introvert who is undoubtedly on the spectrum. She needed a house sitter. So, I am happy to oblige because of my second reason; I am determined to move my mother and her foster kid into my small adobe house in Santa Fe, New Mexico. Here she and the boy, Diego, will be under the protection of my neighbor, Señor Rivera. The truth is that we–myself, Diego, and Mr. Rivera–are probably sitting ducks for the evil that has unexpectedly arisen in our lives, no matter where we are. But damn, I cannot allow myself to linger on thoughts like that or paranoia will hijack my life.

Because my place is a mite *too* cozy for three humans and a dog, I have moved forward on this slightly complicated relocation project, which at first might look, to those who know me, a bit capricious and impulsive, but the last few months of my life have made me cautiously wary and protective. Surrounded by an audience of boxes, I can't help but fuss over the way my life has unfolded. As if the first fifty years haven't been weird enough, the last month has challenged me with a new kind of terror and pain that leaves scars. But here too lies the polar opposite of my wonky personal narrative compass as it was a month that also brought the kind of joy that I never could have imagined: the love of my life, an old man and a young boy who share my proclivities for disembarking into other people's past life incarnations, and the opportunity for a client of mine to become my hero. It is all of this that leads me to the temporary decampment of my adorable little home in a historic part of the city for some time in the country.

The sudden knock on my front door turns Maca into a skittering, tail-wagging, barking, greeter. After all of our years together, I can quickly decode this into 'we know them' or 'we know them not'. This is decidedly her 'we know them' bark. In fact, before I can extricate myself from my cardboard fortress, my friend Graciela sticks her head through the door and starts sweet-talking the dog.

"Good thing I'm no bad guy, amiga. Your damn dog might lick me to death, and I think I could still get away with the kitchen sink." She looks around the room. "By the way, which box has the kitchen sink?"

I'm finally on my feet and hobble stiffly over to her and give her my best bear hug and a kiss on the cheek.

"Those snake bites still got you limping, huh? Have you been going to the physical therapist like the doctor says? Don't think I don't know what you do. The first person you start to neglect when you get these wild hairs for change is you. Even though you're excited about moving, you gotta take care of yourself, corazon."

I can't help but dwell for a moment in her loving admonishments. She and I have had thirty-plus years of sharing this roller coaster ride. The eerie sixth sense that we have with each other far exceeds the ability we humans have to know each other's spirits in one lifetime. Although I haven't found it yet, I know that Graci and I have shared more than this lifetime together. Over the years I have witnessed many glimpses of her past lives, but as of yet, I haven't sensed the presence of myself in any of them. I smile at her. I haven't given up yet.

"Can you believe this mess," I whine while sweeping one of my arms grandly around the room. "I told my mother she could move in over the weekend. It's Thursday already and I haven't gotten a thing out of here." I glance at the Guatemalan mask that is hanging on the wall watching the door for evil. Graci sent me that mask while she was in South America visiting her sons. She felt compelled to get it for me when she started getting these uneasy vibes that seemed to suggest that I was somehow messing with bad voodoo. My words, not hers, but she was right. She was so right. Looking back, so much of it just feels excruciatingly surreal, maybe like it wasn't even my life. But the aftermath of three rattlesnake bites and heroin track marks up and down my arm, is enough of a daily reminder that the whole sordid affair and the abomination who carried out the attempt to end my life are undeniably real. And wherever that devil of a man escaped to, I hope it is as far away from me and my people as is planetarily possible. I decide to leave the mask where it is.

"So, Marta, why you movin' so much stuff? You're house-sitting, right?" I nod and lean back against a stack of boxes, giving her the eye. "And your friend is leaving most of her stuff in the house, right?"

"You're right," I concede, "but you know my mother. And now she's got Diego in tow. Diego will be lucky to find a tunnel to his room by the time she gets all her stuff in here. That room, by the way, took me two weeks to clean out, and then I had to find a bed and a dresser and make it marginally acceptable for a ten-year-old boy." I sight and look up at my friend. "Three months, Graci, that's all I'll be gone, but she will come packed like she's driving a covered wagon and moving west."

"Yeah, you're probably right, about everything except the direction. It's moving north from Albuquerque. The good news is… you guessed it. That's why *I'm* here. I'm at your beck and call for the rest of the day." She runs her fingers through her new short hairdo. At fifty-one her locks are still a mostly enviably raven black except for two matching half-inch wide wicked silver streaks that shoot through her hair like blazing comet tails. "But first you have to woo me with a cup of your strongest brew. I slept terribly last night."

"You worried about me, hermana," I tease as I make my way to the kitchen. "Dark roast?" I ask though I already know the answer.

"So, what I really want is a chance to see this new place of yours," she declares between gulps of coffee. "What d'ya say we take a ride out there later and drop off some of these boxes." With her feet propped up on the coffee table and Maca playing lap dog, half on and half off her lap, Graciela calms me as she always does with her confident, untroubled presence.

"That would actually be great," I respond, "since Cassandra said she was going to leave quite a bit of food in her fridge. She said, and I quote, 'Have at it'. I still need to figure out what else I might need in the first few days. It's not like I can make a five-minute run to the grocer's once I move out there. And your timing couldn't be better. I really need some inspiration here. I'm definitely overwhelmed and getting nowhere fast. I'll owe you big time." I tell her this truthfully, before needling her just for the fun of it, with my best sarcastic eye roll. "And maybe I'm craving just a wee bit of your camaraderie." She gives me her yeah-right smile, but then I see her thoughts pull her away, her gaze turning inward to her inner landscapc for a moment.

"So have you seen Maria lately?" she finally returns and asks, putting the coffee cup down on a box and gently moving Maca to the floor. She walks over to gaze thoughtfully at the mask.

I can tell by the way she lowers her voice into a soothing yet earnest tone, that she wants to open the door to reviewing my most recent events. But she leaves it up to me whether to walk in... or not. Because Maria is a client in my counseling practice, I have to tread carefully, even though Graciela is fully aware of Maria's entanglement with drugs, her drug-dealing boyfriend, and her involvement in my kidnapping. It was her slimy boyfriend who kidnapped me and held me prisoner, all the while working for that madman, Misterioso, who supposedly is an incarnation from some inconceivable past life we shared. It was he who sought to exact a horrifying revenge upon me, for a wrong that I did to him long long ago. Thus, both Maria and I have been living with the aftermath of what felt like a harrowing journey through the land of perdition.

"She's actually doing okay," I say somewhat noncommittally, then amend the bland statement, because I think that this friend of mine actually deserves better than that. "I did meet with her last week. She's going to take another stab at her senior year in the fall, and she has stayed off the heroin. She and I both have to show up to testify against Tomás Moscoso. He's been charged with contributing to a minor, drug trafficking, and kidnapping. He needs to be put away, but the tragedy, as you well know, is that the demon incarnate is still out there and this is making me feel nauseated just talking about it."

"I'm so sorry, Marta. I thought maybe you were feeling strong enough to talk about it a little. We can drop it, but do you think I'd be allowed in the courtroom to come with you? When is the trial, corazon?" I start to answer but she continues. "Actually, it doesn't matter when it is, because if they'll let me in, I'm going to be there. Hell, they can't stop me." Graci turns from the mask and looks in one of the boxes that is completely full. She mindlessly folds the flaps in to seal it up. "Okay, let's change the subject to something less disturbing, but just know that I will find a way to be there with you. Promise. Maybe I can get my cereal box lawyering license. How about that?" she laughs. "So, speaking of ex-lawyers, how's that boyfriend of yours? What's the mad musician up to these days?"

"Geez, has it been that long since we've talked? I haven't told you that John got a recording contract and will be heading up to Denver in a week to lay down the tracks for a real album with his buddies. He really wanted me to go with him, but he understands all my responsibilities here in town, so he didn't press it."

"Ooh la la, Dr. Hooper's in love." Graci croons. "In love with a suave rock star. So has he seen your new digs yet?"

"Nope. Cassandra just left the day before yesterday. I'm the only one who's seen it. It's a sweet little place and a chance for me to see if I like 'country living'. It's not that big. I think she had an architect friend of hers help her remodel it. It's kind of a contemporary log cabin with a lot of nice touches, like a deck with primo views of Shaggy Peak and Lake Peak."

"Did you time how long it takes to get to your office?"

"Not exactly to my office, but it's probably about thirty minutes. It's the dirt road part that takes a while; still, it's not too bad."

"Well let's get crackin' on all this packin', mi amiga. I can't wait to see it." She comes over and gives me a big reassuring hug. I can always count on Graciela.

II

Unbeknownst to me, Graciela has borrowed a friend's small pickup, so by the time we fit the last box into the bed, I am amazed to see that the rooms of my little house look almost empty. Just right for the refitting it will undergo this weekend. It kind of makes me smile inside to think that Diego, my mom, and Mr. Rivera will be sharing this neighborly-hood and a chunk of time together. Already I have seen the potential for a bond forming between my mom and the charming viejo. What a remarkable thing to find out that there is not just one, but actually two other people in this world who share this aberrant facility of mine to dive into other people's past lives. Leave it to my mom to uncover a ten-year-old orphan boy who has been dealing with the same affliction as me, that of involuntarily being sucked into the past lives of friends and strangers alike. Moreover, after all these years, I discover that my neighbor has also been harboring not only these powers but also some sense of how all of our paths profoundly intersected in another lifetime. With the covertness of a seasoned operative, this gentle, eighty-year-old widower neighbor, has secretly designated himself my self-appointed protectorate. Then I find out, kind old Señor Rivera has also had a much better understanding of, not only how we all got these hind-sightful powers, but also of the deception and duplicity that we employed to cast out the fourth member of our little guild, Mr. Misterioso, also known as my attempted murderer. I don't even know his real name in either lifetime, though I have become partial to the phantom of the opera.

"You seem lost in your thoughts," Graci remarks as she guns the motor and shifts into the passing gear to get around a crawling 1980s Ford Pinto that looks like it has bullet wounds and very little of its red paint left. The kid in the driver's seat flips her the bird, but with her usual aplomb, she waves her two-fingered peace sign out the window.

"Just enjoying the scenery that I'm going to be commuting through for the next few months. It's good to know there's a gas station and a convenience store on this road. You know, just in case." I look out the open sliding window behind us, back to the truck bed to make sure my boxes are secure. "So, you need to turn left up here at the light."

We pass through an area of very expensive homes perched high on the faces and tops of the surrounding foothills. "I find that so disturbing," I say more to myself.

"What's so disturbing?"

"All those houses up there, desecrating the foothills."

"People gotta live somewhere, you know."

"Maybe, but I'll wager that half those houses are lived in only half the time. It's a safe bet that most of those people built those monsters as vacation homes or whatever."

"You know, she says conversationally, "I agree with you, but my money's on the odds that if you ever met any of those homeowners, say, out in the streets or through your practice, you'd probably like them just fine and you'd be the first one to find all kinds of admirable qualities in them. Yep, because that's just the kind of sucker you are." Graci turns and smiles at me. "Okay, where to now?"

We have passed through a small village with houses and a church, lined up next to the narrow, paved road as it winds its way higher into the ponderosa foothills. Her request for directions comes just as the pavement turns to a rocky dirt road.

"Just stay on course." I have to speak up as the engine whines a bit climbing upwards and the tires spit out loose gravel. The road continues upward, but after a few minutes turns to softer dirt. "There," I say as I point to an unmarked right turn off this road.

Now just keep following this road. We'll pass a few driveways on the left, but Cassandra's is about another half mile on the right."

Graci bends her head down and looks me in the eye over the top of her sunglasses. "You sure you're going to be okay, way out here all by yourself?"

"Just fine, Graci. Wait till you see this place. You're going to want to have all kinds of slumber parties with me out here. And I haven't even told you the best part. She's got two horses I get to take care of.

The cabin itself is not visible as we turn into the driveway which is about another eighth mile of driving up a gentle hill. Once we are on top, we are looking back down over a meadowy area carpeted with sparse native grasses, snakeweed and colorful wildflowers, all highlighted by a dozen giant elderly Ponderosa pines whose branches are dancing in the wind and whose needles glisten sharply with the sunlight. Downslope from the house and garage is a well-maintained barn with a large, attached corral and just as I promised my friend, there stand two horses, statuesque in their rapt attention at our approach.

"The neighbors have been feeding them the last couple of days," I chatter excitedly. The anticipation I am feeling to be able to call this place my own even for just a few months is tantamount to some of the first Christmas mornings I remember from my childhood. Graci gives me a breezy, indulgent smile which is her typical initiation sequence of caving into my way of thinking, and now it's mixed with the same whimsical wonderment that hit me the first time I saw this place.

Once parked, we both disembark with Maca right on our heels. Greedily and without hesitation or second thoughts, we stand like ancient stumps stilled by the timelessness of the uncultivated world lying bucolic all about us. With a breath, we ingest the pine-scented air, and it brings a serotonin rush to the brain.

Witnesses to a deep cloud shadow gliding across the terrain, are we, and it moves like a balmy yearning across the terrain of our bodies as well. A migrating mound of whipped clouds builds into the impossibly blue sky. Our stupor is broken at the sound of ravens squawking in the trees. But this too is woven into the buzz and hum of summer at 7,500 feet. Cassandra's chimes tinkle from the front porch as the sweet odor of hay and manure is swept up the hill by the migrant breeze.

Graci shakes herself. "Okay then, let's get a look at the house." Maca is dashing around our feet, running twenty yards toward the corral, then hurtling back underfoot again. Doghappy to feel so much uncluttered free range around her, her pink tongue is lolling from the side of her muzzle and her doggy spirit is visibly unbridled. Graci and I, as if we were synchronized swimmers, turn and take in the humble little cabin with unblinking eyes and hands hanging freely at our sides. I can almost smell the fragrance from the hand-hewn cedar logs used to construct this single-story rustic building. Though the building is not large, the covered portal extends the width of the front of its front. Usually furnished with seating and other patio-type accouterments, Cassandra's porch lies barren, without luxury or fuss. To the right, though an oak-colored blind closes off our view, is a very large window which I know is the living room. The smaller window to the left of the door, though I can't quite recall the floorplan, most likely hides one of the bedrooms. A layered stone chimney rises from the right side of the living room wall, architecturally cozy, but a feature I will probably have no use for. A few newly planted aspens quake tenderly in the breeze keeping a measured beat with the chimes. I fumble for the key and make my way onto the porch.

Once inside, it is cool and dim. Not surprisingly, the prevailing scent that greets us is a spicy medley of fresh cedar and Murphy oil. With the blinds closed, the cabin has a clean cool feel to it. The building seems well insulated against heat and cold. It takes a moment for our eyes to adjust, but when they do, Graciela gives a surprised whistle.

"Did she like, truly move out, or is she really this ascetic? Where's all her stuff?"

"It looks exactly the way it looked when I was out here before. I told you she's a different breed of woman. I actually wonder, now that I know her pretty well, how she will ever survive Dubai, the noise and traffic, not to mention all the social interactions that will be required of her." I watch Graciela as she begins her big snoop. "So… what do you think so far?" I ask.

"Did she leave you dishes… How about pots and pans to cook with?"

"Those glass doors on the cabinets make the shelves look pretty empty from where I'm standing," I answer.

Looking around the room I have to agree wholeheartedly with Graciela. The place is acutely spartan. There are three pieces of furniture in this large open room that encompasses the kitchen, dining room, and living room: a leather sofa that is in the middle of the room facing the large picture window, a mammoth bookcase that spans the west wall, that is teeming with books, begging and crying out to be opened, volumes that I know wish to be wielded and read, and a small two-person oak table in what could be a fairly lavish dining area, but isn't. The floors are beautifully finished, with wide, oak planks that gleam with expert care.

As Graciela continues to sleuth about, I check the fridge, which, unlike the rest of the house's restrained décor, is packed with wine, various exotic cheeses, yogurts with French names, numerous packages of smoked salmon and prosciutto, as well as, jars and jars of various kinds of olives. I cannot judge her impeccable taste in her choice of staples. Closing the fridge door I move over to the bookshelves and feel an overwhelming sense of desire as I pull out what has to be a collector's volume of The Iliad and the Odyssey by Homer. I just barely spy a run of poetry volumes when I hear an inelegant exclamation from somewhere deeper in the house.

"Look at this, Marta. I haven't seen one of these in years." Graciela's voice is muffled coming from somewhere in the back.

Reluctantly I walk away from the bookshelf, but not before gently sweeping the bumpy spines of dozens of books with the tips of my fingers. The hallway is impossibly dark and I wish I had opened the blinds before leaving the front room, but I manage to find Graci squatting on one of the three-bedroom floors captivated by the only object in the room besides a twin bed and a simple wooden chest of drawers.

"Come look, amiga. It's a rocking horse," she whispers.

I kneel down awkwardly beside her and she steadies me with a hand on my arm.

"I swear I had one of these when I was a niñita. But it's so weird because I have no recollection of it in my parent's house. Not anywhere, anytime. But it's so clearly there in my memory."

Maybe your abuelos had one for you or you played with one at a friend's house. I don't remember anything like it at your house when I came over."

"It's kind of eerie because as soon as I saw it I knew that feeling of being so little and rocking endlessly and believing it was a real horse, and oh my, the places I would go."

I give the little horse a pat on the head before pushing myself painfully back to standing, but Graci stays down there rocking the little pony back and forth. I can see she's totally lost in trying to place this little guy in her present memory.

"You know, Graci, there could be another explanation." My tongue is still articulating the word "explanation", when I am left dragging the word behind me as I am gently tugged into the familiar landscape of Graciela's remembrances, those buried deeply in her soul.

I feel myself softly alight onto her world, far from Cassandra's room, centuries removed from the woman I know. Vanished are the familiar elements from our time, subsequently replaced by a large room with an oddly woody, perfumed smell. There in front of me, a large stone fireplace crackling and dancing with flames lends solace and warm glow to the room. An elaborate mantel of exquisitely carved wood is embellished with ornamental gold leafing that clings to its frontboard like ivy on a wall. Such opulence, I think. Behind me, I hear the contented off-key humming of a child. A rhythmic tapping accompanies the highs and lows of the sweet voice. I know I can turn to behold this child without disturbing her, but I pause, momentarily spellbound by the serene tranquility of this moment by firelight, by the untroubled ease I sense in the child. On the mantel, there is a large clock perhaps made of black slate. The clock face is round and ticks steadily around beautifully formed Arabic numbers. A sculpture of a muscular black horse, rearing back, with his groom on the rein, tops the mantle scene. With a slight shift of my focus, I can now see a painting hanging above the hearth, a man and a woman, both distant in their gaze and dressed in a Victorian style. Atop the woman's lap is a baby dressed in a lavish frilled white gown.

Finally, shifting my non-existent body so that I can take in the child, I see that I have been listening to a child of five or six years. Her flaxen hair tumbles over her shoulders. Bright green eyes are caught up in the view just outside a window dressed in thick velvety curtains pushed aside to provide a rainy view of a stately but dormant garden. The child who wears the deeply preoccupied expression of someone much older does not surprise me. I smile. Perhaps she envisions the strange woman she will one day be; I really don't understand the machinations of how all this time travel works. I relax, continuing to study the child that will one day become my friend in another incarnation. Her proper green satin dress swishes as she rocks at a crisp measured cadence that matches the melody she hums. Her pony is white with dapplings of gray painted expertly on the wooden body. The mane and tail flow long and thick in an ebony cascade and the arc of the wooden rockers is large enough to render the rider an exquisite rise and fall with a gentle tap to the floor at its apex. I am captivated by her small pale hands that hold firmly to the reins, her leather-booted feet swinging freely along the belly of the horse. There, at the belly, I chance to see a small hatch-like cut-out with a latch for opening and closing. Interesting. I feel languorous and remote as I waver here in this peaceful place, in this faraway home. It's like the beginning of a fairytale. Then as usually happens, the feeling of motion commences without warning. As usual, there sets in the sensation of my insides being pulled outside. It causes a gentle concussion to the scene I am witnessing and with a bit of reluctance, I feel myself riding the white line of the intangible stratum of time. I travel forward, as always drawn to the extant body that I call my own, the one that awaits me in the plain little room in Cassandra's plain little house.

My vision clears slowly, and I feel the need to rub the cloudiness from my eyes, but as they refocus, I see that the setting has not changed. Graciela is still crouched next to the rocking horse, but now she is staring at me, her expression a mixture of curiosity and consternation.

"Where were you, Martha Hooper? Tell me!" she demands.

The nerves of my leg tingle and a deep aching pain rides up my calf. I move to the bed to sit down and then return her look with an amused and secretive one.

"Tell me, Graci, does that horse have a little trap door on its belly?"

"What are you talking about, bruja?" She swings around and looks the horse in the eye, but then slowly drops her hand underneath the toy and feels along the belly.

"You're a scary woman, you know that, right?" she says in her wise-ass tone accompanied by the wise-ass smug look that I know and love.

Moving the boxes from the truck to the cabin left me wilting on the leather sofa even though Graciela did the lion's share of lifting. I'm checking my cell in the coolness of the cabin while Graci and Maca walk down to the corral to greet the horses. I know I should be there with them since Maca has never really been around livestock but at Graci's insistence I put my affected leg up on a pillow and rest for the moment.

Sure enough, I have somehow missed a call from John, but I see that he has left a voice message. "*Where are you, Martha? I know you took the day off. Want to have dinner tonight?* His message is sung in a silly yodeling kind of voice and I chuckle at this. There's also a text message from Maria which I open quickly and apprehensively even though I know she's been doing pretty well. *Dr. Hooper- just wanted to let you know that Chela had her baby. Little Ricardo is here!*

I am so excited I jump up off the sofa as if my leg were as strong and flexible as a sapling tree trunk. Even when I feel the tingling twinge, I keep going out the door and down the hill, yelling Graciela's name. She turns from the corral where she is feeding a handful of grass to the palomino mare.

"What is it, Martha? Wait, I'm coming to you." She and Maca start up the hill at a dash. We meet in the middle, all of us panting and wild-eyed.

"Chela had her baby!" I crow, like one of those noisy ravens. I'm swinging my cell phone above my head like it is living proof of the event.

"Chela had her baby?" she repeats as a question.

"Oh my gosh, Graci," I pant, "I can't wait to see that little guy."

"Well, text Maria back and find out when we can go see them."

Chela is Maria's very best friend in the same way that Graci is mine. It was her passionate desire to be at Chela's side for the birth that fueled her drive to free me from my kidnappers and to devise a plan so that I could be rescued from the rattlesnakes. It also inspired her to get clean from the heroin habit she had developed thanks to Tomás Moscoso. Graciela has gotten to know Maria and Chela through a few spontaneous visits they have recently made to my office while Graci was there.

"I will," I promise, "on our way back to town. I also have a dinner date with John this evening."

"Okay I get it amiga, use me, then dump me, all for your handsome novio."

We start back up the hill arm in arm with Maca happily digging holes every few feet.

"You know it's not like that." I squeeze her hand. "Anyway, you can come if you want. I'm sure John wouldn't mind. I'll ask when I call him back."

"No way, sister. None of that weird third-wheel stuff for me. At any rate, I have my own date tonight. So there."

"With who?" I am starting to really limp as we get to the top of the hill.

"With my telephone and my two boys. They're calling from Guatemala." This puts a smile on her face. Though, I know, there's a caveat to that smile because while visiting them last month, her oldest and his wife Zulma miscarried their first child and I know her sadness around that event runs deep. Perhaps this new baby news will be a balm to soothe her broken grandmotherly heart.

III

It's already past six when my friend unceremoniously dumps me and my dog out on the curb in front of my house. I blow her a kiss and holler out a thank you as she drives away into the sunset. My hero. How in the world would I have made this much progress without her? It's easy to hold on to the magic of the day, but I have only an hour to recoup and spruce up before John shows up for our rendezvous, and still, a few chores to do as well.

Not completely unforeseeable, there is a grinning face peering over the wall between his place and mine, my good neighbor, Señor Rivera.

"Como esta, señorita," he greets, "y hola a tu perro."

"We're great, Mr. Rivera. How are you, señor." I smile back. I grab the mail from my box and unlock the door before turning back to him. "Guess what?"

"I have no guesses, but I hope you are going to tell me something good. Does your perro want a treat, Dr. Hooper?"

When I take a closer look, I can see that he has given his scruffy beard and his head of silky white hair a trim. "She will always take a treat, as you know well enough." I give him a sly sideways look. "You're looking very handsome this evening. Do you have a date?"

"¡Venga! I haven't had a date in years. I'm much too old for that kind of nonsense."

"Really. Is that what you call it? *I* have a date tonight. Let's not call it nonsense, Mr. Rivera," I say with mock vexation.

"Ah, good to have a novio, maybe you two will get married one day." He has managed to lure Maca over to the wall and is dropping small treats into her slobbery waiting mouth. "So, tu madre, Señora Hooper and the boy are moving in this weekend. ¿Es verdad?"

"Yep, it's true. I just got done moving my stuff into the new place. That's when I got the text from Maria with the excellent news... Chela has had her healthy baby boy."

"A baby boy." he repeats. "Ricardo, right? I think it is a brave and hardy name. Is she in her home yet?"

"I don't know, but she, Armando, and Maria are going to try to stop by this weekend to bring the little treasure here for all of us to meet." I call Maca back to the porch. "Will you be around? I'm thinking we should have a little get-together. John is leaving for Denver on Monday and I should be in my new place by Sunday night. Maybe we could make tacos or something. It would be good for Diego and my mother to see you right off the bat, you know, so you can feel really comfortable with each other. I want them to know that you're there for them. What do you say? Saturday?"

"You got it, señorita. I'll make the guacamole. I've got a secret recipe. Now go get ready for your 'date'." He rolls his eyes as he utters the word date. "Hey, Maca can stay with me if you wish. She and I make good company for each other."

"You got it, señor," I call out as I slip into the cool shade of my casa.

It seems like a mere few minutes from the time I closed the door, looked through my worthless mail, and made it through my shower. But there it is. John is knocking on the door and I haven't even fed Maca yet. Damn. Unlike Graciela, John does not employ the 'knock and enter freely' method of entering, so I limp stiffly over and open it.

It is not John. Instead, there is a tall, stunning dark-haired woman framed in the opening.

"Hi, Martha. You remember me? Right?" Looking around nervously she adds, "John's friend Sunny." A half smile that doesn't match the expression in her brown eyes, trembles nervously on her full lips. Her beautifully sculpted face is so incongruous with the emotions that are contorting it. My face must be communicating straight-out confusion because she takes a step back and stutters something unintelligible, then taking a deep breath, I see her vacillate between words and tears. Finally, she begs softly, “Can I come in, Dr. Hooper?”

“Of course,” I say, moving back from the entrance, but I’m not sure I mean it. As she steps in, I stare at her suspiciously. “How did you know where I live?”

I know I must have sounded a little ruder than I meant to because it would seem that it is just the remark and the displeased expression, that removes the final chink from the dam holding back her tears. Suddenly a sobbing woman is standing in my entryway with her face in her hands. I take this moment of distraction to give her the once over. I’ve only met this gorgeous woman once before and at the time I was a little put out by the way she tried to cajole John away from me to be with a group of their friends. He was overwhelmingly apologetic and explained how she was an old family friend and a fragile one at that. Imagine that, I think, as I lead this weeping woman over to my sofa.

“Can I get you a glass of water or a cup of tea?” I ask, but I’m thinking that maybe we both need a stiffer drink.

“Yes, just some water please.” She lifts her face towards me, and I see that her mascara has smeared, and her eyes have instantly turned puffy. Not so gorgeous now; a catty private thought that I should feel terrible about.

“The bathroom is right around the corner if you’d like to freshen up,” I offer.

Sniffling away her tears she somberly takes me up on the suggestion. When we are settled back in the living room, her on the sofa, swirling the ice in her glass, and me on the chair across the room, I think to mention to her that John will be showing up at any minute.

“Oh,” she responds, sounding a little unnerved by that fact. “I wasn’t expecting that. But I don’t want to keep you, anyway. I don’t know what made me think I could just barge in on you like this, but honestly, I just didn’t know who to turn to.” Her eyes are starting to tear up again, so I quickly take over the conversation.

“I can see that you’re pretty upset about something. How can I help you, Sunny?” I ask.

“Well, John trusts you so much and that’s good enough for me. Can I tell you something in confidence?”

I lean forward and hold her eyes for a second. “Are you sure that I’m the person you want to talk to about something that is obviously very painful and personal?”

“Well,” she shrugs off my look, “you are a therapist, aren’t you?”

Now I’m wondering if I’m being manipulated big time and being sucked into a Sunny drama, which John indicated to me is often her modus operandi.

“Listen, Sunny. If you’re in some kind of trouble, I don’t think I’m the person you want to be dealing with. If you feel the need to work long-term on some kind of issue that therapy might be effective for, we can make an appointment and I would be glad to work with you. But…” I stop because her face, like an ancient crumbling statue, goes to pieces right in front of me.

“I’m pregnant,” she whimpers and puts her head down on her knees. “And the father is, you know, like a well-known politician in town here. And he’s married and he’s got three kids.”

So many things go through my mind. Like, how old is this woman? Forty-something, I think. Birth control? A sense of integrity? Is abortion not an alternative for her? Why the hell did she choose to lay this bombshell on me, her family friend’s girlfriend? Then just as I’m about to suggest that she call the Women’s Health Services, I realize that... I am going to play creeper in her deep dark past. I lose my grip on the present and begin the corkscrew excursion through the dim cool tunnel that leads me deeper into this woman than I ever wanted to go. The only words that are pieced together in my unruly propelled brain are: Oh fuck!

The descent is immediate and inescapable, which I have found means nothing as to how far back I travel, where I end up, or how long I stay. In this case, I just hope that maybe, it means I'll be back quick, quick enough to move on from this whole disturbing affair and be ready for the arrival of my "date". The first sensation I feel is air so thick with humidity and mists, that even the flying insects seem stalled in the muted beams of moonlight; its feeble illumination filters through the trees and the gloom. Heavy and portentous is this land and as starless as a night can be. A chorus of crickets confesses their sins, prodding and provoking the rafts of frogs that bellow hellishly from thick green pads that float on the steamy soup, the brew that forms the swamp. It lies all about me, covered in a constantly creeping slime. Spanish moss proliferates riotously on every branch of every black craggy tree that stands rotting in the stew, each fibrous stringy finger clawing desperately towards the murky waters. Everywhere, the scent of putrefying vegetation and decaying life fills the nostrils with death. There, behind the curtain of mist, lurks a small hut balanced above the muck on skeletal stilts. There, on the tilted collapsing stoop, is where she sits, rocking herself in an unraveling cane chair, smoke curling heavily from the bowl of her long-stemmed pipe. On the splintered wooden table in front of her are two things: a chipped black plate with shiny white objects that resemble an assemblage of various-sized teeth and a murky glass of red liquid that I'm sure is blood. At her rubber-booted feet, the body of a man lies still and ghostly. The creaking of the rocker stops as she looks down upon him, then allowing a crooked smile to work its way perversely around the stem of the pipe, the creaking resumes. Beads of sweat pattern themselves upon her large dark forehead. Removing the pipe from her thin lips, the conjurer murmurs a monotone chant of words in an indecipherable dialect. Her tongue is guttural, yet her tone is soothing as if she is crooning to a colicky baby. Every so often, the woman stops and reaches down and gently strokes and pats the body in front of her. The way her dark eyes play over the man makes me think she has found a way to ease his impending plunge into the waters of hell. I watch transfixed and wonder if the rapping I hear is the blade of her rocker against rotting wood or some evil guest at her door. Without changing her gaze, the priestess gently sweeps the teeth from the plate into her palm, then carefully slips them one by one into a small tin can that has been resting on her lap. The fitful shaking of her hand renders a clattering cadence of bone on metal that now accompanies the incantations and begins to mimic the arrhythmia of my heart. The rapping noise that has become intrusive and annoying to me, seems of no bother to her. I move closer desiring only to be lulled and enslaved by this grotesque scene. The voodoo twists through me and tugs within me, compelling my spirit to stay, but a greater force begins to woo me away. Just before it impels me forward, I see a gentle ripple in the fluorescent green of the water near her porch. I am sure two black pupil-ed bumps rise just above the water level and though the scene is fading from me it doesn't evaporate before I see the shuttering curious eye of the alligator. Helplessly, I slither like a water moccasin back through this muggy tunnel of time and wonder at my capacity to be enthralled by a life so nefarious.

Sunny is staring at me. Her eyes are wide with confusion though her lips are slightly curled in an expression of exhilaration. Nervously grabbing and twisting strands of her long dark hair, she flicks her gaze back and forth between the front door and me. I feel unsettled, muddled and so very hot.

"I think John is at the door," she finally whispers in a low voice. "Do you want me to let him in?"

Unwittingly my head is pivoting back and forth implying "no", but my vocal cords say "yes", and the woman moves quickly off the sofa. Why, I think, is Maca not barking? I do not feel fully in this world yet. Maca *is* there, at my feet, her eyes steadily trained on me and she doesn't budge; she is rigid with some sort of dogworry that will not allow her to leave my side nor her eyes to leave my earthly body.

I hear Sunny mumbling something, and then more clearly deliver an apology. I also hear John's reassuring, albeit somewhat puzzled, calm voice enter the room. It is only when I look up and see the concern on his face that I truly snap out of the thrall that this past life experience has me under.

"So, I see you've met my new friend, Sunny," I joke awkwardly as I rise clumsily from my chair. I know the smile on my face is vague and I'm sure I appear unfocused, almost inebriated. "You two have a seat. I just need the bathroom and I'll be right back."

I stop at the no-nonsense tone that John adopts as he calls out to my backside, "Martha, are you sure you're alright?"

Maca is following me into the bathroom so that when I stop and turn suddenly to reassure him, I nearly trip over her. I lean down to reassure her first, take a deep calming breath, and when I straighten up I feel much steadier.

"I'm fine. You and Sunny just chat and catch up for a minute. You know me, here I am running late as usual, and I need to finish getting ready. It'll just take a sec, I promise." I smile brightly and close the bathroom door. I look in the mirror expecting to see some dark evil cipher growing out of my forehead or blood dripping from my eyeballs, but what I see is comforting. My rather pleasant face, tanned, and as of yet superficially unwrinkled, a wild mop of wavy silver-streaked auburn hair. My green eyes appear clear and bright in the mirror thank goodness. As I take a step back from the mirror, I think: Okay, not too bad and this jade-colored, silk blouse is working for me. I scribble over my teeth, run a comb through my hair, and change into some matching wedged sandals. Out the door I step, like the put-together, sane woman John believes me to be.

John is sitting on the couch wrestling with Maca.

"Where's Sunny?" I ask, looking around like she could be hiding somewhere in this small place.

"She said she had to be somewhere. She left pretty quickly, but she did say to tell you that she would be in touch. What's up with her visiting you?" he asks fairly evenly.

"I've got to say, John, her visit was probably more of a surprise to me than you. I don't even know how she knows where I live." I realize I don't have my earrings in and head back to the bathroom as I finish my thought. I raise my volume so he can hear me, "But apparently she's got some problem she thinks I can help her with."

"Sunny's always got a problem," John says, shaking his head. "Did she say what it is this time?"

I know he's casually asking out of his brotherly love for her, but even so, I feel like when people, whether they are clients or not, unburden themselves on me, I become like a private reserve for their secrets. And she did ask for confidentiality. So I tell a little white lie. "No, she never really got around to it. Probably why she said she'd be in touch. Where are we going tonight?" I ask, trying to quickly change the subject.

John leaves Maca to her own devices and walks up behind me. Wrapping his arms around my waist, he buries his face in my hair and then nuzzles into my neck which sends waves of goose-bumping chills down to my fingertips.

"I made reservations at El Farol," he whispers in my ear then moves his lips to my shoulder. "I figured it was such a beautiful evening we could walk there, have a drink on the deck, and just watch the people. But now I'm thinking I should have reserved a room at the Hooper Hotel."

The man can make me literally weak in the knees. He spins me around like we're dancing and begins again gently kissing the front of my neck and moving his fingers through my hair. I grab his face between both of my hands, and we put the finishing touches on this salacious act of love with a deep and lusty kiss because exasperatingly, the 'feed Maca button' keeps going off in my brain as I hear her licking her empty bowl causing it to bang up against the base of the cupboard. The man can read my mind too. His fingers gently wrap around a bundle of my hair, and he softly pulls my head back exposing my neck to more of his fondling.

"This isn't finished," he murmurs into my skin, then releases me. "Go feed your dog. I know where you sleep and I will finish this for both of us," he threatens in a woozy kind of tone.

I'm not sure this human psyche of mine is built to experience such powerful emotional fluctuations in such a short period because now I really am feeling emotionally inebriated. However, I am experienced with inebriation of most kinds, so move on to feed Maca hoping that John and I will intoxicate ourselves further with wine and tapas and the magic of a late summer evening walk before we finish off this night in rapture at the Hooper Hotel.

IV

Waking up to the cool morning breeze rolling through my window and the chitter of finches drifting in like the soundtrack of a happily-ever-after movie, makes it more than difficult to wake the man next to me, to remind him that he has an appointment in a few hours. That was his directive, not mine. I made no appointments for myself on this exquisite Friday morning. Mostly because of packing and moving, but now because I do have this lovely man in my bed who will soon be gone for a month. I gently stroke his long silver hair and arrange it on the pillow around his head so that he looks like a silver-haloed angel. To me anyway.

He stirs and reaches for me without opening his eyes. "What time is it?" he asks, his voice still rough with sleep and maybe a little too much midnight wine.

"Time to rustle up some eggs and bacon, cowboy."

"Really? Cowboy? Last night I think you called me your pirate." Now he is caressing my back with his fingertips.

"Hmmm," I sigh as those little goosebumps break out again. "You are all those things and more," I tease. "Lawyer, musician, superhero, and let us not forget most importantly my own personal Don Juan."

"I am that," he declares as he rolls his body towards me. For just one moment, as he embraces me and touches me in ways that I have not been touched in years, I bask in my good fortune to have finally met the kind of man that I not only have fallen in love with but whose past lives only extend as far back as this one he is living now. Thus my ability to be so absolutely close to him and never be plagued by the plunge into his deep, dark, ancient secrets. For me, it is as refreshing as that breeze that is blowing in the window. And with that auspicious thought, I am lost to the foreplay of passion and the consummation of love.

"We should meet back here at noon," John says between bites of the piece of whole wheat biscuit that accompanies the actual cowboy eggs and bacon I have cooked up. "That way we can drive out to Cassandra's place together, take any last things you can think of and I get a chance to see where you will be while I slave away in the big city recording studio."

I agree to the plan and having finished my own serving of this hearty breakfast, begin to clear the dishes and run soapy water for the wash. I watch Maca through the window frolicing in the small backyard. With her doggie intensity set to frenetic, she pounces upon some scent that compels her to drop to the ground and roll about like a hysterical wild thing. I get a brief but sharp pang of temporary loss as I think about not being in this house and not having this man in my life for a month. I turn around to tell him so, only to find that he has silently appeared at my back. His arms go around me and he too watches the dog's antics.

"I'm so glad that your mom and Diego have agreed to keep TomB. He likes it here and I feel better knowing that he'll be well cared for." Tom is for tomcat and B for Bobcat or bobtail. TomB is John's beloved bob-tailed orange tabby, aka his only ever kid. Tom's first sleepover at my house was the night I was kidnapped by Maria's boyfriend. TomB and I were night-owling it, both of us struck with an unexplainable feeling of apprehension; well I was, TomB was probably just being a prowly cat. I was on the porch holding him when I was brutally abducted and he ended up wandering the neighborhood for two days before he turned up in Mr. Rivera's yard. The memory causes me to feel sick to my stomach. For a therapist, I am woefully short on the skills it takes to get over my own shit. Actually, the therapy I need is right at hand. I simply circle into an embrace that leads to a quick makeout session at the sink.

"You are going to make me late, bruja." he says as he pulls away.

"Hey, that's the second time in two days someone has called me a witch. I'm getting a bit of a complex." I laugh.

"Well, maybe you need to explore that part of your own history a bit. You think there might be a little witchiness in that long list of lives you are toting around like a ball and chain. Because I, on the other hand, am as light as a feather." He kisses me on the cheek and heads for the door. "Hasta luego. See you around noon." And he is gone.

The decision to go into the office was cemented when I realized I had left my laptop there with all my appointments and a few key phone numbers on it. Plus I had this nagging feeling that I needed to pick up messages off of my Mesozoic Era landline that is not ported over to my cell phone. I try hard to honor the separation of work and play. That's one of my rules and I try to stick to it, unless I don't, as in the case of Maria Maestas. There was no concrete reason to break my rule, just a feeling that the teenager needed a port in the storm twenty-four-seven. Looking back, my instincts were good.

That's why I trust that same instinct that leads me here to my desk on a beautiful Saturday morning. Not unexpectedly, the machine's light is blinking.

The first message is from yesterday. As I listen to his voice I get a bit nostalgic. Devin was a client of mine several years ago, that is, until in a classic critical mass kind of way, he had the kind of breakthrough that therapists wish for all their clients. Devin was the quintessential non-succeeder at life. He made it through the first twelve years of school with 'D's that were really: '*D*on't want this kid in my class no more'. He dropped out of college, went to the community college and left after a month, waited tables at almost every restaurant in town, ran through a string of young women, married two, divorced two and along the way picked up an unhealthy affinity for Jack Daniels and weed. By the time he came to me, he was disillusioned, broke, beaten, lonely and only twenty-eight years old. We tried lots of traditional tools and techniques that failed miserably. For whatever reason, I dove into his past lives with an unprecedented regularity and came to relish the crossing-overs and cultivated an absolute confidence that I would find the faulty underpinnings of his long-standing failures and impending implosion. Nothing seemed to click. His depression seemed like it was on the fast track to a bad ending. Then one afternoon as he was relating again what his elementary school years were like, it hit me like a frisbee in the face– he was describing a severely ADHD young boy who was never identified as such, rather, just a little shit, trouble maker (his memory of what he was called by a teacher). And it stuck with him all these years later. Childhood ADHD untreated can turn into unidentified adult ADHD, unsuccessful self-medication with drugs, alcohol or sex; or all of the above. No persistence, no endurance, no ability to plan and organize and follow through. Executive function failure in the brain. Setbacks, defeats, impasses, frustration, anger and depression. The guy needed help. We began the work and an appropriate med. We found a behavioral coach to help him with organization, life skills, time management and setting goals. My job became easier and easier as things began to fall into place for this young man and small successes began to be followed by bigger ones.

His message was an excellent one, an invitation to celebrate his completion of the paramedic EMT program. This path, he went on to relate, "feels like a calling" and "I completed the program with honors." he reported proudly.

I am so pleased.

The second message is from today: *Dr. Hooper this is Catherine Jennings. Hope you are starting to feel better after everything you've been through. I'm calling to make an appointment for Maggie with you. She's been doing so well.* Catherine's voice up to this point has been steady and matter-of-fact, but there is a quaver on that last word, an unsteady breath before she goes on. *Really well... until this week. Early this week she started waking in the middle of the night, crying. I thought maybe she was having nightmares because nothing else seemed wrong. But the night before last, Dr. Hooper, I found her in the backyard standing in front of the fence around the pool. It was the middle of the night. Jack has installed new inside locks on all the doors, still last night,* now I hear the hitch in her breath, *I found her cowering at the foot of the door screaming like she was being torn apart from the inside. My god, Dr. Hooper, what is happening to my baby? Please, can you see us... as soon as possible. You know we appreciate everything you have done for us. I hope to hear from you soon.* Even the click of her phone as it ends this heartbreaking appeal sounds desperate, so I dial her number immediately.

With no answer from Catherine's cell, I try Jack's and have no better luck. I redial Catherine's and once again, with a twinge of guilt in my gut, I break my rule and leave a message urging her to call me on my cell phone as soon as she gets my message, that number that is supposed to be the demarcation line between 'you're my personal peeps and I'm at work now'. I sigh and shift uncomfortably in my desk chair, open my laptop and make a few notes in Maggie's file. I reread the past notes while I'm there.

Doesn't talk to anyone but her mother. Talk is at the level of a two-year-old. Doesn't sleep, eats very little and only three or four particular foods with an emphasis on saltine crackers. Doesn't interact with other children. Cried so continually the first week of school that the teacher and principal convinced her parents she needed another year to mature. Likes to swim. That was our first meeting. I later learned that a past incarnation had been lived out in a Mayan community that had a yearly ritual of sacrificing a young girl to the gods who provided for the ongoing abundant life of the farmers and fishermen. Maggie's father, in that life, was the brother who cruelly offered her up for that position of supposed honor, basically to increase his own political stature. The work that we did uncovering this, and the understanding that Jack gained from it, seemed to be slowly changing the relationship between father and daughter. Currently, it seemed that along with some other professional avenues, Maggie was making progress. Now this new twist. But children are full of twists and turns. It's the nature of a child to bang up against obstacles with a kind of persistence that we adults seem to lose with age. My job, as I see it, is to define this new obstacle.

I check the time and realize that I have been sitting here much longer than I had planned. Scooping up my keys and laptop, I head towards the door and just as my hand touches the knob, the cell phone in my pocket begins to vibrate. I did give them this number. It was my decision, I think as I reluctantly return to my desk. But it is not the Jennings.

"Hello, Mother," I answer with my usual attempt at nonchalance. At ages seventy and fifty our mother-daughter relationship can so easily revert back to that of the thirty-five-year-old single mother and the fractious fifteen-year-old; this despite the fact that I myself was a single mother raising a daughter and Olivia never bumped against me in the same bristly way. But don't get me wrong, I love this woman dearly and have nothing but respect for the way she has navigated her life with poise and independence, as well as, an incredibly sunny demeanor.

"Good morning, sweetpea. How are you feeling today?"

"Not too bad, all things considered. Graciela came over yesterday to help me move some things out to Cassandra's house. So the place should be ready for you and Diego this weekend just like I promised."

"That's wonderful, dear. Diego is out-of-his-mind excited. You should have heard him last night. He's been dreaming up twenty ways to convince you that Maca should stay with us. And you know Mr. Rivera promised to show him how to make these little wooden boxes he creates. You know, dear those ones that have painted clay figures in them. It's kind of like retablo art– I think. Anyway, Diego seems really interested in learning how to do it. Have you ever seen any of Señor Rivera's work?"

"No, but it sounds interesting and I think it's good for Diego to be doing something other than the computer. Did you tell him that John's cat is coming to stay with you two? Maybe that will satisfy some of his pet needs till we work out some Maca visitations."

"He knows, but he wants it all. You know how he is, insatiable for things to love on."

This makes me pause. Makes my heart ache and makes me love my mother all the more for her superpower, that innate insight into human nature that she wields with the ease of a cooking spoon.

"So you're driving your car up with Diego?" I take a glance at the clock on the wall. "And Melanie has a van or something for the rest of your stuff? Oh, and she plans on checking on your place regularly, right? You've got the bases covered, yes, or do you need me to do something?" I realize I sound really impatient, but I need to get back to my place to make my rendezvous with John.

"We've got it covered, Martha. Don't worry about a thing. We should be there about eleven tomorrow." I hear Diego in the background whooping it up about some crazy thing that is amusing him.

"Oh Mom, I forgot to tell you. Chela had her baby. She's thinking she will bring him by tomorrow afternoon so we're informally planning a little get-together to celebrate all these changes in our lives. You think you'll be up for that?"

"Of course, honey, and Diego will love it. He was afraid he wouldn't be able to spend any time with you. So this sounds perfect. See you tomorrow."

"See you tomorrow, Martha!" I hear an echoing little boy's voice from the background.

"Bye Mom. Give Diego a big hug from me."

I sit for just a minute and take it all in. Despite the recent horrific events of my life, I have so much to be grateful for. I sweep my eyes over the photo-covered walls, seeking for a moment, the history in my life that bears out this emotional response. The faces that look back at me from their perfect angles and diverse perspectives are the ones who have always looked upon me kindly, if only to permit a stranger to take their picture. Yet, many are so much more than strangers, the ones woven into the tapestry of my own life in a way that binds my rough edges and ill-fitting pieces together. The ones who encourage me to stay undiminished by the things I have seen and experienced. I nod my head to them all in deep gratitude; then remind myself to pull out my camera when I get home.

V

John is already at my house and waiting on me by the time I get back. Feeling tardy and guilty I offer to make him lunch, but he refuses the offer.

"I've got a suggestion and a change of plans," he smiles knowing that I don't always respond readily to last-minute changes.

I grab a glass of ice water and say, "Then let's move out to the porch. I need a little fresh air. I managed to coop myself up at my office for too long."

"I thought you weren't working today." He gives his head a confused shake. "Anyway, I got a call from Sunny a little while ago. Staying right in character, the woman started right off in an emotional lather and insisted that she needed to talk with you. Now I'm not sayin' I wanna throw you to the she-wolf, but it sure would make my life easier and my cell minutes go down if you would talk with her today." He looks over at me to see if I am staying receptive as I sit in the shade with my feet up and my drink cooling my forehead. I nod. "So I was thinking about our plans to head to

Cassandra's as actually being kind of flexible. Instead of going today, we could both go up there tomorrow night after the gathering and spend the night together and maybe even part of Sunday before I take off for Denver."

"That part sounds really good. Tell me about the Sunny part."

"Yeah, elementary, my dear Doctor Hooper. We meet her for lunch, my treat, delicious food, beautiful patio, dessert of your choice and then you two spend a bit of time together after lunch and voila, it's over." He lays his hand gently on my shoulder. "So what do you think?"

"I think you must be missing your closing arguments in the courtroom. I feel like I've just been lawyered." I chuckle and give him a sideways look. "Did she tell you what she wants to talk to me about?" I ask casually as if I don't know.

"Nope, just that she had a private can of worms she could only talk to you about. I can't say that I'm not immensely relieved not to be a part of whatever this one is, but I'm also deeply sorry to get you involved in her shit," he says with a shady lawyer kind of grin aimed my way.

All that does is reinforce my feeling of just being sold down the river. "Thanks a lot. You know, I'm beginning to have suspicions about just who the wolf is here."

Placing my drink on the table and kissing the top of John's head, I get up and walk over to where the wall meets the house. There is a huge beautiful spider web spanning about ten inches of real estate. Somehow I can't shake the feeling that I am like the fly that's about to unwittingly land on that sticky deadly gossamer. Or maybe I'm the fly that's being tossed into the web by the naughty little boy. I sigh, "Okay, Mr. Sacrifice Your Girlfriend To Save Your Own Sorry Hide, how soon till we leave?"

My answer is a long sweet passionate kiss.

Sunny has arrived before us. She sits elegantly at a cafe-style table with a shady umbrella. From where she sits, she can see all the action on the busy plaza street.

"I ordered you guys raspberry iced tea. I hope you don't mind, but they are my favorite at this place and I figured you'd be thirsty on a hot day like today."

"Thanks," John says before reaching down and giving her shoulder a squeeze and her upturned forehead a quick kiss. "How are you?" He pulls out my chair for me.

"I'm fine. A little hot," she starts to fan herself with the menu, "but it is summer, now isn't it?" If she was lathered up earlier, she certainly seems to have shaved that lather right off her attractive face. In her pretty striped summer dress, with her hair pulled back in a complicated braid, she looks downright cool and collected. "You know John, I haven't seen Sera for quite a while. What is that sister of yours up to these days? Have you met Sera yet, Martha? She and I had our heyday back in our high school days. And I mean high as in high not school and I mean d-a-z-e. It was fun to be so carefree back then." Her voice turns a bit wistful. "When we were young. Right, John?" Her big eyes wax nostalgic, as she places her hand over his.

"Fun for you two. I was already at UNM on the slow slogging track to my law degree," he says while gently withdrawing his hand from hers. Sunny doesn't seem to notice because her eyes are trained on two men sitting at a table near the door.

"Isn't that… What was his name, you know him, John. The really good-looking guy who worked at the print shop over by your old office. Remember, Sera and I went dancing with him years and years ago. Maybe she even dated him for a while. My memory is not what it used to be."

John turns slightly in his chair and while Sunny looks again at the man, John rolls his eyes for my benefit. "Jimmy Sanchez," he says.

“Let’s go say hi,” she says as she rises gracefully from her seat, smoothing her skirt. John shakes his head and grabs my wrist like it’s an anchor that will keep her undertow from pulling him along. It must work because Sunny glides over to the other table without him.

John watches her briefly, then turns to me. “The woman goes nowhere in this city without bumping into at least half a dozen people she knows, per outing.”

I have a very good view of the woman shaking hands and laughing with the two gentlemen.

“She will never be lonely, now will she?” Under my breath, I also mumble, “No wonder she’s in trouble.” I search for any kind of pregnancy bump on that long shapely waist, but see nothing. A breeze stirs the hem of her skirt and she coyly pushes it back down, but not before the man, Jimmy Sanchez, lets his eyes and imagination wander.

John is scanning the menu and begins to point out his favorites when we are suddenly interrupted.

“Dr. Hooper, fancy meeting you here.” I look up to see the smiling face of Jack Jennings.

“Mr. Jennings, this is a bit of unforeseen good luck.” I stand to shake his hand and introduce him to John.

“How so?”

“The phone call?” He looks at me quizzically. “From your wife. You know, about Maggie’s newest troubles.”

The smile disappears from his face completely and his eyes narrow. “I’m afraid I don’t know what you’re talking about,” he says.

I watch uncertainly as his eyes drop slowly to the table.

“Catherine and I are taking a little break from each other.” He glances up at John briefly. And John, bless his sensitive heart, excuses himself to go join Sunny.

“Do you have time to sit down for just a minute? I feel like I need to understand what is going on here.”

“Of course, but I really don’t want to take you away from your time with your lovely friends.” He glances over to where John and Sunny are deep in conversation with the two other men. I see his eyes linger briefly on Sunny.

“It’s okay. Please, let’s sit down.”

He begins quickly after we are settled.

“As you know, Dr. Hooper, Catherine and I have not always seen eye to eye on the most effective means of dealing with our daughter. And that's not to say that your help hasn’t been invaluable. Maggie has made progress in ways that I hadn’t thought possible. And I feel like a different man since the experiences and conversations that you and I have had.”

“But..” I say just to acknowledge that he has my full attention.

“But, on a day-to-day basis, the management of our daughter’s unusual behaviors was and continues to be a source of disagreements that ends up in terribly emotional arguments. Way too often in front of Maggie. I could see how fearful she was becoming and it felt like she might be slipping back away from me.” Jack’s face looks tortured.

“So...” I try to give him time to compose himself, “you and your wife have split up to give little Maggie a sense of peace. Is she spending any time with you?” The waitress shows up and after asking Jack if he’d like anything, I shoo her away.

“Not yet. It’s only been two weeks. Actually Catherine is a master of deflecting my attempts to interact with either of them, so I’ve been throwing myself into my work and I rented a small studio actually located in the same complex that your office is in. Can you tell me what Catherine said to you?”

“I didn’t speak with her directly. She left me a somewhat desperate-sounding message to tell me that she wanted an appointment because Maggie has been having nightmares and wandering during the middle of the night. She didn't answer when I called her back so I left her a message with my cell phone number." I feel it coming on, that stupid urge to give my cell phone number to Jack. "I'd like to give it to you," I say slowly, trying to check my errant ways with no luck at all, "so that you can get a hold of me too. I'm not in the office quite as much as I used to be, at least not until my full stamina returns. I'm sure you understand."

Jack nods and pulls his cell phone out. Once my sacred number is loaded, I hear Sunny's sultry voice returning to the fold. Jack quickly rises out of his seat and smiles brightly at the beautiful woman coming our way. I stand to make introductions and am relieved when Jack excuses himself quickly, but not before giving Sunny one last appraising look.

"Jack looks really familiar to me," John ponders, "I bet our paths have crossed professionally at some point. Does he play music?"

"No, I answer, he's a quite successful architect here in town."

"Oh, are you getting some work done on your little home?" Sunny joins in. She is flushed and animated after her visit with the gentlemen at the other table.

"Nope, just a social visit," I say, with a look to John to keep his mouth shut and not offer up any other tidbits about what he heard.

The waitress reappears and the fiasco of what to have begins. Small talk, good food and even better desserts finish out the next half hour.

VI

Sunny and I find a bench on the busy plaza and sit on either end. John has gone to run a few errands and much to my displeasure, Sunny has offered to drive me home when we are finished chatting. Her mood has slowly descended from highly vivacious to almost morose in the short time that it took for John to say goodbye and us to be seated. Her highs and lows are a red flag in my book.

"So what did you need to talk to me about?" I am nothing if not straightforward with this woman. "John mentioned your can of worms."

Sunny looks at me wide-eyed. "Well, hopefully it's just one worm."

I can't help but let a little smile escape, because that actually was kind of funny.

"There's really not much I can do for you, Sunny. You need to see a physician, have the pregnancy confirmed, if you haven't already, and then make a decision as to what you want to do about it."

"That's just it," she stammers. "I really don't know what I want. I mean this might be my only chance to have a kid. I might really like having a kid. But, you know, I've never really given it much thought before. I just figured I was one of those women who never could or would."

We both stay silent for a moment and watch the teenage couple walking their dog past our bench.

"I'm not going to have that," she nods after them. "I'm a wreck, Martha. Not that I haven't always been. But this is like the icing on the cake. And the slimy bastard who's the father, well you know, he broke it off before I even had a chance to tell him about it. Said his wife was getting suspicious."

I look at her trying hard not to be judgemental, but I can't help it. She's a part of this affair and not taking responsibility for her slimy part in it. Forty-something going on sixteen.

"If you don't mind my asking, how old are you? I only ask because it does have implications for your pregnancy."

"I know," she responds dejectedly. "I'm forty-two. But lots of women have babies at forty-two and older."

She reminds me of a little girl rationalizing why she should be able to keep the puppy that followed her home.

"Sunny, do you want me to be straight with you?" She gives me a silent nod. "You need to grow up. You have now involved another human being in your shenanigans, a helpless innocent baby who has a father who doesn't have a clue or seemingly want one for that matter. You are not, at this time, in a position, at a level of maturity, or in any way that I see, ready to settle down and be a mom. I come from a long line of single parenting, and I have to tell you, it is really fucking hard. It's emotionally, financially and yes, socially really really hard. I feel indescribably upset that a forty-two-year-old woman cannot see the implications of her choices. And I also feel very upset that I am this upset with you!" I look around to make sure no one has been listening to me ream this woman out, then I turn to face her full-on. Sunny's face is pale and her eyes are as wide as one of those Japanese anime characters. I think for a moment she may be thinking of slapping me as her arms suddenly reach out towards me.

"You are an amazing person, Dr. Martha Hooper." Her arms encircle me as she whispers these words in my ear. "If my mother would have lived, I think that she would have been just like you. Nobody," she whispers with a dash of whimper. "Nobody is ever straight with me." She releases her grip on me and sits up ramrod straight. "It's always: be careful with Sunny, she's fragile, she's flakey or unstable. And I am that. I am all of that and worse. I'm unpredictable, I lust after someone to love me, anyone. I self-medicate, can't hold a job or have a decent relationship and you are right, I act like a teenager. But I ask you, could this be the one thing that could change my life? Could this child transform me into the woman I know I could be?"

What do I say to an appeal like this? Here, sitting in a public place, with a distraught woman pinning me to the bench with her brimming eyes, pleading for the categorical decoding of her dysfunctional life. Do I tell her to go have an abortion, to go talk to the father of the baby, to go to the doctor, to church? (I think this as the church bell down the street coincidentally begins to chime.) I am buffaloed. Stymied. And there she sits, quietly and patiently awaiting my response.

"I... I honestly don't know what to say to you, Sunny," I stutter sincerely. "I guess I have to say that I really don't know the 'real' you or the woman you know you could be and because of that I really can't presume to have an answer for you."

She smiles at me with something that surprisingly feels like sympathy. "How about this, Martha? Please let me come see you for the next few weeks as a patient or client or whatever you call your people. I promise I will go see my OB/Gyn and you can get to know the 'real' me, if I can find her. You don't have to tell me what to do, just tell it to me like it is. You seem very good at that and I need that more than anything right now."

There are good ways to say 'no' to people, to let them down easy. I just can't think of any of those ways at the moment, so I look down at my hands and then cast my eyes up to the heavens. I try to muster a gentle refusal, to spit out an unequivocal veto of this insane idea, only to hear myself, as if I am a non-voting onlooker, say to this difficult woman, "Okay. How about next Wednesday?" What the hell is the matter with me?

Sunny's car has been parked under the cool shade of a sprawling elm with all the windows down.

"Aren't you afraid someone will vandalize your car?" I ask.

"Hasn't happened yet," she smiles and slides in behind the wheel. "Besides there isn't a thing in here that anyone would bother to steal and it's my little contribution to putting some positive vibes of trust out there into this sucky world."

"Okay," I say watching her turn the ignition key to accessory and fiddle with the radio dial. "They could steal your radio."

"Like I said, hasn't happened yet." She finds a song she likes and starts tapping her pink polished fingernails on the steering wheel. "Can I ask you another question, Martha?"

"Okay." Again, really? Couldn't the answer be: I'd really rather you didn't?

"The other day when I was at your house and you kind of went, you know, like AWOL in your mind, it was like you were having some kind of apoplexy."

"What?" I laugh. I'm not even sure I know what that means. Where in the world did you pick up that word?"

She actually smiles big and boldly at me. "Oh lordy," she laughs softly, "an old boyfriend used to say that to me when I was so drunk or stoned I could barely talk. I don't know why I said it just now, but it is a really silly word to say out loud." She giggles to herself. "Anyway, was that you having one of those past life things you got from me? You don't have to tell me if you don't want to, but if it was about me, I think I'd like to know."

Through my years of being thrown helplessly into this transcendental portal, I have grown to believe in the higher purpose of a gift that has presented itself to me as both an illumination and a vexation. Before my encounters with Misterioso and Mr. Rivera, whose visions helped to manifest a much less righteous genesis of my superpowers, I became convinced along the way of the need to use these visitations to help people find their path back to some sense of peace within themselves. Though I may not always have divulged the details of my travels, I certainly shared the implications if they were helpful. Now, I am no longer as sure, as I once was, of divine purpose or even the clearcut relevance that once drove me. So, Sunny asking me to reveal her deep dark voodoo soul does not jump out at me as being necessarily prophetic or helpful.

"It's not always helpful." I say cryptically.

"So, you don't want to tell me." She finds a new station on the radio then grabs thc stecring wheel with straight arms, eyes staring rigidly out through the spotty windshield. And we're still not going anywhere. "Does that mean it was something bad? Did I do something terrible?"

I don't know what it is about this woman that makes me unable to 'just say no'.

"Sonny, sometimes the places I go to are very dark and that was a dark place, but it was only a snippet of something that made no sense to me, so chances are it'll make no sense to you either. What do you say we just move on?"

"I know I said you didn't have to tell if you didn't want to, but all of a sudden, I'm getting these 'vibes'," she curls her fingers around this word. "Like maybe this is some kind of message."

I turn and look at this woman closely. She's got to be toying with me.

"Dammit, Sunny, it feels like you're mocking me. You don't have to believe in this stuff. Not important to me at all, but don't mock me. It does nothing for my desire to help you."

Surprisingly she doesn't say another word, just starts the engine, turns off the radio and pulls away from the curb. I put on my seatbelt and glance over at her. She hasn't put her's on, but I manage to keep my renegade mouth shut.

My plan is to jump out of the car as soon as she stops in front of my house. I have this feeling I have made a terrible mess of things, and I don't want to tangle things up anymore by lingering. That was the plan, but it is not what happens.

"May I come in, Martha? Just for a bit. I know John won't be back for a while."

"I'm quickly unbuckling my seatbelt as my right hand pushes the car door open. So close. So damn close to the door to my solitude, the cool dim innards of my sanctum. It's just right there,

Maca and her happy eyes, Graciela's mask keeping away evil spirits, a cool good-natured breeze whispering through the window.

"Sure," I say. "Sure, come on in."

VII

"So do it again," she argues with me. "If it was so inconclusive the first time, then try it again."

"You are not understanding me, Sunny. This is not something I can just do again. I have never been able to control it. It's possible if we sit here together long enough, I might get a whisper, but then again maybe not." I'm taking off my sandals and rubbing my feet as I parley with this woman from the comfort of my sofa. She paces back and forth between my kitchen and living room. "And there's no guarantee that I would end up in the same past life, anyway."

She finally alights on the other end of the sofa. Maca walks up to her cautiously, tail in a slow wag, and her nose on high alert.

"Maybe, I only have one. You know, that one you saw. John says he has had nada before this life. If that's true, then you'll just jump right back in, right? Isn't there anything we can do to trigger it?" she pleads.

"No." There I said it. And it felt so good that I just have to say it again. "No, not at all."

"Okay then, Dr. Martha Hooper. Then just tell me what you saw. You can see I'm not joking around or pooh-poohing your special gift. I really believe in it. What if what you saw in the past can help me with my present predicament."

I hate that she said those words. I hate that those words, which have been the parenthetical dogma of my professional life since I became a therapist with this peculiarity, no longer hold the same meaning for me. I barely trust the ground that I walk on anymore, let alone the belief that I was born to guide the fragile and disoriented ones. It's just not fair.

I sigh and get up off the sofa. "Do you want something to drink?" I ask like a beaten woman because I know I'm about to cave, and it irritates me that I no longer feel sure that what I'm about to reveal to her will make anything in her sorry life a whit better.

I bring us both back drinks, a small glass of white wine for me and a bottle of Perrier for her, curl back up in the corner of the sofa and look into her unreadable gorgeous brown eyes. When she finally blinks, that's when I begin...

When Sunny finally leaves, she leaves with new baggage bound to weigh her down on her path to redemption. It was impossible for me to read her reaction; she listened so intently, quietly managing to keep an impassive expression throughout my storytelling. She did finally ask if I thought that she had killed the man beneath her feet, to which I gave her the answer she didn't want to hear. "I don't know, it was not conclusive."

Now all I want to do is to lay in my bed and let the breeze wash over me. I need a spirit cleansing. That woman exhausts me. I guess the midafternoon glass of wine didn't help either. Within minutes of sprawling across the top of my bed, I can feel myself drifting peaceably into a hazy gossamer sleep.

I dream about a baby. Tiny and wide-eyed, it drifts helplessly in a sea of fluid. Its eyes reach out to me, implore me to do something. But unable to articulate what it is that will help, it simply moves its lips in a sucking motion. All I can do is swim slowly and gently through the thick clear swells of brine to reach out and pull the child into my arms. There we rock, pulsed by a heartbeat and buffeted by the tides. Here, I make some tiny pact with this old soul, some wee unknowable agreement that puts my heart at ease.

A Reconstructed Life

I

My mother and Diego arrive right around eleven on this blissful Saturday morning.

Despite Sunny's sunless cloudburst yesterday, I awoke this morning to a sunrise shot through with fiery orange tendrils, smudged with goldenrod and lightly brushed with the green of sea foam, all splashed onto an ephemeral canvas of blistering blue. I awoke alone, with an uncharacteristic energy that undoubtedly was spurred by the anticipation of a new adventure and the notion of gathering together all those I love in the spirit of change and sanctuary. Braced with the challenge of re-shaping the context of our small lives, I got to work in those early morning hours preparing for all that this halcyon day might bring.

Eleven AM brings the arrival of the first car. Diego hops out of the passenger door, a frisky pup looking to roughhouse with the wild canine who willingly enters into a complicit pact to make that happen. Maca the Traitor. In lobo-kinship, they navigate paths to bring blood back to the pack, the clan that is slow to assemble on this bright cerulean morning. Just to emphasize her commitment to the moment, Maca knocks the boy backward onto his hindquarters, steals the cap right off his head, and runs for safety behind my knees.

My mother on the other hand, scoots out from behind the steering wheel looking a bit worse for the wear. I immediately go to my guilty place and wonder why in the world I didn't go down there and help her get packed and drive her up here.

"You look a little tired, Mom," I say as I walk quickly to the car and slide my arm through hers. I give her a kiss on the cheek. "How was the drive?"

"Very entertaining, Sweet Pea. Diego gave me another little personal history lesson about my life from the sixteenth century. Ever heard of Nicholas Copernicus? Apparently I knew the man intimately."

"Is that so?" The smile on my lips hides my own intelligence on this little story. "And did you help him understand that that big ball of fire in the sky is the center of the universe?"

"That and so much more, all the way from Bernalillo to La Bajada. It was quite the saga. I'll have to tell you about it later on. Highly diverting, I must say. How are things here?"

We make it to the porch, and I settle her onto one of the chairs. "Things are great, Mom. Are you sure you still feel up to the little get-together I've arranged for later?" I sink into the chair next to her.

"Oh my, I wouldn't miss it for the world. You're telling me I get to see a little baby, and I can't wait to catch up with Señor Rivera. Graciela and I have some catching up to do as well." She sighs. "You know, spending time here in Santa Fe, in your sweet little casa, is like a summer vacation for Diego and me."

"Well, let me get you two something to drink, and how about a little snack, Mom. You do look a little worn out." I slip into the house just as Diego completely tackles Maca to the ground and starts scrubbing her belly with his fingers. "Hi Martha!" he yells out as I disappear.

At least I had the foresight to make sandwiches and some fresh lemonade in those early morning hours. I grab a bag of chips and one of the carrots, then suddenly remember I need to check my cell for messages, so the cell goes between my teeth as I keep moving forward holding the door open with my foot. Diego has seated himself on a chair, placed his cap next to him on the table and with Maca at his feet seems completely at home. My mother's chin rests on her chest, her eyes closed, but her color looks surprisingly more cheerful. Diego speaks softly.

"I'm starving. Can I open the chips?"

"Yes, if you eat a couple of carrots first," I whisper back. My parenting skills come back to me like riding a bike. Amazingly, without complaint, he picks up the carrot bag and starts munching away and in between bites asks if Maca can have one.

"Sure, carrots are good for dogs, too," I answer. "So, what's new Diego?"

"Well, Alice has been taking me to the pool. I took a few lessons and the guy said I picked it up real fast, so I kinda stopped taking them. But I taught myself how to dive and I can find a penny in the shallow end without running out of breath. Oh yeah. We've been going to the library in the evenings. Alice has been researching some top-secret thing and I've been reading all these really cool Japanese graphic novels. I'm learning to draw my own characters. I'll show you some of my pictures after we unpack them. Can I have some chips now?"

"Absolutely."

I'll take some iced tea, dear." My mother has opened her eyes and sits up a little straighter in her chair.

"Iced tea, or lemonade, Mom?

"Oh iced tea, please. Lemonade has far too much sugar in it for me. By the way, where's John and Graciela?"

"They'll be here sometime after one. Maria, Armando, Chela and the baby should be here around two or three. So we have time to unpack and relax. I've got all the food prepared. You can even take a nap if you want. I changed the sheets and you're ready to go." I pick up the tray of sandwiches. "Here, why don't you start with one of these while I get your tea." Just as I open the door my cell phone starts to buzz on the patio table.

It's a text from Catherine Jennings. *Sorry I missed your call. Thanks for giving me your cell number. Maggie's doing better. How about Tuesday at one o'clock?* I immediately text her back confirming the time and set about pouring up iced tea. One for me and one for her. When I get back outside, I see that between the two of them, they have gobbled up most of the egg salad sandwiches.

"Sorry, dear. We didn't have much breakfast. Oh look, here comes Melanie with the van."

Let the games begin, I think to myself.

II

The extraordinary number of belongings that come out of the car and van do not surprise me. And somehow, Melanie and I manage to get every piece to magically fit into each room, turning Hotel Hooper into a cozy little bungalow for a seventy-year-old woman and her ten-year-old foster kid. In fact, Diego completely disappears for at least an hour as he arranges his room with my mother's computer, his drawings and books and the boxes of clothing that somehow have come his way.

As I peek in on him, I see that the boy is placing a framed photo of Maca and me on the second-hand dresser, a gold nugget I found at a garage sale last week. "John and Graciela are here," I say softly so as not to startle him. My heart does a bit of a flutter at the thought of how desperate this kid must be for a real family. Before I can open my mouth to address him further, John snags my arm and pulls me into the kitchen. TomB is nestled in the crook of one of his arms and as I take a quick measure of the kitchen, I see that there is a small heap of Tom's belongings in the corner. A bag of food, a box of litter, a cozy kitty bed and a litter box, all speaking to new adventures for the cat, but also new territory for my mom and Diego.

"So, how's it going?" he asks as he circles my waist with his free arm drawing me close for a quick private nuzzle. Tom B takes advantage of the distraction to free himself and launches into his feline inspection of every nook and cranny.

"Excellent. Everybody seems like they're settling in well. My mom looks a little washed out, but I'm sure she'll be fine. I should have helped her and Melanie with all the packing. Am I a bad daughter?" I ask a little contritely.

John kisses me on the lips and lifts my chin to meet his eyes. "Never."

I smile and lean into him but don't surrender to the feelings that are heating my blood. "Is Graci on the porch with her?"

"Yes, and that reminds me. We need to drop Graciela off at her house this evening before heading up to Cassandra's. If that's okay with you?"

"Of course," I snap a little testily, "like I would ever mind doing anything for my friend." Where that came from, I have no idea. "I'm sorry," I say and give him a quick peck on the cheek. Grabbing his hand, I say, "Let's get Diego and go out and join the party."

He pulls back a little. "I'll be right there. I'm just going to find a home for all this Tom B paraphernalia and add two last instructions to my encyclopedia of cat care for Diego." He grins his heartbreaking grin as he disengages and turns to the pen and paper on the counter. "Just a few more chapters." I hear him laughing as I turn the corner.

Out on the porch, my mother is happily surrounded by Señor Rivera on her left and Graci on her right. Melanie has pulled a chair up to the patio table to sample the chips and guacamole, and Diego finds an old dog toy to start a game of tug of war with Maca.

At this moment my heart is full. A moment, I think, one like this, has so much power in it. The agency to sweep away bad memories, to heal painful wounds and to give hope where hope might be wilting like a black flower in a bloodthirsty swamp.

Right at two o'clock, just as John is setting up the extra table for all the taco fixings, I hear the deep purr of a tricked-out low-rider. As it comes swinging broadly around the corner, the low-slung, baby blue '63 Chevy Impala edges carefully to the curb. When it stops it does a few gentle hops.

"Híjole! That's my kinda ride!" Diego scampers over to the car and stands beside it, hands on hips, whistling through his teeth. I watch him turn his cap from back to front to back again, a sure sign of unabridged car worship. Around his neck, swinging from a wide strap is my thirty mm camera. It only took a few minutes of instruction, and he handled it like a pro. Now he has become the event photographer and begins clicking off multiple photos of the car. I say a little grateful prayer for the invention of digital photography.

I, on the other hand, walk briskly to the front of the car where I see Maria's crooked grin through the open window. As she maneuvers her way out of the almost ground-level front seat, I move to wrap my arms around this teenage girl. Everything about her aura tells me that she is still okay, from her clear bright eyes to the healthy glow of her skin, to the confident way that she returns my hug. Over her shoulder, I see that John has moved over beside Diego and together they admire the ride.

“Let me help Chela get out of this death trap,” Maria laughs as she pulls away from me.

“Yeah, *somebody* let me and Ricky outta here before we expire. I only ever liked back seats for other things, you know. Oh yeah. That’s how little Ricky got here in the first place. Kinda full fucking circle. ¿Bien, Armando?” She snickers while unsnapping the car seat. Maria carefully unstraps the carseat and using meticulous care withdraws the newborn from his royal blue lowriding throne.

Maria razzes her best friend, fully well knowing that no amount of chiding will change this wild girl. “Hey, watch your mouth, Chela. There’s babies and kids around,”

In fact, I see very little that has changed about this girl. Maybe a new tattoo or two, a new piercing, but Chela’s ways of coming on to the world are all the same. The girl doesn't even have an ounce of pregnancy fat on her. How does that happen?

Graciela steals up beside me and together we peer at this tiny pink scrunched-up human being with a head of jet-black hair. There’s just no way of not falling instantly in love with a brand-new human being. It's like its own kind of sorcery.

“Chela, he’s beautiful,” Graciela coos. “Ricky is just like a work of flawless art.”

“He is,” I agree, and watch his tiny fist open like a flower blooming into five perfect little splayed finger petals. Then it happens and I can’t help it. It comes on like a stiff breeze blowing me back against the car as I watch the three women chatter and marvel over the babe in the basket. *But it is no babe, and the basket is a wooden bucket, and the young man carries it to the stone well. His feet shuffle but his whistle is practiced and melodic as he swings the bucket keeping time. I hear sheep baa-ing in the distance and see mounds of heathery hillside. Suddenly a young woman in a peasant skirt and a kerchief covering her dark hair sneaks in from behind and playfully grabs the bucket from his unsuspecting hand. He turns and captures her wrist before she gets away and they walk like that up to the well. I turn my head to get a better view of their faces but am cascading back through time and when I focus. I realize this was a journey of seconds and not a soul noticed.*

That is not a soul except for John who catches my eye over the roof of the car and nods slightly, acknowledging his recognition of my gentle journey.

“Amiga, come see his eyes, they're open now and so clear and watchful.”

I press forward to see these bright little eyes, but my renegade eyes see the past, see the sincere boyish eyes of the happy-go-lucky peasant youth in love with the pretty little hayseed of a girl.

“A happy handsome lad,” I say, and they all turn to look at me in amusement.

“My tia says she thinks she knew your wife, señor.” Maria is sitting next to Mr. Rivera. I watch his eyes grow moist with an instant sting of grief, but he hides it well with a quick look up to the heavens.

Turning to Maria, he brightens and says, “My wife was an extraordinary woman, a rare woman indeed. Smartness, strength and a heart full of goodness only. Añe could be tough as nails if it was called for. Nothing shocked her, only demanded her attention and perhaps that she must fight harder for her truth. She changed lives. And my life has not been the same since she passed on.”

Maria’s expression contains that tender mix of sorrow and embarrassment. “I’m sorry. I didn’t mean to bring back sad memories. It's just that my auntie is sure that Señora Rivera was her high school English teacher and one of her favorite teachers. If she is the one, she is the reason my tia stayed in school and graduated."

"It is true that my wife had the gift of charm over young lives." He shifts in his chair so that he can look more directly at the young woman. "It is much the same way that Dr. Hooper has helped you, Maria." He puts his hand on her shoulder. "Muchas gracias, señorita. It always helps me to hear of Añe's effect on others.

"Dr. Hooper did save my life. Who knows your wife may have saved my tia's." Maria looks down at her fingers that begin to nervously lace and unlace.

"It is one of those miracles of life, is it not, the way that people show up in our lives just when we need them most? It is a lesson my Añe taught me. It is one that is full of truth. As I said, she was a very wise woman." He reaches over and takes Maria's nervous hand in his, then places it over her heart. "You, like myself, have been helped by this truth. Am I not right?"

Maria allows a small smile while her hand lingers on her chest. "Yes," she nods. "I do know. It is true."

He settles back into his chair with a contented look.

I listen to these conversations of souls crisscrossing and connecting, and as always, I find myself preoccupied by the randomness and relevance that brings people together. It remains such a curiosity to me this unpredictability of how humans arrive at these junctions, a chance opportunity, a fickle breeze that curls through the heart and soul. Are we guided by some deficiency in our own condition? I can only have faith since I cannot know if there is some kind of master plan.

I look around and don't see Diego. He was here to say goodbye to Chela and the baby. He let Maria and Chela sandwich him into a hug before they burrowed their way back into the Chevy. He even got Armando to loosen up a bit as they blew off some steam with a bit of boyish jostling and fist bumping that ended in a sealed-in-spit pact that a ride in the Impala would definitely be forthcoming in Diego's future. But now as Graciela glides about folding chairs, picking up dishes and uneaten food, and my mother and Señor Rivera talk quietly in their lawn chairs, I realize I haven't seen the boy for some time. John has no insight as to his whereabouts. He is focused on giving Melanie directions that will take her through the Ortiz mountain pass and the scenic old mining town of Madrid on the back road to Albuquerque.

I finally locate Diego. He is back in his little room lying on his bed. TomB is sprawled on his chest. The purring is audible from the door frame where I stand. It may be the reason why I am, as of yet, undetected by either of them.

"Some watch cat," I snort.

Diego looks up, his cap tilts on his head. His silver front tooth gleams as he gives me a sleepy smile.

"You know Maca may not be pleased about this budding new friendship. She is a bit of the jealous type when it comes to cats." I watch him caress TomB's soft fur for a moment. "Can I come in?" I ask.

"Yeah," he looks down at TomB and smiles at the cat. "Seems to be okay with both of us."

I walk in and since there is nowhere else to sit, I lower myself onto the foot of the bed.

"So, John and I are going to be leaving soon to take Graci home. How're you feeling about being here?"

"It's okay. I'm really used to moving around. And I do like my new room." He scans the room through sleepy eyes. "Just in case you were worried, me and TomB are gonna get along great. You should leave Maca here, too, don't ya think?"

This is like the fourth or fifth time he has brought it up today. "Same answer, stinker. I think I'm going to need her company more than you will and you'll have your hands full taking care of TomB, my mom and Mr. Rivera.

"Martha?" he whispers without looking at me.

"What, sweetie?"

"You're gonna come and visit us, right?" He turns onto his side and the cat flops over like a floppy stuffed Garfield. Diego rubs his belly and the displaced cat purrs. The boy keeps his eyes on the ceiling while he waits for my answer.

"Of course I will. I'll be here in town a lot because of my work, and I plan on having you guys come out there a lot. You know, Cassandra has horses out there. She swears they are super gentle and easy to ride. I really want to find someone who can give me and you a few lessons on how to saddle up and drive one of those things. What do you think?" I ask, trying to get a rise out of him.

He sits all the way up and looks at me through squinted eyes.

"Right, Martha? You're gonna drive the horse? Riiiight!"

"Well, that's how much I know about horses, but we can learn together." I shift on the bed and give the lazy TomB a stroke on his soft warm belly. I thought I read somewhere that cats don't like to be touched on their bellies. "So Diego, I've got a question for you." I look at him straight on now because finally I seem to have said the right things and he is giving me some eye contact. "I need to know if you have had any kind of communication from that creep that kidnapped me. Even the tiniest stirring that he's trying to get into your head."

"Shit, don't you think I'd tell you, Martha? That man's messed up and I'm pretty sure if he ever comes round us again, I'll kill him!" His eyes flash.

I close my eyes. I've got to be more careful with this boy. How quickly I forget that like the spark that sets off a wildfire, his street kid heat can ignite and reduce his recent progress to ashes. Diego's wounds are still smoldering below and above the surface. I move closer to where he is sitting by putting the cat in my lap.

"Diego, I just want to know if that man makes any contact with you or Alice. You know my mom is not as strong as us superheroes." I put my hand softly on his shoulder. "I got you a cellphone so you can call me if you need me. From anywhere." I pull a small smartphone out of my back pocket. "It's charged and activated and ready to go. Do you know how to use it?"

I know this is a ridiculous question for a kid of this day and age. And the answer comes as quick as his dancing fingers on the screen. Without looking up he thanks me twice.

"This is so badass! You're awesome, Martha. You already got your number in here and John's." He's up on his knees tapping rapidly through the screens. "Can I load some free apps? I promise I'll be responsible." Now he's rocking back and forth so vigorously that TomB decides to ditch us for more peaceful climes.

"You can load free stuff, but no bad stuff. I mean it. The phone goes away if you abuse the privilege." I turn his cap sideways on his head. "Got it, kid?"

"Got it! Promise! Did I tell you how badass this is, Martha?" He laughs.

"Okay, Diego, look at me for a minute." He does with wide eyes, so I continue. "It's for fun, yes. But it's also our weapon against evil. It's our superhero protection tool. Right?"

He jumps straight from his knees to a standing position on the bed and salutes me. "Got it, Captain."

"So, anything else you need to know before we leave? There's plenty of food in the fridge. Oh, and watch for the UPS guy. I ordered you a couple of new books. I think you'll like them. And no, I won't tell you what they are. It's a surprise. What else?"

"Nothin' so far, Captain. But I'll be in touch," he raises the phone, "if there's anything to report."

"Okay, kiddo, then why don't you come out and say goodbye to Graci and John and then see if Alice needs help with any last little things? You know I'm counting on you to take really good care of her."

He gives me that silver-toothed grin that is melting a defensive buffer that I now realize I have been keeping cushioned around my heart. I take a sharp breath in with this unexpected discovery about myself. Why am I not freely letting the boy into my heart, like my mother has done? Why do I feel so guarded? I'm so adrift in this thought that he startles me by jumping to his feet on the bed almost bowling me over. As he leaps off the bed, Diego shoves the phone in the back pocket of his shorts, turns to give me a quick hug and bolts out the door. Again, I ponder, as I walk slowly out the door myself, why can't I shake this feeling there might be something not right with my heart? Is it broken?

III

"You have to come in just for a minute," Graci begs me. "I've got a housewarming gift for you that you have to have on your first night out there."

John looks over at me from the driver's seat of his old pickup truck.

"You better do what she says," he laughs. "This friend of yours is a force to be reckoned with. Not someone *I* would choose to say no to."

Graciela gives him her no-nonsense hands-on-hip, dramatic bow of the head and nod of approval. So, what choice do I have, despite my eagerness to spend some time alone with my man in my new digs before he abandons me for his second paramour, his passionate affair with his guitar?

"All right, all right," I surrender, while I awkwardly and a bit laboriously climb down from the bench seat.

Graci is already unlocking the door to her sweet little house in this quiet out-of-the-way part of town. Her front yard is a Southwest House and Garden dream. The color of her thumbs and all the rest of her fingers on both hands are green, green, green, green. I pass through an arbor that is laden with morning glories of the royalest blue imaginable. On either side of the river stone walkway is a riot of blossoming colors. Stalks of purple hummingbird mint, bright yellow sprays of tiny flowers exploding like skyrockets, African Daisies bobbing bright orange heads in the breeze, and pink and purple stalks of cosmos. A small black wrought iron tea table with two cushioned chairs is strategically placed under the cool shade of an ancient Catalpa tree, positioned just so the sitters can view the various bird feeders and the bubbling fountain while sipping a libation of their choice.

Passing through the painted bright blue door of Graciela's house is just a continuation of her floricultural wizardry. Harvested from the garden in the backyard, bundles of herbs are hanging from the beams of the ceiling drying in the kitchen, and sending out earthy aromas. More herbs and medicinal blooms sprout from indoor and outdoor window boxes, as well as the vegetable garden plot in the backyard. It's surprising there's nothing blooming from an old boot or toolbox.

"Sit down, Marta." she commands, then disappears into her bedroom.

I do so obediently, but also yell at her backside, "Remember, John is waiting in the car so be quick about it, Graci." As I am feeling the rigors of a day spent meeting the needs of all my partygoers, I actually do relish lowering myself onto the antique serpentine settee that she found on Craigslist. One of her many self-taught talents– she learned to reupholster it herself, choosing a forest green fern-covered fabric. I rub the ache from my snake-bit leg that throbs beneath my touch. The bite to my forearm never feels quite this bad.

"Get a move on, Graci," I yell again. "We want some daylight left to feed the horses and to explore the place."

Looking around, I see that Graci has brought a mask for herself back from Guatemala, hers looks quite different than the one she chose to guard me. Hers, which hangs above the kiva fireplace in the corner of the room, has the dark wrinkled wooden face of an old man. Attached to the chin is a long thick goat-like beard. Graci told me just recently that these masks are not intended to hide the identity of their wearer, but are made so that one can inhabit the elemental nature of the image that the mask represents. It's a moment to live inside the skin of another creature or being, taking on the spirit in a magical transformation.

"Here we go," she says as she re-emerges from her room. She releases a loud sigh of relief, "I really had to pee. Like my mask?" I nod wordlessly in my suddenly lethargic state.

"It's called el viejo máscara, the old one. He looks so enlightened, but sly, don't you think?"

"So do you wear him around the house and become wise and sly?" I ask. "On second thought, you don't need that mask, you're already a wise ass and sly as fox can be."

"Ahh, Marta. Never lose your whimsey." she sighs again and comes over flopping down on the settee next to me. "Okay. So here it is. A bottle for this evening." She holds up a rather large shapely brown bottle of liquor as if she's waving around a coveted Oscar trophy. "It's rum. Zacapa rum from Guatemala, slow aged in the high mountains. Guaranteed to make this an interesting evening for you and your novio."

"Okay," I laugh a little hesitantly. "Knowing you, I was expecting your latest healing potion. But I'm guessing this is potent enough to cure what ails me."

"Well, it will at least humble the things that ail you. But funny you should mention that because my second gift is one I have concocted that *will* cure what ails you." She hands me a small tincture bottle with an eyedropper top. "Hold up a sec, let me get you a glass of water so you can start it right now."

"What is this stuff?" I call after her as she scurries to the kitchen.

"It's a healing potion." She gives me an impish smile, "And of course, all ingredients are perfectly safe, and Graciela tested and approved. Actually, I found this outstanding curandera up near Coyote and she has been working with me in some of the areas of preparation I was lacking in. But for this, I grew everything myself and made the tincture exactly as I was taught. It will heal the nerve damage, corazon. Do your physical therapy and take this in water two times a day and you will be stronger than ever." She takes the bottle from my hand and sprinkles several drops into the water. "Bottoms up." she coaxes.

I sniff, I swirl, I take the tiniest sip, then swig it like an old sot. "It tastes like weeds smell when you pull them out of the dirt, and then maybe dip them in alcohol. You sure this is good for me?" I smack my lips and roll my tongue around in my mouth. "I guess you have to develop a taste for it, but not as bad as the last thing you made me take." I look at her warily. She's looking back at me like I'm a lab rat. "I think I'll need a chaser next time. You know like we used to do with bad liquor." This makes her laugh heartily. "Yup," I continue, "now, if only you had something that could heal this PTSD dread in my heart."

"Oh, but I do," she crows, "but that is for another time. In the meantime, you and John have some rum fun and..." She gives me a two-armed hug and a kiss on the lips. "And I will call you in a day or two to see how you're doing." Taking the glass from my hand, she sprinkles the last few drops on her tongue before helping me up from the settee, then practically pushes me out the door with my tincture and my bottle of Zacapa. I look back at her as she waves to John from the door.

Hobbling through her psychedelic garden of floral stimuli, I wonder what else this woman could possibly have up her sleeve.

IV

Cassandra's back deck faces the southeast. Despite its unvarying habit of setting in the west with admirable regularity, the setting sun projects its evening kaleidoscope show onto the cloudy mantle to the southeast. This evening's spectacle with its woolpacks of bleached white puffs and decidedly animal configurations is turning into crimson and amber plumage, peacocking against the backdrop of the ever-deepening sweep of turquoise. All this is best viewed from the deck where we sit propped on the descending wooden stairs, with glasses of rum on ice and a lover's arm wrapped around a shoulder.

Momentarily silenced by awe and alcohol, no hindrance to bliss is to be found in Cassandra's spartan lack of outdoor furniture. Not on this deck or on the front porch or anywhere else on the visible parts of her twenty acres is there any outdoor furniture. Thus, with exhaustion setting in, after a light dinner of cheese and olives, feeding the horses and walking perhaps one half of a half of an acre while playing soccer with large ponderosa pinecones, we have sunk contentedly onto the wooden steps for the evening's diversions.

As the sulky twilight sets in and washes the color from the world, I am renewed by finding myself bewitched by the half-light and the growing shadows all around. "That which subdues the light reshapes the very objects that we trust to be substantial," I softly wax poetic. "That which we think of as the real world is recreated by the dusky light fading. Eclipses of shadow and silhouette, echoes of a day passed, suggest regard for the spirits and enchanters hiding behind every tree, those who push the wind to sing in our ears." Only a few or more sips into Graci's rum and I am feeling an unearthly peace of mind and an unusual feeling of deliverance from my prevailing anxiety. A period of tipsy, gypsy poetic grace.

I look up to see John staring at me. If I am reading him rightly in the half-light, he is smiling with wonder. I feel his face hover over mine for a mere flash, then his lips are on mine resulting in a long sultry kiss. "You truly are the whole package, Martha Hooper," he finally mumbles woozily against my cheek. "Healer, lover, poetress, an old soul and a traveler in time. How is it that I found you and fell so profoundly under your spell?"

I barely have time to devour his affections and his words when the serenity of the moment is split wide open by coyote song. Less like a song and more like a chorus of banshees yodeling, yipping and yelping, a wail both chilling and exhilarating at the same time. The uncivilized feral spirit always lurking just below Maca's dog skin compels her to answer with a mad song of her own. With a tortured convoluted impersonation meant to answer the call of the wild, her cries send John and I plunging into yodeling hell.

"Make it stop!" John cries out with rummy breath and withdraws his hands and drops his glass to the step as he places his hands over his ears. Laughing I stand up teetering for a moment and call her in, petting her to soothe the wild out of her. Returning to the steps, I snuggle in between John's long legs and lean back. We sit like this for many moments taking it all in with renewed appreciation of the quiet. Now the sound of crickets and a night frog somewhere down by the corral can be heard and soaked up.

Out of the blue, his voice a husky whisper, John asks, "Do you ever feel like you have chosen to have a relationship with a child?"

"What do you mean?" I tip my chin upward so that I can look back at him in response to this curious question. His fingertips, cooled from holding the rum glass, brush a few stray hairs from my forehead, but his eyes do not meet mine.

"I mean, in addition to your mystical powers of seeing into the past, there is no question in my mind that you are an old soul. One that has collected many savvy, enlightening, and perhaps a savory one or two, experiences throughout your colorful past lives. I on the other hand seem to be an infant in this process. So, in a nutshell, you are robbing the incarnation cradle. Or something like that." He takes a sip and laughs at his own metaphor.

I turn back and stare off into the dark bank of clouds that linger almost invisibly on the horizon. A muted bolt of lightning flashes deep within the thick cumulus, lighting it up inwardly.

"I really haven't ever thought about us like that. You do?"

"I do. I think about it a lot. I worry that there is no depth to my soul, that I might seem shallow or unevolved to you. That you might grow bored with me." I hear the clink of ice in his glass as he takes another sip above my head.

Well... I think Graci was right about her rum making for an interesting evening. But he has stirred thoughts that flash like silver minnows in and out of my stream of consciousness. One of the things that I welcome about this man is his quiet soul. It holds no enigmas for me, no esoteric webs to get caught up in, no tidings from the past to console, and still continues to draw me inexorably to him. Seduced by his... innocence? I turn around so that I am kneeling on the step below. I face him and draw his face towards mine.

"If there is some kind of inherent rule in the universe that dictates the number of lives required between lovers, then I say, we will be renegades against these time lords. One lifetime... the hours that your one life has collected, your wealth and wisdom that is banked for the future, it's all your shiny commodity in the present. You are a man of complexity and depth to me in every way."

Turning away from me, John's face is unreadable while he ponders my words and the distant flashes of lightning.

"Maybe for now," he replies after a while. "But that's the thing about relationships, the 'for now' is always in constant motion forward, assumptions of this moment don't necessarily travel unbroken into the future. I know this well enough from looking back at the sorry road of broken affairs I've already traveled. I just kind of want this one to last."

"What?" I shake my head as I wrap my arms around his shoulders. "I'm either suddenly very intoxicated or you just tried to soft-sell me on some temporal ideology that is running rings around my brain. So, wait a minute. Let's remember that we are here right now in this incredible place. Together. Tomorrow you leave for Denver and in four weeks you will be back. What do you think will change in that time?" My knees are starting to ache.

"Maybe nothing in that bit of time. It could be three months from now. Maybe a year from now. Or maybe," he looks down at me smiling up at him, "maybe we do have something here that's stronger than the inherent rules of the universe. Maybe what I need is a little more Graci juice and a little less apprehension."

Stretching upwards and pulling his face closer I kiss this man deeply and with longing. The wash of rum that taints our tongues only kindles the wildfire that has ignited. It's hard for me to comprehend, through this rummy fog, the desire I am feeling, and John's uneasiness about souls. This is the most untroubled relationship I have ever been in.

With an abruptness born of need, he suddenly stands and helps me to my feet. His eyes are full of a hunger I know I can satisfy. So the thick-walled tumblers of half-filled rum are left sweating on the steps. John reaches for the bottle as we pass by the deck railing where earlier, in the pink light of sunset, he had carefully poured the golden elixir into our glasses. Now, in the deepening twilight, he takes a swig straight from the bottle and offers it to me like a sacramental sealing of our incongruous collusion in this love affair. Swinging the bottle above my lips, I taste the brimstone fire at the back of my throat, the sweet molasses mixing with vanilla on the flat of my tongue. In this fiery mix of booze and passion lives the elements of tonight's delirium, the primitive electricity of ecstasy coiled with an alcohol-inspired dose of recklessness. A current that sends us reeling into the bedroom that I have prepared with candles and scented sheets for our parting night together.

In the middle of the night, we are both awakened. Probably the call of nature, since I head to the bathroom, and he moves to take care of his business out in the blackness of night. But I, too, feel the call to wander back out onto the deck. Checking the clock, I see that it is 3:00 a.m., and much cooler than it was a few hours ago. I grab the blanket off the bed and head out the door.

"Breathtaking, isn't it?" he whispers as he awkwardly finds his way over to me in the dark.

I answer him as I try to put the blanket around both of us. "A little cold, and spooky, too. I'm not sure I've ever experienced so much darkness all at once. Even with enough stars to light up New York City, it feels like we're twenty thousand leagues under the sea. I can hardly breathe." I shiver. He pulls me closer, and we just stand like that, our chins tilted heavenward and our eyes scanning the sky.

Suddenly I am remembering a time, a time of this much darkness and with it came a horrifying desperation. The memory moves through me slowly as slowly as the realization that this is why, suddenly, I can't breathe. I feel those walls rise up around me, confining me, paralyzing me, and in the far away, I hear the chilling rattle of viper tails. And there it lies, just beneath the thin lids of my closed eyes. I am alone, and I am going to die. The shivering turns to spasms of shaking and I can't catch my breath at all.

"Martha, what's wrong? Here let me wrap you back up in the blanket." He bundles me, swaddling my shaking body like an infant. Turning me back towards the house, he is speaking words to me.

Soft words, calming words, but I can't hear them over the rattling that is echoing in my ears. My arm and leg are throbbing, and though I feel John pushing me along, I no longer have control over my wobbly legs. Suddenly, the shadow of that monstrosity is hovering over me, his wine-stained face and evil leer carving at the heart of me. Mr. Misterioso. "John!" My scream is muffled and choked. I feel his presence both outside of me and inside my blood and bones. He is here. He is in possession of my mind. He inhabits my mind and is whispering in my ear, the voice of a venomous viper. So foul, like a poisonous hissing, it coils through my body, "I am still here, Master Turnbull," says the viperous woman's voice. Madam. I can barely breathe.

I am being carried. I am being saved. A shield between my flesh and a monster's control.

The shaking won't stop, even once I am in bed next to John's body covered in a mountain of down he has dug out of the bedroom closet. Finally, he slides out from under the tomb of blankets and reassures me he'll be right back. His absence hollows me out even more and now the shaking is accompanied by uncontrollable tears. Enough, I tell myself, but there is no controlling it, and I realize that it is the fear and anger and horror that I have been bottling up for the past month that has found a crack in my carefully fabricated veneer. The deluge is brutal. My body feels ravaged and powerless against the torrent of nightmarish memories, against the tsunami of tears. Where the fuck is John? The paroxysms and the unstoppable tears feel like they may never end. I'll lay this way for years, get wrinkled and old and die in a sopping wet pool of suffering and wet duck feathers. Where could he be?

Then he is here. He lights the candles. I smell the distinct aroma of chamomile tea.

"I put some ginger in it to help warm you," he murmurs, as he finds a place to set the mugs. He helps me sit up and wipes the tears from my face with the sheet. I think I won't be able to drink the tea because of the shaking, but with his help, I manage, and just as he predicted the warm liquid moves through me like a hot bath from the inside. It soothes and begins to restore a sliver of my self-control. John sits next to me, his face, the picture of compassion and concern, all of which champions the beginnings of calmness. Little by little the storm that has thundered through my body and mind moves off to sea, leaving me drained and exhausted, but thankfully sedate.

"It was him. He was here." I insist.

"Who? Who was here, Martha?" He takes the empty mug from my hands and returns it to the bedside table, moving to blow out the candles.

"Please," I beg as I slump back down into the bed. "Leave them burning for a little bit longer. The monster who kidnapped me. I swear he was out there in the night whispering to me. In my ear. Or maybe just in my mind." I sigh and pull the covers up to my chin. "I can't believe that the police haven't been able to locate him yet. It's the one goddamn thing in this world that stands between me and a true peace of mind. Everything else will heal or mend or I can rebuild, but I really don't know what to do with this fear that he is coming back to hurt me or you or my family."

The candles are left burning and John slips back under the comforter with me. With his head propped on the pillow, he turns to face me and softly strokes my hair.

"They will find him," he reassures me. "But until they do, I truly believe that you have taken all the precautions that will keep him from finding you."

"But what about Diego and my mother? He may know where I live and come looking for me there."

"Not without the police getting wind of him. Don't forget that they have promised to patrol the area regularly until he is apprehended." He shifts us both so that he is cradling me in such a way that I feel like a ravaged ship coming into safe harbor.

"I'm not sure that you understand even now what an unearthly creature he is. He is full of power and sorcery that no human being should ever be in possession of. It makes him illusive and treacherous and terrifying. And nameless."

"He's Mr. Misterioso, the phantom of the opera, right?" John makes an attempt to lighten the mood with a reference to the name that one of the monster's cronies gave him.

"Or Madam, the other horrifying creature he was in my past life with him," I add.

"Would it help if I didn't go to Denver?" he asks.

"Oh god, no. That would be the worst thing. Do you want me to wallow in guilt, as well as terror and self-pity?" I finally laugh, feeling a trifle of warmth and calm flowing through not only my body but my mind as well.

"Well, I'm not feeling so good about leaving you if you think that that creep is near and coming after you. You know you're going to be spending a fair amount of your time alone and who's going to be here to do this," he says as he moves his lips onto my neck.

"Let's get one thing straight, buster," I say, as I pull away from him in mock irritation. "I'm no lily-livered pansy. Subject to panic attacks, yes. Predisposed to falling hard for musician types. It happens. And yes, possibly a little too unorthodox for my own good, undoubtedly. However, I have, with the help of my friends, been doin' it on my own for a lot longer than you, baby. And I'll be okay," I give him my hardest glare, but at the feel of his touch I am drawn back to the warmth and comfort of his body. "As long as you find your way back to me in four weeks." Pushing back the blankets, I stroke his bare back.

"Is that a fact, my savvy sexy lover. Let's see what all those lifetimes have taught you about pleasing a man." He moans as he pulls me on top of him and buries his face in my body.

V

The sun is streaming through the window. How late is it, I wonder as I turn over in bed. It suddenly dawns on me for a disoriented moment, that John is not in the bed with me. I touch the rumpled sheet on his side of the bed and there is no warmth to it at all. I stretch leisurely and call out his name. When he doesn't answer, I feel compelled to get my sorry ass out of bed because the man must have gotten up some time ago while I was here sleeping the sleep of the dead. I almost step on Maca when I swing my legs to the floor. She doesn't have that frantic 'where's my breakfast' look about her, so it's a pretty good bet that John has already fed her. I get a whiff of coffee and that's just what it takes to get me to throw on a robe and barefoot it into the kitchen. The coffee pot is on and there is half of a pot of coffee just waiting for me. I find a mug, pour it up and prepare to find my lost man when suddenly I see a yellow tablet of legal paper on the small wooden table. I finally glance at the time on the wall clock in the kitchen. It's a quarter after ten.

The tablet, I notice, is brand new, the handwriting is printed not cursive and is crisp and easy to read. It covers the full length of the page and ends with, I Love You, John. I hug my mug of coffee into my body. I dare myself to go to the front window and look at the driveway.

After a small debate on the virtues of dealing with reality, I move slowly to the window and open the drape. Reality sucks. John's truck is no longer parked where it was. I linger at the window, sipping my coffee, watching the breeze push the pine branches back and forth, and try to recall each and every second of last night. When I've covered it from beginning to end, returned to it and relived the best parts, pondered the embarrassment of the worst parts, and finished the last drop of coffee in the mug, only then, do I feel prepared enough to walk over to the legal pad, pick it up, and settle onto the sofa that faces the empty driveway.

It starts: *Dear Martha, I guess we all have our failings. You may have touched upon what you might consider one of yours last night. But be assured that if you are thinking that I disagree most vehemently. I see it as quite the opposite. The way I see it, experiencing fear and anger as deeply as love, joy, and bliss is just the manifestation of a person who is a human fledgling, strong enough, smart enough and ready to fly to even greater heights. You are so much more evolved than most of us. That is the Martha Hooper I know and love.*

Now onto my flaw. I have never learned to say or carry out a proper goodbye. To be honest with you, I thought I could do it. I lingered quite a while feeling brave. I thought I could give you a lovely, until-we-meet-again farewell, a morning toast to the future with clinking coffee mugs. But in the end, I just had to leave. I promise you, if I've left you feeling hurt or jilted, or really pissed off at me, I completely understand. But know this, woman, I will so make it up to you when I get back because I am really good at homecomings. You'll see.

The lover's treatise goes on to say that Sunny will be bringing my car to me with a friend of hers around noon. He hopes that she won't be too much of a burden in his absence because she seems to have grown quite fond of me and my therapeutic ways. This is a slightly distasteful turn of events, but I can hope that because she has to come with a friend, she will talk little and leave swiftly. I put the legal pad aside and get up to pour another cup of coffee. The clock reveals a bit of bad news. I have only an hour and a scattered mind to work with. I have to shower, eat and prepare myself mentally for Sunny's arrival. I look down at John's note. He had finished the epistle with promises of frequent calls, texts, emails, and notes by carrier pigeon and the instruction that I should do the same. I smile because, for just a flash, I feel like a young woman with a boyfriend who is maybe going off to college or war, or better still, off to make his fortune, in this case by making a CD. And of course, he will come marching back to me complete with wealth, stories and undoubtedly with longing made sweeter by the passage of time. I decide disappointment will not be long lived in this house, not in my unmistakably newly reconstructed life.

Slipping into Solitude

I

Sitting under the front portal on one of the two chairs from the dining table provides me with a view of the incoming driveway. While the wind dries my freshly shampooed hair, I spot a rather large healthy cottontail that manages to nibble a tuft of grass not forty feet away, without catching Maca's attention. It's at that moment that I realize, her attention is focused on the sound of my Subaru chugging up the road, a sound that was inaudible to my human ears until I see it climbing up the hill just short of the drive. I'm sure this sound must confuse the dog who owns it since she is sitting next to the woman who should be driving it.

Sunny pulls in, sets the park brake and hops out with all the windows down. Her jeans are designer and form-fitting. The blouse, an exquisitely delicious plum color, compliments the high flush of her cheeks. Her hair carefully divided into two long dark braids makes her look half her age and the whole look is accented with a pair of western boots that have plum-colored tooling on the leather uppers. Those long legs carry her quickly to my throne, where she leans down and throws her arms around me. She smells like freshly washed laundry that blows on the clothesline from a springtime breeze.

"Oh Martha, it's so good to see you. Look at this place!" She releases me and stepping back twirls herself in a circle like Marlo Thomas spinning on the streets of New York. That Girl. Except this girl is a forty-two-year-old pregnant woman.

"How are you, Sunny?" I ask, with my usual reserve, a reserve built from skepticism that this altruistic act of bringing me my car does not come without some ulterior motive. "Soooo…" I tilt my head inquisitively, "how are you getting back into town?" I look up at her while running my fingers through my damp hair with a nod to my own car.

"Oh, that's no sticky wicket," she laughs as she gives the house another appraising look. "He'll be along shortly. He wanted to stop at that little store on the way here to pick up a pack of cigarettes or something. I really love this place. Do those horses down there come with the place?"

I look down at the barn, but my ears are trying to hear sounds only dogs can hear - the sound of another vehicle coming up the road.

"Yes, those are Cassandra's horses. I'm caring for them while she's out of town."

"You know, I used to ride quite a bit when I was younger. A friend of mine had some horses that her family kept on a ranch north of town and we would ride in the mountains. I swear, it was one of the best times in my life."

"Were you good at saddling and all that kind of stuff?" I ask, entertaining the flicker of an ulterior motive that ignites in my own selfish brain.

"Oh yeah, and I'm sure it's like that old 'riding a bike' thing; you never completely forget how once you learn." She comes and sits cross-legged on the wood planks next to my chair.

“Here,” I say standing up, making an attempt at being a good host, “have a seat. I can get the other chair that's in the house.”

“Don’t do that, I’m perfectly fine, Martha. So, John’s off to Colorado, huh? I really hope this is his chance at a big break. He’s been a musician as long as I’ve known him and he’s, you know, like really really talented. I bet you’re going to miss him.”

“It’s true,” I agree with her. “Someone with his musical gifts should be able to share them with the world. A CD is definitely a step in the right direction. And yes, I will miss him, but I think I’m probably going to be pretty busy over the next month, so the time will go by fast.” I sit back down in the chair and turn my ear to the road again. This time I am rewarded with the faint sound of a distant motor.

“Sounds like your ride is coming up the hill. It was really nice of you to bring my car all the way out here, Sunny.” The sense of relief I am feeling is like a rush of oxygen to my brain.

“Oh, no problem. When John texted me this morning, I got really excited. I thought it would be great fun to take a ride into the country, and also, I just wanted to see you.”

Oh great, I think, trying not to let the trepidation show on my face, but here it comes; that demanding childish solicitation for attention and problem solving that she is so obviously dysfunctional at.

“No really. I just thought it would be interesting to see the country girl in you. It suits you, you know. You seem really calm and like you belong out here. Personally, I don’t think this is the life for me. I like to have my cafes and entertainment and shopping nearby. But,” she shrugs, “to each his own.”

“Well, it is temporary,” I respond, a little bit too defensively. I don’t know why.

The deep growl of a powerful engine rounds the corner, and a shiny black truck becomes visible through the trees.

“Is that your ride?” I ask.

She rises from that cross-legged sit in one graceful movement and proceeds to raise her arms upwards, twisting and stretching like a slinky feline.

"Yep, that's Jimmy. He just got that new Ford 250. What a monster. Again, personally, I prefer a snazzy little sports car, but he likes to go fishing in the mountains and stuff like that."

Jimmy...that name is ringing a bell, but not quite loud enough that I'm remembering the association.

"Hang on Martha, I'll be right back." She casts a quick glance to me that is full of secrets, then swings her hips in a spirited swagger over to the truck. The man, still not visible to me, leans his head just slightly out the window, and she gives him a light kiss on the lips.

Wow, my mind careens for a moment like a runaway car. Already? Does this woman have any principles? And I find myself getting even more disturbed as I watch the man hop several feet down from the cab of his big truck. Jimmy is... 'good-looking Jimmy' from the restaurant. The one that she flirted with. They walk hand in hand back over to the porch, and as I stand up, Maca greets them with tail wagging, no restraint.

"Martha, you remember Jimmy from the other day, right?"

"I do," I respond as I offer my hand for a shake. His face is open and friendly and very good-looking. Somewhere in his forties, I think, as I take his measure.

"Jimmy Sanchez," he smiles broadly. There's a humorous sparkle and a depth of living in those saddle-brown eyes. For a moment I feel a little disarmed by the man.

"Well, I'm happy to meet you, Mr. Sanchez and glad to know that Sunny has such a generous friend. I have to thank you for helping me get my car up here."

"No problem, Ms Hooper," he smiles. I can see in the set of his jaw, and the gleam in his eye, that he is immensely amused by something in this conversation.

"What?" I shake my head. "Did I say something wrong?"

He tilts his head. "Well, first off, can we just be Jimmy and Martha? And secondly, I guess you don't remember me. Which doesn't surprise me at all."

Now I look even more closely. Measure every inch of his being because I can't stand puzzles like these. I shake my head stumped.

"Well, Martha. Is it okay to call you Martha?" I nod mutely. "Let's call it ten years ago. And let's say you were taking a walk, oh, maybe to clear your mind or to get a little fresh air. Imagine, and I know you can, that you came across some down-on-his-luck derelict who had OD'd himself on some really persuasive drug, because he really couldn't give a flying fuck about whether he lived or died.

"So, there *he* was waiting for the devil at the bottom of some arroyo and suddenly there *she* was... a storytelling angel, who lifted his feet out of those fires that were tickling his toes. And just for memory's sake, let's say that storytelling angel stayed by his side and kept him from sinking back down into fire and brimstone by telling him truths from some long-ago past life, a tale in which that wretch was a man of valor and gallantry. Spun that tale out of golden strands of enchantment, she did, cloaking the nearly dead man in notions so brilliant that by the time the ambulance came to take him away, he already had a kernel of hope growing in his gut."

I look over at Sunny. This story is not news to her. Her face is interested but passive. Mine, I'm sure, is the embodiment of dumbfoundedness.

"James?" I move my eyes back to the man. Squinting, I stare like it will help me see the man he was, more clearly. "You are you? I mean him?" I say stupidly. Then suddenly, the James I had once offered solace to materializes in my mind's eye. He who has obviously cast off his deathwish, was once a startling skeleton of a man with deep saddle brown eyes fringed with dark lashes and a look that was laced with poison. His drug of choice was whatever he could get his hands on. His tangled mass of brittle black hair and beard that mice might have been living in, served only to make him achingly possessed by his demons. But now, I remember him well. I recall pulling his frail body onto my lap and locking my eyes onto his, just to hold him in this world until help arrived. And unwillingly, I had invaded his forgotten days of yore. But as I did it, I spoke of every step he took and every detail I encountered. Murmuring and chanting like a monk, I had whispered the stories from the archives of his past life. I remember how I had pleaded with him to let my words save him. Pressed every word into his ears. A savior in a suit of armor I had told the dying man in the present. Words to bind this man to his life.

I look up to see him searching my face as I am flooded with the memory. His smile is genuine, but I can see it is haunted by the same memories.

"You were nothing if not my guardian angel," he says candidly. Turning to Sunny, he continues. "I didn't tell you about the way that she sat at my hospital bed and let me rave like a madman about my rabid life. Later she visited me regularly in rehab, until, I'm guessing, she felt I was strong enough and connected enough with other support, to cut me loose."

"Imagine that! It's taken until now for our paths to cross again. I can't believe it." This feeling of wonderment is reinforced by the transformation I see in front of me. I am humbled and suddenly ashamed of the petty thoughts that I have been harboring for Sunny and this man. In the presence of this restored human being, there would seem to be no place for such triviality and unkindness. I am reminded of my own axiom that I have let disintegrate with recent events: within us all, there lies the seed of redemption, and if not in one lifetime, then in another. There within lies the chance for growth, healing and evolution towards our greatest fulfillment.

"Hey," I say, gathering my wits about me, "would you two like to come in for coffee and see the place? If you have time, we could take a walk down to the barn."

Sunny chimes in, "I was really hoping you'd ask." She grabs Jimmy's hand with both of hers. "Do you think we have time? I know you wanted to go have lunch, but we have all afternoon. What do you think?"

I see by his expression he is easily swayed by her appeal. So, I open the door and invite them in.

The coffee maker chugs along, spitting out a fresh pot of brew. I find a couple of clean mugs in a box I haven't unpacked yet and place them on the counter while I listen to the murmur of conversation coming from the couch in the living room. Turning around, I lean against the counter and watch them. If it wasn't for Sunny's stormy disposition and her pregnancy by another man, I think I would gladly celebrate the beginning of this charming relationship between two fetching unattached souls. But that is not the case, and I worry that this will be just one more of Sunny's follies and Jimmy will have to circumvent a mismatch for his heart, if not a broken one. I lose track of that thought and feel myself for the moment pleasantly drifting on the smell of fresh coffee, the idle talk and the feeling that I'm simply floating along.

It's not until I feel that familiar rough landing, that I realize that I've unwittingly maneuvered through those channels of time again. I don't even know whose. I'm just suddenly... where?

I try to clear my vision, but I seem to be surrounded by blackness, a sensation that brings on a familiar sense of panic. It's a blindness I do not wish to revisit. In that way that I have, of swimming through the archival tide, I move myself to find sight, to find my bearings. A dim light in the blackness draws me to it as if I am a moth in the night until finally I sense the outline of two walls, a narrow tunnel that I force myself to pass through. When I reach what seems to be the end, it opens up into a larger space, lit by one burning torch. Beneath the torch, a man sits, blank-faced and drowsy, his eyes remain open but unfocused. Around his waist is a belt that holds an iron ring of large keys, while a cudgel made of a large bone or a smooth curved piece of wood balances casually between his bare muscled legs. The weapon is crowned with a large, rounded rock attached with leather thongs. He pays no mind to the moans and cries of pain that echo through the otherwise damp cold silence. All around me, the rock walls are overgrown with moss and mold, and thick condensation oozes from the walls and ceiling. Here the air is thick with a noxious effluvium and the miasma of rotting human spirits. It is some kind of prison.

Her cell is small and dark, and other than a small filthy reed mat and a wooden bucket, there is nothing. The dress she wears is of a rough colorless fabric and cinched at the waist with a thin cord. Her feet wear nothing but the accumulation of the filth and muck that muddies the stone floor of her cell. When I move closer, it is as if I have created some kind of unearthly breeze that she can sense. I see her look about the cell and shiver. Her dark braids resemble the braids she has so frivolously styled into her hair in the present. But these braids, though as long and dark as Sunny's, show the foulness and slovenliness of much time spent in this dungeon, as does the patchwork of grime and deep bruising across her cheeks, her bare shoulders, her arms and legs. Suddenly with that same air of sensing me, she stares into the space where I feel like I am and begins to speak. It is a tongue incomprehensible to me, but as I watch her face and her fearless eyes, I sense that she is reprimanding the very gods that have led her to this terrible moment. Removing a small sharp object that was well hidden under her dress between her breasts, a contorted smirk and one whispered word parts her lips. "Frith!" she cries out. Then the blade is plunged into her own chest with a purposeful and deadly aim for the heart of her. Though she crumples to the stone floor, blood pumping from her chest and a hideous cry issuing from her lips, her eyes are trained on me, locked in a way that paralyzes me. And yet with sickening and desperate relief, I feel my grip loosen on this world, and I fade and tumble forward through the convoluted burrows of time that lead me back into my own kitchen.

Sunny is staring at me, leaning her head on the back of the sofa. Her eyes meet mine in a meaningful way, but her voice is cheerful and neutral as she calls out, "Can I help you with the coffee?"

"No, I'm fine," I call back, trying my best to be in this world and this one only. "I've got it. Do either of you want cream or sugar?"

II

Monday mornings have always been full of busyness, commitments and often intriguing work with clients whose dilemmas help to grow the width and breadth of my abilities to decode the human equation. This workload has been considerably less, since my obligation to heal myself both physically and mentally from the kidnapping ordeal. Today, on this particular Monday, that sense of responsibility to my avocation is virtually nil. I wake up to a day brimming with nothingness, a blank page of my story that I am free to write in whatever way pleases me.

It pleases me to start my day by feeding the horses. The smell of the hay, the contented sound of large teeth grinding their way to satisfaction, the sound of snorting and blowing and hooves shuffling and stamping upon the packed dirt. The simplicity of it takes my breath away. I find the mucking fork and begin to remove the manure from the enclosure, hefting shovel-fulls into the wheelbarrow. It's true that I limp and hobble my way through this activity, but when it's done, I feel like I have awakened muscles from a long-dormant sleep, while my mind, in direct contrast, is blissfully quiet.

Maca finds her own amusement sniffing out mice from under the large mountain made up of hay bales in the barn. As an excuse to linger a bit longer here in the warm morning sun and the sweet-smelling air, I decide to retrieve one of the brushes and try my hand at horse grooming. I start with the palomino mare, the gold color of her coat glistening in the sunlight. She stands calmly as I run the brush over her large belly and back to her muscled hips and thighs. Maca has wandered back and stands at the gate, observing this interaction with her own brand of dogenvy. The mane of this horse is soft, wispy and white. I carefully run the brush down through it, all the while wondering what it would be like to sit upon this beast.

Yesterday, when I had brought James and Sunny down here, Sunny had shown a totally unexpected competence around these animals. Even James had looked at me with a hint of wonder when she slipped through the corral slats and both creatures immediately found their way over to her, nuzzling her shoulders and flapping their lips at her as if they were relating some long-held secrets to the woman. Laughing like a child, she maneuvered with confidence and ease between the two, giving hugs and kisses without a hint of favoritism. When I questioned her again about her riding background, she tilted her head with a glint of amusement in her eyes.

"Why, Martha, are you, in some roundabout way, trying to ask *me* for help?"

"Well, maybe," I had answered with more than a little apprehension. "I would like to try a ride at some point, but I really know nothing about horses."

I could see the wheels clicking and turning inside that beautiful tricky head of hers.

"You know, I'm always up for a good trade on services. What do you say?" she answered cryptically.

At this point James or Jimmy as he now calls himself, looked from me to her and back to her again. I knew then that he really didn't know this woman at all, and especially the rest of her story. But then neither do I, the difference being that I really don't want to.

Now as I think back on this interaction, I wonder what I might have gotten myself into. She was adamant about meeting me back out here next Friday to have a lesson and go for a ride. I had tried to backtrack with excuses of my injuries, of the possibilities of appointments, of chores undone, and of family commitments. She would hear none of it. The deal was sealed in her mind. What my part of the deal will be has not yet been revealed. I feel a hint of anxiety wriggling into my beautiful morning. So, I return the brush to its home in the barn and roll the wheelbarrow out of the paddock, around to the back of the barn where these droppings can join the mounded hill of decomposing dung.

Jimmy, I suddenly remember, as I begin the climb back to the house, had made another reference to my tinkering about in his past life.

"You know," he had said, "I always thought if there was such a thing as reincarnation, that each consecutive life would be built on the good deeds of the last one." We were sipping our coffee in the unadorned living room. He was perusing Cassandra's bookshelves as he spoke. "I guess I'm referring to the whole concept of Karma, which, perhaps, I don't really understand." He set his coffee cup on the floor and pulled a book from the shelf. "Even this lady, Cassandra, seems to have some interest in the afterlife." In his hands, I saw a tattered copy of Edgar Cayce's - Story of the Origin and Destiny of Man. I wondered then, as I wonder now if he has read this book. I have.

Thinking I might turn the conversation away from this subject which seemed to hold an obsessive curiosity for Sunny, I had artfully replied, "Cassandra obviously has volumes and volumes of interests. She has, what I have to believe is, a first edition of Sylvia Plath's - Ariel. I'm sure that one is worth a pretty penny."

"But this thing about Karma, I'm curious about it, too," piped in Sunny.

"So, in both Hinduism and Buddhism, Karma seems to be tied to the actions and deeds of one's life," Jimmy went on, as he returned the book and picked up his mug, "determining the consequences or the evolution of the spirit for the next life." He then turned his attention to me specifically, as I sat in the straight-back wooden chair I had brought back in from the porch. "I think about things like this, Martha. All the time now. I wonder about what you told me. You understand I heard and remembered every word that was ringing in my head in those moments. I was on the raggedy edge of my life, but your voice was in my head, leading me like a lamb to some truth. It's still in my head, like a character from some history book, that lion-hearted soldier of the civil war who worked ceaselessly to bring wounded soldiers off the frontlines, risking life and limb to bring the wounded to Clara. Me, you said, without a thought for my own safety, weaving through musket fire and cannon barrage to carry the dying to Clara. So why then, would I backslide to such a dark place in this particular life, if I truly had earned brownie points in a past one?"

"Who's Clara?" Sunny's question dies unanswered in the palpable silence that follows.

I lose myself in my thoughts. There are no straight and undivided paths in any life. That is a fact I am willing to stake this life on. But I am no expert in this stuff. I only have the small bits of insight lent to me by the experiences I have had. And in this big scheme of religion, philosophy, metaphysics, Karma, transmigration otherwise known as life and death and life again, I am naive and perhaps even simple-minded.

Today, I feel burdened by rethinking these heavy thoughts and find myself stopping mid-hill and turning back to face the barn. Carefully, I lower myself to the ground as I work to calm my breath. Cautiously, because my newly awakened muscles are not as hardy as they once were, I find a comfortable position to sit in. For a moment, I look down upon that bucolic scene. I long to hold on to those few moments, those elusive minutes when my mind was free from fretting and overthinking. If only I could gather them together like blissful seeds and bury them in my heart where they could grow into a wild garden of serenity. And there I could live out the rest of my days.

Suddenly, I laugh out loud. Maca is stalking an outrageously large grasshopper and formulates a game plan that includes an attack in an all-fours-off-the-ground assault. I groan just a bit, as I lift myself back up and she comes to join me. Looking down at my carefree companion, I laugh. "Ahh Maca, such is the solitary life. We ascetics have always been burdened with the weight of our musings. And grasshoppers."

In the end, I answered his question in the only way I could. "Do you really believe for a moment that there are cosmic rules that define this process, a formula that is intrinsic and followed precisely for each and every human being on this planet? I think not. Good people stumble and die, babies breathe their first and last breaths in the first seconds of their life, bad people are rewarded with riches and fame. There is no miraculous equation, no spiritual road map, no predictable ascension of man. There is only the struggle, the pursuit to find peace and happiness and love. And the bravery it takes to move through each moment." I braced myself for the backlash as they both stared wide-eyed at me, the peddler of disillusionment.

"This is it!" Sunny gushed. "This is why I love this woman. She tells it like it is." And she threw her arms around me.

III

Finally, still huffing and blowing, sounding a bit like those horses down below, I am back at the house. Checking my phone, I see three messages have come in, in my absence. Two voicemails and a text from Diego. This time as I feel that familiar flutter of panic that arises with news delivered via my phone, I make myself revisit that vision of my garden of serenity. I firmly place the seed of pastoral peace in the loam of my heart and pat it down, then open Diego's text.

All is good here, Martha. I'm going to Señor Rivera's after lunch. TomB slept with me all night and woke me up this morning to feed him. Do I really have to clean a cat box?!? Can I come out there pretty soon?

I text him back. *Yes, you have to clean the catbox. And yes, you get to come out here soon. Tell the Señor I would like him to come out here too. Take good care of Alice and I'll stop by, maybe tomorrow. Martha*

I realize before I pick up the other two messages that I forgot to take Graciela's magic potion this morning, so I make my way into the kitchen and fill the dropper with the amount she showed me. As I sip it down, I realize that maybe I do feel a slight decrease in the weird nerve spasms that plague my leg. Could it be this concoction? I hold what's left in the glass up to the light that is streaming through the kitchen window. The dark thick amber-colored droplets have formed swirling patterns that pirouette slowly in the water. It is a mesmerizing dance that I put an abrupt end to by swallowing the rest of it. And the woman calls me a bruja, I laugh silently.

The first voice message is from my mother. She, like Diego, reports that all is well and that she slept beautifully last night without the backdrop of sirens and overhead jet traffic. Her voice sounds much more animated today and I know all is back to normal when she ends her message with: Deepak Chopra says, "All great changes are preceded by chaos" and honey, remember, "Cinderella is proof that a new pair of shoes can change your life forever."

The second is from John: *"Hey Martha, sorry I missed you. And wow, I miss you! Made it to Denver. We're setting things up in the studio today. The Airbnb we rented is perfect, big enough to accommodate all of us comfortably and some nice restaurants right down the street. I'm really hoping you can make it up here for a weekend. It really is a fun city. Anyway, I'll try to call back this evening. I hope you understand how badly I hate goodbyes and just couldn't stand the thought of creating that moment with you. Please, please forgive me. I'll try to explain it better later. Love you."*

See... I tell my heart. It's all good.

Suddenly, I realize that I am feeling the tug that all good pioneers feel when they first set their boots on lands unknown. It's time to explore. Maca senses the change in my mood immediately or perhaps she responds to my frantic search through boxes and bags for my pack. When I finally locate it, I begin to unceremoniously stuff it with a rain poncho, snacks, water bottles, binos and a light jacket. I search unsuccessfully for my camera and realize I probably left it in the hands of the nouveau mega-talented photographer, Diego. Maca's little pack also seems to have fallen into the realm of unfindable objects, so I finally give up and offer up a short lecture to the panting dog on the virtues of self-sufficiency and carrying your own weight. Her indifference towards my lecture is completely overpowered by the notion of an adventure in the wild.

I remember the hand-drawn map that Cassandra provided me with, the one she sketched with details of the areas that surround her property. I find it folded neatly on the kitchen counter. There, with a large red tracing of a property line, lies the dominion of the landowner that Cassandra adamantly contended was a curmudgeonly old rancher who just might sneak up on me with a shotgun, should I find myself trespassing on his land. She did reassure me that he had clearly secured his territory with a sturdy barb-wire fence and No Trespassing signs.

I refresh my memory on the lands that lie to the west which belong to Ventana a Los Pinos. Cassandra had called it a rural eco village that was settled at the very end of the road in a small valley that was blessed with an active spring. Here, she told me, lived about thirty or so hippie throwbacks who were employing some of the most ecologically innovative designs and methods for living off and with the land. Cassandra was less than enthusiastic about the "hippies" and their temperament for communal habitation, but absolutely obsessed with their technologies and strategies for green living. Here, a green circle on her map, outlining the boundaries of their acreage, wound erratically around illustrated hills and sketched out arroyos, with symbols for a variety of buildings. In all, she estimated they incorporated about fifty acres. Even the spring was symbolized with a squiggly arrow and in crisp blue lettering the words: Coyote Springs. Should Cassandra ever lose her footing in the world of finance, I dare say she might have a future in cartography.

The National Forest creeps down off the mountains and foothills into the backyards of these outliers, but there are several swathes of unowned land that pass between natural egresses that allow hikers free passage into the forests. One such pathway is marked on the map in blue marker. Across the passage, again, in perfectly formed tiny blue letters, Cassandra has penned: *Arroyo Coyote*. On one side of the arroyo is Ventana A Los Pinos and the other side, marked by the ominous red of her marker is the old badger's barb-wire fence line. One has to wonder how well these two neighbors coexist.

"So," I say looking directly into the keen eyes of my hiking companion, "Arroyo Coyote, it is!" I carefully fold Cassandra's artwork and tuck it into the back pocket of my jeans. Just as I'm turning away from the bookshelf, a slip of a volume catches my eye. It is the author's name that attracts my attention and rouses an association that I can't quite place, but I grab the volume by Gary Snyder and scan hurriedly through the columns of words that make up his poetry. Something for a sunny rock, I think, then slide it into my increasingly heavy backpack.

IV

I have passed through the lands of several immediate neighbors, undetected. Though Maca is nearly deranged by her enthusiasm with the new scents and animal noises, I call her in frequently and keep her close. I do not wish to give my new community reasons for animosity. It isn't until I am well down the steep brushy hillside with a clear view of the sandy arroyo below me, that I start to feel less paranoid. I am, however, feeling a deep ache in my calf and ankle from the work of sliding downhill on ponderosa needles and cones and circumventing the attacks of prickly cacti and yucca. I have ceased to use my energy to call in the dog and use it all on calling into play a sense of strength and balance. Finally, the flat bottom of the canyon is underfoot.

Catching my breath, I look around trying to spot Maca and am rewarded with the view of her backside wriggling in the air while her nose is six inches into a burrow of some kind. I call her in. and we begin our trek into the wide sandy arroyo bed.

On either side of us are tall ponderosa pines and tangled junipers with their thick thigh-sized roots pushing out from the banks. We pass one set of roots that have been exposed far below the still-thriving cedar that grows six feet above. The root bifurcates into two perfectly formed bark-covered legs that disappear into bedrock at the ankles and hips. I wish I had my camera. To me, there is a buried forest gnome just waiting to be freed. I begin to notice another oddity as we make our way down this sandy highway. Every hundred yards or so there are regularly spaced rocks that stand out from the rest of the terrain by virtue of their size, the smoothness of their surfaces and their unusual uniformity. Like skulls without features, they balance on the flat surfaces of other rocks. I stop and inspect one. A little bit unnerving for some reason.

Moving on, I decide to simply acknowledge them with a sideways glance, and we do pass a few more of them along our way.

It's not unlike me to fall victim to wayward thoughts and memories when I am wandering alone like this and it takes a sudden gust of dusty wind blowing detritus in my face to make me realize that I have been walking or standing, for quite some time without any thought as to time or place or the whereabouts of my dog. Instead, my mind had decamped to a time when I was a small girl. It was a sunny afternoon, and my father was still living. He and my mother were working feverishly to fumigate a stand of their avocado trees that had been contaminated with a fungus of some sort. They were adamant that I was to be as far away as possible from the fungicide they were applying to the trees, so I took the opportunity to wander out of the grove and into a wooded area. There, a small creek flowed under a massive sprawling canopy of evergreen oaks. Moist emerald-green moss carpeted the embankment and boulders. It wasn't hard to imagine the limbs of the trees to be dark gangly arms twisting blackly from the sturdy oak trunks, to picture the leaves as fettering spells to keep the creatures anchored in time. Beneath the gnarled trunks, the deep creeping roots channeled deep into the earth that held onto unfathomable secrets that dwelled right under my bare feet.

Now I remember a memory buried so deeply, it spooks me to do so. Spooks me because, for the first time, I realize that was the place, the time, and my very first brush with evil. Madam, Mr. Misterioso, or whoever or whatever he was back then, is the same evil presence who wishes me tortured, worsted and dead some forty years later. How is it that until this moment, my brain has been unable to evoke this one memory when it has led me down the path to so many others?

"Who are you?" I had asked of the apparition back then. Frozen in my tracks and believing, as many six-year-olds do, that a twisted tree could materialize into a twisted man, I had asked, "Are you from the tree?"

"I am," he had answered, his voice as cavernous as a hollowed-out tree trunk. His black coat hem had brushed across the gnarled roots as he lowered himself awkwardly to a knee and uncoiled a crooked disfigured hand out to me. The black wide-brimmed hat that shaded his features dipped even lower as I involuntarily took a step forward, faltering for only a moment, to raise my small hand toward his outstretched talon. Underneath my toes, the ground so familiar, had magically reshaped itself into a mire of writhing worms and sinking mud. "Come closer, child. Let me see who you have become."

I remember now, the way his head had slowly risen, how out of the deep yawning shadow of his hat, his face had emerged, red-stained, as if colored by the reddest paint in my box. His hand clasped onto mine and his eyes beamed the most bewildering images into my mind. It was a storybook place with shadowy fairytale people, but most of all he had made me see him, as

Madam, in her flowing black layers topped with a sinister black hooded cloak that hid her face. I remember the way I had clutched at my chest as I felt my six-year-old heart beat erratically like the thud of a flat tire. He felled me to my knees that day, a child without memory or sin. When I awoke, I was an abandoned ragdoll left to the devices of the burbling creek. Soaked to the bone, my skull pillowed on a moss-covered boulder, I had gathered my wits about me and ran my bare feet over rock and briar to find the shortest path home. A small trickle of blood was drying from a cut on the edge of my hairline where I must have struck the boulder. I saw this in the mirror as I washed myself and changed into dry clothes. My mama and papa sprayed fungicide praying to kill an evil that wished to kill our trees. I looked in the mirror and wished for a fungicide to spray on the evil stranger.

I never went alone into that oak forest, again. I never spoke of the man to my parents, nor did I ever complain of the wound to my head or the trauma to my childish heart. All that had occurred on that terrifying day was thrust deeply into some secret recess of my brain, holed up there like a dormant spore, surviving unfavorable conditions, until what? This day? Why this day? Where is that damn fungicide?

The wind has picked up and I am being pelted with dust and debris as I stand in the middle of the arroyo. For how long I wonder. I cover my face as it swirls around me, but it quickly moves on its way down the arroyo. Just a dust devil. In its wake, all is once again calm and sunny.

Moving more quickly up the dry riverbed, I try to leave behind the plaguing feelings that this memory has left me with. Fortunately, Maca has not wandered far because to my right, as the bank flattens out a bit, I see the strong rusty strands of barbed wire that indicate I am passing curmudgeon-ville. A smile flickers across my face as I realize that according to Cassandra, I am standing in the arroyo that divides good from evil, dark from light, ecovillage from eco-terrorist. From where I stand, I can see zero evidence of Ventana a Los Pinos. I figure it must be one canyon over, tucked into the embrace of, a rare for this terrain, verdant ravine, which would make the buildings unseeable from here. However, to my right beyond the barbs of wire, perched on a small mesa top in the distance, I can just barely make out the outline of some type of cabin or outbuilding. It is a reminder to move on quickly, and I do.

The arroyo has led Maca and me to this seductive rocky canyon that is a slight detour off the main artery. It is much narrower, with more undergrowth but bordered by fewer tall trees allowing the warming sun access to the lithic boulders that have tumbled and jumbled themselves here at the bottom. Here the canyon walls rise up with a dramatically steeper incline, scaling upward with only cacti and yucca clinging for life on what could look like the outer wall of a great fortress. It offers no easy ascension. I imagine the upheavals, the water, wind, and ice that has reconstructed this land over many eons. Even a shallow sea had once covered this area and when it receded, in its wake it deposited the pale limestone, red sandstone and black shale that can be seen. There are formations from an even deeper past that have been exposed, as outcroppings of granite and quartz. They intrude from the magmatic layer deep within the earth. I choose the surface of a large flat-topped granite boulder lodged into the vertical earth to carefully climb up and spend some time basking in the sun. The rock beneath my jeans feels almost alive with its sun-baked warmth, so much so that the muscles and nerves of my calves begin to relax and feel soothed.

I unpack my goodies including the small volume of poetry, Turtle Island. I remember now that the poet, Gary Snyder was a friend of Jack Kerouac, both being authors of the Beat Generation. This volume of poetry was copyrighted in 1974, well after the Beat

Era. On the cover I see it is noted that he won a Pulitzer for this book. It pleases me mightly to open the volume and find title names that reference nature and ancient native people, children and zen. And so, I prop the small book in one hand, quench my thirst with the other, and feel the sun kissing my toes as I wiggle them unhindered, no longer confined by my boots. Occasionally, I lift my eyes from the text to check on Maca who stays close but explores the ravine below.

After a few poems chosen randomly, read slowly twice over and reflected deeply upon, I feel my inner world shake loose a piece of the cutting torment I have been harboring and torturing myself with. The sense of profundity and enlightenment for a world gifted by both pieces of ancient and present wisdom heals me. I take a break and search through a few snack options. Maca returns immediately upon hearing the crackle of a cracker wrapper, so while I continue to chew upon these enriching word morsels, I provide the dog with a snack of her own. She spreads out companionably next to me and we dwell for a time in this Xanadu created by nature, companionship, and another human's perceptiveness and insight.

I turn back to the Introductory note and learn that he has chosen the title of the book, Turtle Island, by borrowing it from ancient myth. The legend, one that teaches amongst other things, that the continent of America, or in some cultures, the world as a whole, is supported through eternity on the back of, or within the belly of, a great turtle. It would seem to be a cautionary tale that Snyder saturates his writing with; we humans have an obligation to find harmony with animals and plants, with the teachings of history and nature, with each other and the planet itself.

I drink large gulps of water and lure Maca momentarily away from her bone to offer her water from a bowl made out of a ziplock bag destined to carry our trash out of this place of beauty. When she returns contentedly to her bone, I return, in the same spirit, to the book, leisurely picking out poems at random, closing my eyes to fully digest the heart and nuance of each. I punctuate his words with brief pauses to just let my mind wander.

The first small pebble bounces from my head and rolls casually onto the granite slab I am sitting on. It is enough to startle me out of my daydreaming. Maca stands up with her bone dangling haphazardly from her teeth. Her eyes are trained on a point far above my head. A low growl issues from deep within her chest, which only serves to exaggerate the wild beating within my own chest. More pebbles shower down with a cloud of fine dust and grainy sand. Covering my head with my hands, I wait. I think that some large boulder will be next, and I will surely be flattened. But nothing more happens except one startling loud warning bark from Maca. I shake the dust from my hair and shirt and quickly stuff my belongings back into the pack.

The scramble from the rock ledge is precarious because underfoot, the small rocks are like ball bearings rolling my feet out from under me. When finally I stand with Maca and stare up to where she stares, I see nothing but the top of the canyon wall. It all looks so undisturbed and peaceful, and I would believe this if it weren't for the intensity that remains in Maca's eyes. I pick up her bone from the dirt and stuff it into the pack. A fitting time to head home, I decide.

With no further disturbances, we make our way back out into the main arroyo and begin our return trip. It's easy to recover that carefree mood as Maca dashes about chasing squirrels and the sky is endlessly blue above us. My only concern is the feeling that I have pushed my bum leg just a little too hard already, and we have a number of hard-earned steps still in front of us. I try not to limp or favor that aching leg, but it becomes a bit of a battle. To distract myself, I think about John and his music and the way that he has awakened a long-slumbering desire in me. With these calming thoughts, I meander down the arroyo no longer connected to my discomforts. At some point, I realize that Maca is out of sight. I don't really fret, just give a sharp whistle to bring her back in. Instead of her return, I hear the sound of her barking, the type that usually means she has found something to warn me about. It pumps just enough adrenalin into my system that I find myself jogging, though somewhat painfully, down the arroyo. A klutzy floundering, graceless lumber to be sure, but it brings me quickly to the source of the disturbance. Maca stands her ground in the middle of the arroyo as a man sitting upon his horse on the other side of the barbed wire fence looks down at her. He carries a rifle snuggled under his arm but not in a position to use it. I arrive huffing like an asthmatic steam engine. I quickly get a hold of Maca's collar and snap the leash onto it. She gives a last disgruntled snarl and looks up at me with a disconcerted whimper.

"It's okay, girl," I wheeze, then bend over to catch my breath and rub my calf. When I look up, he is still sitting there. Both he and the chestnut horse he is riding are as still as a bronze statue I once saw at a gallery in town. In fact, as I take a better look, I am convinced that he and that horse must have been the models, the master plan, for that bronze statue. He is a convincing mix of old-timey cowboy and Grizzly Adams.

"What are you doing out here, lady?" he asks gruffly. At the sound of his voice, Maca's growl erupts again, a grumbling volcano waiting to explode. I pull her lead firmly.

"We're just hiking the arroyo," I answer curtly, finally regaining some sense of composure and normal breathing.

"You from that commune over there?" He nods towards the lands of Ventana a Los Pinos.

"Not that it's any of your business, but no, I'm house-sitting for a friend of mine." I try to look him straight in the eye. Absurdly, I feel like putting my hands on my hips and sticking my tongue out at him. The rude bastard. But I don't. Instead, I look him up and down and what I see is a man who looks like he's in his sixties, a large bear of a man, with a full gray and white beard that tumbles onto his chest. A crown of long, unkempt gray hair crops out from under an Outlaw Josie Wales-looking cowboy hat, stained with who knows what. The broad-brimmed hat dips well over his brow so that it is difficult to look him in the eye. Though it's a warm summer day, the man sports a long-sleeved denim shirt with suspenders that attach to his dusty faded jeans. Cowboy boots with spurs finish out the bigger-than-life portrait of an old cowpoke curmudgeon.

We seem to be caught in a standoff.

"Hey," I say suddenly. "Were you just down the arroyo? You know, a little bit ago, up on the mesa above a side arroyo? Was that you, trying to scare off me and my dog?"

"No, ma'am. As long as you weren't on my property, I got no cause to try and scare off you and your dog. I will give you fair warning, though. There's plenty of coyotes that run up and down this arroyo, not to mention an occasional bobcat or cougar. A couple of years ago we had a black bear that was roaming around causing all kinds of havoc. So, if I were you, I'd keep that dog of yours close. A pack of coyotes could take that little dog down purty quick."

"Thanks for the advice," I say a little sarcastically. "I think we better get going. Sorry if my dog bothered you and your horse." I guess I must be feeling emboldened by that rusty fence that stands between us. I readjust my pack after that jarring jog down the arroyo and turn to walk away.

"Hey," I hear him call after me. I turn back to face him after a few limping tottering steps. "You twist your ankle or something?"

I think about just ignoring him and walking away, but something in me just can't leave it alone. "No, it's an old injury. I got bit several times by rattlers." There, see how tough I am.

I see him turn on his mount and pull something out from behind the saddle. For just a moment I think my insolence may have provoked him to gun me down, just like in an old western movie.

"Here, catch!" he calls out and throws a large stick at me. It lands in the sand at my feet. "You can keep it if you want to, or just lean it up against the fence right here and I'll pick it up some other time." He gives two clicks with his mouth, then slapping the reins gently against the horse's neck, he turns the beast and within moments is out of sight.

I look down at the stick lying at my feet. It is an intricately carved walking stick. At the thicker top, a hole has been drilled into the wood and a leather cord threaded through. I pick it up. It is smooth except where patterns like petroglyphs have been expertly carved into it. For its size, it is amazingly lightweight but sturdy. I lean into it with all my weight, just to test it out. Maca's nose explores it from every angle she can reach. Peering back to where the man and the horse had stood, I shake my head. Acts of kindness can come packaged in the most unusual wrappers. I plant the stick firmly and use it to meander at a much steadier pace down the path. And temperament.

As we near the turn in the arroyo that precedes the steep climb out of the dry stream bed, the sun sinks behind the high mesa to the south. It is not anywhere near sunset, but the sun's shine and warmth are now reserved for higher ground. Maca seems more sedate, having had plenty of running. We meander our way slowly, moving towards that hill that will take us home. Twice now, I have seen fresh scat in the sand. It is berry-filled and easily identifiable as belonging to a coyote. And though the old man had tried to scare us off, I have hiked coyote country all my life, and neither Maca nor I have ever once had an incident. That scat and those thoughts are not what makes the hair on the back of my neck stand up like porcupine quills.

It is the skulls of white rock that had been scattered randomly along the arroyo on our approach into this dry riverbed. Now, there in front of me, lies a congress of chalky white craniums in the middle of the path. They form a collective circle. Twenty or so pale rocks, all the size of human heads, communing and consorting in that way that only preternatural rock skulls are apt to do. Maca is unbothered, while I am spooked to my core. If I were a dog, my hackles would be erect, and a low growl would issue from the pit of my chest. However, I am but a human woman who, though she believes in things preternatural, prefers to think that most things have logical explanations, so I place the walking stick between me and the heads and cautiously circumvent the parley of skulls by making a very wide detour around them. When I am a good distance away, I look back to see if any spectral emanations are arising from the scene, and though there are none, I do catch the flicker of something red far up the hillside amongst a very congested stand of ancient ponderosas. I decide then and there and whisper my resolution into the breeze, "I'll be back, my spooky little friends."

Back in the City Different

I

A Tuesday morning that feels like a Monday morning is not always a good thing. As I sit here at my office desk, I find myself absently staring at the walking stick lying across the desktop in front of me. I have listened to all the messages that seem to be constantly cluttering up my answering machine, including the one from Sunny reminding *me* that we have an appointment on Wednesday. There was also a confirmation call from a new client that I will be seeing later today, as well as a call from a school counselor confirming that the man had actually made an appointment. After reviewing all my notes and the history of my first client of the day, I realize that I am more than eager to find out what exactly has been going on with this little girl. All paths to healing are paved with progress and setbacks, that is pretty much a given in my line of work, but I can't help feeling like I'm missing something with Maggie and her family.

In the end, I find myself awaiting their arrival, perusing the remarkable etchings on this walking stick. Some of the symbols appear to be similar to Native American petroglyphs, but others resemble ancient Egyptian script. Halfway up the stick, an intricately carved rattlesnake curls upward around the stick until it reaches a few inches from the top. It's at this point that the triangular head with its venomous cheeks and small dark eyes have been etched in meticulously. The viperous forked tongue slithers up around the handhold. What should unnerve me, surprisingly, seems to have given me a sense of edification. Yesterday, on the difficult climb back up the hill, with the pain of those bites rippling up my calf, the strength and balance of the stick, and perhaps some kind of exorcism that happened with that carved creature at my wrist, summoned the kind of sturdiness I needed to climb out of the arroyo. Subsequently, I have been making use of this stick and as I am at this moment, mulling over the man and the stick.

Just as my thoughts shift to the man, I hear a light tapping on my door. I also detect the whine of an agitated six-year-old girl being subdued by her mother's patient reassuring words. Propping the stick in the corner behind my desk, I quickly make my way over to let them in. It has been a while since I have seen Maggie and her mother, which would explain Catherine's awkward inability to make up her mind as to whether a handshake or a hug would be the most appropriate. Ultimately, I make the decision and grasp her hand. Then I offer the same to her daughter who surprisingly offers me her pale little hand. It's like lifting the wing of a small bird. Again, astonishing me, she doesn't let go and we are holding hands as I walk the two of them to the back room. Suddenly Maggie stops and looks up at me with her doll-like sea water blue eyes. With her free hand, she makes a motion which I can easily interpret as waves on the ocean. "Do you want the dolphin or the kangaroo or both? She nods her head vehemently yes, so we walk back to my desk, and I pull her two friends from the bottom desk drawer. We meet Catherine back in the other room.

"How are you, Catherine?" I ask, finally releasing the little girl's hand. "Can I get you anything to drink? How about you, Maggie?" I kneel down on the feather of a chance that I might catch her eye again. "Would you like some juice?" With a stuffed animal in each hand, Maggie regresses and buries herself deep into her mother's skirt.

"Here, let me help you up, Dr.Hooper," Catherine offers as she watches me struggling upward from that position. "I just can't imagine what you have been through since we last saw you. I swear Maggie knew something was going on with you, while Jack and I knew nothing. She kept bringing us avocados and saying, 'Hooper. For Hooper.' As a matter of fact," she reaches into her purse turning quickly to the child clinging to her backside. "Here, Maggie, would you like to give this one to Dr. Hooper?"

I can't help but smile as she maneuvers both animals into one tiny hand, grabs the avocado and offers the bumpy little piece of green fruit to me.

"Does she still like to eat them?" I ask.

"Obsessively. But the pediatrician says they're really good for her and to let her have as many as she wants. She's actually gained about five pounds, and he thinks that she is less anemic than she was."

I turn away from them for a brief second and cast my eyes to the ceiling. Thank you, Papa, I whisper in my mind. Then turning back to the two of them, I raise it in the air and say," Shall we, Miss Maggie? I think your mommy and I would like a snack, too."

Catherine nods in agreement and I search out a knife and some little plates. "Would you and Maggie like to go in the other room?" I ask as I prepare to cut up the avocado. "I pulled out some of her favorite books. I'll be there in just a minute with our snack and some drinks."

"I understand there have been some changes in your life just recently. Just so we're being straight with each other, I did want to tell you that I bumped into your husband a few days ago and he informed me that he is not currently living in the house." I look over at Maggie. She is nibbling on her avocado pieces like a chipmunk and slowly turning the pages of the book as if she is deeply contemplating each word. Her favorite beanie babies, the dolphin and the kangaroo are snuggled into her lap. When I look back at Catherine, I have trouble reading her expression. It is somewhere between embarrassment and panic

"It is true," she whispers. "We've just been arguing too much."

"Jack seemed to indicate that many of your disagreements had to do with Maggie. What were some of the issues that provoked your quarrels?" I watch as she sips the tea that I have made for her. The slice of avocado that Maggie gave to her remains uneaten on the plate in front of her. Her eyes meet mine briefly, then turn longingly towards her daughter.

"Dr. Hooper, I hope you don't think less of me, that you don't feel that I am dwelling pointlessly on the situation that you brought to light. But the aftermath of that revelation has devastated me. I can't seem to think of anything else when I see my husband. I mean, I see Jack and who he is, the man I fell in love with, the father of my daughter and this little guy in here." She places her hand protectively on her abdomen, "And yet, I obsessively search his soul day in and day out, seeking out the man who could coldly murder his beautiful young sister."

Catherine shifts in her seat, removes her hand from her abdomen and nervously combs her fingers through her hair. She glances at Maggie, as do I. We both, despite conversing in low tones, realize that Maggie might be listening. But she seems happy in her make-believe world babbling in her own secret language as if she is reading the books to her friends.

Catherine seems reassured that Maggie is quite preoccupied and so continues. "I have become wary and distrustful of every minute that he spends with our little girl. He accuses me of being overprotective and coddling her, but it's all because I can't let go of that picture of him in my mind's eye."

"Have you tried talking to Jack about your feelings?"

"Oh no. I couldn't. It makes me nauseated just to feel those feelings inside of me. But the worst thing is that now Jack is questioning this pregnancy." Tears are beginning to spill, and I reach for the tissue box, offering one as I peek at Maggie, who continues to be fully engaged at the little table. "He is starting to believe that we are not prepared to be good parents to Maggie, let alone ready to bring a second child into our lives."

It's a little late to start thinking like that," I say sympathetically.

She shakes her head with a hopelessness that is heartbreaking. "And he continually questions me; what if we have another child with the same difficulties as Maggie?" Her eyes begin to well with tears. "I tried," she softly sobs, "to make him understand that it's not genetic, that Maggie has come so far and with more therapy will progress even faster. Our second child will be fine," she says fiercely, "but he is utterly pragmatic and as hard-headed as they come. Even with everything that you have done for us, there is still a part of him that is searching for a medical answer to her problems, an objective reassurance that it won't happen again." She pauses and wipes her eyes and checks on the little girl who continues to chatter and turn pages. "Do you mind if I use the restroom?"

"Of course not, you remember where it is, right?"

Maggie looks up and watches Catherine walk from the room. Carefully she places the two stuffed toys on the table and picks up the book and walks over to me. I see that her tiny pale fingers are sticky green from the avocado as she hands me the book.

"Let's wipe your fingers and I'll read you the book," I say quietly as I take a tissue, wiping the bright green from her hands. "Come on up here, honey. Mommy will be back in a second." She allows me to lift her onto my lap and I spread the book out in front of us. "Show me which page you would like me to read."

Startling me completely, Maggie throws the book with all her strength onto the floor and with her hands folded between her legs she stares down at the book as if it has offended her.

"Maggie, honey, tell me what's the matter." Her face remains emotionless but her eyes glare at the book. "Was there something in the book that you didn't like?"

"Want Daddy." The fierceness in that tiny voice that is using real words catches me off guard.

"You want Daddy to come here?" I ask, remembering suddenly that he has taken up residence somewhere in this building complex. I turn her in my lap so I can see her face more clearly. Though she continues to sit on my lap, her body is now rigidly defensive, yet she doesn't struggle against me. "Are you missing your daddy, Maggie? Do you want to see him?'

"See Daddy," she says in a flat voice.

"Were you remembering when Daddy was here and read that book to you?" I wait to see if she will respond, but she doesn't. Instead, she slides off my lap and walks back to the table. She stands staring at the dolphin and kangaroo until Catherine comes back into the room.

Catherine leans down and picks up the book. "Did she throw this book?" she asks apprehensively.

I don't know why I am less than truthful. I answer, "No, she just dropped it when she was walking around. Listen, Catherine," I say, "I really feel like I need to talk to you alone. Is there anyone who can watch Miss Maggie so you come in solo? I'll be back in the office tomorrow if you think you could arrange it that soon."

"Is there something really wrong?" she pleads in a soft voice.

“No nothing like that. It’s just that I want to talk to you about you and your husband and it’s probably best not to have little ears about.”

“Oh, Dr. Hooper, I don’t think she pays any attention to these conversations. She’s usually lost in her own little world. But if you think it’s best, I’ll try to arrange something. What time tomorrow would work for you?”

The only other client I have tomorrow is Sunny and I scheduled her for around two, knowing fully well I would be ready to go home right after her trying confabulations. “Do you think you could make it in around eleven?” I’m quite sure I will be in need of a sabbatical after Sunny’s visit.

“I’ll try to make that work. If it doesn’t, I’ll text you, if that’s okay?”

I’m so busy watching Maggie, I barely hear her answer. Maggie has walked over to the window and is using her finger as if she is writing messages on the glass. Little tiny gestures are punctuated with eloquent movements as if she were penning out an elaborate scripted message to the hummingbirds that are darting among the trumpet vines that are in full bloom on the wall just outside the window.

“Catherine, I know that we’ve talked about this before, but is Maggie still not interested in drawing?” Maggie creates a few large figure eights, then returns to tiny little scribbling motions. Catherine is now standing beside me as mesmerized as I am.

“I’ve never seen her do that before,” she says, and I can hear the astonishment in her voice.

“Try giving her a really large piece of paper and a paintbrush. Or big fat markers if she prefers and see if she will give it a try. Tape the paper to a wall or a window.” I say this as I am walking over to the little girl with sea blue eyes and skin like an oyster’s pearl; a child so fragile and so full of mystery. My heart aches to help her cope and to find the puzzle piece that will bring them back together again.

"Hey Maggie," I address her softly. She stops but doesn't look at me. I kneel down next to her and whisper near her ear. "Will you draw me a picture, honey? When you get home, Mommy will give you some paints or markers and you can make a picture for me." I gently turn her towards me. Again, her frail little body is compliant while her eyes are cast like steel beams to the floor. "A picture, okay? Show me what you want me to help you with. Your Mommy can bring it to me tomorrow." I look up at Catherine.

"Ready to go home Maggie?" she asks. The wisp of a child runs over to her mother and in just the same manner that she came in, she grabs her mother's skirt and buries her face in it, clinging for dear life.

Once they are out the door and well on their way, I pick up my cell phone and with an uneasiness born of guilt, I touch the screen and dial Jack's number.

II

Angelo, as he insists I call him, showed up about thirty minutes late for his appointment. I had actually tired of waiting on him and had started to gather my things, ready to call it another early day. But no, no hooky to be played today.

At this moment, Angelo De Arco quietly paces the perimeter of my outer office. It's not a frantic pace, rather one with a more contemplative and measured stride. He had formally introduced himself, shaking my hand and in that moment I caught the fragrance of weed and incense infused into not only his hair but in the fabric of his Afrikan Dashiki style shirt. When I had offered him the opportunity to enlighten me on the purpose of his visit today, he had looked at me thoughtfully then slowly began to wander about the room. For a moment I am struck with the idea of creating a labyrinth on the open floor for clients with movement needs such as Mr. De Arco. When he makes no attempts to break the immediate silence, I shift from my desk over to the coffee table and make a cup of strong tea for myself. Without looking at him, I ask if he would like something to drink. I hear his steps come to a stop behind me, so I venture a slight turn and glance. His smile is disarming.

"I would love a cup of tea. Do you have anything grassy?"

Turning to face him, I ask, "I'm not sure I know what you mean. Would chamomile do?"

"Sure. I usually only drink alfalfa or lemongrass. I do like chicory, but I do give my kids chamomile before bedtime. So yeah, that'll do."

Angelo is thin, maybe five foot ten. A handsome man with black hair that is tangled into dreadlocks that are pulled back into a ponytail. He looks like he is possibly in his late twenties. His facial hair includes an untrimmed black mustache and a soft, thin beard that compliments his deep brown eyes which already have those crinkles formed by much smiling and laughter. I brew a cup of chamomile for the man and hand it to him, returning to my desk with my own cup.

"Mr. De Arco," I begin as he continues to stand sipping the hot tea and gently staring in my direction.

"Angelo." he corrects me.

"Okay, Angelo." I smile. "I'm not completely sure of what brings you to my office this afternoon. I did get a call from your children's elementary school. It was the school counselor, I believe. Her name was Mrs. Cruz. I didn't have a chance to talk to her directly, but the message said that you are required to…" At this point, I look up and see that he is again smiling broadly at me.

"Go on." he encourages.

"Well, I think she was indicating that your little boy and girl missed a lot of school and came in late most mornings last year. Summer school was recommended, yet they never showed up. Apparently, you've racked up enough offenses with their school, that they are now threatening to turn you over to CYFD, Children, Youth and Families Division, for the possibility of neglect in the home."

"That's right," he sighs, but says no more.

"So, they offered you the alternative of seeing a therapist?" I ask, a bit dubious.

"Again, you are right. You seem to be a very insightful woman, Dr. Hooper."

Had those words left the lips of most other clients, I would have flinched at the possibility of sarcasm, but this man seems guileless. His sincerity is simple and unaffected.

"I see." is my pointless response.

"What is in that other room, if you don't mind my asking?" His mug is held firmly to his chin as he takes deep whiffs of the warm moist aroma of manzanilla, the Spanish word for chamomile.

"You're welcome to step in there. It's the room that I prefer to do my therapy in. Maybe we could go sit in there and you can tell me a little bit of background on this problem you're having."

He chooses to sit comfortably cross-legged at the low table that has been recently vacated by little Maggie. I join him but stand at the window contemplating for a moment the nature of hummingbirds. They are such tiny creatures, yet so seemingly erratic and aggressive. How is it that these aerobatic little air divers are so adept at capturing the attention of us big clumsy humans? My feeder hangs, always fresh and full in the warm breeze. In legends, the little bird is often portrayed as a healer, a spirit being who with lightness and tireless resiliency is symbolic of the journey back to vitality. For a moment Angelo glances out the window and watches with me.

"My wife left me," he begins. "She was an amazing artist. A glass blower. Having our first baby slowed her down quite a bit, which made her not so happy. We had Jaden first, and Lola was initially content with just being his mom and trying to blow a few pieces in quiet moments. She was able to show her work in several galleries around Madrid, and during that time, a few started to sell. But within months she found out she was pregnant again. She was dreadfully sick this time and exhausted from sunup till sundown. I did the best I could to help her out, but our life was not an easy one." The young man sips his tea and for a moment closes his eyes as if he is compelled to retreat for a moment. "You see, we live off the grid. Without electricity, heat, and running water, our work is cut out for us, just doing the daily stuff, like firewood and hauling water, well...you know."

"What happened when your daughter was born?" I slowly lower myself to the floor on the other side of the table. He looks down and absent-mindedly turns the pages of Maggie's little book.

"A lot of things happened. Jazzie was born prematurely and when we were finally able to bring her home...well, you can imagine, caring for two babies is overwhelming, but caring for a feisty two-year-old and an irritable high-needs preemie was mind-boggling in our situation. Lola was not well either. She had lost a lot of blood during delivery and came home weaker than ever. I took on every possible role I could, but that meant I couldn't be counted on by the people who would employ me for odd jobs, and the money stopped coming in. We had to sell all of her glass materials and tools, just to survive."

"I take it neither of you had family in the area to help out?"

"No, Lola was in the foster system as a kid. The last family that took her in were the ones who taught her the glass-blowing business. They were an old couple ready to retire, but they loved her immediately and recognized the magic in her. When Lola moved out and in with me, they finally pulled up roots and moved to Florida. We haven't heard from them in years. My family is in Arizona, but none of them have any more resources than I have. Anyway, not the point. The point is, Lola abandoned us three years ago. Her descent into depression was persistent, pitiless and unstoppable. She tried twice to take her own life. Then one morning, when I finally was able to secure a day's worth of work, she took the kids to a neighbor's house on the pretense that she had a doctor's appointment in Santa Fe. You can guess the rest."

I can see by the slump in his posture and the heartbreak in his eyes. His revelation has taken a lot out of him. I say to him softly, "My guess would be, that you haven't seen her since, and you have been the sole parent for Jaden and Jazzie since that day."

Suddenly he looks up at me with such an abrupt change in his mood, that for a moment, I think he has been possessed by the spirit of a madman. Jumping up from the table he resumes his pacing and seems to be deeply caught up in the inescapable web of his thoughts and memories.

"But you see, Dr. Hooper," he continues as if there had been no intermission at all, "these are not the reasons or the problems that plague my family now." He sees me struggling to pull my own self up from the floor and immediately offers a hand to my arm. "No, the problem is with expectation and policy." Once I am up, he smiles largely at me. "Look, these are my children and I know them as little people with their own minds and potential. If they ask me to take them to the mountains to fish for trout for dinner, I say to them: what a fine day for fishing. And we go. It might be a school day, but it's a better day for fishing." Angelo's eyes flash around the room like they are following hummingbirds that are darting here and there inside my room.

"I do think I understand what you are telling me, Angelo." I walk over to the sofa and sit down leaning my elbows on top of my thighs for support. "I have a daughter. She is grown now and living away from me, but for so many years, it was just her and I. It was hugely difficult for me to let her go away to school eight hours a day to be under the influence of people other than myself."

"You've almost got it, Dr. Hooper. You see, I am not opposed to school. The school is full of rich experiences and wildly interesting people who have so much to share with my children, but schools and their rules and their agendas are not everything. They are positively not everything that my children will need to survive in this world. The school is just a fraction of what they must learn and experience. I resist the notion that their presence is required every single day. Each morning these children of mine wake up with an unbridled enthusiasm for the day that is about to unfold. They relish the mystery of each and every one, including the ones when they do go to school." Angelo comes and sits next to me on the sofa and searches my face with those profoundly poignant brown eyes. He whispers emphatically, "I will not take that away from them."

I genuinely grasp the nature of his dilemma. Angelos's reasoning is not unsound, and I in no way feel his situation is one that indicates neglect or bad parenting. In truth, I feel quite the opposite. He and his little family are merely outliers in the world of rules and regs. The public school system's policies and statistical record-keeping don't take into account folks like Angelo and his kids. His eccentricities and nonconformity to conventional requirements have put him at risk for legal intervention. However, knowing that children do benefit from some predictability in their lives and being aware of the unforgiving nature of the school systems, I see that we have some work to do to find a compromise.

"Angelo, when Jazzie and Jaden are at school, do their teachers feel that they are able to keep up?"

"I have never gotten a bad report on either of them. Their teachers always say that they are bright and imaginative, and if they didn't have so many absences, they would probably be in the gifted program. Everyone who meets them is astonished by how kind and gracious they are. But I don't need other people to tell me that they are stellar little people. In a lot of ways, Jazz and Jaden are already more resourceful and self-reliant than many grownups I know. My kids know – sometimes you just have to push back against the man. I taught them– listen to what your bones and your heart are telling you is truly right for you."

I watch as the man caresses the children's book beneath his fingers. I say softly, "And what are your bones and your heart telling you about this situation, Angelo, because it could get very unpleasant if we make the wrong decision."

The man smiles at me, finishes the cup of tea and says, "My bones told me– be resourceful." Gazing thoughtfully at me, he strokes his beard. My heart told me, find Dr. Martha Hooper. And I did." He laughs easily and rises from the table and stands by my side watching hummingbirds dart with exquisite precision. "And now my bones and heart and the rest of me, we're all satisfied that we have made the right decision."

"We need to find a compromise, Angelo." I say. "Have you ever looked into other kinds of schools outside of the public schools?"

"I have. Private schools are too expensive. Charter schools seem to have the same bureaucracy as public schools. Homeschooling doesn't offer them the opportunity to be around other children and adults."

"It seems like you have done your research. But I'm not convinced that our community doesn't have an educational opportunity that is a better match for you and your children. Let me do a little investigating. I will also talk with Mrs. Cruz and see if we can get a hold on any action that she feels like she has to take with CYFD."

Again, he gifts me with a smile that lights his face like an internal lantern. "I never expected anything less from you, Dr.

Hooper. My children and I are eternally grateful for your help." Angelo places his hands together in a prayer pose and bows slightly, then offering a handshake, takes a few steps towards the door. "Oh," he turns back to me, "should I make another appointment with you?"

I follow him to the door. "Let me see what I can find out. Would you mind filling out a quick paper with some contact information for me? Then I can call you when I find out something."

I'll give you this number," he says, as he pulls a very beat-up-looking phone from his pocket, "but you'll have to leave a message because we have no cell service out where we live."

While Angelo leans over my desk filling out a quick form, I rinse out our cups and think about contacting my mother's friend, Melanie, the school social worker.

"Oh, by the way," I say as I turn to see if he's done, "do you mind if I ask, how you came to make your appointment with me?"

"Dr. Hooper," he laughs, "your reputation precedes you. All of my peeps know about your revelations and visions. I was actually a little intimidated by your reputation, but now I see that you are gracious and compassionate. And I didn't feel a thing."

"What do you mean?" I ask, suddenly completely confused by his words.

"I mean, you did reach back into my past lives, didn't you? You know, my past incarnations? I never sensed a thing. You can tell me if you like."

"No. That never happened," I say a little defensively. "It doesn't always happen." I fumble with my words and my emotions.

"Well, maybe next time." He hands me the paper and ambles over to the door. "My friend, Tasha, who's a regression hypnotherapist insists that I was a follower of the ancient Chinese philosopher Lao Tzu. I think she only says that because Taoism runs through my veins, and she knows it. But you might already know this." He winks and closes the door.

"Dios mio," I sigh out loud. "I am blessed with a curse!"

III

"So, tell me about Denver," I say, slightly distracted, as I kick off my shoes, grab a bottle of Cassandra's rosé and pour a sizable portion into one of her smoky-gray stemless wine glasses. John is on speakerphone. Gathering up some cheese wedges, crackers, the wine and the phone, I head barefoot to the sofa. The horses are fed, Maca has had an adequate walk and in a moment of pure ecstasy, I collapse on the sofa.

"Did you just groan?" John interrupts his own diatribe on the insanity of Denver traffic at rush hour.

"I did. Long and zealously. It feels so good to be home." Out the window, the day is putting itself to sleep. The gauzy gray veil of dusk steals over the trees and grass and wildflowers. I've left the small window open, and I can hear the crickets cranking up their jam session. The blinds clatter gently in the breeze, and I wiggle my toes as I stretch out.

"So, it feels like home. Already? That's good, you know. Except that, I wish I was there with you."

"I wish that, too."

"How are your mom and Diego getting along?"

"I stopped by after I left my office today. Diego was over at Senor Rivera's. They were working on these beautiful retablos. Diego wouldn't show me his. He said it was a present for me, so no previews. He looked so happy, and Mr. Rivera was lording over him just like a doting abuelo. You know he has no grandchildren close by, so I think this is a match made in heaven." I take a long sip of the cool wine.

"How about your mom?" he asks. A few male voices drift in and out of the background.

"She was baking cookies. Chocolate chip and I ate some of the dough."

"You what?" he teases. "Get ready for salmonella sorrow. Actually, again, I wish I was there. So, we've got the studio set up and we'll be ready to work on the first track tomorrow. The guys want to start with Sunset Disposition. What do you think?"

"Hmmm." I try to cover up my yawn. "It's pretty new and according to you, you all haven't worked all the bugs out yet." I take another sip of wine.

"That's my thoughts exactly, but they feel like being under this kind of pressure will force us to be ready and more likely to figure out what those bugs are. You sound tired."

"Happily so. I have an appointment with Sunny tomorrow. She's insisting on being a client of mine."

"I don't even want to ask. Just be careful. She loves drama and sucking other people in."

"Ya' think!" I turn the speakerphone off and bring his voice closer to me. "I miss you, John. I keep thinking about what a great reunion you and I are going to have. You know, when you get back. I'll still be out here. Maybe we could go riding together."

"You've been riding?"

"No, not yet. In fact, Sunny has offered to give me lessons." I hear someone call John's name in the background and I hear him mute his answer.

"That was Omar. We have reservations at some music club downtown. They're stepping on my heels. I guess we need to wrap this up. You know, when Sunny was a kid, she actually did several events every year at the Rodeo, like barrel racing and roping, or some such thing. Won some ribbons as I recall. Anyway, be careful, especially with that leg of yours."

"I'll be careful. You be careful too, small town boy in the big city." I hear him sigh.

"Love you, Martha."

"Love you, too."

Suddenly there is the click and then nothing. A silence filled only by the a capella fusion of the crickets.

I'm not sure what wakes me up so abruptly. The room is dark and cool. It's just that... I woke up so suddenly. I sit up in the bed and try to clear my head and focus on the blur of Cassandra's alarm clock that I put on the dresser across the room. It looks like 1:45. Reaching over to flick on the bedside light, I realize I don't hear Maca's breathing. Instead, a low threatening growl comes from the living room that shoots me up and out of the warm bed like a bullet from a rifle. I reach for the walking stick that is propped against the wall and lean heavily into it as I do a stiff hobble into the living room.

The room is as dark and quiet as the bedroom, with the exception of a small amount of moonlight filtering through the window. I must have unintentionally left it open before going to bed. In that shadowy light, I find Maca in her hypervigilant stance, hackles up, ears twitching, and her eyes riveted on the open window. My own heart skips a beat and hearing another deep growl emerge from her chest, provokes my own hackles to rise. I'm sure I am hearing a rustling sound just outside the window and a snap, like a small twig breaking. Then nothing. For what seems like an eternity, Maca and I remain frozen, eyes fixed on the small rectangle of muted light, ears straining to hear something more than crickets and the breeze.

It's not until I see Maca's stance soften and her tail swish easily, that I take a partial breath and release my own muscles from a tautness that made me feel like an overstretched rubber band ready to slingshot into space. What I actually do is race over to the window, glancing back at my faithful guard dog who jumps onto the sofa and curls up burying her nose in her tail. Spreading two slats of the blinds and peering guardedly into the darkness provides no further clues. Nothing. The hush of solitude and the unilluminated dead of the night seem almost vacuous. Then suddenly, from the hollows of a more distant darkness, the rise and fall of a single note. A coyote howl shatters the silence. The haunting cry ends with dissonant trilling. Now that it is over, it has left the night almost unbearably quiet. Maca adds a disconcerted whine and I close the window, pad across the cool wooden slats and plunge back under my blankets, overcome by the gravity of oblivion.

IV

Morning breaks with a gloom that causes me to oversleep. Thick gray clouds have moved in during the hours between the "coyote concert" and "now-I'm-late" o'clock. It's easier to blame the clouds for altering my natural alarm clock and denounce voodoo as the source of my brain fog. The wine bottle next to the sofa is lying on its side and curiously emptied of much of its content. So maybe it's the alcohol. Whatever the case, it is causing me to almost forget to feed the horses. Getting dressed, I mindlessly fall victim to my most annoying peccadillo, the haunting habit of choosing mismatched footwear. And as I am leaving with my purse, laptop, cellphone, Maca and car keys, that is when I notice the shoe faux pas. Too late to do anything about that, but as I pull out of the driveway, checking boxes off my mental list, I realize that I have also forgotten to lock the front door. Two is the charm, back I go.

It would have been an easy thing to miss, but for the fact that as I stomp back to the door, I glance over to make sure that I have closed the living room window. My composure takes a leap like a jumpy bullfrog, and I make my way over to the window. Everything else about this muddled morning fades away like the end of a really bad movie. Now here is a mystery that both stokes me and frightens me. An oddity centered squarely beneath the window in a bare patch of dirt. I can't take my eyes off the precisely balanced spherical chalky-white rock sitting on the flat of a rectangular rock, one that has been shimmied securely into the dirt. It, like the others in the arroyo, is exquisitely extant in the size and shape of a human skull. Has it, I hypothetically fantasize, broken away from the consortium of other chalky heads and come to visit me? Or- more realistically, did Cassandra, as odd as she can be, pick it up and put it here herself? Upon its upturned face, someone has skillfully drawn in a pair of very convincing, inquisitive eyes using something like a pastel crayon. The beautifully rendered peepers look up at me with some sort of haunting enlightenment. Though creepy as hell, somewhere deep inside me, there seems to be a vestigial organ with a sensitivity to all things unfathomable, as I am eerily sensing a presence emanating from that rock, a vibration in my bones tells me so. Thanks a lot, Angelo. Well maybe it's true, after all these years I'm finally cracking. If I were a spiritual phone therapist, I giggle to myself, I might say this bodiless cranial rock is reaching out to me on some kind of ethereal hotline. A dopey lopsided smile freezes on my face, partly because I am amused by my crafty flight of fancy, but also because now I really am starting to wonder if such a thing can communicate. All this weird and wonderful diversion is suddenly cut short as a much more rational and cautionary thought hits those same neurons with a wild scream. "You moron," it forewarns, "that was not some coyote at the window last night. It was some*one*."

Chains

I

Traveling to my office is an exercise in distracted driving. Between the rain beginning to fall and the growing apprehension about bogeymen dropping skulls off at my house, I nearly miss my turn, and realize too late, I would have liked to have stopped for some strong coffee. Thus, my arrival at the office feels slapdash and dripping. Maca and I both shake off the drops and get down to business. I make the strongest possible pot of hot coffee with my drip maker and Maca seeks out the warmest corner to curl up in. Out of the corner of one eye, I see that, blissfully, there is no light blinking on the answering machine. Zero messages is some kind of blessing from the gods of the airways. By the time I have flipped on the lights to brighten up the oppressive feel of this dark morning and poured a cup of not-so-state-of-the-art coffee, there is a firm knock at the door.

"Good morning, Dr. Hooper," the man says as he turns to shake the raindrops back out the door from off of his dark umbrella.

"Kind of an unusual morning for us here in the Desert Southwest, wouldn't you say?"

"Yes," I respond, as I take his damp raincoat and hang it on a hook near the door, "so unthinkable that it definitely has me in a mood this morning,"

"And what mood would that be?" Jack Jennings smiles as he pulls up a chair so as to be closer to my desk after I have seated myself unceremoniously behind it.

"I guess I would have to call it slightly discombobulated, Mr. Jennings. But hopefully, this cup of coffee will do the trick. Would you like one?" I offer.

"Thanks, that would be great."

After handing him a cup, apologizing for the bitterness of too many grounds. I settle back into my chair. For a quiet moment, we both find comfort in sipping the pungent brew and listening to the rain batter against the door. The wind whips it to an amazing ferocity and there's even a distant rumble of thunder.

Finally, I break our companionable silence. "Your wife should be here in about fifteen minutes, but I wanted to speak to you first." I look up at him to see his reaction which remains quiet and contemplative. "How are you feeling about seeing her?" I ask.

"I really don't know. I guess I'm still angry at her and…" It seems hard for him to go on.

"And…" I encourage him.

"Well, I guess I'm missing Maggie and feeling pretty crushed that my own wife would try to stand between me and my daughter. As if I would do something to hurt her."

"Do you think that's why she's keeping Maggie from you? She thinks you'll hurt her?"

"I really don't know what happened, Dr. Hooper. Things started to get so much better, then it felt like Catherine just went off the deep end, you know, like she wasn't really thinking clearly. I know that I was really unsympathetic to her, which just made things worse. And of course, Maggie was caught up in the middle of it all." He pulls his chair closer to my desk and sets the half-empty coffee cup down on the corner. "I know it has something to do with her not trusting me around Maggie. And I know I said some things to her that probably were pretty cruel, but it didn't seem to matter what I said, she became impenetrable until finally, as you know, I just gave up. I moved out."

I look at him. His tightly controlled expression belies the woundedness I hear in his voice. I never would have believed him capable of depth of emotion and revelation, especially when I think back to our first meeting.

"As I said on the phone, your wife came to see me with Maggie yesterday. Spending time with both of them convinced me that this estrangement is taking a toll on Maggie and also led me to believe that it is a mendable situation, but the sooner the better because these kinds of misunderstandings can take on a life of their own. If left to their own devices, misunderstandings can harden into hostilities that are irreparable. You two need to talk. Honestly and openly, but gently, Mr. Jennings. Hurt makes us say all kinds of cruel things in the name of protecting the breakable parts of our heart. Get past this, Jack. If you want your family back, stay compassionate and forgiving."

"Do you mind if I warm up my coffee?" he asks.

I nod. I know that the brain does not take in all the nuances of a conversation in the moment, and it's clear to me that this man needs a moment. Easy enough to provide. I excuse myself to the restroom.

The hesitant knock on the door takes us both by surprise. As Jack thumbs absently through a magazine, I scratch out a few notes to myself at my desk. We both look up a little startled from our deeper thoughts. In the moments it takes me to traipse to the door, he has moved quietly to the back room.

“Catherine, so good to see you. It looks like the rain might be letting up a tiny bit.” She too comes with an umbrella and shakes it gently to shed the clinging raindrops. As I lead her into the room, she immediately spots her husband’s raincoat hanging on the tree.

“Is he here?” she asks with a quiver in her quiet voice.

“Yes. I asked him to meet with us this morning, Catherine. I know this might feel like an unkind surprise at the least and maybe a betrayal at its worst, but I was convinced yesterday that you would not agree to a meeting with him. I feel so strongly that the well-being of Maggie is dependent on you and Jack talking this thing through. I really hope you can forgive the deception. I promise you my motives are sound.” I reach out my hand, offering to take her raincoat, an offer that I hope she will accept as an indication that I will meet her halfway. Her pale face, which is rivaling her daughters, has the high-strung look of panic.

“I really can’t stay long,” she says, pulling the collar of her coat tighter around her neck. “Maggie’s sitter can only watch her for so long.”

“Then just for a few minutes,” I say. “Come into the back room and let’s talk.”

“Oh,” she suddenly remembers something. Out of her coat pocket, she pulls a thin sheet of paper that has been folded many times to make it fit. “Maggie drew this for you last night,” she says stiffly, handing the paper to me. Her feelings of betrayal are evident by her flat tone and unwillingness to meet my eyes. I take the paper from her.

Jack is standing at the window. This morning there are no hummingbirds. There is only the splash of rain off the vine-covered wall and the continuing lackluster light that filters weakly through the thick bruised purple clouds.

“I only have a few minutes,” she says again, this time loud enough for Jack to hear as we move into the back room. And when he turns to face her, she wraps her arms around herself as if she is shivering with a bad chill and then says his name like an accusation. "Jack."

For an endless moment, he says nothing, just stares at her. In that sinking moment, I start to doubt my instincts for these kinds of situations. Finally, he moves slowly from the window and gently takes her by the arm, leading her to the sofa.

"Catherine," he says softly. "I think we should give Dr. Hooper a chance. Please let her help us figure out what went wrong."

Catherine's icy expression begins to thaw. Her eyes take on the thunderous blue of this morning's storm. Steeping in salty brine, the tears begin to pool and then escape down her cheeks. She makes no attempt to wipe them away.

"You were such a cruel, cruel man," she whispers fiercely while shaking her head. It is as if by doing this, she can shake the mental images from her mind. The obsessive vision she is consumed with, the images of her husband, the father of her child, dropping their daughter to her death into a subterranean abyss. It is exactly what she must free herself from.

"Catherine, look at me." He lifts her face tenderly until they are eye to eye. "That is not who I am. If I *was* once that person, that cold bastard, I swear to you that I have evolved. I love our daughter. You and Maggie and ..." he places his hand tentatively on her abdomen, "and this child that is coming, you all are my whole world. I think what you might be picking up from me is the constant state of worry and anxiety that I live in. Now. That, somehow, I will never be enough for all of you."

I watch as she pushes his hand away and turns from him. Her shoulders shake from her silent sobs. He looks up at me. I know he is looking for guidance, so as unemotionally as I can, I encourage him to give her some space. As Jack moves back to the window, I watch an uncharacteristic slump settle into his shoulders.The rain rattles against the window in another outburst driven by a blast of wind.

When her own torrent of emotion seems to have quieted, I move to sit next to Catherine. Unfolding the paper she had given to me earlier, I smooth it out onto the sofa between us.

"Have you looked at it?" I ask as I look at it for the first time.

Without turning back to me, the woman nods.

"Tell me, Catherine, what do you think Maggie is trying to say in this drawing?" I look down at it again. Maggie has, in her childish bold lines, recreated my office and the little round table. There, three stick figures sit with their branch-like arms and hands entwined as only a child could draw. I have to smile. On the table, scribbled with a dark green crayon, are four plump avocados. I look up at Jack and know that he too wishes to see the drawing, but I give him a quiet signal to stay put. "Please, Catherine, turn around and look at the picture with me."

It takes my breath away, the way I submerge into her tunnel. It is like the reverse of being sucked backward through an airlock into space. *When her world opens to me, I am greeted with the scour of salty sea air and black thunderous clouds. The ship rocks and teeters upon the massive waves, its sails snap, bellowing in the brutal winds. I turn as I hear a blood-curdling scream from the bow of the ship. The officer is violently wrenching a bundle from her arms but has not lifted the whip that flails at his side to her bare back or shoulders that shine nakedly beyond the confines of her thin shift. The shredded and filthy fabric has nothing left to cover the top part of her dark emaciated body. Shifting the bundle to her other arm, the woman attacks with a ferocity unanticipated by the slaver. The wind lashes out at the two of them thrashing the boat from left to right. "The bairn is dead," the man roars against the thundering waves that crash against the listing hull. Through her avalanche of blows, he gains purchase with his fingers on the twisted rags that cocoon her infant. With a vicious yank, the slaver wrenches the dead infant from her bare arms and hurls the bundle into the maw of the beastly waves. Agony infects every fiber of my being like a deadly disease. I try to move closer to the shattered mother who crumples like a spineless ragdoll onto the slippery planks of the rime. The black iron chain that bites into the bone of her ankle thuds, then with a heavy clanking, the rusted links fall upon themselves, and the man falls upon the woman, dragging her back to the hold. It does me no good to attempt to follow. I am ripped from the scene with an electrifying jolt.*

There are times that I would like nothing better than to tear this black sorcery from my impaired soul. My heart can't take it. My arms are still reaching out, imploring the slaver to let me comfort the grieving mother, but it was not so and will never be so. Catherine turns suddenly towards me and collapses into my open arms. Her renewed sobs rain teardrops down onto the piece of paper that lies between us. I hold her tightly and try to conceive of a way to cleave the chains that bind her.

II

In the unearthly quiet of a storm passed, I kneel at the round table, my aching calf tucked back under my skirt. I smooth out the folded paper once again, this time onto the surface of the table. The sky is brightening and the leaves from the trumpet vine glisten with beads of moisture. A few hummingbirds dubiously flit through the drenched space. In the drawing, Maggie has included the little hummers.They are really no more than round airborne circles with pointy sticks for beaks and pairs of tiny circles for wings, but I would recognize them anywhere. I look back out the window. It took Catherine at least a half hour more of sobbing and ranting, till exhausted, she merely sat with her hands folded in her lap. I decided then, and agree with myself now, that I will not tell her about her past incarnation. The brutality of it will not serve her in any way, I am sure of it.

Jack had slumped against the window, speechless, in the face of her tirade. He neither attempted to rebuff her accusations nor did he try to soothe her. In the end, his composure and my encouragement had a positive effect and Catherine calmed. They spoke softly with each other, and Catherine was able to speak of Maggie's yearning for her daddy. They agreed to meet with me again but acknowledged that they were not yet ready to cohabitate. Catherine, however, did agree to let Jack come over and spend a little time with Maggie.

Though not a complete reversal of course, I am content to see things moving in the right direction. I look back down at Maggie's picture. I think I may try to find a frame for it. It is amazing the way that a child's art, so simple and uncensored, can move a person emotionally. Suddenly, as I pause and muse over the directness and spontaneity of the little waif's drawing, I see a small blurry image in the far corner of the drawing's depiction of my window. All around are her little hummingbird creatures, but there too, is an odd black crayon smearing in the bottom corner of the window. I take the picture with me as I awkwardly rise and move from the backroom to my desk where I keep my readers. Propping the glasses on my nose I look again.

The blur is slightly clearer through the magnification of my glasses. I know what she drew. What I don't understand is who tried to smudge the black crayon. That is what I mull over to keep myself from experiencing a visceral state of panic. There in the corner of the crayon window is another stick figure with a crudely drawn black hat that obscures the head of the figure. I am not being very successful at holding onto any semblance of calm. What the hell? Why is Misterioso in Maggie's drawing? I know it's him. Or maybe I'm wrong, maybe she just saw a dark shadow and imagined a person with the shadowiness of this fiend. None of it makes sense. I quickly fold the picture and place it in my desk drawer.

Maca has been comatose throughout the rainy morning and the stormy people inside. Finally, she stands and stretches at the sound of the drawer banging shut. Arching her back like a cat, she produces a noisy, dramatic yawn, and pads over to me, licking my trembling fingers. Was he here? Did Maggie see him through the window? I put my fingers on the cell phone in my pocket as I fight the temptation to call Catherine and have her bring Maggie in here. I think better of it and instead, bury my face in Maca's soft fur and breathe in her familiar doggy scent. It helps. Fresh air is what I decide we need before Sunny arrives, so snapping on her leash I lead Maca to the door. When we step out, the air that greets us is washed and cool. The sun peeks out from a fast-moving cloud and when I chance to look down, I see a happy dogdance in advance of the impending walk. We take off down the rain-washed streets.

III

"So, you haven't told him anything yet?"

"Why would I tell him, Martha? We aren't really even dating. Not in the usual way." Sunny is sitting on a chair against the wall. Her long legs are crossed, and she nervously kicks her leather-booted foot back and forth.

From my desk, I try to respond to her calmly and professionally. "It seems to me that James...I mean Jimmy, has been through enough. Unknowingly, falling for a pregnant woman might not be his healthiest option. I mean it, Sunny," I say suddenly irritated with her, despite my promise to myself to stay business-like. I take a breath. "So have you seen an obstetrician yet?"

"Yes. You should be very proud of me. I had a full exam, even blood tests and everything is in perfect order," she says, standing up and doing a little twirl in front of my desk. "The baby and I are in awesome shape. We're going to have an ultrasound in two weeks. Dr. Gonzalez thinks I'll be about eight weeks, then." There is an unmistakable glow of exhilaration about the woman. Whether it is hormones or mania is anyone's guess.

"No morning sickness?"

Sunny shakes her head and smiles. "Nope. Have you heard from John?" she suddenly changes the subject as she sits back down in the chair.

"I have. He seems to be having a really good time exploring Denver and they're ready to start recording today." I'm trying to keep up with her quick diversions.

"Are you worried?" she asks, still smiling and resuming the leg kicking thing.

"Worried? I have no idea what you mean, Sunny." I look at her questioningly.

"Oh, you know. It's just that he's a really good-looking guy, an amazing musician, in a city with lots of beautiful women. You know, like, the whole temptation thing."

"Really, Sunny. Is that what you want to pay me to talk about? Me and John? I was under the impression that you wanted some guidance in making some hard decisions regarding your own circumstances."

She tilts her head, and her long black hair falls over her shoulder. The smile disappears and she drops her foot back to the floor. With her hands folded in her lap and her eyes downcast, she looks just like a freshly scolded schoolgirl.

I curb the smile that is bewitching my lips because it is not necessarily a kind one. "Listen," I say, "It sounds like you have made up your mind to go through with this pregnancy. I feel no need to argue with you about your decision, only to give you two pieces of advice. The first is what we were talking about earlier. You can't hide the pregnancy for much longer, so very soon, you are going to have to be honest with the people around you, like Jimmy and John. Being candid with people in your life will help you to weed out the superficial ones and hopefully leave you with the ones who will support you on your journey into motherhood." I watch her carefully. She raises her face up and stares back into my eyes, her face the picture of passivity. "Secondly, you need to make a hard and fast decision about the father of this baby. In my way of thinking, fathers have the right to know that they have a child in this world. I don't know this man that you had a relationship with, but I do think you need to consider allowing him the option of taking some kind of responsibility. If he refuses and you're alright with that, then proceed on your own." She is still staring at me, so I get up and walk over to sit next to her. "Sunny," I say softly, "I really don't usually give advice in my practice. At the heart of advice is just someone's opinion and it's not terribly professional." I put my hand on her shoulder. "So, let's just say I'm giving you a little friendly advice. From a friend. And I won't charge you," I smile.

I seem to have a talent for making people cry. For the second time today, I am looking into eyes flush with unwieldy tears. As they break, Sunny tries to sniff them back, while wiping the offenders with the back of her hand.

"All I ever really wanted was for you to be my friend," she whispers.

"Well," I say to my own surprise, "that is kind of what I'm saying. Let's give this thing a clean slate, a new start. What do you say? You can teach me to ride a horse and I'll teach you a thing or two about being pregnant."

Sunny is nothing if not demonstrative. She turns to face me and wraps her arms around me. I am suddenly reminded of the fact that this woman lost her own mother at a very young age and is probably sorely in need of some mothering modeling. My therapist brain starts ticking off some possibilities. But for the moment, I try, I try really hard, to just be Sunny's friend.

IV

Graciela's house sits back from the curb looking all the world like the peaceful, ensorcelled, cottage of an enchantress. The problem is the lady of the dwelling is not home. Looking down at the clock on the dashboard of the Subaru, I realize that she is probably working. The afternoon is still young and though her hours can be unpredictable as a self-employed practitioner of the healing arts, I should have called first. Tapping my fingers on the steering wheel and glancing over at Maca who is curled up on the seat, I weigh out my options.

I steer the car into a parking position next to the curb at the little house that was once mine alone. It appears as deserted of inhabitants as Graci's. I find myself briefly enduring an unsettling feeling of abandonment. Still, I bother to amble up the walkway with Maca on my heels and tap on the door. It would seem that my mother and Diego also have somewhere else to be. I look down at the dog and shrug, "I guess it's just you and me, kid." I turn back down the sidewalk.

"Senorita, you're back so soon. Everything okay?"

I look up and smile. Mr. Rivera's silvery head bobs just on the other side of the wall.

"Yeah, I'm okay. Just thought I'd check in on my mom."

"Well, she had some errands to run, but Diego is over here. And so is TomB. Would you like to come over for some café and galletas? Your mama baked us some fresh biscochitos before she went on her way."

His grin is infectious and his invitation attractive in my current state of lonesomeness. "That sounds great."

The inside of Mr. Rivera's little casa is cool and bright. Skylights bring the sun into the room, but not the heat. A sofa with a worn deep brown jacquard pattern shares the biscuit-colored wall with a group of framed family photos, some of which depict relatives who are, I am sure, long gone. But amongst the group, I quickly spy an old sepia-tinted wedding photo.

"Is that you and Señora Rivera?" I ask as I move closer for a better look."

"How did you know?" he laughs. "To me, it appears to be a completely different hombre. Though my Añe would look just the same. She was one who never lost her beauty."

The young man and woman stand against the wooden carved door of one of the small northern New Mexico churches. His raven black hair is slickly laid back against his scalp. A well-trimmed mustache complements his full sensuous lips. A slight upturn to the corner of his upper lip and the liquid brown of his dark eyes, reveals that this young man is flush with the joy that the universe has just bestowed upon him, the answer to his every desire. She donned in an intricately patterned Spanish-style wedding dress, leans her head back onto his shoulder. She, a pale flower with equally dark hair twisted into a labyrinth of coils, possesses the expression, which is at once delicately winsome and yet, sultry and inviting. Bringing my face right up to the picture, I peer into this woman's eyes and what I see is intoxication fueled by desire and the dawning of her new life. It is so startlingly intimate, and yet unpretentiously innocent.

"What a beautiful photograph," I whisper thoughtfully. Moving on to a much more recent photo of a young man standing amongst a group of cap and gowned graduates, I ask, "Is that your son?"

The Señor, standing on the opposite side of the room answers, "That is Mateo, at his graduation from the University of Hawaii. My first ever trip across an ocean."

"That must have been wonderful. You said he got a Master's in Education, right?" We both find ourselves sinking deeply into the fatigued springs of the old sofa.

"Oh yes, Señorita, he followed in the footsteps of his mama. He keeps threatening to come back to New Mexico." The old man chuckles. "I tell him yes. When hell freezes over. But I also tell him it is good to give back to the community that has given him so much. I know how it is for him. He is settled and has his own family. So restless is that one, busy all the time. Dedication is his nature."

"Not to change the subject, but where is Diego?"

"Oh, you see, I bought your muchacho a bicycle. It is from a friend of mine. Diego has it in pieces in the backyard. It is his new project. I believe he calls it 'tricking it out'."

This makes me laugh, and at the same moment, I hear Maca scratching at his back door. To head off any damage to Mr. Rivera's wooden door, I decide, it would behoove me to wrestle myself from the comforting clutches of this sofa and see what the boy is up to.

After the initial furry greeting from Maca, and after tripping over the metal parts of bicycle rubble, Diego rushes to the stoop to give me a hug.

"What gives my friend? It looks like you've turned Señor Rivera's backyard into a metal scrapyard."

His grin is electric as he looks up at me still keeping his arms wrapped around my waist. "You'll see," he says, "I've gotta plan. Can you believe I get to do this?" There is an old toolbox lying open in the damp grass. The tools are lined up in an orderly fashion on a rectangle of old newspaper.

"Looks to me like Señor Rivera might have found your calling. How do you know what's what in this mess? Have you ever done anything like this before?"

"Nah, I've never even had a bicycle before. But it just all makes sense to me. Don't worry, the master plan is in my head." Diego taps his finger against his forehead.

I smile at him, return his hug big time, then sit down on the step. "So, where's my mom this afternoon?" I ask, as the boy picks up a wrench and works on a rusty nut holding what looks like a fender brace.

"She said she had a doctor's appointment," he grunts.

"Here in Santa Fe?" I do not hide my surprise.

"I don't know. She just said she'd be back by dinner time. Did you get a biscochito? They're awesome. Maca likes 'em, too."

Just then I spot TomB lounging next to the wall. Maca has been busy sniffing around all the bicycle parts and seems to have missed the covert kitty. "How's TomB adjusting?" I ask, with a nod toward the drowsy sun-drenched tomcat. It is at this moment that Señor Rivera steps out of the door with a plate of cookies in one hand and a bright blue cup in the other. With a gentle groan and a bit of arthritic restraint, he lowers himself onto the step next to me. "That cat makes me want to get one of my own. Ese gato es muy amigable," he says as he hands me the blue cup of coffee.

Diego looks up from what he is doing. "Rafael is saying that the cat is really friendly." He looks down and continues to loosen the bolt.

"I believe it is very important for the boy to use his first language and not forget. We forget too many things that bind our pasts to us. My Añe used to say, 'You cannot know who you are if you do not honor all that has come before, the clay that you were molded from, the ground from which the clay was dug and the bones of your ancestors buried in that ground whose dust prepared the clay.'

I take a sip of the coffee and then admire the thick blue handpainted lines that create abstract depictions of big blue flowers. "Muchas gracias, Señor Rivera, por el café." I smile at my awkward attempt at speaking Spanish.

He leans very close to my ear and whispers, "I will tell you this now and only now, Martha Hooper. Mi nombre de pila es Rafael. Rafael, por favor." Now it is his turn to smile as I nod obediently and take a sip of his rich Mexican brew. "Rafael," I say, feeling relaxed and cheered by his companionship."

His eyes light up and I see the edges of his slightly stained front teeth through his gray-white mustache. "Tomás is a friendly cat." He offers me a biscochito, then nibbles at one himself. "I've been thinking that maybe it is a friend I need, but now suddenly, I have so many. You and Diego, your mama, Maca and Tomás. Suddenly my life is filled and no longer pitiful. But still a cat…" He puffs a breath slowly and softly as he leans back, closing his eyes.

I turn to look at Diego. He seems so distant, so far away. A wavering vision, then gone. The journey begins and I feel a sigh of frustration release from my lungs, but my movement is such that I quickly leave it behind as if it really never belonged to me and I once again descend into someone else's past. This journey somehow feels different. This one comes with a strange feeling of surrender, of passively giving up something for something else. Planet Hooper in retrograde, I try to say, or maybe just think. The winding labyrinthine descent makes me dizzy and sick to my stomach, and voices echo all around me reverberating and unintelligible. The landslide of my atoms seems to slow and maybe stop. I really can't tell as the nausea swells in me.

At first, I think that I'm alone. Am I blind? I see nothing but darkness. A hand on my shoulder. A breeze on my cheek. Beneath me, it is my own legs that keep pace to some unknown rhythm. I raise one hand to my face and stop in my tracks as it brushes up against a full beard and I open my closed eyelids. Inside my head, surrender is complete.

"Ah, Master," his voice rumbles from behind me, "what a splendid day you have chosen for travel. Paris, mon ami, will welcome us with open arms. Though we shall have to proceed clandestinely, like downy feathers under the wing of a goose. Not a soul shall suspect our mission of merchantry."

Though I am steeped in confusion, a deep bewilderment of disposition, I know unerringly, the face I will see when I turn around. And just as was divined so very long ago, my companion's face smiles up at me as I turn about. "It is true, Master Devereaux," I say, "the day couldn't be finer, howbeit, all at once, at the whim of some impish wind, I am feeling quite unhinged. Could you offer your shoulder for just a moment?" I look him in the eye then unsteadily catch hold of his arm. He is such a fit and robust man, that Percy Devereaux. "As I see it, we still have yet a day's travel ahead of us and I fear at this time, I am ill fit for the journey."

"Rufus!" the man bellows. "Bring about the horse. Master Turnbull has been laid low." The boy, most nearly a man, moves out from behind a stand of billowing green-needled umbrella pines, dragging a pony, one of questionably harmonious nature. As Percy takes the reins, I lean heavily upon the dogged little horse. The path that we follow, I see now, cleaves its way like a whimsical snake separating wild forest on the right from the tamer farmland and tillage on the left. Presently, as I set my bearings, the wrinkle of disorientation seems to settle and smooth. Yet, I am much content to lean upon the pony who bears our barren haversacks that will not bear so lightly on our return trip. Thanks to my companions, she sets a slow pace forward, as in the meanwhile, my heart beats with goodwill born of brotherhood and fresh country airs. Each of us has abandoned our prattling to the speculation of the providence of our quest, which like the grapes upon these

bucolic vines along the pathway, we hope to find good fortune from pip to fruit. Our combined minds do so swell with anticipation.

"Master Devereaux," I finally exclaim, as I jostle the bags that lay flaccid against the sides of the pony. "When these are fulfilled to brinking with cinnabar and brimstone, how is it that we will bear the perils of the dirty-doers and the vexations of purloiners on our return voyage? Full pouches are an indubitable proclamation of profitable goods in transport."

"Tis true, my good man," Percy Devereaux answers affably while leaning firmly into his staff with each step. He keeps possession of the pony's reins with his left hand, while smiling broadly and begins to lift the heavy pikestaff that boasts a keenly honed tip. My august companion shakes it ferociously at the heavens and roars with good-natured aplomb, "He willst not only get our brave band from one place to another but will at length, get us from here to hearth, unharmed and with chattel unmolested." There is a moment of awed silence before the rupture of mirth and howlings fill the aire.

"I'll be safe, as well, Master," belts out Rufus, who is ambling a few paces behind us. He pulls a gleaming blade out from the Netherlands between his broad, leather waist-belt and the borders of his baggy breeches, then begins a swashbuckling farce of sorts.

"Take care, son," I shout, "should you find yourself at the tip of your own blade. For then there will be only two on the road home. But, I daresay, I am happy to be in the company of such richly implemented gentlemen. Was there no implement that you trusted to a man of my nature?" I question with mock perplexity.

"Most assuredly, not, William. Of your many talents, weaponry is not one of them," Master Devereaux contends.

"And yet you see fit to drag me along on this perilous journey."

"Tis a journey of your own making, my brother. The boy and I do avail our protection to you, while you hold the reins of science

and alchemy, the beasts that will bring us three to the threshold of immortality."

"Hush man! The trees and vines themselves have the eyes and ears of every unbeliever and opposer of our thaumaturgical science. If you are so free with that tongue now, what of your garrulity once we trod upon the busy cobblestones of Paris. It is not out of the question that we could find ourselves buried most deeply below the city in the abominable pits of their dungeons." I lean a little more laboriously onto the pony's back at just the thought of it.

"No, William, it will not be so," he answers me, his voice suddenly grave and deliberate. "We will succeed at every turn. I feel it in my bones, and dream of it each and every night."

Rufus sheathes his blade and without being requested to do so, takes the reins from Percy. His youthful vigor infects the pony to a more sprightly step.

"Listen, my brother," Master Devereux utters softly into my ear as he keeps pace with my trudge, "I have heard from a traveler that the whole city whispers of alchemical symbols embedded in the walls of the cathedral at Notre Dame. There are some who say that the walls themselves are undisguised stone tablets of alchemy brought in by the Templars." Mayhap, a visit would prove fruitful for inspiration."

"The uncovering of the philosopher's stone, might be that to which you speak?" It is a wishful sigh, not even words that I am aware of uttering.

But Percy picks them up, each word, and tosses them back at me. "Unmasking the Stone. That's right, my master. The city also sibilates with the story of Nicolas Flamel, the man who transmuted mercury to gold. Aye, it is said that he holds the philosopher's stone in his hand, the same stone whose cousin we too shall bring to light. I can barely deny the rhapsody that my heart is beating to."

"I too suffer this delirium for our ambitions, but I beg you, sir, I entreat you with a fearsome earnestness, do not allow your enthusiasms to betray us within those city walls, to those who would just as soon see our kind rotting beneath the earth with worms cavorting about our sockets."

"Indeed, we do understand with the very blood that we wish to continue throbbing through our hearts. It is quite so. Do you so agree, Rufus, my lad?" He taps the boy's back with the blunt end of his stick to secure his complete accord.

Rufus looks back at us with a smile, one that charms with its humble innocence. He opens his mouth fringed with the blonde peach fuzz of adolescence, to offer a response, but suddenly I fear I am suffering an apoplectic spell of greater seriousness, as I no longer hear the words of my companions clearly. It's as if I float away from them! My eyes, too, suffer disjunction. All that is or that should be, pales and befogs. Away I am swept. So persuasively. So cheerlessly. My dance with Death? Does the reaper banish me from my earthly realm in a same wont as the womb expels a slippery babe. Sadly, I will be lost to my most treasured companions and my rapacious designs for immortality. I most humbly confess to sin...

"Cool!" Diego whispers. My blurry eyes turn his way as he shakes his head and clears the past from his soul. At the same moment, I feel Senor Rivera's arm enfold about my shoulders. The instability of my very atoms plagues me as it has never done before. No other foray into the past has ever left me feeling as though I have not brought all of the pieces of me back into the present. This, this ascension that I have done hundreds of times has never left me so undone and has usually left me with explainable insight, not this feeling of bewilderment.

"Is she okay?"

"Si, hito, she will be fine. Just give her a minute."

The words are too complicated, the voices profoundly heartbreaking, and my bones, they feel like they have turned to dust one by one. At my feet, shattered on the ground below me, the blue mug leaves a gruel of mud and coffee. I cry. Mostly for the broken mug and the lost coffee. Maybe for my missing pieces and the distress that I see on Diego's innocent face.

"Qué tal." Raphael mumbles as he shakes his head. Cautiously the man stands up and brushes the dust from his baggy pants. "How about that?" He pats me on the head like I am a small child. "I'll go get you a tissue, my friend." Gingerly he climbs the few stairs to the door and opens it, but before he disappears through it, he turns back to Diego and me and mysteriously declares, a note of duplicity woven into his words, "It does seem, now doesn't it, that we three might have shared some history together."

What of the Road

I

"What of the road not taken?" I ponder.

Then choose to reread the stanza. The volume lies open on my lap turned randomly or perhaps intuitively to this verse titled, *The Road Not Taken*. Having reclined my kitchen chair haphazardly back onto the trunk of a giant ponderosa, I promptly chose the medicine of poetry to detox against the miasma of deepening insanity. Since emerging from my car and re-seeing the chalky orb with a face still sitting owl-eyed beneath my window, I have convinced myself that there must be some kind of voodoo afoot. Yet, as unnerving as it all is, I don't sense any kind of immediate threat. Instead, I feel more curious as to who this trickster might be and why so inclined to bring such a peculiar gift. The lateness of the afternoon inspires my time-out with a book and a tree. So far it has been mostly successful at drawing my mind away from all the disconcerting events of the day. I glance at the poem again and draw meaning from the next two lines. Yes, one path divvies into two, divvies into four and how do we not get lost? So seems to ask the musing Mr. Frost. But for some reason, the idea of a lost opportunity, a path not followed, just makes me sad. Aren't there always more paths, more journeys, more choices, than we can possibly choose from? Perhaps, but that doesn't make me feel any less deprived. I stand up with the book balanced on my palm and walk slowly around the tree. Is it not true that some days I feel burdened with choosings? Yes, and that's not such a good thing. "Right," I say out loud and close the book with a soft thud. The sound wakes Maca from her doggie dreams, and since she's now awake I continue with her as my audience. "Let's take Sunny for example. She has chosen her path, and it *could* be called the path less taken for a single, 40-something, troubled woman. The child will be born, and Sunny will take up her role as its mother. Why this disturbs me so deeply, I cannot seem to fathom, but it does. Why I react to her in the way that I do is also unexplainable.

"My own passage into motherhood was not so different. A daughter born from what seemed to be a miscalculated blunder. A father, who, like Sunny's lover, was unable and unwilling to take part in the journey. And so, against all odds and the objections of the father, I chose to have my daughter and gave myself the greatest gift of my life. So why not believe it can be so for Sunny." Maca puts her head between her paws and closes her eyes, not at all interested in my musings. Unless it were to include a hike down one of those paths or dinner for two, she is unwilling to get involved.

And so, I continue to brood quietly to myself, pondering this other winding road, this ancient road from my own past life. A trek to Paris, some dangerous adventure undertaken not only by myself as a man named Turnbull, but with companion incarnations of Diego and Señor Rivera. Raphael. A road I chose that may have launched lifetimes of repercussions. This has never-ever happened to me in any of my experiences mucking around in lives once lived. And the wildest notion of all is this seemingly random reunion of our souls in this life. What is it that we chose back then that could have the inexplicable consequence of bringing us back together again in this life, in these body-souls that we are presently inhabiting?

What of the road *chosen*? What of that path we forged back then? The implications are ... The implications are a man who wants to torture me, longs to destroy my life, and if possible, extinguish my soul for good. Is that even possible?

Back inside the cool simplicity of Cassandra's house, my laptop offers me a different kind of solace. I type in *La Ventana a Los Pinos*. Amazingly a very extensive website pops up. I settle into the comfy sofa to do a little research on this neighboring ranch.

I read: *La Ventana a Los Pinos (The Window to The Pines), is a prototype, grassroots eco-village, a rural community of people who strive to integrate a supportive social environment with a low-impact way of living. To achieve this goal, we integrate various aspects of ecological design, permaculture, ecological building, green production, alternative energy, community-building practices, and much more.*

Our village is a living model of sustainability. It represents an effective, accessible way to combat the deterioration of our social, ecological, and spiritual environments. We value community living opportunities and as a people are constantly striving to maintain independence from corporate, state or federal funding, for our water, housing, agriculture and other basic necessities.

Los Pinos provides its inhabitants with facilities for research, innovative approaches to farming, greenhouse technology and energy production as well as opportunities for production of customary products, trades and craftsmanship all of which are green, functional, and put into use in the everyday lives of our residents.

Our people have a strong sense of shared values and offer many experiences for the public to participate in both educational and recreational enlightenment.

Contact information is included at the end of this website. We welcome visitors and have several docents available to take visitors on an informative tour of our village.

Scrolling through the rest of the website arouses a curiosity that I feel like I shouldn't deny. I look at Maca and chatter happily, "I got nothin' better to do tomorrow. No appointments, no rendezvous. And us country women shouldn't be driving all the way into town just to entertain themselves." The decision seems really all too easy. I have met the dark lord, on one side of Arroyo Coyote. Tomorrow seems to be the perfect day to make a neighborly visit to the people of the light and educate myself in the ways of the forward-minded.

With this intriguing plan taking shape in my mind, I manage to avoid the otherwise stressful thoughts that could ruin an evening alone. I gather myself and Maca and we set about to do the evening chores on my own little ranch. It isn't until I am making my way down the hill to the barn and horses, that I notice the distinct swagger in my gait. My stride is longer, and my pace brisker than it has been for weeks. Though I can still feel a slight tenderness and tingling along the nerves of my calf, I have to believe that Graciela's magic potion is doing something wonderful. I fill my chest with the balmy air of the evening breeze and put even more purpose in my step. Inside the corral, the nickering horses burst into a playful equine friskiness, celebrating their own muscular beauty by ricocheting from one corner of the corral to the other. Their exhilaration is infectious, and it takes Maca no time at all to become inspired to join in the fun. She dashes off in her own Olympic-style frenzy. Meanwhile, I take the more sedate joy of gazing back to the west, where the seductive orange and red fire of a New Mexico sunset animate my mood into new heights and depths. I am waxing foolishly quixotic as the ball of fire slowly slips behind the flushed quilt of pink clouds, then drops behind the bulk of the shadowy mountain. I scurry to get the chores done.

II

I am a guest. The sign says guests park here, but where are the guests? There are no other cars in the dirt lot. Feeling a little hesitant and fighting back against the twenty reasons I should turn around, I instead make the long journey to the closest building, the first indication of civilization. It's a downhill journey of many buried railroad tie steps. I can't imagine that this is the only way that building materials, supplies, wheelchairs, fragile people or any other necessities make it down the hill. However, it is the pathway with arrows, so I navigate the stairs. I arrive breathless and sweaty at a wide-open door with a wooden sign that spells out 'Visitors Center' in a colorful mosaic-style inlay of stones. The unfinished walls of the structure show what I'm guessing is straw bale construction. This must be the starting place, so I poke my head in through the open door. The room is a large, open space, furnished with a few makeshift desks and two rather old but comfortable-looking sofas. There are paintings and framed photography on the walls and a large water dispenser with pale green cucumber slices floating in it like jellyfish in an aquarium.

"Hello," I call softly, "anybody here?" Without an answer or any sign of humanity, I walk over to one of the large-framed photographs on the wall, a black and white that captures a snowy day, perhaps here in this compound. Several buildings pictured are buried in the white stuff all the way to the bottoms of their window panes. Yet, they are so cozily lit frome the inside. Veils of ghostly smoke exhale from chimneys, giving off a cold icy air of enchantment, while just beyond in the foreground, Ponderosas rise up with blooms of snow blossoms decorating the needles. Deep snowbanks engulf a small, bundled child attempting to raise a booted foot higher than the drift of snow that stands before him. "So lovely." I sigh. I see a small price tag hanging off the bottom right corner, but as I lean in closer to see it, I hear footsteps behind me.

"Oh... hey there. Sorry, I didn't realize anyone was here. Sofia's normally here but she was called away."

I turn around to see a petite young woman with boyishly clipped blonde hair, squinting at me.

"I think I left my glasses in here. Somewhere," she mutters as she fumbles through some items on one of the desks. "Are you here to check the place out?" she asks. A smile transforms the sober expression on her face when she successfully finds a pair of large dark framed glasses underneath a stack of papers. With her glasses perched on her small, upturned nose, she looks up at me more confidently. The glasses actually look striking on her pixie face.

"I *am* here for a visit. I read on the website that it was okay to drop in and I had some free time." I walk over to her with my hand extended. "My name is Martha Hooper and I'm house-sitting at a place not too far from here. The owner had mentioned this community here and I found myself really curious after looking at your website." She gingerly shakes my hand, with what I interpret to be distraction, not unfriendliness.

"Of course, Ms Hooper. I'm Maya." She tilts her head to the side as she looks at me. "Like I said, Sofia usually covers our guest tours. She's also in charge of the herb garden and that's why she's not here right now. They're getting ready to harvest some of the herbs and she needs to be there."

"Oh!" I say with enough enthusiasm that I unwittingly startle her, "I have a friend who is mad about herbs. I would love to visit the herb garden. Would it be possible for you to take me there?"

Maya ponders my request for a moment, then answers, "Actually that might work out really well. Since Sofia's over there, I can introduce you to her and she might be able to get away for a little while. I would love to show you around, but I'm due in the kitchen for a cooking class. I'm pretty new here and I've signed up for the culinary arts program. Maybe Sofia can bring you over to the cafeteria later. You know, to sample a few homegrown snacks and to tour that facility."

I'm glad I thought to get my camera back from Diego before leaving Mr. Rivera's yesterday, and equally glad, as we walk a well-trodden dirt path away from the Visitor's Building, that I thought to tuck it in my backpack this morning. "Maya," I ask, having a hard time keeping pace with her business-like gait, "what is your photo policy here? Am I allowed to take pictures?"

"Well, get this confirmed with Sofia, but I think it's okay to photograph the place. The thing is, if it includes people, I'm pretty sure you have to get their permission." She smiles at me, her round eyes owlish through those big glasses. "You can take mine if you want, you have my permission."

And I do.

As we press forward down the path, we pass by several large two-story cabin-like structures with solar panels and water catchment systems, large barrels with water levels that probably got recharged with yesterday's shower. A small area with children's swings and rope climbs and bridges, a convoluted tunnel created from canvas and a wooden treehouse is in use. It seems to be a popular place and is echoing with little voices and the instructions being called out by the two adults who appear to be responsible for the ten kiddos.

"Are they residents here?" I ask.

Yes. Some of the families live in communal residences like those two big buildings we just passed, and others choose to have their own places and those are built a little further down the valley. But all the parents share childcare, especially during the summer.

"Are the kids homeschooled here?" I ask.

"A few are, but some go to different schools in town. Sofia will tell you, but residents are totally free to come and go and make their own choices about living and families. What Los Pinos does offer is a chance for people who believe in certain eco-friendly ways of living and share an understanding of the importance of social connection and community, to participate in ways that are not easily available outside of this community." We pass by several individuals, some my age, some her age, but all greet her warmly, smile at me and then continue on their way.

The path curves downward, and suddenly I am looking down upon the tops of several greenhouse structures, surrounded by a variety of gardening plots and some kind of complex watering system. Several people work each plot, harvesting, pulling weeds, picking insects off the leaves and tossing them to some free-ranging chickens that wander in and out of the patches.

"We're almost there," she reassures me. "The herb garden shares some of that second greenhouse and also the plot that's behind it. Sofia should be there."

It's a good thing my gimpy leg has started feeling better or I might have wilted on this last portion of the journey under a sun that is companionable with life forms filled with chlorophyll, but less so to a slightly afflicted, flesh and blood, fifty-year-olds. I should have brought my hat.

Maya points to a young woman who is kneeling between rows of what looks like lavender. "Hey, Sofia! You have a visitor." she calls out. Sofia stands, placing a bundle of freshly cut blooms in a tall tightly woven basket at her feet. The glisten of a shiny curved blade, like the slip of a new moon, reflects the sun just before she seamlessly slides it into one of the pockets of her gardening apron. Moving easily among the tall stalks, she carries the basket with ease. She sets it down at the corner of the plot.

"Sofia, I really have to run. I'm late for my class, but this is Martha Hooper." Maya and Sofia both turn towards me. "She was hoping to get a tour of Los Pinos today. Do you think you have time?"

Beads of sweat begin to trickle down Sofia's smooth dark forehead. She swipes at them with the back of her hand. Her long dark hair falls in waves around her narrow shoulders. "As you can probably tell," she smiles, "I am ready for a break. So go on to your class and I will accompany Martha Hooper."

"Thank you, Sofia. Nice to meet you Martha Hooper," Maya laughs at the use of both names and turns to trot back up the hill.

For a moment, I worry that I am intruding upon this young woman's very important work and start to apologize, but before I can even get the words out, her dark eyes turn to me with a look that startles me. It's as if she can read my mind and is slightly amused by it. "Do not worry Martha Hooper."

"I beg your pardon?" I say somewhat stupidly.

"Follow me. Let's put these stalks in the greenhouse and get a cool glass of water. It's a warm morning, don't you think."

I follow obediently. "Your lavender garden is magnificent," I say. "I can't wait to see the rest of the things that you can tease out of this barren New Mexico soil." We reach the greenhouse door, and she holds it open with one hand while balancing the basket on her opposite hip. I notice now that underneath the apron she wears a simple cotton Mexican skirt and white peasant blouse. Her arms are slender, muscular and browned by the hot sun, hard work and heritage. "I have a friend who loves to grow and work with herbs." I repeat my story.

"It was my abuela and my mama in Mexico who taught me everything I know about plants. In my village, my abuela was the curandera. Do you know what that is, Martha Hooper?"

As endearing as it sounds when she joins my two names together, I say, "Yes, she was a healer who worked with plants. And please, you can call me just plain Martha."

There is a glint in her eye when she answers, handing me a glass of water, "I do think Martha Hooper a more lovely choice than Just Plain Martha."

I am surprised by the spontaneity of my own laugh, and lacking any answer that could be as witty as hers, I raise my glass in a toast to her playfulness.

The greenhouse is hot, as it should be, so without much of a look around, we retreat to a bench on the north side of the building. A gentle breeze adds to the cooling that the shade provides.

"Are you thinking about joining our community?" she asks.

"No, not at this time." I answer. "I just had no idea that a place like this even existed, so my curiosity got the better of me." I finish off the glass of water as I tell her about house-sitting and taking care of the horses and learning a little bit about country life myself. She inquires about my profession, and I explain my therapy practice and what I do. This seems to strike a chord with her, causing a momentary pensiveness that quietly takes her away from me. The easy humor of a few minutes ago drifts darkly to a faraway place.

I often get a lot of questions about my work, but not the one that she asks me now.

"Why do you do this work that you do?"

I want to say, why do you do the work you do? I want to say this because the therapist in me wants to turn this interview around. And in a way, that's what I do say, as I look out across another flourishing crop of herbs planted companionably with marigolds and beautiful layered cabbage plants. I say, "Why do you do what you do? Your grandmother, now you, have been called to the job of working with healing plants, I'm guessing." I shrug. "For me, I've been called to the profession of listening to other people's problems. Therapists and bartenders," I laugh, "we have a lot in common." She looks at me with a slightly unsettled expression. "It's just an old joke." I say.

"What would you like to see?" she asks, changing the subject abruptly, but seemingly revived from her momentary musings. "There are the residential areas, the building where craftsmanship and creativity combine to make beautiful and useful things come to life. There are the livestock barns, the recreation and community center, and the theater. We also have a large area for cooking that includes the classroom spaces where Maya went and a communal dining area. Do any of those areas grab your attention?

I watch as a few gardeners with gray hair and slower locomotion move into the plot in front of us. One carries a basket of similar weave to Sofia's but shallower while the other wears a sling with a large, cradled pocket that swings near her waist. They move carefully up the row of plants, squatting down and rising in an effortless dance as they pick and preen the crop that is unfamiliar to me.

"Before we leave, I just have to ask you what you are growing in this garden in front of us."

Sofia rises and calls to the gentleman with the basket. "Daksha. My friend here, Martha Hooper, would like to know more about what we are growing here." Daksha pulls a small spade from his basket and kneels next to a particularly busy clump of three-foot plants that are covered with blood-red berries. Carefully he extracts a woody root with the tenacious berried plant attached and as if it is a tender infant, carries it over to us. Daksha has piercing black eyes that peer from a face that is dark like the earth that the plant just came from. His clipped Indian accent identifies the plant with no squandering of language. "Ashwagandha."

"It is an herb from India, useful in Ayurvedic medicine." Sofia adds.

Daksha hands the plant to me for examination. Running his free hand through a thick swatch of his graying, once-black hair, he offers a slow nod, much like a bow, then speaks. "The root is washed and dried then pulverized into a powder. Very useful for many disorders and complaints."

"It is one of our crops that we are able to sell to herbalists and practitioners all over the United States." Sofia smiles broadly at Daksha. "He has taught me many things about growing and using this particular herb."

I bow back to the man, then return the bushy plant to him. "Thank you, Daksha. I wonder if you would mind if I take your picture in the garden?" I ask. With his permission, I pull the camera out of my bag and snap several pictures of the garden and the man.

As we turn to leave, I call back, "It was nice meeting you, Daksha."

"It was nice meeting you, Martha Hooper."

I smile at the sound of my new name.

III

There is nothing quite like the loneliness that follows a day of inspiring camaraderie and awakening of the spirit. In the quiet of the late afternoon, my thoughts digress. Though the day ended with a heartfelt invitation to return at any time, it felt sad to say goodbye to my new friends. It was a revelation to watch happy people doing work that they felt passionate about. Every person that I met was possessed with a genuine commitment to the principles and mission of this community. In the artistry workshop, I shrugged off my bag and rolled up my sleeves to join Sara as she taught a class on how to throw a clay pot on a wheel. My hands felt like clumsy instruments that squeezed and pressed and massaged the cool wet clay until something that resembled a drunken vase emerged. This beginner's achievement was praised by more than one of the students and I couldn't keep the proud grin off my face. Picking strawberries from a thriving patch was hard, sweaty work, but in the end, we were able to bring a substantial basket to the kitchen where she and I created refreshing smoothies that we drank while watching Maya's cooking class.

There were wooly little lambs, and goats to be milked, honking geese and wildly feathered chickens wandering underfoot. "Dorkings and Frizzles and Leghorns," Tom had instructed me, while I dodged the rather formidable, feathered beasts. But I cheerfully raked animal dung which he told me would be used to fertilize the garden plots. "Do you like goat cheese and milk? There's plenty to be had in the kitchen. This is only part of the herd. We make enough to sell at the farmer's market, and it pays for their upkeep and makes a bit of a profit."

In retrospect, the big takeaway from my tour was the seemingly happy, peaceful, coexistence that this group of people have been able to create. It is, in my mind, a Shangri La. I did not meet one person along the way who was not eager to sing the praises of not only their own accomplishments but also of the Los Pinos community as a whole. Taking my camera and laptop over to the sofa, I curl up with Maca at my feet. I click the SD card out of my camera and slip it into my computer. Knowing that the pictures that Diego took are still on the card, I reverse the order of my perusing and look at the newest first. It produces my desired outcome and drives away the "aloneness" as I recreate the experience. When I get to the picture of Sofia that I snapped as I prepared to leave, I pause. We had been sitting beneath a tree just outside of the Visitors Center so that I could catch my breath and sip some cool cucumber water before beginning the ascent to the parking lot. My face felt flushed and maybe a little sunburned, my muscles contentedly exhausted and my mind charged and inquisitive. We talked a bit more about the community, but then Sofia had stared at me, wordlessly, and for a long moment. I could see her brewing a question she felt uncomfortable with.

"Is there something wrong?" I asked, worried that maybe in my enthusiasm I had unwittingly committed some personal act of tactlessness.

Her eyes grew darker, and it seemed as if she was truly conflicted about asking me something.

"Please tell me what it is?" I said gently.

Finally, she tilted her head and smiled nervously. "Martha Hooper, do you know anything about schizophrenia?" An uneasiness diminished her otherwise strong musical voice, a gravity so uncharacteristic of the girl that I had spent the day with, that I too was weighed down.

"I do." I answered simply, all the while looking at her curiously.

"I just wondered," she said as she quickly looked away and swallowed the rest of her cucumber water.

"Is there something about it that you would like to know?" I asked, trying to draw her back in. But I could see she was unwilling to go any further with this topic. "Sofia, if I can somehow pay you back for this wonderful experience you have provided for me, by offering you some information or counsel, please let me know." I dug around in my bag for a moment until I finally came up with one of my cards. I stared at it for a few seconds before handing it to her. "That's my office number in Santa Fe," I said slowly, knowing full well as I said it, what I was getting ready to do. I reached back into my bag and pulled out a pen, "Here," I say, "let me write my cell phone number on the back." Sofia took the card, and with a solemn look, she thanked me.

Diego is a fine young photographer. I download all the photos and begin to scroll through his pictures of the party. How he managed to capture the essence of all of us with such candid shots is a subject I promise to raise with him next time we are together. It would seem he is in league with those small prodigies who are able to play Mozart at age 3 or sing opera or name every president and their dog. These photos are remarkable for such a young first-timer. I particularly like the one of my mother and Graci sitting in their lawn chairs, pulled intimately close, their heads bent in the arch of juicy gossip. And the close-up of Maria. Those eyes restored to a shiny clarity of dignity and innocence, her smile untainted by sadness or the guilt of our recent fiasco. It makes me smile as I click through at least fifteen shots of the car. And it makes me lonely when I see the one of John and me, in what I thought was a private embrace. Sneaky little coyote with a camera.

Suddenly I feel Maca licking my toes and with a jolt, I realize that my chin has dropped to my chest, and I think I even heard myself snore. In a state of fogginess, I come to realize that I was sound asleep. Looking down at my laptop which is still balanced on my lap, I smile as I see Señor Rivera's face looking up at me with his roguish smile lighting up his whiskery face. Behind him is the blurred-out background of the wall that separates our two yards. Suddenly my smile fades and I bend closer to the screen and hit the magnify button. There is a vague outline of a person there behind the wall in his yard. I see black. A large black hat? A dark cape or coat? It's all so fuzzy. I magnify it even more, but that makes it worse, only less definitive. Jerking to an upright position, I startle Maca and she jumps off the sofa.

I click quickly through all the pictures and try to find another with the shadowy figure, but there is not one. "Fuck!" I shout to no one. I feel hell breaking loose in my brain and gut. Leaving the laptop behind, I begin to pace frantically. Should I call someone? Mr. Rivera? John? Officer Martinez? Then suddenly another thought emerges. What did I do with Maggie's drawing? That innocent drawing with the smudged black figure in the corner. Is he here stalking us? The picture, I suddenly remember, is stuffed in the desk drawer at the office. Without an ounce of clear thinking, I grab my purse, keys and laptop, and with a sharp whistle to Maca, head out the door.

IV

Before I head to the office, I decide to drive by Graciela's place again, hoping against all hope that she will be home this time. When I spot her car parked along the curb, I feel a sense of instant relief, like some kind of tranquilizer flooding through my veins. It's enough of a calmative that I'm able to remember to pick up my bag and laptop, let Maca out and walk calmly up the pathway to her door. Like the prescient spirit that she is, Graci seems to have known I was coming and opens the door with her arms out before I even get there. Wrapping those arms around me, she murmurs, "What is it, Marta? What happened?"

I feel my legs begin to buckle underneath me, but I work really hard at maintaining the pretense of sanity. Shoring up my strength, I invite myself in. Graci follows me to the sofa. I feel her apprehension and as soon as I sit down. I steadily lose that little bit of self-control that I had previously tapped into.

"It's him. I'm sure of it. He's back. That black-hearted son of a bitch is back, and you know he wants to hurt me," I sob. She lets me ramble from one broken unintelligible sentence to the next. I babble on through tears like a broken pipe that gushes endlessly until finally, I just run out of words. And still, she sits quietly beside me, holding my hand.

“What should I do?” I finally break the silence with a plea for help. Looking up, I fixate on her face, so calm and thoughtful. For a moment it makes me angry that she can be so calm. But as I look deeper, I see the gears turning behind those quiet eyes. I see her blueprinting the design of my ramblings and adding her own notes. Reaching for my laptop, I bring up the photo that has me in this state. I place it on her lap.

“So, Diego took this picture on the day of our get-together,” she says. It is not a question, but a statement of fact, information that she is collecting. She bends to look more closely, just as I did, and hits the magnification, in the same way I did. “And what is the other picture you’re referring to?”

“I need to go to the office to get it, but it's a drawing that my little six-year-old client made for me. He’s in that, too.”

“Well let’s go get it,” she says firmly, closing the laptop cover. “I’ll drive. I just need to get my keys.” She bends over as she gets up to give Maca a thorough rubdown. It hadn’t occurred to me that I probably freaked my dog out. Her doggyradar would have picked up on my panic easily enough. While Graci goes to find her keys, I too give her a reassuring cuddle. Already, my hysteria is draining away, and I feel my rational self starting to return. I splash some cold water on my face from the kitchen sink and use a comb that’s lying on the countertop to tame my unruly hair. By the time we head out to Graci’s car, I am feeling less the victim and more the huntress.

My office feels stuffy and uninhabited as we enter. I leave the door open to let some fresh air in. Since I’m here, I check my phone messages, which thankfully are minimal and not so important. In the spirit of a good self-scolding, I remind myself how often I have been giving out my cell number lately.

The folded paper that possesses Maggie's drawing is in the drawer just where I left it. I spread it out on the desk for Graci to see.

"So, walk me through this. What am I looking at? It seems like a really sweet child's drawing."

"Okay." I respond. I am determined to make her understand my fear. "I had this client draw a picture of what she wanted. What she drew was a picture of her family, all of them together here in the therapy room. See how she drew the hummingbirds. She watches them out the patio doors. But in the corner here," I point to the smudge, "if you look closely, you can see she drew a dark figure with a black hat. I don't know if she tried to smudge it out or if it was an accident, but look, Graci, it is right outside of the window. I feel like she drew him looking in."

Graci grabs the readers off my desk and slips them on. "Well," she pauses, "it doesn't take a stretch of the imagination to see that she was drawing some kind of dark figure. But knowing her, can you think of any other person she might be portraying? You know, like some nasty uncle or an unfriendly little boy that she dislikes."

I feel exhausted and plop down into my desk chair. I look up at her. "No," I say definitively. "I know I probably sound paranoid, Graci, but I've just got this feeling that he is near and biding his time, waiting for another opportunity to strike out."

"I'm not questioning your assessment of the situation, amiga. I'm taking measure of the intent of his messages. I don't believe either of these pictures was an accident. I think we need to stop by the police station and talk with your officer. Let's just let her know what's up. We can show her these and hopefully they'll be alert to the possibility of his presence."

I am a woman of great bounties. This amazing friend of mine is one. By the time she has walked me through the unnerving process of reporting this new information to the police and supported my theories as to why all this might be a real threat and not just my paranoia, I am feeling steadier as we go.

At her suggestion, we stop by a favorite taco stand on the way home and sit at the picnic tables, fill our bellies, toss tidbits of chicken to Maca, and talk only about the things that amuse us. I tell her about Sunny and how she is coming out tomorrow to teach me how to ride a horse. Graci finds this monstrously amusing.

"You, on board a horse?" She wipes her hands on her jeans and then casually uses them to comb her short hair backward. "Not that I don't think you can't do it. I just can't picture Dr. Hooper as rodeo queen Hooper."

"Get over it, Graci." I laugh. "Lots of people ride horses and they're not all cowpokes and rodeo queens."

"So how is it that Sunny is your choice for a riding instructor?"

"Not my choice, really. She actually kind of muscled her way into that job. But John swears she actually was a "rodeo queen" and knows what she's doing. He trusts her. And I trust him."

Graciela is looking at me with her sideways not-the-whole-story expression.

"Look," I say, "it's complicated. She offered. I accepted. She's complicated."

"Okay, I get it, but I can't wait to hear the after story."

We both take a breather and watch the sun setting. The cool breeze that whips the loose trash around feels good on my face and it's fun to watch the parade of cars whizzing up and down the busy road in front of us.

"So, there is another reason I'm feeling a little edgy," I say as we head back to the car. She lifts her eyebrows and nods like she knew I was holding back on something. "Señor Rivera and Diego and I shared a past life experience together yesterday. You know, like a three-way," I try to laugh. "Actually, it was wildly distressing for me." She opens the back door for Maca to jump in, then hustles me into the front seat.

"Was it the same for Diego and the Señor?" The engine purrs as she buckles in.

"It didn't seem like it. Diego just thought it was cool and Raphael was the epitome of calm. It was his turn to scrape me off the pavement."

"So, tell me about it," she says as she pulls out into the traffic giving the engine a little rev.

"Well, the thing is Graci, these experiences are so different from my experiences with other people's pasts. You know, like when it happened with Señor Rivera the first time and when that black devil made it happen when I was kidnapped. It feels more like… like I lose Martha Hooper and I'm replaced by this man, this William Turnbull. I don't know how to describe it except that I am him. I'm not watching him. Anyway, when it happens this way, it makes me feel kind of sick inside." I turn my head to read her reaction, but she is concentrating on the traffic. The whole experience for me, and it would seem for me only, is disorienting and disturbing."

"Okay, but tell me what you saw and what you did as this Turnbull guy? Did you do anything unsavory?"

"No, not this time. The three of us were just traveling on foot to go buy something. I guess something valuable. In Paris. I have no idea where we were coming from or exactly what happened, but it has something to do with alchemy and something to do with the past life conjuring that Misterioso, the fiend, dragged me into when he kidnapped me." That gets her attention.

"Alchemy? Wow!

I spend the rest of the ride to her house trying to recall the details and unfolding the tale to her. It actually feels therapeutic and even a little fun to explore this adventure with Graciela and, before I know it, we are back at her house and there sits my little car next to the curb.

"You okay to go back to your mountain chalet, all alone?" she asks as we exit the car. Maca dashes eagerly up the sidewalk, intent on extending our visit. "You can hang out here. We can have a slumber party. I can even go out there with you and keep you company if you want."

"No," I say, as I come around to her side of the car, "I feel so much better. I really think I'll be fine. Just keep your cell phone on, okay? And tomorrow, I suspect, Sunny will be there bright and early."

She gives me a hug and calls Maca back for a goodbye neck scruffing. Dusk is settling in, and it makes the world look like an old hazy black-and-white film, which persuades me to get on the road. I don't like driving in the dark all that much anymore.

I do feel calmer. Even when I notice that the white rock with the face is missing from under the window when I get home, I stay calm and chalk it up to neighborhood pranks. I am almost cheerful as Maca and I follow the beam from my flashlight down to the barn and quickly feed the ravenous horses. I even start to hum a little tune in anticipation of giving John a call this evening. I brew up a warm cup of tea for myself and give Maca a piece of rawhide to chew on. All is lighthearted and serene while settling myself onto the sofa with the volume of Robert Frost poetry, my cell phone and my tea. All is calm until…

Four raps on the door. They are rapid and insistent intruding upon my hard-earned serenity in an instant. Maca abandons her chew for the work of boldly taking a stand at the door and barking with deafening obsession. I jump frantically from the sofa, only to land with an emotional paralysis of my own making. It is only the increasing volume of Maca's insanity that finally dissolves my suspended animation and moves me forward. I grab her collar and try to calm her while yelling to the rapper on the other side of the door.

"Who is it?"

"It's your neighbor, ma'am, Charley Walker." I hear the gruff voice that sets Maca off into a frenzy of barking again. He tries again through the barrage of noise. "You know, we bumped into each other down in the arroyo the other day."

"What do you want?" I ask, not so sure I want to calm Maca down at all.

"Just wanted to give you a warning about a prowler?"

"About a what?" I yell over the doggybedlam.

He raises his voice to a level that I'm sure can be heard a mile away. "About a possible prowler in the neighborhood."

"Why are you coming around so late to spread this news?" I shout back.

"I promise you, ma'am, I'm just trying to let you and all the folks up here know I got broke into. Just trying to be neighborly."

I snap the lock open and crack the door about an inch. "I don't see a car, Mr. Walker. Did you ride your horse up here?" I ask a little sarcastically.

"No, ma'am. I left my truck at the end of the drive and walked in. Just didn't want to scare you."

"Well, that ship has sailed," I counter, my heart still pounding. I lean down, this time making a concerted effort to calm the dog. Finally, with a stern command, I get her to quiet down and back off. "So, what is it, Mr. Walker? What news that couldn't wait till the light of day?" I ask. I open the door just enough so that I can see the whole of the man who is standing on my porch. Sure enough, it is the so-called curmudgeon who I met in the arroyo. The large man is dressed in a clean western-style shirt with his hands tucked into the pockets of a pair of faded but crisp blue jeans. His long gray and white beard flows down over his chest and he has his cowboy hat in his hand, freeing his bushy gray hair to go wild in the nighttime breeze. This man squints doggedly at me, despite the bright light that must be streaming glaringly into his eyes.

"Maam, I've been having problems for some time now with someone gettin' into my barn and movin' things around, and once or twice a few things have turned up missin'. Nothin' of any consequence, so mostly I been turning a blind eye to the goings on... until today."

"Yes, Mr. Walker, so what happened today?" The expression on this man's face is resolute and sincere. Looking down at Maca, I see she has suddenly become instantly curious and quiet, sniffing the scent of him through the crack in the door, taking in his information and formulating her own opinion. Unwittingly or maybe based on her calmness, I open the door wider. Maca boldly slinks out onto the porch to get a better sniff.

"Today," he says gruffly, "this packrat of a human being has changed his tune and decided to become a full-blown bandito. While I was out huntin' down a few of my stray cows, that sneaky son of a bitch jimmied my window open and got into my kitchen and stole a hunk of elk meat right outta' my freezer, a loaf of bread off my counter. A full gallon of milk- gone. Just vanished right outta' my fridge. Not to mention my favorite bedroll has turned up missin' as well." He shuffles his boots around like he's going to carve his frustration into the dust on my porch floor. "So, you can see, Ms…?" The man looks at me expectantly.

"Hooper." I give in to the carelessness of not staying anonymous.

"We gotta problem going on here, Ms. Hooper, and who knows which one of you folks will be next."

"Well, you do have a point, sir. Did you report this to the police?"

"I did. And that was a goddamn waste of my time, if you'll excuse my rough language. They've done less than nothing, except to say that they'll keep an eye out for the missing items and let me know if there's any more reports of stolen items in the area." There's a sudden slump to the man's shoulders and a slight hanging of the head that I sense is a mixture of fatigue and the feeling of futility.

"So, Ms. Hooper, I just felt the only thing left to do was to warn all the folks. You're last on my list which is why I'm showin' up so late. I do apologize."

Against my better judgment, I say, "Can I get you a glass of water before you get on your way? You look like you could use a little something."

"Oh no, mam, I'm not one to impose on folks. Just felt like it was my duty to come round and let you all know." He turns his large frame and starts down off the porch.

"Mr. Walker," I call out to his backside as he swings that ghostly head of hair and that lofty white beard back my way, "I insist. Do you drink tea, Mr. Walker? The kettle is hot. Let me make you a cup. Here," I quickly retrieve a chair from just inside the door and set it out on the porch, "sit down and I'll just be a minute." I watch his deliberation for only a second before I ease back from the door and into the kitchen.

The kettle is still warm, and it only takes a minute to heat it back up. I choose a sturdy mug and call out through the open door, "Do you take honey or sugar?" For a moment, I suspect that he has refused my invitation and gone on, but finally, after a cricket-filled interlude, I hear the creak of the wooden chair and the soft groan of a tired man settling in.

"A little honey would be most pleasin', mam," I hear him say.

I glance at the clock from under the covers. It's almost midnight.

"Really John, you're being way too fussy," I say to the cell phone lying on my pillow. "He's not such a bad sort. He kind of reminds me of a big fluffy white wolf, with his white beard and wild hair. He told me that, in his younger days, he was a bronc rider on the rodeo circuit all throughout the west. He said it took a -calamitous-, his word, accident and a beautiful woman to finally make him part ways with the only way of life that he could ever imagine doing. Apparently, she had some kind of voodoo that settled him down."

"I know that breed of woman." I could hear him chuckle softly. "So, where's this beautiful woman now? And by the way, you know you kind of set me up to believe this was a burrow-dwelling old badger you unearthed down there in the arroyo."

"Stories change," I smile to myself. "So, here's the sad part. Apparently, she saw him when he came through Santa Fe with the rodeo and made it her mission to meet the young bronc rider."

"This is starting to sound like some old western movie I once saw." I can't tell if John is being sarcastic, but his voice hints at his curiosity when he adds, "Go on, how did they get together?"

"Well, the woman, her name was Camila, apparently broke all the rules getting to him back by the bronco pens. He was just getting up on his bronc when she climbed up on the slats. Then just as he chanced to look down at her, she placed her little rosary cross in his hand. He took it and put it in his shirt pocket and nodded thanks to the beautiful dark-eyed woman and rode his heart out that evening. He won the competition."

"Imagine that," John remarks, "I swear I've seen this one."

"Oh stop. So, when he and the rodeo show moved on to their next stop on the circuit in Tucson, apparently she showed up again. That's when he became completely 'besotted'- again his word- by the woman. They spent time together for the next few days and he was convinced she'd put some kind of spell on him because he could do no wrong. He invited her to come to Denver with him to his next event, but she refused and stayed in Santa Fe. He went on to Denver, nursing a broken heart and feeling like he was losing his direction. So, on the last day of his Denver event with the championship in the bag, his distraction was extreme and despite his bronc riding expertise, he somehow found himself lying sunny side up beneath the hooves of the most savage horse he'd ever ridden. He admitted to a sudden loss of substance and recalled just surrendering to the pummeling until his body broke and his heart stopped beating." I pause and listen to John sigh on the other end of the line.

"Are you getting the eerie parallel here?" he finally asks.

"Not!" I answer quickly. "You'll be just fine… unless your guitar falls on your head. Do you want to hear the rest of the story or not?" I grab the phone from the pillow and take it off speaker and move it close to my cheek.

"I do, but it better have a happy ending."

"Okay." I pull the blanket up to my chin. "But not all of it is so very happy. Apparently, he woke up from a coma that lasted for a week or so, only to find Camila in his hospital room, straightening up a vase full of roses, humming a tune, then turning to smile at him as she had never been anywhere else except by his side. Charley says the whole thing remembers like a dream, the way she took that little crucifix that was hanging back around her neck and came over to him with a real sexy smile, and placed it back in his hand. And because he was not in his right mind and he knew he wasn't feeling his body right, he was sure he had died and gone to heaven to be with an angel.

"They got married in that very hospital room a few weeks later while he recovered from broken bones and damaged organs and legs that he was told would never work right again. Everyone thought he was going to be a paraplegic. Everyone except Camila. According to him, she dealt out some pretty potent persuasions to motivate him to mend and become a whole man again. So not only did he live and heal, but because of her dogged belief in him and her utterly mysterious ways, he did learn to walk again."

"Now that's my kinda' woman," John interrupts, then, "You must have spent a lot of time wrestling this story out of the old curmudgeon."

I can hear a hint of suspicion in his voice, so I just keep on going. "Well, here's the sad part, John. Of course, he could never rodeo ride again, but he learned some carpentry skills and worked at cabinetry while she worked as a waitress and a bartender at a place that used to be called Angelina's, here in town. Then Camila got cancer. He said she was just forty years old when she died of it. He said he had no magic persuasion for her and the road to death was short and harrowing."

"That's incredibly lousy and not the happy ending I was hoping for."

"I know," I say quietly as I recall the defeated sadness and anger I had seen shifting across his weathered features while he finished the story.

"Did he ever remarry?" John asks while trying to stifle a yawn.

"No, he never did. Charley Walker said he moved up here into the mountains as soon as he could find a small ranch that he could afford. He told me that his life these days adds up to nothing more than a handful of cows and a few horses. He encouraged me to come and see his place if I ever felt like it."

"Well, now, I think, I'm worried in a whole different way. You make it sound like this busted bronc rider might have a crush on you." His tired laugh loses even more of its life coming through the phone.

"John, I really miss you," I say, changing the subject.

"I know," he says softly. "This is hard on me too. I thought maybe I could drive down for the weekend, but now I don't think that's going to be possible. Any chance you could get away and come to Denver?"

"Sadly, not this week, John. I just don't feel like I can, and I've got the horses that I'm responsible for."

"Yeah, that's pretty much what I thought. But we'll get through this, and I'll be back in Santa Fe before you know it. The album is coming along really well, and we actually got booked for a weekend gig up here at a pretty swank bar."

"Well, just don't go getting all popstar on me, okay? I don't want to have to fight off all the groupies just to get you back in my life."

"Ha! I won't mess around with the groupies if you don't go sporting around with that rough and tough cowboy. How's that for a deal?"

"I'm good with that. Consider the deal sealed." I sigh, suddenly feeling overwhelmed by a serious drowsiness. "I think I better go before I go dopey on the phone here."

"Yeah, I'm pretty done in, as well. We'll talk again in a few days, okay?"

"Love you, John."

"Me, you." he whispers, and the phone and my brain go silent.

The Weight of Expectancy

I

The warm morning delivers sun and the shifting breezes of anticipation and apprehension. Having eaten a light breakfast, dressed and redressed three different times, unsure of what one wears to ride a horse, I finally settle on jeans, sneakers, my oldest green tank top and a lightweight denim shirt. I pull my hair back with a clip, wash my face, forgo makeup and move to the porch to wait. Leaning up against the side of the house is the carved walking stick that Charley Walker gave me on my first meeting with the old cantankerous cowboy down in the arroyo. Last night I had tried to return it to him, reassuring him that, thanks to my friend's magic potion, my leg was feeling much better. He in turn argued that it was a gift, and I should hold on to it. He fortified his position, divulging that he had carved quite a few of these sticks in his free time, enough that he was well covered for the occasional recurrences of his own accident-related twinges and cricks. "Besides," he had cautioned me, "rattlesnake bites have a mind and a timetable of woe that is all their own." I had then sarcastically thanked him for his glad tidings and offered him a glass of rum. I reach for the stick and hold it on my lap, running my fingers absentmindedly over the carvings.

Sunny will undoubtedly be late, though we did leave the meeting time pretty open. I decide to give Diego a call while I wait.

"Hullo," a child's sleepy voice answers.

"Are you still sleeping, Diego?" I ask.

"Huh? Martha? No. Well, kind of." I hear him groan, then the sound of a cat meowing several times.

"Do you want me to call you back later? Sounds like you need a few, to get it together. I was just checking in to see how you and my mother were doing. Nothing earth-shattering."

I hear a few thumps and another groan, then, "No, it's okay, Martha. I'm up. We're good here. So, what's up?" His boyish voice is much more animated this time.

"How are you? How's my mom?"

"We're good. We went and saw a movie last night. A late one. I think your mom's still sleeping. You ever see the Star Wars movies? We saw the latest one. She said it was the first one she's ever seen, but she liked it a lot."

That makes me smile. That mom of mine keeps an open mind.

"I'm getting my first riding lesson this morning," I tell him. "Sunny should be here soon. I'm kind of nervous, but then I remind myself, the sooner I figure all this out, the sooner you can come out and I'll teach you. What do you think?"

"I think you better get it down quick, 'cause I wanna do it really soon," he chatters excitedly.

Oh, to be so young and able to go from zero to sixty emotional miles per hour in thirty seconds or less.

Then he says, "So are you okay from the other afternoon?" His tone and choice of words seem that of a much older child. "You were pretty messed up by that past life thing we did. You left Señor

Rivera's house so fast that I never even got to tell you how totally awesome it was for me, but it scared me that you got so upset." He says this to me like an old friend, one who knows me well.

"I know, Diego. I was pretty shook up. It's really weird experiencing a past life, our past lives, that way. You know the way it was, us all being there together, as if we were actually living through it, and not even just looking in on it. Having you and Señor Rivera right there with me, pretty much freaked me out. Something about it just turned me inside out, you know. But it didn't seem to affect you that way. Have you ever had that kind of experience before?"

"Nope, not ever. That's what made it so cool. Like being an actor in a movie. No, even better, 'cause I didn't even know I was an actor. Did you see that knife I had? Now that was badass! Did you really feel that awful about it?"

"No, not now anyway. I think I need to look at it more like you do. Like a movie." I don't reveal to him that this particular movie does not end so well. It did seem to me like that little episode took place before we had ever met the dark and evil Madam. And our happy camaraderie at the time was undeniable. I think I just have to let it go. "So, tell me, do you think Alice is adjusting well to living in Santa Fe? The house is working out for the two of you? And how about that TomB?"

Diego fills me in on little details that make me laugh and also in the end reassures me that I have made the right decision. Just as our conversation is winding down and Diego finishes describing TomB's antics with Poppy the female calico that lives a few houses down which indicates to me that the boy knows way too much about romantic overtures, I hear a car sputtering up the hill. He and I sign off with a few fond words to each other, and slipping the phone into my back pocket, I shake my head feeling a little taken aback by how attached I'm getting to that boy.

II

Standing at the corral, leaning against the split rail fencing, I can smell that pungent cedar fragrance of the wood. I watch Sunny brushing and coddling the two horses. The two horses, in return, nuzzle her and rub their big flat faces against her shoulders. With her long tan arms that emerge gracefully from the sleeveless denim shirt she is wearing, she gently picks up each hoof, inspecting it carefully and using some kind of pick to pull out unwanted debris.

"Would you like some help?" I call out.

"In a minute Martha. It's really great just getting to spend a little time getting to know these girls." She peeks out at me from under the brim of the western hat she is wearing while squatting awkwardly to one side with a heavy hoof in her hand. "My take on this little palomino, Sol, is that she is a bit of a mischief-maker. Reminds me a bit of me. Luna, on the other hand, seems to be a follower. And very calm." She finishes the hoof inspection and gives them both a pat on the rump. As she walks over to me, I notice that her boots which glistened with fresh polish on arrival, are now thickly coated with dust. "So," she nearly sings to me, "are you ready for your first lesson?"

The irony of this woman being in the driver's saddle of this venture is not lost on me. I am feeling unsettled in the role of Sunny's pupil. Still, I give an enthusiastic nod and climb over the rails, landing clumsily, but upright, on the other side of the fence. She looks me up and down, from pulled-back hair to blue tennis shoes and gives me that broad Sunny smile. In that smile and those eyes that fluctuate like mercurial clouds, I cannot tell if I am seeing a bit of mockery for my incompetence or the thrill of being the master. At any rate, I rally and move towards the horses.

"I think you'll be more comfortable on Luna," she says, "but of course, it's up to you. So, grab a halter and let's lead them into the stable."

Sunny proves to be a remarkably patient teacher as I falter uncertainly at each step. Mishandling each piece of equipment, I fumble absurdly as if the two hands connected to my very own wrists were fused into boxing gloves. Luna also demonstrates a bucket full of tolerance and self-control, responding with only an occasional snort and full-body shudder when I have to retry things like the whole bridle thing... three times. In the end, after repeating every step to the edge of flat-out frustration, I actually feel like I might be able to do this on my own. When Sunny turns her smile back on me and raises her hand, I swear she might flip me a dog treat for a job well done. But instead, that hand reaches out to give the stoic pony a knowing pat.

"Left foot in the stirrup," she instructs. "Now give a little jump and swing your right leg all the way over the saddle." She stands back with Maca at her feet, chuckling. "Nope, you can't pull yourself up with the saddlehorn. Here, let me show you, Martha."

This time I stand back with my arms folded resentfully across my chest and observe this limber woman mount Luna as if she were executing a perfect ballet move, but it does provide me with a better picture of what I was doing wrong. Third time's the charm and Sunny leads Luna with me in the saddle out to the corral. Sol, who remains in the stable munching on some hay grass, seems untroubled by being left behind. I look down at my blue tennis shoes which are now gray with a fashionable hint of green manure.

"Hold the reins a little steadier," Sunny says firmly, as she walks us in a circle around the corral, "and you can let go of the saddlehorn now." I watch her cowboy hat bob as she walks along beside us. "Your thighs need to press gently into her sides, and Martha, try to sit a little straighter. Your back is going to really be sore if you don't." I make the adjustments that she has asked for with great concentration, and when I look back up, I realize that she is no longer walking with us. For just a few seconds, I feel a panic surge from my toes to my hair follicles. An image of this gentle horse bucking me off and stomping me into tiny little pieces flashes into my mind. But then I hear her reassuring voice.

"That is so excellent, Martha. You're a quick study. Now give her a little squeeze so she picks up the pace a bit and keeps a loose but steady rein. It lets her know you're confident all is well."

Luna picks up the pace, not a trot, but a quick little walk. "Sunny?" I call out. "Do I just pull back on the reins to stop her? I can't find the brake pedal." The horse, burdened with her hesitant passenger, swings past the woman and does another turn. She is leaning against the rails with a piece of grass between her teeth, hugely enjoying the spectacle of inelegance that I am while I try to keep upright in the tight turns.

"Really, you're doing fine, but if you want to stop her pull lightly on the inside rein. Just enough to direct her head around and down and she will stop for you." She pauses, and watches. "No Martha you're pulling too hard and on both reins. That's better."

Luna stops. But suddenly my heart is pumping. "I did it!" I pant, as Sunny walks over to us.

"You did. Wanna try a trot?"

Sunny runs us through our paces, walking, stopping, walking, trotting, stopping, walking and stopping, till my head is spinning in the circling orbit we've been making around the corral. After a bit, she seems to feel I am not a total trainwreck and can manage the basics, and she scurries off to the stable and leaves Luna and me to practice our thing. When at last, Sol and Sunny join us, my thighs are aching, and I am ready for a break.

"Sunny?" I ask politely. "How do I get off this thing? I think my ass has fallen asleep."

After a hilarious dismount that gets Sunny laughing so hard I think she just might fall off her own horse, I make it back into the barn to the hitching loop. I almost cry when I take my first few steps.

"Keep walking it off, Martha," Sunny shouts back to me as she gracefully puts, the more contrary Sol, through the same paces I have just been through.

III

Arroyo Coyote seems wonderfully unchanged since my last visit. I know that it is inherent in nature that all things eventually change. Sands shift, trees fall, little by little mountains are worn down to ant hills, but to my inexpert eye, from my seat on this beast, I thrill at the sight of the recognizable landmarks and geography. Sunny, too, appears confident and untroubled. However, as we move the mares forward along the sandy bottom, I do take note of one departure from the similarities to my last visit. The chalky white skulls are nowhere to be seen. And that, I decide, is a good thing.

"How are you holding up, Martha?" She rides ahead of me, and just as she predicted, my little Luna is content to be a follower.

"I can feel the aches that are going to plague me tomorrow, but for now I am absolutely enchanted. "I'm not sure why we ever invented cars. Thank you for this, Sunny."

I hear her chuckle, then ask, "Should we just follow the arroyo?"

"I think that would be best. I really don't know this area all that well.

As we walk the horses at a casual pace alongside the bank of the arroyo, I keep an eye on Maca who has seamlessly taken on the role of trail dog. She parallels our path weaving in and out of the trees, but always staying within visual range and checking in on our progress with no bother towards or from the horses. The afternoon sun is high and warm, streaming from a perfect turquoise sky. A more blissful person could not be found at this moment. The floppy sun hat I was able to dig up is a saving grace even though it makes me look more like a gardener than a cowgirl.

"How have you been feeling?" I ask, then add, "I mean with the pregnancy?" Why would blissful me ask such a question? No doubt a subtle self-scolding is in order. With a sharp shake of the head, I take myself to task for my habit of opening cans of worms, especially this one. She hesitates just long enough to make me think that I might have finally stepped over that line with her or maybe she didn't hear me or maybe she is appalled by my audacity to dig into what I hope she thinks is her private life. Maybe we have reached detente. But…

"Actually, I don't think I've ever felt better." Sunny twists easily in the saddle so that she is looking back at me. "And before you bother to ask, no I haven't talked to the gentleman who helped me with this happy accident."

"Happy accident?" I echo, mildly annoyed by her choice of words. "Well, there's still time, if you decide that it's the right thing to do, you know."

"I know *you* think it's the right thing to do, and don't get me wrong, Martha," she slows Sol down and pauses so that our horses begin to walk side by side, "you know I have a lot of respect for your views on most situations, just not this one."

I toss her a stern look. "So, how's Jimmy?"

She throws her head back and laughs easily. "Martha, I know what you're doing. I get it. Really, I do. But I've made up my mind. This is my deal, my child. This baby has made me feel stronger and more whole and more purposeful than I have ever felt in my entire life. Seriously, I feel some need to reassure you, so I will." She tips her cowboy hat back away from her eyes and stares into mine. "I am absolutely sure that I am capable of being this child's parent and taking care of him or her."

I nod and offer her a reluctant smile.

"And since you asked, Jimmy is fine. He and I both agree that for now, we have other things to pursue. Other than each other, that is. He did ask me, to ask you, if he could call you sometime to talk about more profound subject matters than I would ever care to talk about with him." She slides her hat back over her eyes to protect them from the bright sunshine. With a click and a gentle nudge, Sunny urges her horse forward until once again she has a good-sized lead. We drift along in silence, Sunny with her newfound direction and confidence and me with an inexplicable feeling that I have somehow driven off course.

We have ridden out about as far as I feel comfortable. The arroyo begins an uphill incline, and a smaller drainage bed joins in with the one we are riding in. It seems like the perfect place to pause for a few minutes before turning around. We both dismount, Sunny, as competently as a seasoned jockey, me as awkwardly and painfully as the hapless loser in a bar room brawl. She holds the reins to my horse while I stumble around trying to get the feeling back into my gluteus maximus as well as movement back into both of my legs.

"Maybe a bit too much, a bit too soon," she comments while rubbing her face on Luna's wide soft cheek.

"No, I'm okay," I finally laugh, knowing I must look like a hundred-year-old crone, the way I am hunched over and limping circles into the sand. Even Maca seems to see some kind of humor in my pain, as she crouches down with her tail sweeping like a metronome, baiting me to start up a game of tag with her. That is until her attention is diverted by something that suddenly arouses one of her senses. I stop my crippled dance and straighten up. The horses also take note of something that neither Sunny nor I have yet to sense. I think nervously about the warnings Charlie Walker gave me about bears and cougars the last time I was in this arroyo.

“Here, come take Luna’s reins,” Sunny says. Though Luna is alert, ears twitching, nostrils flaring, she stands quietly. Sol on the other hand is nervously stomping her hooves and performing small dance steps in the sand. Taking the reins Sunny hands me, I also call Maca to my side and try to soothe her with a few calm strokes, afraid that if she starts barking, Sunny’s horse might choose to execute a full-blown equine panic attack. Sunny, however, soothes the savage beast with soft reassuring words whispered into those velvety twitching ears.

Then without warning, one of those round chalky skull rocks comes tumbling down off the steep canyon wall on our right. It bounces and careens around tree trunks until its ricocheting path brings it to a rolling stop just a few feet from where I am standing. Now, both horses are jangled. Sol rears up, but Sunny keeps a firm rein and brings her back down and walks her in circles. Luna is taking nervous side steps and snorting in alarm, so I follow Sunny’s lead and stroke her neck and whisper sweet nothings in her ear. Maca also begins to bark, her hackles erect, her nose pointing up the hillside to the origin where the rock may have been launched from.

Despite the fact that my horse is dancing the two step on the other end of my reins, my eyes are riveted on that point of blast off. When at last I am able to drop my gaze to the rock that has tumbled into stasis in the loose sand of the arroyo, it is as I fear; haunting painted eyes appealing to me from the pale face of the chalky white skull rock. There is not a shred of doubt in my mind. I know it’s the very one, the very one that had been under my window. And a sense of the insubstantiality of reality washes over me.

If Rocks Could Talk

I

To be sure, I never would have predicted that the fiftieth year of my rather circumspect life would become ground zero for the reeling upheavals that have shaken me to the core. Do I believe that there is a divine reason for these psyche-concussing quakes? I do not. Do I believe that we can learn from shockwaves such as these in the same way that we can from the calm seasons of our lives? I do. Well, I think I do, and I know I used to. I built my practice trusting in these kinds of assumptions. But what if one can no longer make sense of any of it, no longer put the pieces together in a meaningful way? The earthquakes. The Misterioso Days. The Sunny Ahumada days. I find myself longing for a remote beach with the soothing crash of salty waves. A place where not one solitary character in my life, nor any troubling event, can have the power to shake the solid ground under my feet.

I lean back in the wooden chair and picture Sunny as she had slowly become aware of what the cause of all the ruckus was, as she calmly led Sol to my side, and allowed the two horses to knicker and nuzzle each other. She placed her hand gently on my trembling shoulder. “What in the world is that?” she had asked, seeming slightly amused by the pale upturned face in the sand.

In a quivering voice, not quite my own, I forced a smile and answered, “Child’s play. A spooky spirit rock.” And as my voice grew steadier, I added, “It’s probably just somebody’s idea of a joke. At any rate, we should probably head back, don’t you think?”

With the sharp toe of her boot, she had rolled the chalky skull so that its face was abruptly planted firmly in the sand. It was in that moment, when her eyes were cast attentively downward, that my own eyes angled to the heights of the canyon wall and there saw a figure squatting on a rock outcropping. At first, embraced deeply by the shadow of a tall pine, his was only the outline of a man. Then while I laboriously worked to calm my jittery nerves, the silhouette stepped forward out of the shadow. A young man with an eerily familiar face. One with a head full of tangled black hair marginally tamed by a red bandana tied about his head. In a most guileless gesture, he had lifted a hand to the level of his chest, palm turned out with fingers splayed. A guarded gesture of a greeting that seemed outwardly shy and friendly. And then another gesture, a scooping motion accompanied by a nod. As I try to focus my mind on the face of the man, I realize he was much too far away to really distinguish anything like that at all. I'm not even sure how I decided his hair was tangled and black, because remembering him now is like peering through a mind-bending kaleidoscope.

“Sunny,” I had whispered, “pick up the rock and hand it to me please.”

For once she asked no questions, just leaned down and picked up the rock while my eyes remained riveted on the young man who was backing away from the ledge and dematerializing like a wisp of smoke or a mythical jinn. I am simply left with an unreliable memory of perhaps a ghost or maybe a hallucination.

The small chalky skull that I now hold on my lap, balanced like a toddler on my thighs, is a thing of mystery. The appearance of the person that happened after the rock tumbled down is an enigma that preys on my sanity. I bounce the head up and down on my leg, a throwback from soothing babies or a nervous response meant to soothe my own frayed nerves. I look down the driveway in the direction that Sunny has cheerfully driven off into. With a casual wave of her hand out the window, she left me to the solitude of my crumbling rationality. Luckily, she did not sense my unease. Probably because I'm frequently irritable around her. "Let's do this again, soon, Martha," she shouted back towards me.

Should I call someone? Sitting here is unnerving me. I could call John or maybe Graci. Both would understand. I think. Maybe I need to tell my mom. I look down at the rock. The painted-on eyes stare back with just the slightest look of sympathy. "Tell me, what would you do, my friend?" At the sound of my voice, Maca lifts her head, tilting it curiously, searching my face for a sign of some kind of call to action. Seeing none, she returns to her well-earned nap.

I look down again at the rock. Remembering.

We had been quietly working our way back down the arroyo. Both Sunny and I lost in our own private thoughts. Propped between my thighs and the saddle, I strove to keep the chalky skull balanced with one hand while holding the reins in the other. I tried, as we rambled along, to remember the details of the young man I had seen lodged on the rocks of the cliff, but this encounter did not follow the rules. The particulars that I thought I might have seen were fading fast. Yet, I was sure I had seen that face before, even though I'm quite sure I never *really* saw it at all. As I strained to recall, even just a piece of clothing he was wearing, I chanced to look up distractedly and my gaze settled on the graceful portrait of Sunny and Sol as they paced peacefully in front of me. Her long ponytail bobbed under the dip of her cowboy hat and her lanky torso swayed and wove so naturally in sync with that of the horse that they seemed to be one being united from two. Possibly because I was already vulnerable from the rock incident and also lost in a reverie about the legend of centaurides, the female centaurs of Greek mythology, the beings mythologized to be half woman and half horse, that I became unaware of the fact that my soul was being sent down the proverbial backslide of time.

So, without warning, another tide was set in motion. I only wished not to fall from my horse as I plummeted once again into this woman's past. Closing my eyes against the swirling patterns of time, I felt the reeling and sliding that plunged me into the backwoods of her lives. Why, I briefly wondered, was I once again being dispatched into her murky waters? And only when the transit fell still, did I dare open my eyes. This I do relive in vivid detail as if it is happening again.

To my relief, no cold prison walls rise up around me, no fetid swamp waters lay before me. The sun shears its way through the narrow shiny leaves of an orderly array of large verdant trees all laid out in premeditated rows. Each is ladened with the burgeoning clusters of plump green alligator fruit that bob from the branches in the warm breeze. As if pierced, my heart feels stricken and though I cry out with the surprise of it, I know no one will hear.

This place was once my own. I move beneath the treetops, low to the dusty ground, yet try as I might, I cannot reach out and touch the rough bark of my beloved trees. Impossible. I bear the burden of my gift angrily. I long to hold the cool bulbous fruit in the palm of my hand. The intimacy with which I remember each dusty row of this grove sings in my blood and in my bones. The yearning inside me is ravenous. To be a child again.

I sense his presence long before I am able to lay eyes on him. His DNA sparks like a current of electricity conducting and transmitting through genes, DNA, brain cells and memory, burrowing paternal tentacles into the fibers of my soul. I seek out the ladder that I remember, the one that leans precariously against a thick tree trunk. And I listen. Through rustling leaves, Papa's voice swells larger with the tune. My papa's voice. Slightly off-key, yet balmy and tropical. He sings. He sings like the whirlpools of memory eddy:

"Come, Mr. Tally Mon, tally me banana
Daylight come and me wan' go home
Come, Mr. Tally Mon, tally me banana
Daylight come and me wan' go home"

Suddenly his face emerges, free from a jumble of leaves, his expression alert as if he has heard me call his name. Did I call out, Papa? Maybe I did. He peers down to the pathway, expectation furrowing his dark brow, blue eyes bright. So free his young face is of the worry lines that I would later come to know. "Alice?" he calls out, raking a swathe of black hair from his forehead. "Is that you?" Answered only by the whisper of the breeze, his handsome face withdraws, back into the leafy vegetation, but the song continues:

"Six han', seven han', eight han', bunch!
Daylight come and me wanna go home
Six han', seven han', eight han', bunch!
Daylight come and me wanna go home"

Then she is there. Mama. Waddling down the path between a row of trees, carrying a basket balanced high on the rounded bulge of her ninth-month abdomen. It's a beautiful insanity to watch her free hand rise up and press gently against the rippling movements within her, the rolls and twists that are destined to be the baby me. I move impatiently within her.

Sorting all this out is maddening. But it is him that I was there for. My Papa. He who left us far too soon. It is he that pulled me into this memory. It is a staggering, mind-boggling fact, that this was not Sunny's memory I had plunged into. This memory belonged to the embryo that floats passively and innocently in Sunny's womb. Speculations that might be cajoled by wild dreams, or childish fantasies shiver through the gutters of my brain and sweep away anything in my thoughts that smacks of a normal reality. Sunny's baby is an incarnation of my own father. I feel myself groan helplessly as I stand up from the chair and walk over to the ground outside the window where this chalky head had resided. There is nothing that this rock can say, nothing that can make me consent to this collision of souls. I glare into its all-seeing eyes though it remains mute, and I drop it back onto the ground.

II

The phone is ringing inside my office while I am outside fumbling the key into the lock. Dropping my bag and purse just inside the door which I leave standing wide open, I hobble on my knotted horseback rider's thighs to my desk and breathlessly answer the phone only to hear the drone of a missed call. Maca ambles casually in the open door while I attempt to catch my breath.

Good grief, I say out loud as my cell phone that I have left in my purse buzzes relentlessly. So again, I scramble trying not to miss another call. I think I need a secretary or at the very least, a life organizer. This time I do make it in time and answer breathlessly.

"Hello, Dr. Hooper?"

"This is her." I answer with a modicum of courtesy.

"Oh, how are you, Martha Hooper? This is Sofia Villalobo. We met last week on your visit to La Ventana a Los Pinos. Do you remember me?

"Of course I do," I answer quickly. "How are you, Sofia?" I settle into the chair at my desk.

"I'm very well. Thank you for asking. I was just wondering if I might be able to speak with you? Perhaps not on the phone. Could you see me, maybe at your office? I need some information. Possibly some advice."

My therapeutic acumen turns on and I listen carefully to the tone of her voice. I don't hear distress, just some kind of concern. "I'm actually in the office right now," I respond, "and will be here for most of the day. Would you be able to come in sometime today?"

We set up an appointment for later in the afternoon. After we end our call, I sit for a moment, contemplating what might be going on with this young woman. I recall our parting conversation that day when I visited, the one that prompted me to give her my card with my cellphone number. "Martha Hooper, do you know anything about schizophrenia?" Now why would a seemingly healthy young woman, living in a wonderful place like Los Pinos, want to know about schizophrenia? Yes, I think to myself, it feels good to sink myself into someone else's conundrums and to distract myself from my own emotional baggage. Feeling temporarily buoyed, I open my laptop and begin to work. I revisit the information I took from Angelo De Arco's session. I scratch out some notes on the pad on my desk and look up some phone numbers, jotting them down, too. I feel the way my work pulls me into that safe and comforting realm where I regain my footing with a sense of control and competence. "This is good," I sigh, as I begin to dial a number.

By lunchtime, I have traveled far from my own little hell. I have found, with the help of my mom's friend Melanie, the names of several schools outside of the public school domain. With the possibilities of scholarships, the promise of rich flexible curriculums, and tolerant absenteeism policies, I feel a perfect match coming on. I text Mr. DeArco the details and reassure him that he is welcome to make an appointment with me, should he have any further questions or concerns. While nibbling on cheese and crackers from my lunch, I contact Catherine Jennings to see how things are going with Maggie. I sense a cheerful relaxed mood in the way that she answers the phone and greets me warmly.

"I just wanted to check in on how things are going for you and Maggie." I say. "Also, it might be a good idea to schedule your next session, if you are still feeling the need for it."

"Well, Dr. Hooper," she answers eagerly, "a really wonderful thing happened this morning. I've actually been bursting to tell someone about it, so your call is very timely."

"I'd love to hear it. What's going on, Catherine?"

"I had an ultrasound this morning. You know just to check on how the baby is doing, not because anything is wrong. Jack met Maggie and me at the clinic and we all got to be in the room together. I have to tell you, Dr. Hooper, as soon as Maggie heard the heartbeat, her little head tilted back and forth and suddenly she got the biggest smile on her face I have ever witnessed in that child."

"Catherine," I acknowledge, "that is wonderful. I know you were concerned with Maggie's seeming indifference to your pregnancy."

"But that's not all, Dr. Hooper. When the sonogram picture finally displayed on the monitor, she rushed over to it pointing exactly where the squirmy little thing presented itself. Her eyes were as big as saucers, and she was absolutely hypnotized by it. And Dr. Hooper," she pauses and takes an audible breath, "it's a boy!"

“Oh congratulations, Catherine. I am so genuinely happy for you and the new big sister.”

“Jack seems so truly thrilled, as well. But here’s the most amazing part of all of this.”

“Do tell.” I settle back happily in my chair.

“Before Jack and I separated, we had casually tossed around baby names, both boy and girl names, which, of course, we abandoned once things started going badly between us. Well, the nurse gave Maggie a photograph from the ultrasound as we were leaving. She was obsessed with it and wouldn’t take her eyes off of it, turning it round and round and touching the spot where the baby was. Suddenly she looked up at Jack and me, and as clearly as she has ever spoken anything, she said, ‘Baby Jacob.’ That was one of the boy names we were considering.”

“That is truly wonderful progress, Catherine and as your therapist, I have to say that Maggie seems to have made a healthy connection to her new little brother already. This just might be a real win-win for your whole growing family.”

“I know, and honestly, Dr. Hooper, we are so grateful for everything that you have done for us. I knew you were the right person to help us, and I will always be thankful that I followed my intuition to you.”

“Well, you all are doing the hard work,” I say, a little flustered by the high praise.

“Oh yes, and also Jack and I would like to make another couples appointment with you. We know we have a few more issues that we need to work on, and your insight and understanding would surely be helpful.”

“Of course,” I answer, and we find a mutually acceptable date. “I do hope you bring Maggie by sometime soon. I would love to see her, too.” I say as we end our conversation.

I pick at my lunch while contemplating how resourceful and resilient people can be when encouraged to navigate the toxicity in their lives. I don't make the changes happen that can lead to successful outcomes. I paint a picture of the path to healing and as they choose to tread on those restorative soils, choices are made, patterns are uncovered, and authentic dialogues begin to happen. Unconscious repression and conscious suppression are such reflexive responses that we all use to help cope with suffering, fear, sadness and despair. But those measures can only temporarily turn off the distress. Sometimes the wounds heal on their own, sometimes not. How do I know this? Not my degrees, not even my therapy experience necessarily. I carry my own burdens and what I strive to heal in others is just the tip of my psychological iceberg. Physician heal thyself. I consider the stressors of the last few months, stressors that are both positive and negative, but they all cause a certain change in our chemical makeup. I smile and check the clock. I make some notes for Jack and Catherine's next session.

If Jack and Catherine succeed at saving their marriage, despite the odds against them, the odds that show forty to fifty percent of marriages in this country end in divorce, then that will be a justified reason for me to celebrate my methods and practices. So, while I do want to feel invigorated by this morning's developments, I will reserve my certainty for another day. On the other hand, the weather outside is sunny, the streets rainwashed and full of life and would it be so naughty to call this an early lunch? I decide to take my stiff aching legs and my increasingly restless dog and go stroll around the busy plaza.

III

I guess because it's a Monday and not quite the lunch hour, the Plaza is not nearly as busy as I thought it would be, but in comparison to my reclusive sulking country weekend, it's a veritable hullabaloo. Maca seems to agree and walks close to my knee. We collect smiles from people we pass along the way. Dogs are a great magnet for social interaction, so in spite of my earlier inclination towards brooding, I let a little light into my heart and a nonchalance to my step. Maca exchanges greetings with a few dogs and their people. Turning towards the green lawn of the old Federal building, there is a companionable air to the pre-lunch picnickers, Tai Chi practitioners, and other dog walkers, all taking advantage of this halcyon morning. We pass by a young man picking a tune on a guitar and I feel a desire to be walking here, in this moment, with John. He would unshoulder the guitar he is carrying and serenade me as we sit on the mowed grass smiling at the folks who stop to listen. I am pulled from this lovely fantasy by the low thunder of Harley motorcycles turning the corner in front of us. Maca cowers between my legs as thunder rumbles and the earth beneath our feet quakes. It's as colorful and loud as a parade. Tattooed riders pass two by two slowly navigating the pedestrians and the narrow street. Sleeveless shirts, heads bedecked with colorful do-rags, skull caps and skeletal facemasks, they resemble nefarious nomads traveling along the highway to or from hell. Between the deafening explosion of the eight-hundred-pound beasts being revved and the haunting specter the riders create, the sight is more than a little breathtaking. Surprisingly, they are exceptionally courteous, stopping for pedestrians, waving to the children and allowing for passing cars. One skeleton even throws me a hand gesture that I had interpreted in the past as something to do with the devil until Diego said it means rock on. I nod back nonchalantly. As the choppers rumble on by, leaving for more daring compass points than this innocuous crowd, they leave behind an echoing contrail of sound that lingers in my ears long after they're gone.

Maca and I loop back around to the plaza. Just as I seek out a bench to rest on for a few minutes before heading back to the office, I find myself a little stunned at the sight of a familiar figure. There, in her lime green floppy hat and matching tropical sundress is my mother, sitting with her back ramrod straight against the wrought iron bench. Serenely poised with a paperback book on her lap, her eyes are fluttering closed. She turns her shaded face to the sun. I wait to approach her until her eyes blink back open.

“Fancy meeting you here,” I try to say as benignly as the shock allows for. Maca moves in for her customary mollycoddling.

My mother smiles a little blankly at me, her face still tilted upwards. Another pause before her eyes clear and she says, “Oh, sweetie, you spooked me. I think I must have been daydreaming, I didn’t even hear you walk over here.” She reaches down and scrubs Maca’s furry neck with her fingertips, topping it off with a kiss on the top of her brown-speckled head. I lean down and kiss her cheek, settle onto the bench beside her and take a hand in mine. It feels so cool, despite the heat of the day.

“So how are you, Mom? Everything going okay?”

“I’m fine dear, just thought I’d take advantage of this beautiful day. Diego and Señor Rivera are off on a fishing trip together. I think he said they were going to the Pecos River. They promised me a fresh trout dinner tonight,” she says. The smile on her face does not reach her eyes.

“Are you sure you're feeling alright?” I ask. She looks so pale under that bright green hat. “Have you eaten lunch yet?” She squeezes my hand with hers.

“Of course, dear. I actually feel bright-eyed and bushy-tailed on this beautiful morning. Oh, but is it lunchtime already?” She seems slightly confused by this.

I smile at her use of that old saying but am unnerved by the daze she seems to be in. "Yes, Mother. It's lunchtime and you probably need to eat something." I look at my watch. "How about I drive you back home? You drove here, right?"

"Oh no sweetpea, I don't want to bother you. I know you must have better things to do than to keep me company. Aren't you supposed to be working?"

"It's lunchtime, Mom. Where's your car parked? I'll go with you back to the house and we'll have lunch together. Okay?"

We walk the block back to her car, which she parked close to the Central Library.

"I love this old library." she comments. "I got my card so easily. Such nice people. They said because I already had one for the Albuquerque library, I was eligible. I've been coming over here a lot. Diego likes the other one better. The one on the south side of town, but I find this one so peaceful.

She insists on making me lunch. While she sheds her sunhat and hangs her purse on the coat rack, Maca and I take a peek in Diego's room. The boy is compulsively neat, though his room is filling up quickly with all kinds of projects in progress and drawings tacked to the wall. On the little desk, is a pile of graphic novels and drawing books that I see are from the library. The cat, TomB, is sprawled across the bed and seeing Maca, he gives a perfunctory hiss, changes position and otherwise ignores us. Not one to be ignored, I go over and lift him into my lap as I sit on the edge of the bed. I give him the cuddling that I wish I could give to his owner. Next to my picture, on the boy's dresser, is a new picture. It looks like a selfie. Diego and Mr. Rivera are both grinning, looking slightly deranged with their tilted heads leaning into each other. Somehow, it instantly transports me and brings to mind the intimacy and companionship I had felt as the three of us traveled the road to Paris in that long ago lifetime.

"Would you rather have a turkey salad or a sandwich, honey?" Her voice sounds stronger, more in charge coming from the kitchen.

"Just a salad, but I'll be there in a sec, Mom. Let me help you." I lay the cat back down on the bed and make my way to the kitchen.

"Do you miss your place, hon?" She asks as she pulls greens and veggies from the fridge.

"A bit, I guess, but Cassandra's place is pretty amazing. I even went horseback riding on Friday. I rode the little mare named Luna."

"Not by yourself, I hope, in that strange place." She starts chopping some tomatoes.

"No, I went with a friend who's a very capable rider." I wince ever so slightly as I realize I have just referred to Sunny as my friend.

For a few minutes, both of us become completely absorbed in the task of filling two big bowls with all kinds of fresh salad fixings. Instead of sitting at the table, when we are done with the prep, we decide to balance our bowls on our laps and sit in the living room on the comfy sofa. I look up and spot the mask that Graci had given me.

"That thing doesn't bother you, does it?" I ask and nod towards the mask while chewing on the crunchy goodness she has prepared. Her mouth is full too, so it takes her a moment to answer.

"Not at all. In fact, I kind of like it. There's something so fierce and protective about it."

"You're very intuitive," I compliment her. "That's exactly why Graciela sent it to me all the way from Guatemala. It's also why I left it here with you and Diego."

"Well, I certainly hope I'll have no need for that kind of protection." She smiles and takes another bite.

"Hey, Mom, do you remember a song that Daddy used to sing when he was working the trees in the grove?" The question had popped out of my mouth like a snake hiding in the grass. I have no earthly idea why I would bring it up. Especially right now. But it's out, so I wait for her answer. I watch her eyes take on that pensive introspective expression she had had earlier.

"You know, sweetpea, there were a few songs he loved to sing, especially while he was working. But if I remember correctly," she sets the salad bowl to the side of her, "the one that you loved to hear him sing when you were a little girl had something to do with bananas." I keep my eyes on her while I continue to chew vigourously on the salad. I want her to fill in my missing memories.

"Oh yes, now I remember. It was an old folk song. Perhaps from some Caribbean country. I'm not sure, but I loved that song, too. It was the way he sang it, belting it out with a voice that I never heard him use for any other song. It might have had something to do with the fact that it was a song about the work and how hard it was." She looks at me with a wistful smile and misty eyes. "I tried so hard to never show my worry, but sometimes his acrobats at the tippytop of those trees, well, it scared me to death. Then he would sing. The spirit in that particular song would just fill him up, soothe my uneasiness and–" she says, placing her hand on my arm, "it made you dance like a wild forest creature around the tree trunks." She drifts away for a moment. "Such a beautiful memory, my love."

"Like this?" I start to hum the melody and sing the words that I can remember.

"That's it!" She claps her hands and tries to sing along. We both fumble terribly with the lyrics and end up breaking into fits of giggles.

"Oh honey, I miss that man so much, always have and always will. He was the love of my life. People say, that's not the way of it. That there is always someone else out there for you. But not for me. I have never found anyone to love in that same way." She laughs. "Except for you, Martha. I love you that much." It brings tears to my eyes to hear her say this and to think about the memory I had witnessed of my tender fledgling parents and my unborn self. She moves her salad bowl to the floor.

"Come here, sweetpea," she says softly while patting the sofa next to her. I put my bowl down and scoot over to her. Her arm enfolds me, and I bury my face in her shoulder. "You know," she says, her voice just barely above a whisper, "your father has visited me almost every night since he passed on. You might say, in my dreams, but it has always felt so much more real than that." My eyes fly wide open, but I dare not lift my head for fear she will stop talking. "He has given me the strength to go on when there have been so many times I just wanted to quit. Quit and go to him. But he would always remind me that he lived on in you and I had to be in this world to love you." She stops talking and strokes my hair. "The thing is and a strange thing it is. A few months ago, he said goodbye." Her voice starts to quiver. "He came in the night and said, 'I love you, Alice. See you soon, sunshine. Goodbye." I see a tear land on her summer dress, right on the leaf of a palm tree, like a drop of dew. "It's a cold and empty feeling, my daughter, to finally lose him altogether." I add a few more drops to the fronds on her dress and take a ragged breath.

"Mama," I say, just as I used to when I was a child, "I miss him, too."

IV

For some reason, I left the dog with my mother for the afternoon. Maybe it had something to do with the fact that when I went to look for Maca, preparing to leave, I found her curled up on the end of Diego's bed, sharing the space companionably with the infinitely more relaxed TomB. Or maybe, it was my irrational attempt to fill up my mother's emptiness with as much life as I could provide in the moment. Whatever the reason, I now plan to stop by there again later, see how the fishermen did, and pick up my dog.

I have a few minutes before Sofia arrives, so creating tasks to keep my mind from straying, I heat up some water for tea and straighten almost nothing in the backroom. Opening the sliding patio door, I let in some fresh air. I rearrange Maggie's favorite books on the round table and arrange the floor cushions in a different pattern. I pour and brew the tea, then finally settle at my desk to check emails and texts.There's a brief text from John professing his insatiable unsatisfied desire for me. I sit back and wonder if he is the one. The one like my father was for my mother. It feels conceivable, but only time will tell. And now I wonder what John will think when I finally get up the nerve to tell him that Sunny is carrying the incarnation of my father in her womb. Will he find my aberrations and preposterous claims too much to stomach? So far, he's hung in there admirably. Again, time will tell.

She is punctual. The soft knock on the door marks the clock at promptly four o'clock. When I open the door, I do a classic double take. Why? Because now I have seen that beautiful face in two settings and my mind is suddenly reeling. Gathering my wits, I greet Sofia graciously and offer her the chair that I have set in front of my desk.

She smiles at me generously and says, "I'm so glad that you were able to see me this afternoon." Taking the chair I offer, the young woman nervously pulls her long black hair back behind her head, as if to make a ponytail of it. "I apologize for taking advantage of your good nature and asking this of you, Martha Hooper. Here you were just a welcome visitor to our village and now I take advantage.

"Please don't apologize, Sofia. This is what I do and I'm also really glad to see you again."

"Should I call you 'Doctor'?"

"Whatever you feel comfortable with, is fine with me."

"Okay. I am usually very direct, but I find myself extremely nervous in this situation."

"Would you like a cup of tea?" I ask. "We can also move to the back room which is a little more casual." I add.

"I think I would like that, Martha Hooper. Sorry, Dr. Martha."

I flash an affectionate smile at her.

Once we have settled around the table with our cups of tea and Maggie's books, Sofia seems to feel calmer. We sip quietly for a moment while Sofia casually turns the pages of one of the books.

"So, how can I help you, Sofia? Oh, before we get started, I just wanted to tell you how much I appreciated your tour of Los Pinos. You live in a truly wonderful community. I really hope that I can come visit again." I take a sip of tea and look at her deep brown eyes that take me in as I soak up her gentle charm. "Also, you were a splendid tour guide, Ms Sofia. So, thank you, again. Now what is it that brings you here?"

"May I tell it to you like a story, Dr. Martha Hooper? I feel as though I should give you some history and the context of the situation I find myself in. I have been told I'm a good storyteller." Her smile is confident though her eyes now reflect a preoccupation, an immersion into the repository of deep memory, the province where all good stories dwell.

I give her an encouraging nod and softly say, "Of course, that is often the best approach."

She looks down into her cup for a moment, then swishes her teabag around. "My mother was a reader of tea leaves, as well as a curandera in the tradition of my abuela. She only read my leaves one time and that was during the time that my papa tragically disappeared. My mama feared for the lives of my brother and me. She feared for all of us. And so, she felt the need to consult the leaves to see my path." Pausing, she looks up from her cup and briefly holds my gaze, then continues. "Have you ever had your future told by tea leaves?"

"No, I can't say that I have." I smile. "I tend to dabble more in the past."

Sofia nods. "We lived in a very poor but magnificently beautiful, rural village in the state of Michoacán, Mexico. Around us, the Sierra Madre mountains rose up to meet the heavens. Most of the families were chile farmers, but just a few miles away lay the cartel's poppy fields where the seed is planted for opium, harvested then turned to heroin to be sold to this country. Not only did the strong men from our village begin to disappear, but the older children as well. The cartel's insatiable need for more and more labor to grow their operations and replace the dead, sent them into the villages to kidnap the children and seize the able men. Women were also targets and really, Dr. Martha, no one was safe."

Sofia looks up briefly, and I see in her eyes that she is reliving the horror in the telling.

"It was decided by my mamá that we too, should disappear into the night, but unlike my papá, this was for our own safety and survival. It was also with sadness that I say, my abuela, who was suffering from swollen legs and could not walk far, refused the journey and chose to remain in the village in the care of our elderly neighbors. The raiders would not be bothered with los sequestradores, only seeking to take the young and the strong."

When she pauses again, I gently ask, "Could I ask what your mother saw in the tea leaves?"

"Yes, you may ask," she smiles, "and I will tell you that my mamá would not reveal all. She sternly cautioned against the sealing of a fate with too much knowledge. What she did confide was that the paths of my brother and I would, and must, remain inseparable for a good long time. She called my brother into the room and repeated those words to him, then said to us both, 'A time will come, and you will know when it has arrived, for parting. It will be a sweet sadness, but also a time of great opportunity.' I will tell you now, before I go on, that my brother is my twin. We are so much the same, in so many ways, but where I have been one who has always had her feet well planted on this earth, my brother has always been one who moves between worlds, sees and knows that which to the rest of us, is unseeable and unknowable. In our village, this was considered a great gift, though as we came to know the world outside of our own, it became apparent that others considered it an illness. Schizophrenia, Dr. Martha. The hearing of voices in his head." She tilts her head to watch for my reaction.

"Well, that answers one of my questions. I wondered why you asked me about schizophrenia when I visited you. Your situation is becoming clearer to me with your very good storytelling. So where is your brother, now?" I ask cautiously.

"In just a moment I will explain that, but I would like you to hear the rest of our story first. Is that okay?"

"Of course." I nod.

"We disappeared into the night, just as my mamá said we would do. My brother and I were twelve years old at the time and leaving our abuela and our home was the hardest thing we were ever asked to do, except for bearing the hopelessness that came with our papa's abduction. For two days we traveled by night and slept during the day in dry riverbeds. We covered our bodies with the boughs of trees that prickled and scratched our skin just so that we would not be discovered. It was not unusual for us to hear the jeeps of the cartel as they came roaring up the mountain and the rapid firing of their guns as they ran down the deserters and drug thieves. We avoided the areas where the smell of death would come to us. Having crossed the path of a rotting body more than once, we wished not to repeat that horror. My mamá fed us peeled cactus paddles, and when she could find them, a bowl full of crickets, grasshoppers or grubs that she would cook on a small fire during the day.

For almost a year, we drifted from one village to another. We survived only because my mamá could trade her services as a curandera and a seer, for food and places to sleep. My brother and I would do whatever chores people were willing to trade for. As we wandered ever northward, we at last came to the city of Morelia. Here, among thousands of people, my mamá found opportunity. Here, she became a cook in the cafeteria at the Universidad Michoacana de San Nicolás de Hidalgo. It was also, in this vast city of Morelia, that Gabriel and I went to school and because my mama said it was a part of our futures, we learned to speak English. The tutor of English was a handsome man from Los Estados Unidos, a man who befriended my mamá and unofficially adopted us as his own. When my mama became fatally ill and passed away, it was this man, Joseph Alameda, who brought us into the US. Though we all mourned the loss of my mother, my brother and I were excited to see Joseph's other home in Los Angeles. He was not rich, but he continued our education and got us the papers we needed to be in the United States. Sadly, he too was lost to us when he was killed in a car accident while driving the freeway of Los Angeles."

"Gabriel and I once again learned at the age of sixteen to live as vagabonds, however this time in the so-called underbelly of LA. Homeless and penniless, we were well prepared by our mamá and Joseph Alameda to survive, but as time passed, Gabriel seemed to be living more in his other worlds and speaking more with his ghosts. It became harder to keep him present in my world, the one that required the finding of food and shelter every day. It became harder and harder to leave him alone so that I might find the things we needed, let alone leave him to find work. Then one day I secured a spot in a homeless shelter for us. I chose that day to venture out to do such a thing as find work. And on that day, Gabriel tumbled fully into the other world that was calling to him more strongly with each passing day. The people at the shelter called an ambulance and he was admitted to a hospital."

Sofia has been looking at me this whole time, watching my face, studying my reactions while skillfully weaving her story. Now, she pauses and looks down. I can only shake my head at what must have seemed the finishing blow of desperation. Clasping her hands together she continues.

"Without money for transportation, and I did not own a phone, it took me three days to locate the hospital where the ambulance had taken my twin. When I arrived at the hospital, filthy and exhausted, I found that my brother was in what was called a psychiatric unit. A doctor, a medico of the mind, came to talk with me in the waiting area before he let me see my brother. He asked me a lot of questions about our family and questioned how long Gabriel had been suffering from schizophrenia. Offended for my brother, I told that man that my brother had not suffered at all until we came to this city. Finally, he let me see my brother. He was in a foul-smelling room with four other patients who were either tied to chairs or moaning in their beds. Gabriel was in his bed, not moaning, but not asleep. His eyes were fixed on the ceiling, one with peeling paint and drops of dew on the exposed pipes. His wrists were bound to the side rails of his bed and his fists were closed and knotted with the hopelessness of this world that he found himself in. I went close and whispered in Español, 'Are you well, hermano?' His face turned slowly towards me and that which I saw in his eyes, and felt in my twin soul, scared me more than all the cartel monsters in Mexico. My brother was like a dead man who could still move. I grabbed for his hand that was tied to the rail. His fingers were gray and cold, and that hand did not clutch back at my own. When I finally looked up, the Doctor was standing at the end of the bed watching me. 'Will you be able to care for your brother?' he asked. 'Yes, sir.' I answered. 'Can you make sure he takes his medicine?' 'I will, Doctor.' I answered. 'Then please go to the waiting area and I will have the nurse get him ready to go with you.' 'Go where?' I asked myself, beginning to panic."

Sofia takes a sip of her tea that must by now be quite tepid, but as I watch her, I am sure she is not even aware. "You and your brother have been through so much," I say. My voice has dropped to a whisper that is almost more to myself than a response to her. Then more clearly, to her I say, "I can't even imagine what you did next and how you ever ended up here in Santa Fe."

"Yes, it was unimaginable to me, too. But I was determined to get him away from that place of madness that had broken his soul and stolen his brilliant mind. When the assistant wheeled my brother out of the big doors, he handed me an orange bottle with colorful pills in little plastic coats. The man asked, 'Where will you go?' 'Back home,' I had answered confidently though I knew my face betrayed my lie. The old man had kind eyes. He pulled a wallet from the back pocket of his scrubs and handed me some dollar bills. 'Take the bus that stops over there,' he advised and pointed to a dirty bench with an overflowing trash can next to it. I turned to thank him, but he had taken the chair and was moving briskly back through the doors to hell. Gabriel stood next to me, hunched and pale, filthy hair in strings, his empty eyes leveled on the ground, holding nothing, asking for nothing.

"We rode the bus for the rest of the day, watching the people get on and get off. The bottle of pills bulged in the pocket of my jeans, and I swore my brother had forgotten how to speak. At last, as the final passengers emptied from the bus, and the streetlight poured its yellow light onto our seat spreading across our thin weary thighs like a devouring disease, the driver walked to the back where we sat. Though we were nothing more than shadowy spirits, he ordered us to get off. Like the zombie that he had become and the derelict I felt to be, we stumbled to the front of the bus and out the door. It was only when the man yelled towards our hopeless backsides, that I turned and looked at him. He was holding that orange bottle of pills."

"Those do not belong to us?" I yelled back angrily at the man. It had taken the full day of self-argument, but I had decided that the pills were better off lost. The driver of the bus thought differently about this decision and walked the pills over to us. Sternly he asked where we were going to go. I knew my eyes were filling with unshed tears and my brother stood like a lifeless corpse next to me. We stood that way locked in the impasse of the moment. It was the bus driver who finally broke the standoff. "¡Ay, caramba!" the man said as he tilted his head back and slapped his hand to his forehead in exasperation. I remember how it made me laugh to hear those words of irritation leave his lips. "Come with me" he said with such authority as he nearly pushed us back into the bus. After parking the big bus in a lot with many other buses, he drove us to his little home in the city."

I watch how this memory plays across the features of her young face. Every nuance seems to carry such weight. I want to somehow comfort her, but for now, the comfort is in letting her finish her story.

"This bus driver and his wife offered us showers, clean clothes and a comfortable place to sleep. His wife, Carolina, was from Mexico originally, though Mr. Bustos was not. But she, speaking to us in our own language, lulled me into telling our whole terrible story, all the while stuffing us with burritos and sopapillas and cinnamon horchata to drink. Gabriel continued to be withdrawn and silent, yet Mr. and Mrs. Bustos seemed unperturbed by his seeming absence of spirit. I, on the other hand, had grave concerns. Carolina spoke with us deep into the night; Mr. Bustos went on to bed; I pulled the orange bottle out of my pocket, smacked it onto the little wooden table that the three of us still sat at, while the cheap plastic clock on the wall clearly showed the little hand was inching its way past the two. Carolina put on her glasses and read the label and I watched the corners of her mouth turn down. A sigh of great feeling boiled deep in her chest. She blew it out like a bad wind across the table. 'No more of these,' she advised and when I nodded in agreement, she got up and spilled them like a little waterfall down the kitchen drain."

"I'm so sorry, Doctor Martha, but may I use the restroom." Sofia suddenly said. Her request startled me from the spell of her story. "I promise to be more brief when I return. You have been so patient."

Rising stiffly from my seated position on the floor, I say, "Please let me show you where it is, and Sofia..." I pause and wait for her to rise and meet my eyes. "I hope that you will continue your story and leave nothing out. There is no doubt you are a master storyteller, and I am a captivated listener."

When she returns, we decide to move out into the little courtyard. Sofia graciously waits till I am seated before she sits down. Turning her bright smile on me, she comments, "Dr. Martha Hooper, this is a beautiful patio. You also are very lucky to work in a beautiful place."

"Lucky is right. Most of these places so close to the plaza are way too expensive, but long ago, I got a deal on this little spot, and I have stayed a long time by the grace of the ever-changing landlords."

"Someday I hope to feel that settled." she remarks.

"So, your brother Gabriel, tell me what happened without the medication?"

Sofia rearranges herself in the chair and for a moment watches a hummingbird hover over the two of us. "Carolina had to be one of the real angels chosen to watch over lost souls in a city full of poser angels. She allowed us to stay in her little home for weeks. We both watched anxiously for the return of Gabriel's mind into his body. And it did happen, though very slowly at first, and during that long wait, I cried every night as I lay on the sleeping bag that I had placed on the floor next to the bed where he slept. Every night I told him stories from our happy childhood to remind him of who he was and how missed he was in my world. He would only rise out of the bed when I prompted him to do so. He would only eat when Carolina encouraged him to do so. But on the ninth day, when I awoke, Gabriel was standing at the small window in the bedroom. He turned to me and in our language, he said, 'Our mama wishes me to tell you that you are loved and to never forget the spirit and the gifts of a plant. Our papa wishes you to know that Mama is at his side, and they will be leaving soon.' I began to cry and to sob my brother's name over and over again. When he turned to look at me, I knew by the heat in his eyes– Gabriel was back in his body again. I grabbed his hand and dragged him to Carolina so that she could truly meet the enchanting spirit-talker who was my twin brother."

I pull my chair closer to hers so that I can take her hands in mine because she has moved me to tears. "You yourself are a rare and enchanting young woman," I say. And I mean this with all sincerity. Really. "Please go on. I want to know how you got to Santa Fe."

Her eyes have no tears, only the fiery spark ignited by reliving the joy of having her brother back.

Sofia smiles at me and we release hands. She brushes her dark hair away from her face with her fingers. "Well, this saint who went by the name of Carolina, she had cousins who lived in Tucson, Arizona, Cousins Fernanda and Jose who had friends who lived in Albuquerque. These friends knew a young man and woman who took in homeless teenagers. The arrangements took a few more weeks, but soon enough, Gabriel and I were back on a bus, this time headed for Tucson."

"How was Gabriel's mental health holding up?" I interject.

Sofia cocked her head to the side and gave me a look. With a furrowed brow, she reminded me, "My brother has a gift, not an illness. His mental health was and is fine."

"I only meant after the fiasco with the hospital and the drugs. Sofia, I truly meant no disrespect and it just so happens that I have a little insight into this world of "gifts".

"My apologies to you, Dr. Martha Hooper. You treat me with nothing but kindness. I just often find myself being overly sensitive and protective on his behalf. But let me go on. As I finish this long tale for you, you will finally get the answer to your original question.

"The bus took us to Cousin Fernanda and Cousin Jose. They too, were saintly people who lived in one of the oldest and poorest barrios in that city. But every day was full of life and tradition for them and their community. For the few days that we stayed with them, I worked in the garden and helped in the kitchen and felt so at home. There was a part of me that never wanted to leave. Gabriel played with the barrio children as if he too was still a child and read books and revealed more happiness than I had seen in him since we were young. But Fernanda insisted that in Albuquerque, another couple awaited our arrival with eagerness, so Gabriel and I once again found ourselves on a bus, this time bound for New Mexico."

"To be cared for and to have regular meals and a place to sleep must have felt remarkable after living on the streets of LA. I can see why you might have wanted to remain with Fernanda and Jose." It was just a therapy tool, a way of letting the client know I heard what they were saying and knew how they were feeling. Yet as soon as the words left my mouth, I could see by the look in Sofia's eyes that she perceived them as less than genuine. It made me laugh to be exposed this way by an obviously intuitive girl. I met her eyes, "I'm sorry, but you have to remember I am a therapist, and a therapist like a gardener sometimes relies on the same old tools. Please, Sofia, this story of your life and that of Gabriel is much more complex and powerful than those words conveyed. Please continue."

Her face relaxed and I could tell she forgave the misstep. "It was a girl named Willow who met us at the bus station. Gabriel and I, being pretty raggedy from the travel, stepped off the bus with our new backpacks and followed her to an old red pickup in the parking lot. The girl kept her eye on my brother. The truck coughed and choked three times before it finally spit something out of its clogged throat and came back to life. Willow, like her name implied, was slender in stature but called the shots with that old truck. She would slam that long metal shifter into gear, mash in the clutch and gun the engine till it roared, then sweet-talk it until it purred like a little kitten. Thirty minutes later we arrived at a large house with rooms on the bottom and rooms up above. It was on a lonely dirt road with a few other houses and pretty cottonwood trees. Bernie and Josh were outside waiting for us. Bernie wore a skirt that you might see in Mexico and a striped shawl. Josh had hair so red and so long that its curls bounced off his shoulders like a model in a magazine. They rushed to the truck giving us hugs of welcome and hurried us up the steps and into the house. I should say their home because it was very alive with voices and the smells of food cooking and great mounds of messiness everywhere. I have to say it was an unusual place to find ourselves in, but the importance of this new home turned out to be that both Gabriel and I were able to finish high school. Gabriel received therapy that did not include those terrible terrible drugs so that we once again found people who cared about us and gave us the opportunity to live like a family again. And the final turn of events came when Bernie found me the opportunity to live and work at La Ventana a Los Pinos."

"Well, I certainly like this part of your story," I say, rising from my chair. "When you think about it, your lives could have taken so many other paths, some perhaps, not so lucky. But I can tell you have good instincts, and you make thoughtful decisions." I sit back down and rub my legs. "And you have taken your mother's advice by doing the work you do with plants. That must feel very satisfying. As your grandmother foresaw, you and your brother's paths remained together through the worst of things. Sofia, you took excellent care of your brother, protecting him and his gift through a very formidable journey. And now, here you are."

Sofia rises easily from her chair as if a bit of her burden has been shared and feels lighter. Taking a few steps around the patio, she does seem happily distracted by the trumpet vine climbing up the wall and the songbirds that warble just above us in the old elm tree. Her eyes flit here and there. As for me, some days I just can't seem to soothe the ache that stabs like a cruel memory of those rattlesnake fangs sinking deeply into my flesh, a haunting that my legs choose to hold on to. I find myself sitting and stretching and rubbing until she returns to her chair. For a moment she remains quiet watching me with a sympathetic look that slowly wrinkles into concern upon her forehead.

Finally, she begins again. "So, I believe it to be fact, as my abuela always taught us, stories and lives have no true endings. Not the stories of our lives, not the ones that carry on after we die. Many have been taught that our stories are finished with our last breath, but that is not what my abuela teaches. She says there is always more to a story, unfold as it will. So, Doctor Martha, I'll unfold to you what happened next in this life for my brother and me. Soon you will understand that which has brought me to your door. Then I will be able to answer your question as to where my brother is and reveal to you why I believe I could use your help."

"You have my full attention," I respond, though a part of me is deeply preoccupied with the young man's face I saw in the arroyo. Because now I know with absolute clarity, that it is without question the same face as that of the young woman sitting in front of me. The tiny hairs on the back of my neck tingle.

"Gabriel came with me to Santa Fe. We were given accommodations for two, and each of us had work to do, a small paycheck, and opportunities to share in the many projects that benefit the residents of Los Pinos. Here my brother began to shine in ways that surprised even me. He quickly picked up on every pursuit and skill that was offered to him for learning and in return began to give back by imparting the wisdom he had gathered from the other world, the realm of those trapped in the in-between, the spirit world that his mind often travels in. In some ways we began to live a life that I began to trust could be ours for the rest of our time on this earth. At least I wished it to be so.

"While I became absorbed in adding to my knowledge of herbs and healing, Gabriel began to learn about life in this new forest, how to camp, and how to travel through it with little impact and a quiet foot. He wanted to survive amongst the trees, to eat from the land and to sing with the coyotes. There was no weather that seemed to drive him home and his wanderings became his passion. The more he learned, the more drawn into wildlife he became. It was at this time that my brother began to slip away for days. When he would return, he was always overflowing with chatter that would keep me awake long into the night. His plans of a different kind of living became his obsession and he would go over the details without end." She stops as if just telling me about this has taken her breath away. She steadies her breathing and softens her voice.

"Dr. Martha, I have not seen my brother for several months. He has not visited me or made any attempt to contact me." Sofia's eyes are fixed on me with an intensity that leaves me speechless.

She adds, without taking her gaze from me. "This, this is the thing I seek your help with. I believe you have the knowledge and experience to help my brother. I know in my heart, he is okay, and

I don't wish to involve police or any others who might scare him off or give him drugs again should they catch him."

I can tell she has brought herself to a very precarious edge of unshed tears that make her eyes glisten.

"Sofia." I hesitate. I want to choose my words carefully. "Your brother…well, how do I say this? I think maybe Gabriel has already made contact with me." I let the words slip out of my mouth and immediately wish I could slip them back in.

Her pained expression rearranges itself slowly into a look of stark confusion, and suddenly her dark eyes are probing mine for an explanation for something so outrageous. "What are you saying?" she demands. "Tell me about this contact."

I meet her gaze quietly as I try to think of some way to mitigate my stupidity. "Yes, well, you know that I'm house-sitting, Sofia. It's a house that shares the same large arroyo as Los Pinos. Arroyo Coyote," I say. "I told you this when I visited last week. I think I caught sight of him. It was when a friend and I were horseback riding out there." I keep my eyes steadily on hers, only to watch her shake her head in disbelief and vexation.

Finally, I see a shift in her whole demeanor. "Maybe," she begins with slow deliberate words, "he has somehow led you to me or me to you. Perhaps he uses you, to let me know he is okay." She pauses. "Does he look okay? Did he say anything to you? Do you think you could find him again?"

"So that's the thing Sofia. I only caught a glimpse of him, but I believe he has been trying to make contact with me, and…" I feel like if I don't choose my own word carefully, it'll be me sounding like a nutcase. "I know this sounds weird, Sofia, but it seems like he's been trying to communicate through these round chalky rocks. He drew a face on one and left it under one of my windows. I think. I mean– I think it might have been him."

Sofia tilts her head skeptically, then a slow smile spreads across her face. You are right Dr. Martha Hooper. My brother, as a child, believed rocks sometimes possessed lost spirits. He said the restless dead sometimes found comfort in the body of a rock. Sometimes, he would convey a message to a relative in our village from one of these or maybe deliver an inspirited rock to a place where the soul, without fear, could be released. It appears my brother has found his own work in the forest. But I still need him to get in touch with me."

I sit back in my chair and chew on the pen that I brought to take notes on the pad that lies unused on my lap. The fine gray lines have not a word written on them except 'Sofia and Gabriel' at the top. It takes a few moments for the intuition I count on to click in, but when it does, I locate my smile and let it work for me. Like a small warm flame, I sense the light that illuminates the odd consortium of chalky white skull rocks that spooked me on my hike into the arroyo. I had stumbled upon Gabriel's spirit rocks. "I believe I'm beginning to see your dilemma," I answer, "but I'm not sure how I can help."

Well, you seem to know a lot of people and I'm wondering if you might know an understanding person who could search for Gabriel and deliver a message from me, one that I feel sure will bring him back to me. I would pay them what I can for their time in the forest."

It's funny how the mind works, taking unexpected leaps without prompting. Before the request has even left her mouth, an image of Charlie Walker with his prolific gray beard rises like a puff of smoke. Charlie Walker, who knows the area and travels by horseback. And then, yes, there's also his story of the thief in the night. Could that have been Gabriel? A connection perhaps.

"Maybe." I hedge a bit. "I might know someone who could do a bit of searching, but I don't know him well, so I would have to really explore this option before I can give you an answer."

"It's hopefully not as urgent as I make it out, except in my mind. But if you wouldn't mind asking this person, I would be so grateful. It is necessary for this person to be calm and understanding if you take my meaning. Gabriel has obviously gone back to living in this other world for the present and that will take a person with some compassion."

"I understand, Sofia, and I will do what I can. I'd be happy to call you as soon as I know something." I glance at my watch, remembering that I need to get over to see my mother and pick up Maca. Sofia observes the small deviation of my eyes and stands abruptly.

"I know that I have taken up much too much of your time. I apologize for that and thank you from the bottom of my heart for helping a stranger. You too have the spirit of a saint, Dr. Martha Hooper. I am blessed by your kindness."

"I am happy to do what I can, but remember, I can't make promises regarding the cooperation from this person I barely know. Also, Sofia, I think it's your own grace that draws good people into your life. I hardly think I'm a saint, just a good therapist. She smiles and I walk her to the door with one last promise to call her with any news.

V

The fishermen are back. Diego is scruffy, reeks of fish and sweat, but is absolutely brimming over with stories to tell. His chatter is incessant. Mr. Rivera, or Rafael, as I am to call him from now on, looks contentedly weary. My mother refuses the fishy mess in her kitchen, so Rafael offers to cook the trout at his place. Of course, I am invited to dinner, and other than getting back with enough daylight to feed the horses, I have no reason to refuse. My mother and I prepare rice and vegetables while Diego takes a quick shower, then races over to Rafael's house to help with the fish.

"Was Maca good company?" I ask as I chop squash and potatoes.

"Of course she was, but she did seem a mite more interested in the cat than me. How was your afternoon, dear?"

"It went by really fast with the new client I'm seeing." My mother knows better than to ask me about my clients, respecting the whole professional confidentiality thing.

"Well, I'd ask you if you'd like to spend the night here, but I assume you have responsibilities at Cassandra's place. Plus, one of us would end up on the couch."

"You're right. I do have to get back in time to feed the horses. But we can still have this lovely dinner together."

Together, we go about our cooking tasks. Then, out of the blue, while my mind is focused on oiling and seasoning the veggies in a big ceramic bowl, I catch Alice softly singing the Banana Boat song in her beautifully pitched voice. I feel the shiver of a ghost in the room or someone walking upon my grave. Every lyric, every note, perfect, she has forgotten nothing. I stop what I am doing and listen. When she is finished, I turn to her and wrap my arms around her, feeling just how frail she has become.

"That was beautiful, Mom. That song brings back so many memories." As I say this to her, I drop down into a chair at the table and picture my daddy in the tree, peeking through the branches and my mama swaying and balancing the basket on her abdomen. I am overwhelmed by the weight of so many years behind us, time that has been eclipsed by the persistent biddings of the present. The young innocence that was once my parents has now been colored by death and old age. I wipe away the tears before she can see them, but she must sense them.

"Don't be sad, little one," she whispers into my hair as she places her hand on my back and rubs it like she did when I was a weeping child. "You, more than anyone, know that we never really lose our loved ones. All life moves in circles. Not in straight lines.

The wind, the seasons, trees and flowers and irrepressibly so, we humans. Circles and loops. We are all somewhere on that great wheel." Her hand squeezes my shoulder, "You and your daddy have schooled me well." The side of her face lays sweetly on my head then abruptly pulls away. She says with a sudden different kind of resolve, "The skillet is ready for your vegetables, dear. Why don't you let me finish in here and you go check in on those fishermen." When I try to refuse, she insists and hustles me out the door with Maca playfully nipping at my heels.

Diego, of course, commands the dinner conversation, his energy far outweighing any amount that the three of us older folks can muster.

"I know it sounds like a fish tale," he giggles. "Señor Rafael told me about fish tales today. Anyway, I threw my line in and when I reeled it in it felt like one heck of a fish. See I didn't use the word 'hell'. Señor Rafael says it's impolite, but I pulled and pulled."

"Get to the gist of your tale, hito." Rafael says in between exuberant bites of fish and veggies."

"Okay, okay." Diego lifts his arms as if defeated by the old man's impatience. "I reeled in the string and Señor Rafael held the net and guess what we caught?" He scoops a spoonful of rice in his mouth and makes us wait again while he chews noisily. "A five-pound, wait for it… tennis shoe! A brown one to match these brown trout." His giggles are like a contagion, and we all end up laughing so hard our stomachs ache with it.

"I think I have a little ice cream for dessert. Any takers for ice cream out under the portal?" Rafael offers.

"None for me." I answer quickly. "I think I'll work on the mess we made, then I better get going before it gets dark." I look up and see Diego's eyes meet mine and I know he's got something up his sleeve. "What?" I ask with mock irritation.

“Well, you know,” he draws out these first words, “I could help you feed the horses if you’d let me come with you and spend the night. In the morning, too.”

“I’d love some ice cream,” my mother says to Rafael’s question, ignoring the boyish conniving that’s going on. “What do you say, you and I go relax on the porch and let these two work out their arrangements. Diego can help Martha clean up the kitchen. By the way Rafael, where did you learn to cook fish like that? It was delicious.”

He rises from the table and pats his belly, as he works his way to the freezer. “It’s an old family recipe. Just a touch of chile, garlic and ginger.”

When they have settled themselves on the porch, Diego spoons his bowl of ice cream while carrying dishes to the counter. “Please, Martha, I’ve been waiting to see the horses forever. And I think I’ve been pretty patient.”

I smile at him. “Here, scrape these dishes into the trash and I’ll load the dishwasher.”

“Please,” he begs with his adorable puppy dog eyes and silver tooth gleaming.

“Let’s get the work done and then I’ll make up my mind.”

How We Fall

I

Of course, I've always been a sucker for small begging children. Especially ones that work as hard as he did at getting the kitchen cleaned up and spotless.

"Wow, Martha, they're so big," he observes as he clings to the rails of the corral. "Do they bite?"

"Only little boys who wear their caps backward," I tease. Before he can catch the joke, he yanks the cap off and tucks it under his armpit.

"Right," he laughs, patting his cap back into place.

"C'mon, Mr. Tenderfoot. Let's go get the hay and a little grain for these girls. Oh, and the white one is Luna, and the palomino is Sol."

"Which one did you ride?" he asks.

"Luna. She's a bit calmer for a beginner like myself."

"Well, I want to ride Sol. That is when you finally let me ride."

"You like a good challenge right off the bat, huh?"

"I just like the way she looks. Like she's made of gold."

"Well, we will see," I answer inwardly unconvinced.

As we walk back to the barn, he says, "Maybe your friend Sunny can give me riding lessons."

"Maybe," I sigh, asking myself again, when did Sunny become my friend?

It's well past dark before we finally make our way indoors. Diego had to explore every square foot of the immediate property, taking time to throw a stick for Maca and tackling her recklessly every time she swerved close enough in his path. He collected pinecones from underneath the giant ponderosas and piled them up near the car intending to take them home with him tomorrow. We sat out on the back porch stairs and sucked on tootsie pops that he had begged me to buy when we stopped at the gas station on our way home. With the sucker lodged in his cheek, he decided to count the stars as they began to pop out in the darkening sky and gave up promptly after twenty, when suddenly, the whole black sky was filled with them.

Now that we are back in the house, I make him go wash up, brush his teeth and put on his pajamas. He seems like his tank will never run out of fuel as he sits on the sofa and chatters on about fishing, putting his bicycle together, working on his retablo project with Señor Rafael, and some things that I don't even hear as a peruse my emails and phone messages on the sofa beside him. Then slowly I become aware that the room has become so quiet, I can hear the crickets chirping. Glancing over the top of my reading glasses, I can only shake my head and chuckle. The boy is curled up like a little puppy, sound asleep with his cap at a crooked angle on his tousled head of hair. I figure I'll get him to bed in the guest room in a little bit. Meanwhile, I feel myself unwinding and enjoying a little playtime on my laptop. It's nice to peek over on the other side of the sofa and see a little human being dreaming peacefully, filling up the room with his presence, even in his sleep.

There is an email from John that looks long and sweet and worthy of my full attention, so now that the lad is asleep, I open it and begin to read. He writes that in a moment of desperately missing me, he was overheard by his band members, playing the ballad that he had written for me soon after I came out of the hospital. They insisted on hearing it in its entirety again and agreed amongst themselves that they wanted to work on it and include it on the album. The email goes on to say: *we stayed up long into the night working on the composition so that it will include the talents of the whole band and the magic that they can bring to the song. In the end, meaning in the wee hours of the morning, we had it. I'm including a sound link. If you click on it, you can hear what we've done. The final word is yours, Martha. I let them know that, and they agreed. You be the judge. Click on the link and give it a listen.* There is more but I really want to hear the song and his voice. I click on the link. The song track is there, listed as Hooper's Junction. I don't want to wake Diego, so I make the effort to rise from my seat and retrieve my earbuds. Sinking deeply into the sofa, I click on the little blue link and close my eyes. His guitar moves through me fiercely, the singing of his fingers on the strings moving me to tears of longing. I miss him so much and when he begins the vocals, caressed by the heartbeat of the percussionist and the bass player, I think I have never heard anything so beautiful; that is until the provocative strokes and arcs of the violinist are layered in and at that moment it is clear to me, my heart will never be the same again.

Oddly, as if I were gently drifting into a dreamy sleep, I note that the music is fading, being spirited away from me, and it evaporates. I feel myself yielding to something more compelling, yet wishing it to stop, wanting to turn back before it's too late. It is in fact, the tumble down the tunnel into the vanished past. Into the past of the sleeping boy beside me.

II

"Master?" I hear him say willfully, from behind me.

A hasty jab to the ribs brings me around most tellingly. The boy continues, "He wishes to know the amount you are wanting to purchase."

Taking a swift look around, I find myself in a small sweltering room infused with the satanic smell of burning sulfur. Before me, an aproned gentleman awaits with his fist suspended in the air, his fingers laced tightly around a scoop loaded with small and medium fragments of yellow brimstone. He stares at me expectantly, chewing carelessly on the fringe of a bushy mustache while awaiting my response. Not able to prompt one blessed word in this ceaseless moment, I make do with a show of understanding by offering a vigorous nod.

"Master, are you sure that will be enough?"

With a forced cough, I compel my pipes to respond, "What do you think, Rufus?" My voice chafes against the metamorphosis. The young man comes full round, to the front of me where he can survey the confusion on my face. I observe the uneasiness on his.

"Sir? Are you quite alright?"

"Mayhap, it is the bouquet of brimstone that befuddles the brain and chokes my breath," I mumble, fighting to take a full breath.

"We will take what you have there, Monsieur," the boy bids to the man with the apron. Following an impatient grimace, the shopkeeper drops the load into a large leather sac and secures it with a thong.

I prompt myself to hand over the payment, the one that I find in a pouch about my waist. Turning towards the door, the unevenness of the stone tiles catches the toe of my boot. Rufus grabs my arm while taking the purchase from my shaking hand, slides it down the front of his frock and leads me out into the street. Once out of the shop and taking in the fresher air, I pat my chest heartily and feel more fully embodied.

"Where is Master Devereaux?" I ask, finally in control of my breath and my befuddled wits once again.

"Do you not remember? Methinks sir, you left him at the cathedral. You said, 'One fox slinking about the hen yard is bound to bring about less suspicion than three.' And so, sir, we took our leave."

He sizes me up again, appearing thoroughly bedeviled by my memory loss and I, as a matter of course, am thoroughly embarrassed. Yet when I look into his worried face and see that fledgling's innocence, that boy that I would happily call my own son, I am stirred to a passion so great that I embrace him, abruptly and bear-like. A contagion of nervous laughter erupts from him, and I surrender to the same.

"Of course I remember, you scoundrel. Let us make haste with our plunder secured and fetch Master Devereaux, this before the man discharges our design to all of Paris."

As we near Notre Dame, the deep sonorous sound of the Bourdon bell vibrates the very air we stroll through. A gathering of disciples cluster upon the shallow steps, pausing with rapt features riveted upon their temporarily silenced clerical tutor. Ravaged beggars litter other steps, pock-marked faces upturned, and their withered limbs stretched out humbly in petition for any proffered alms that a more prosperous fellow, perhaps ones such as ourselves, could bestow.

"When we left him, he was studying the 12 bas-reliefs located on the portico of the cathedral. You see my boy; these wits are not so bungled. Shall we begin our quest for the mislaid man there? How thinks you, Rufus?"

"I am sure that I already see him, Master Turnbull. Look." And he points toward a section of the portico near the central columns that surge regally to the heavens.

"Aha," I grumble as I begin the long trek up the vestige. "It would not surprise me if this dear friend of mine is quite the cause of my untimely death." My breath becomes increasingly ragged with each step upwards.

When finally we reach the man, he does not, a misstep make. It is as if we had been standing at his shoulder the whole time. Without a glance in our direction, he directs his forefinger to an area above the large doors, then expounds rapidly, as if enraptured, "See there, my good sirs. The top row depicts each stage of the evolution, each a remarkable inductive work of art and enlightenment." He shakes his head as if in disbelief, "Withal, the continuation thus displayed below for all to see, unveils the results, that of which we too shall obtain, the magnificent alchemical consummation of elements. It's here, mes amis, depicted in stone, the science, the process, which like our own mission, ends with the exquisite amalgamation, the bearing of infinite gold, and the elysium of forever life."

In curious amazement, Rufus and I stare at where he points, William's words having as much consequence on our ambitious souls as the sight of the symbols.

And notwithstanding my earlier warning, the man raves on. "If only for my quill and parchment. There is an almighty want in my soul to bestow this marvel to memory. Rufus!" he demands. "Transpose each pane with all its exquisite detail into your unencumbered virginal mind. Let it become forged with all those latitudes of pubescent lust and longing. Stare long and hard, son. Consume every cipher and entrust it to thy intellect, lad. Oh, William, if we but recreate this masterpiece when we return to our own humble abode, closer to perpetuity we shall find ourselves."

Rufus, to his credit, casts his eyes even more intensely in the direction of the symbols, while I turn my head with a wry smile, away from my fervidly unhinged brother. That is when I hear the air behind us cleaved by the slow percussive clapping of hands.

"How so?" a voice asks, fondling the very air with its inquiry. The clapping ceases, a precipitous fall into silence. "What fortunate wind brings to me three such unassuming travelers who appear before me with so keen an interest in this sorcery?"

I feel the blood drain from my face. In an attempt to abscond from panic, I clear my throat with a mighty huff and swell my chest grandly like a threatened raptorial beast of prey. William and I turn as if yoked by some mysterious concord. We two arrive in our unexplainable forced half-turn, useless and coupled, and face the voice that is so sensually female, yet potently deep and powerful. Rufus, spellbound and obedient still, continues to gaze faithfully at the wall.

The proprietor of such a voice falls to a woman garbed altogether in layer upon layer of black drapery, which nevertheless, allows for the spectacle of her waist, an abnormally narrow and constricted affair, like that of a waspish insect. Overlaying upon this whole semblance of witchery vestments is a fluttering gossamer cloak of which the cavernous hood shrouds the creature's face neatly.

"Have I rendered your tongues tied and useless, moreover your manners decamped? I, Messieurs, am Madame and I wish to know your interest in these panels. You may speak now."

As if some force releases our imprisoned tongues, we both begin to babble like widowed crones at a table d'hôte. I know not what I say, nor can I make out the words of my companion, but when our tongues pause in their wild gibberish, the woman seems quite pleased and lifting her hood, smiles beneficently upon us. Though her nose be a bit narrow and hooked, her lips pursed with a cunning upturn, and her brows thickly fringed in a flamboyant crow-black arch, she is not altogether unpleasing to the eye. One might say 'riveting'.

"You both please me greatly." She bestows these simple words upon us as if they were a magnificent gift from one of great eminence. "Call in your boy, and follow me, messieurs."

Coming along would seem to be de rigueur. The woman leads us through narrow alleyways, past sordid shops and crumbling homes. The streets smell of animal and human offal and there is a hungry look upon every face we meet, though no one solicits our small party as we sweep through the wretched gloom. Finally, we arrive at a low narrow door that necessitates odd contortions to maneuver through its small opening. As passage is being accomplished, we blindly stumble through a dank blackness, in that upon sudden arrival into the dimly lit chamber, we blink like waking bats obliged to stare into a beam of sunlight. With a flick of her finger, our sinister hostess alights the room with a hundred-fold flame and candle, which serves to further our bat-like bewilderment. In a bloodless fashion, we are subjected to the contents of this sanctum of alchemy, this asylum of inquiry, as if it is her wont to detect our familiarity with the measure of all that lies vested upon her tables. She scrutinizes our every stirring and mien. There about us roost crucibles, flasks, spirit lamps, fastening rods and metallic rings. I spy an aludel, for condensing vapors, a Moor's Head still, an alembic for distilling, and a bronze mortar and pestle. On the walls are illustrations of Akash, Air, Fire, Water, and Earth, brilliantly drawn onto large pieces of parchment. In script across the bare wall are painted the words: Matter, Energy, and Consciousness. A trove of manuscripts are stacked on almost every surface, with the leaves of a bewitched few turning as if invisible fingers or an imperceptible breeze seeks the cryptic message within.

I turn suddenly, espying the young Rufus slumped against the door, a puny sickened expression impoverishing the youthful blush of his face. He watches the woman, gripped by her powerful presence. Suddenly he croaks as if just having exchanged pipes with a frog, "We should take our leave, Masters. This is a baneful dungeon of black sorcery. I beg of you, my Masters."

Madame nods at the boy and with a torpid moan our companion's body crumples into mortal oblivion. She moves towards a large cage in a dark corner. Opening the hatch, the witch withdraws a massive black bird with eyes like obsidian beads and a thick black bill that clacks repeatedly as she strokes its shaggy throat feathers. "Monsieur Turnbull," she addresses me with a voice as sinuous as the curl of gray smoke from a pipe, "is this apparatus familiar to you and your companions?"

As if my brains have been scattered at the door, I respond with witless enthusiasm, "Oh yes, in every way." I look about hungrily. "Recognizable and abundant. Who is the alchemist who has amassed a workroom of such scope? This auspicious gentleman must be prosperous indeed." The imbecility of my words is not lost on me. Say what has inhabited my soul, I harrow?

She moves effortlessly, with the weighty bird perched on her narrow shoulder, drawing closer to me than my personal comfort does allow. The bird tilts its head one way permitting it to gaze at me with one eye, then turns completely to the left to view me through the other eye.

"There is no such man," she says, continuing to stroke the breast of her creature with fingers narrow and impossibly long. She, as doth her bird, eye me with an intensity that lacks orderly emotion. "I possess all of this and more. Doth that surprise? Does it tantalize you, monsieur? Like-minded, we might be kinsmen in the name of alchemy and her higher design." The hand stroking the bird moves like a slow-moving wraith towards my face and when it arrives at its destination and the witches finger takes a long slow sensuous path down my cheek onto my neck.

"William!" I hear Percy thunder from the other side of the room. "You are under her spell. Shake out of it, my godly man."

The woman's head swings around with such ferocity, I urgently fear for my friend's bodily safety. But she merely looks at him curiously and asks, "Why do I not hear the same ardor in your voice as just moments ago when you so thoroughly studied the panels of the Notre Dame?"

Percy's face looks flushed and volatile, and I suddenly worry that she will put him in the same state as Rufus, who continues to drowse next to the door. Then she purrs, "Monsieurs Devereaux and Turnbull, I assure you I am only innocently looking for companions to assist me in my own quest which seems to be on the same path as your own. I do not intend to endanger your friend nor you. I have no desire to inform the church nor the authorities of your spiritual leanings. This is merely the good fortune of concordant beings finding each other for a collective undertaking. I have," and at this juncture, she shifts her gaze back to me, "reached an impasse with my own practices and have reason to believe that you may have surpassed that which has thwarted my progress."

Those eyes trespass upon the boundaries I have enacted to keep desire at bay, and I feel my own face flush for very different reasons.

"Master Turnbull, it is your prowess and skill that I have long been seeking." This Madam seems to speak with a brazen double meaning. "I possess any resource, whatever apparatus you might desire, and it lies freely at my fingertips. And should I be able to tantalize you with this alliance, you will find that my talents rise far above even these mundane treasures." She sweeps her arm in a gesture to include all that is in the room. This extravagant motion startles the bird and squawking, it cries out in a voice horrifically sounding like the wail of a human child. A human child in distress. A sound that is so disturbing to me that I feel my wits leaving for good this time, and fear I am about to swoon into some kind of death. And swoon I do, all the way down into the contorted

chambers of the labyrinth of ages. Me, Martha, I feel myself beginning the work of finding my way back into my own time and my own body and not least importantly, reinhabiting my own mind.

III

Beside me, Diego squirms in his sleep. Jumbled, wounded sounds issue from his mouth then suddenly it stops and his whole being quiets. I lean over and raise him to a sitting position and when I feel a trembling that seizes his whole body, I wrap him tightly in my arms. Eventually, his eyes flutter open, and I coo soothing words while I rock him back and forth.

"Your back. You're right here with me, Diego." I've knocked off his cap in the process of picking him up and he pats his bare head with his hand. "It fell on the floor, buddy." He smiles wanly up at me with that gleaming tooth, and I soften my hold on him. Though his eyes are blurry with – what? With the spell of a witch? And his voice is hoarse, I witness the boy's sensibilities return to his gaze. His smile becomes more deliberate, and his eyes take on the light of realization.

"That was awesome, Martha." he croaks breathlessly and disengages from me so that he can lean over and sweep his cap up from the floor. "Who was that woman? She was like some kind of goth witch, right?" He swings his feet to the floor. It confuses me for a second that the boy does not know who Madam is. It is only I who have met this wicked apparition before and experienced her incarnation in the present, as well. The horrifying experience of being kidnapped by the seriously evil man who claimed to be her was my encounter only. Diego, and most likely Mr. Rivera, do not know the whole sordid tale. I don't know how I will protect Diego from it and his death in that time, if every time we're together there is the chance of reliving this experience.

I give him another hug and say, "Listen, let me go make us some hot chocolate and then I'll help you get settled in the guest room."

"Can I just stay here for a minute? I'm feeling kind of strange," he asks, and lays back down with his head propped on the sofa arm."

"Of course, honey. I'll just be a minute, with the drinks." Thank goodness for microwaves and those neat little packets of chocolate. "You want extra milk in yours?"

"Yes, ma'am." He really does sound a little woozy. I pick up my laptop and the earbuds and see that the song that John sent has played through. I'll listen to it again when I'm in bed, I tell myself.

Outside I hear the wind picking up and a distant rumble of thunder. Anything's possible, so I go around the house and close up all the windows. Picking up the mugs as I pass back through the kitchen, I hustle Diego off to his room. Once there, after tucking him in, we sit quietly and sip our sleep elixirs.

"So, Martha," he begins, and I hear a question coming on, "did I think that woman was a witch? I mean like was she a real witch?" He pauses, takes a sip and his eyes narrow in thought. "This was all real, right? But from another time in our past lives?" He shakes his head with a grown-up's sense of disbelief. "It's way sick, but…" he pauses again and looks at me. "It was kind of scary, you know?

"She was not a good person." I answer vaguely, then add, "You were smart to sense that about her. You didn't trust her from the beginning."

"Did Señor Rivera trust her? I mean Master Devereaux?"

"No, I don't think so. He seemed very cautious around her."

"How about you?" he asks.

"I think I was too interested in my obsession to be bothered with her decency as a person. She was someone who could help us to do the things that we wanted to do in that time, so I believe, I, not so honorably, used her as she did me."

He takes a few more sips of his chocolate and hands me his cup. He snuggles deeper under the blanket. "Martha?" he says sleepily. "Why is it only us, me and you and Mr. Rafael? Do you think there is anyone else in the whole wide world who can do what we do?"

I stand up and put the cups on the bedside table so that I can lean down and take his cap off and place it next to him on the bed. "I can't say," I answer, without looking him in the eye. "I'm sure it's possible, but probably not something we should wish for. It kind of makes life complicated, don't you think?"

"Maybe," he mumbles with his eyes closed, "maybe that woman is out there in this world. Maybe she will find us." His voice slurs into the realm of sleep. And as I watch his sweet face and rhythmic breathing, I wish adamantly against his words. I wish that Madame never came into our world.

When Rocks Can Talk

I

While Diego is still sleeping, I search all the little scraps of paper and sticky notes that I have accumulated throughout the house. Somewhere, on one of them, I wrote down the phone number that Charlie Walker gave me the night that he came to visit. Normally, I would transfer the number from scrap to either my little book of numbers or to my computer, but with things not feeling exactly normal, I have done neither. I find titles of books, to-do lists, grocery lists, and doodles, but no Charlie Walker. In frustration, I give up for the moment and sip my coffee and listen again to the recording that John sent me. If only I deserved that kind of praise because, at this moment, I just feel like a forgetful old woman. Then just as the song ends, I remember. I had written it on the back of a magazine that I left on the porch. I hop up to find the magazine.

Suddenly, Diego makes a show of it, shuffling half-awake into the room. "Where's Maca?" he asks while he continues on to the front door.

"She's out and about on this beautiful morning. Where are you off to in your PJs and bare feet," I laugh.

"Nowhere. Can I have some coffee?"

"Does my mom let you have coffee?"

"Yes." he answers adamantly.

"No." I counter just as firmly. "How about some hot chocolate?"

"I guess that'll do." And he slips out the door.

"Aha," I rejoice as I spy the magazine peeking out from under the sofa. "There you are." I check on the boy through the window and see that he has reunited with the dog and Maca is receiving a thorough belly rub while they soak up the sunshine. I pick up the phone.

"Hello." I hear his deep voice, a set of vocal cords that sounds like they could belt out some kind of country western bar song.

"Mr. Walker, it's Martha Hooper. How are you?" There's a long pause, and I'm afraid he either doesn't remember who I am or doesn't care too.

"Sorry," he mutters, "could you hold on for just a minute? Then he's back. "Damned if I didn't get broke into again last night. You'd think I would'a heard something. Anyway, what can I do for you, Ms. Hooper?"

"I'd like to ask you for a favor, kind of an unusual one that I'd like to have the opportunity to explain to you in person."

"Well, unusual seems to be the flavor of the day. Your unusual just might fit in with the rest of the fracas around here. Want me to come on down to your place?"

I walk back over to the window and smile as I watch the boy and the dog snuggle into each other. "Well, sir, I had this thought that... maybe, I could take you up on seeing your place and we could have a chat."

I hear clattering noises in the background as he answers me. "So long as kooky don't scare you off. That damn varmint left a rock the size of a human skull on my kitchen counter. Drew a face on the goddamn thing and took off with stuff outta my fridge again. But you're mighty welcome to join in the tomfoolery that's takin' over things here. Do you remember how to get here?"

While I am having an 'aha' moment, I answer, "I think so, Mr. Walker." But he repeats the directions anyway.

"Listen," I say, "one more thing. I've got a youngster staying with me. Do you mind if he tags along?"

"No problem, this place could use a bit of youthful energy."

"His name is Diego," I add for no real reason. "Does around eleven sound okay?"

"Yes, mam. Sounds fine. I'll see y'all then." And he hangs up.

As my little Subaru chugs up the dirt road and Maca pants excitedly out the window, I notice Diego being uncharacteristically quiet.

"What's up?" I ask as I glance back at him. He looks back at me with eyes that are nearly tearing up.

"C'mon Diego, spit it out. Something's making you feel bad."

"Yup, something's making me worry that you might be mad at me."

"Did you break something? What's up, buddy?"

"No, I just think I lied to you last night."

"What do you mean?" I ask as I make the sharp turn onto a one-lane, unmarked dusty road that I have to skirt some pretty deep ruts on. Maca makes an epic leap into the backseat and settles with her head on the boy's lap.

With an agitated expression, he stares at Maca like she might be the cause of his woe, then, wrapping his arms around her body, the boy hauls the rest of her onto his lap. Laying his head on her back, he looks pitiful as I peek at him through the rear-view mirror.

"I acted like I didn't know who Madame was, like I'd never met her before or the creep that she is in this time. You probably don't remember me telling you, cuz you were in the hospital and not doing so well, but I told you then. That guy found me too and made me see all that stuff that happened when we tried to get our lives to last forever. He showed me who he was and how you wronged him and how I... you know, how I died. He said I didn't really die because he pulled me back through and saved me." He looks up at me. "Are you mad, you know, because I lied?"

I take a deep breath to calm myself. "No, Diego, not mad. Just beyond furious at that horrible man and so terribly sad that you have had to experience things that are that horrifying. I don't know how I can make it so we don't have to relive that nightmare every time we're together."

He gives me that Diego smile. "You know," he says as he scratches Maca's neck, "all of it wasn't so bad. When it was just the three of us, it actually was pretty good."

I want to stop the car and give this amazing boy a hug, but I have to make the final turn. As I do I begin to notice how much higher we are and how there are actually a few aspens hiding in the ponderosas.

Before we arrive at the Lightning W Ranch, I do finally pull the car over to a wide spot on the road so I can concentrate on my words and the effect they will have on Diego. "Listen bud, we can talk about this some more, probably a lot more, because I think it would be good for both of us. But, I need you to understand this, Diego. You and me, we're in this together. All the way, just like we talked about when I first got to know you. Remember... we're like superhero partners. So, part of that partnership is going to be that we are totally honest with each other from here on out. That means me too, because sometimes I'm not totally truthful with you, either. I worry about you. I just can't stand the thought of anything or anybody hurting you and that's because you are so important to me. Do you get what I'm saying?"

His tear-streaked face is turned up to me and I watch the weight of who we are, chip away at his innocence and what is left of his childhood. Then suddenly Diego's dark eyes intensify with some kind of powerful understanding and his face reflects his enlightenment as his lips form a slow smile. "Are you saying you love me?"

I swallow hard and hold tightly onto the steering wheel. I nod and smile back.

"Is it okay," he stutters and tries to find the words he wants, "if, you know, I love you and Maca back."

"Oh Diego," I sigh, the tears start gathering in my own eyes, "it's totally okay for us to love each other." I start the car back up. "Got it, amigo?" I laugh.

"Got it." he answers.

The number of structures on the ranch is more numerous than I had pictured. There's a sprawling single-story ranch house possibly built in traditional adobe style and what appears to be a large vegetable garden back behind it. Two outbuildings, a barn almost as large as the house and some kind of workshop with benches and an array of tools that are visible through the large open doors, give the impression of a fully operational ranch. Beside the barn, a generous stockpile of neatly stacked firewood and a separate mountain of stacked hay bales are neatly arranged beneath two open-air storage sheds. Beyond those, a little way down the hill, are a variety of corrals and fenced-in areas, and though I can't see them, I can hear cows mooing and horses neighing through my open window. Just as the car rolls to a stop, Charlie Walker strolls out of the building that looks like a barn and throws up a hand either to stop us or maybe an awkwardly bestowed greeting.

He doesn't smile through that big beard, at least not one that I can detect, but his eyes are welcoming, and he thrusts out his hand to Diego as soon as the boy jumps out of the car.

"How ya' doin' son? Looks like she got ya' here in one piece. Diego, right?" Diego nods with an ear-to-ear grin on his face, while his hand is being pumped vigorously. He lets go of Diego's hand and comes around to my side of the car and opens the door for me. As I unfold a little stiffly, he tips his dusty hat my way. "And how's Ms. Hooper doing this fine day? Any trouble findin' the place?" he asks politely.

"Nope, none whatsoever." I answer, flaunting a bit of pride in the fact that I made it here on all those back roads, on my own.

"Hey, how 'bout a little coffee? Still got some in the pot from earlier. And the boy, can I offer him a soda? You know I just don't get much company way up here. Sorry if I seem a little nervous."

I smile at him. "Well, that just makes this visit all the more special, and sure, I'd love some coffee. Diego? Would you like a soda?" I ask.

The inside of this bachelor's cabin is not spotless, not even particularly orderly, but it feels homey and well taken care of. While Mr. Walker pours up the coffee, he tells Diego to go in the fridge and pick himself out a soda.

"So, what did you do with the white rock you found on your counter?" I ask as he hands me the mug of coffee.

"Oh, that thing. I pitched that son of a bitch out into the garden. Spooky damn thing." He leads me over to a throwback of a kitchen table. It's like a fifties red formica-topped oval table with the metal banding around the outside rim. The chairs are metal with that red puffy plastic covering. In the middle of the table sits a huge piece of petrified wood.

"I like this table. It reminds me of one my grandma had. Always did like that vintage furniture though it's not so popular here in Santa Fe. Not enough Southwestern style I guess." I run my hand over the table and look up as he fits his big frame into the old chair. "So, do you think I could see that rock you threw away? I know that probably sounds as weird as the rock itself, but there's a good chance that it has something to do with what I came here to talk with you about."

"Sure. Can I send the boy out in the garden to look for it?" I nod and he tells Diego where to go out and how to get into the garden. Diego, with the dog at his side, pushes through the kitchen screen door and trots off to the garden to complete the mission.

"Do me a favor," Mr. Walker sighs as he sits back in his chair with his arms folded over his chest. "I'd like it a whole lot better, if from this point on, you called me Charlie. I'm not much for standin' on formality if you know what I mean."

"Got it, Charlie," I smile. "Martha will do it for me, as well." I watch as his clear blue eyes light up and he does raise that mustache a bit with a crooked but perfect smile. Suddenly, I feel intrigued by this solitary bear of a man.

So, what's first Martha, the tour of the place or you wanna' lay that favor on me?"

"Well, I'd like to see the rock, but I think I can start by telling you a little bit about me and how *I* got mixed up in this predicament." I go on to tell him all about my therapy practice, minus the part about dropping into people's past lives. I explain to him the visit that I got from Sofia and how she lives and works at La Ventana de Los Pinos. Because she gave me permission, I go on to give him some background on her and her twin brother. It's just as I'm finishing up that part of the story that Diego and Maca return, he with the white rock in his hand and Maca with her tongue lolling.

"Hey, let me get some water for your dog, there. She looks to be about as thirsty as a duck adrift in the desert. Come here, pooch." he calls, as he pulls a big bowl out of the cupboard and fills it up.

"Oh yeah," Diego chimes in, "she chased this rabbit the size of a dog all the way down to the arroyo behind the house."

Charlie rolls out a long chuckle, "That would be Bugsy. That ol' Jack has been trying to find a way into my garden for the last five years. Just between us, got so I kinda' like the old fella. Sometimes I even throw him a carrot or two. Bad habit, though. Just encourages the son of a bitch." He slides easily back into his chair.

While he does that, Diego brings the rock over to me and plops it in my lap, face up. "Looks a lot like the one that's sitting in the chair at your house," he remarks thoughtfully.

"Yeah, it sure does," I say and turn it over in my hands. "I didn't know you even saw it," I remark, but the boy has already been distracted from this mystery, as Charlie Walker tells him that he and Maca can go and explore the barn and workshop as long as they keep their hands and paws out of trouble. Like The Flash and his loyal companion, they disappear instantly. I turn back to Charlie just in time to see him smile wistfully after them.

"You know, me and Camila always wanted to have a boy of our own, but that just was not in the cards for us. Did I tell ya' I just lost my dog? He was a stubborn son of bitch," he says as he gets back up and pulls a wrinkled old photo off the fridge. When he walks back over to the table, he sits down a little heavier than the first time. "Lived a good long thirteen years, he did," his deep voice rumbles like soft thunder, as he passes the photo to me. "I keep thinkin' I should get me another one, but somehow it just don't seem right...yet." When I hand him back the photo, he gives it a long look then says, "So tell me more about this Sofia and what she's got to do with me."

I ramble on trying to keep some order to the story of Gabriel's special powers that seem to have been diagnosed by the medical world as hearing voices, maybe schizophrenia or maybe bipolar issues. I tell him how the young man has not checked in with his sister and has been living rogue in this area for a month or more. I also tell him about the encounter I had with Gabriel while horseback riding in the arroyo. That makes him smile.

"So, you decided to change your mode of transportation from two-legged to four, eh? Gotta' admit I'm right partial to sittin' a saddle myself rather than wearing out the soles of my ol' boots. But then it's more a way of life with me."

When I seem to have run out of any more details to give him, he downs the last of his coffee, checks to see if I'd like some more, then quietly, as if he's processing all that I have just told him, walks over to the sink and with his back quietly turned to me, washes and dries the two mugs. While he's putting them away, I take note of this old cowboy with a bit of admiration for his careful way of working through my words and Sofia's request. Suddenly looking back at me, he asks, "So what's the connection to that damn rock? And are you thinking that this is the fella who's been breaking into my house?"

I like the way he's connecting the dots. "I think there's a good possibility that Gabriel's your thief. He might have picked you out as a means for getting the things he needs to survive out there on his own." I have to smile at the consternation I see on his face. I continue, "So then there's the rocks. They seem to be a part of his illness, or as Sofia would say, his way of communing with the dead spirits around him."

"So, you think that damn boy has got my dog in one of those rocks?"

I laugh outright as I lay the white chalky rock on the table between us. "Any resemblance?" He just grins at me through that beard.

"C'mon he finally says, "Let's go find your boy and your dog. We can walk and talk."

Outside the day is warming up, but huge wooly-white clouds are springing up against the boundless blue of the sky.

Occasionally they drift across the sun, giving us a little respite from the heat. "So," I say, as we shuffle down the dusty path to the barn, "if you would be willing to ride out and help find Gabriel, then hopefully, we can assess his state of mind and his ability to care for himself. It would ease that poor girl's mind immensely."

With his hands in his pockets, Charlie Walker pauses and turns to look at me. "Well, missy, I might be willin' to do such a thing, especially if I can put a stop to this thievery business. However, I'm no shrink and probably not particularly sociable and even less so, approachable, if ya' know what I mean. What I'm tryin' to get at here, is... I'll go, if you'll go. It'd be no use for me to track the boy down, then what?" He gets us started back down the path again. "I'll provide you with a nice gentle pony to ride and you can bring along some grub. We'll make a day of it. Now don't that just sound like a real fair business deal?" He hooks his thumbs into the leather belt around his waist and straightening up his big frame. He gives me a sideways glance that contains just a little bit of mischief in those clear-blue eyes like he's finding this bartering amusing.

I have to admit, as much as I enjoyed my first ride, I'm a little leary about putting my still-achy bones back in the saddle so soon. But I do see his logic. Clearly. "When could you do it?" I ask, feeling vaguely apprehensive, but also intrigued by the idea of spending a day with a genuine cowpoke.

"We can head out tomorrow morning if that's what you want to do. I've really got no pressing engagements," he smiles. "I got a few stray cows we can check on along the way. Kill two flies with one swat."

I take a deep breath. There are probably plenty of good reasons to rethink this whole crazy scheme or at the very least, postpone it until I can think it through more rationally. I really haven't spent enough time with this guy to feel like I really know what kind of man he is, and I'm pretty sure that a rider as inexperienced as myself will turn out to be more of a hindrance than a help anyway.

However, as is often the case, none of my rational thinking seems to hold any bearing on the words that come tumbling out of my mouth, right before Diego and Maca come tumbling out of the barn.

"I think tomorrow should work out just fine. The sooner the better as far as Sofia is concerned. Tell me what I need to bring and what time I should show up," I say, with totally false confidence. Diego comes dashing up to me and grabs my hand.

"Come look, Martha. You gotta see this!" He pulls me along while Charlie Walker follows calmly behind me.

It takes a minute for my eyes to adjust to the dimness of the barn, but it doesn't matter because Diego still has me in full tow. When we finally come to a halt, it is in front of a large mound of straw in an empty stall. "Look, Martha. There's three of them and I watched every one of them be born just now." They would look like soggy little mice to me if it wasn't for the beautiful black mama cat that is curled around them cleaning these slimy balls of fur and turning them into fuzzy little mewlers.

"Well, I'll be," Charlie laughs. "Here I thought my pretty little barn cat had done gone off for good. I haven't seen hide nor hair of her for days. Well, now ain't that quite the sight. You say you saw it all, boy?"

"You bet I did, and it was pretty gross and disgusting. But cool. Do you think I could have one when they get old enough?"

"Well son, that decision wouldn't be mine to make, but when the time comes, I'd be happy to help you do some persuading."

"Can I come and visit them?" He looks up at me with those pleading eyes.

"We'll see, Diego. Right now, I've got some business to take care of with Mr. Walker. Do you want to come walk with us?"

"Can I just stay here with the kittens, Martha? I wanna try to pick out my favorite one."

Charlie and I pause for a moment, looking on like a pair of proud grandparents, then make our way back out of the barn and as we work out the details of tomorrow, we continue our trek around his mountain ranch.

II

The early morning air is cool, the sun just barely breaking the horizon, and I sip my coffee on the back porch overlooking the sloping bank that sweeps to the barn. Thick wisps of clouds flush with a deep coral hue that makes the sun's climb even more spectacular. The horses are fed, sandwiches made, and my pack is full of what I am sure will turn out to be unnecessary paraphernalia. The only things Charlie recommended were a rain poncho, a hat and plenty of water.

The drive back out to Charlie's ranch is a lot easier this morning, now that I'm sure of my way, but it's a bit lonelier without Diego tagging along. Yesterday, when I took him back to town after our visit, he seemed to flip back into that moodiness of yesterday.

"Hey, buddy, what's wrong now," I had asked.

When he looked up at me there were tears in his eyes again. "I really want to be with you, Martha. I mean all the time. Your mom and Señor Rafael are cool and everything, but me and you, we get each other, you know. We're superheroes, right? It's like we belong together all the time."

"Diego, all of that is absolutely true," I had answered, "but I'm just not in a position right now to be able to be with you and take care of you the way they can. Besides, I really need you to keep an eye on them for me. They're both getting older, you know, and they need a kid like you to look after them."

“Yeah, but what about when Alice and I have to move back to Albuquerque? Then what? Who’s going to keep an eye on Señor Rafael then? Who’s going to watch over *you*?” He had said this with more than a little challenge in his tone.

“You know what,” I had said, “We’ve got plenty of time to work all this out, Diego. Right now, I just want you to chill and enjoy your time with all of us.” As I said this, he had circled Maca’s neck with his arms and burrowed his face into her fur. He was quiet for the rest of the ride and when we arrived at the house, he jumped out of the car quickly and without a word.

My mom walked over to the car before I could get out. “You should get on back up there, hon. It’s getting dark and you don’t want to be on those dirt roads after dark. I’ll take care of Diego.” She said it like she knew exactly what was going on, and as I shook my head, she leaned in through my car window and planted a reassuring kiss on my forehead. Turning slowly away from the car, she began a slow amble back to the house.

“Hey Mom,” I called out as I leaned over and opened the passenger side door, “Do you mind if Maca does an overnight with that sad boy of ours?”

She smiled and leaned down clapping her hands to get Maca’s attention. I watch the two of them fade away into my happy little home, just like a sappy ending to a sappy movie.

Worrying about all this is diverting my thoughts from today’s mission and that’s not really the frame of mind I want to arrive at Charlie’s in. So, I roll my window down, take a deep breath filled with the fragrance of the ponderosas, and focus on what I might say and do to convince Gabriel that he needs to come down off the mountain. That is if we even find him.

III

The trail that we are following from Charlie's ranch is a longer and much less direct route down into Arroyo Coyote than from Cassandra's place. I figure that's good because Gabriel could be anywhere and there's a lot of ground to cover. At one point, Charlie had pointed out some tracks that he said looked a lot like shoe prints. "Possibly from the boy coming up to help himself to my larder," he had commented a little sarcastically. We rode on in silence for a while.

The horse I am riding is larger than Luna, but just as gentle and maybe even more affectionate. His name is Cody, and Charlie explained that he's a gelding which makes him calmer. The horse was all full of head-rubbing flirtations on our introductory meeting. Charlie gave me a few carrots to come on to him with, though I don't think they were needed. Cody, according to Charlie, is a buckskin, kind of golden color, but with a black mane and tail. Charlie is on the biggest, shiniest black horse I think I've ever seen in person. It's how I always pictured Black Beauty when I was a kid. The trail is actually taking us further up the mountain, away from the arroyo and when I comment on this, Charlie explains.

"Better to cover as much ground as possible, and I did see some evidence back there of someone using this upper trail. Then there's those damn stray cows. There's a meadow up on top of this mesa, where they like to hang out." He turns in the saddle and looks back at me. "You doin' okay?"

I smile from under the actual cowboy hat that he lent me for the occasion because before we left, he had declared my sun hat downright impractical and obnoxious. Digging through an old trunk, Charlie had found one that would fit me. "I'm great," I give a very cowboy-esque nod. "I was just thinking about all this land up here. Land that you own?"

"I do. With not a soul to leave it to when I meet my maker." He seems to take in his kingdom with a slow sweeping scrutiny. "You know, I got an old heifer, who the last time I laid eyes on her, looked pretty heavy with calf. It's possible if we locate her, she just might have a surprise for us." He chuckles softly, like just the thought of it is pleasing to him.

When we reach the high meadow that he referred to earlier, I think my eyeballs just might burst before they can take in all the beauty. The grass is tall and green, dotted throughout with the humps and rough gray contours of rocks and boulders. Butterflies rise up gracefully from the yellow and orange wildflowers. Beyond, far on the horizon are the real mountains, the Sangre de Cristos, looming large against a sky that is seeding white mushroom clouds that stack up like great celestial towers. All of this perfection, but no stray cows. The horses wade through the sea of long grass, disturbing grasshoppers and bees and tiny birds that have made this their home. Breaking out of the meadow, Charlie leads us back down to the trail, reimmersing us into the cool shade of the ponderosas and firs.

"Have you seen any more signs that might be Gabriel's?" I ask after we have been on the trail for some time. I guess we both have been lulled into silence by the gentle motion of our walking mounts and the extraordinary quiet of the forest.

"Maybe," he answers, looking back at me as he takes his hat off and runs his fingers through his thick gray hair. "But I can't say for sure. Broken twigs, a dusty print too windswept to be certain, a new trail that could be deer, coyote or maybe a boy. We're gonna need more than this to track him down. There's a ridge up ahead, a flat rocky cliff about another half hour away. We'll stop there and take a break. Sound okay?"

Just as I'm about to answer, a frightening bellow slips out of the forest in front of us. As Charlie turns us toward the distressed sound, I feel Cody stiffen into an alertness that makes me nervous.

"Well, I'll be. There you are, you slippery little deserters." He leads us off the trail and all the while I'm watching the muscles of his horse bunch and swell as it plants its hooves steadily in the loosely-packed rocky soil of the uphill climb. Holding onto the saddle horn, I lean nervously forward. Cody follows the leader. Within moments, Charlie has located five cows milling around in a fairly flat area that resembles a small shelf on the hillside.

"Look," I holler up to him. "She had her babies." There amongst the three adult cows are two leggy, big-eyed, brown fuzzy-bodied, white-faced baby cows. One of them bawls loudly and the other echoes those sentiments. I can't help but laugh at their newborn awkwardness. I yell out to Charlie, who is inspecting the small herd of cows, "If Diego was here, he'd surely be asking if he could have one of those calves, in addition to the kitten." Cody pulls up next to the big black horse.

"Well, they look to be in great shape. This ol' mama knows how to bring those little scallywags into this world, and she'll protect them with her life." He gets down off his horse and wrestles one of the little ones into his arms, checking here and there, confirming his conviction that his cows possess tenacious parenting skills. When he is satisfied that all is as it should be, Charlie remounts his horse and gives the signal for us to move on. "I'll come back and drive them back up to the ranch tomorrow."

"They'll be alright out here, with the coyotes and such?" I ask.

"Yeah, they should be fine. These cows are hardy critters. They've been scrabbling up and down these hills all their lives. Let's keep on going. We're almost to our lunch stop."

When we reach the outcropping that he has been talking about, the sun is straight up and beating down on us fiercely. We find a stand of closely knit trees that provide a nice umbrella of shade. After the horses are settled and tied, munching on a few meager patches of grass, Charlie walks back over to the overhang.

“Hey, Martha, come over here a minute,” he calls back to me. I am unsteadily trying to walk off the new torrent of muscle spasms that are momentarily crippling my land legs, but I hobble over to where he is squatting down.

“Lookie here. I think maybe our boy has spent a little time here recently.”

When I get closer, I see that he is kneeling in front of the remains of a small ashy campfire. The area is patted down by a good many tracks. I would like to squat down next to the man to see what he is poking at in the fire pit, but I’m sure I would tip over like a drunken sailor, so I stand next to him and peer down.

“There’s still some warm ash here at the bottom,” he remarks thoughtfully. He rises to standing with a nimbleness that defies what I have guessed are his sixty years. He studies the footprints and other impressions left in the bare dusty perimeter of the campfire ring. I can see by the faraway look in his eyes that he’s processing the information and gaining some insight that these remnants are giving to him, so I stay quiet until his steps lead him back to our shady lunch area. I fiddle with the sandwiches and other treats that I have brought until he is ready to sit down and tell me what he’s thinking.

We lower ourselves onto an old log that has lost all of its bark. On the smooth surface between us, I spread out the sandwiches and fruit, as well as some chips and bottled water.

“So do you think that’s reliable evidence that Gabriel was here or do other people come up here and camp,” I ask, in between hearty bites of my turkey sandwich.

“Well, I wouldn’t bet my last sip of whiskey on it, but I think it’s a pretty fair hunch. Looks to me like he’s thrown in with some kind of dog. Did his sister say he had a dog?” He unwraps his sandwich. Because my mouth is full, I just shake my head, no. “Well anyway, both human and canine tracks are reasonably fresh and the warm ash in the pit makes me think it's probably from last night."

"That's great news," I finally mumble through the food in my mouth. "And it's so early in the day, maybe this will work out."

Charlie studies me for a second while he sets about eating his food. "You know," he says, "it's near impossible to find a man in these mountains, who doesn't want to be found. That fact's not lost on you, I hope. It just won't serve any good purpose, for you to go gettin' your heart broke over this boy, if we come up empty-handed at the end of the day." He looks back over towards the remnants of the campfire.

"I think I know the odds," I say. "But if there's even a small chance that we can help out these two… well, you know, they've lived through so much hardship already. I'm hoping Gabriel just needs a little psychological tune-up, and maybe he just needs to know how terribly worried Sofia is."

"Well, I gotta say, you've got a much sunnier outlook than I've ever had. I guess in some ways I've never gotten over expectin' the worst and not trustin' the good things. It's probably my skeptical disposition that's taken me down over the years. But should this lone wolf be curious or feelin' kinda homesick, I guess I can admit to a sliver of a chance that this undertaking will succeed."

Out of the corner of my eye, I see him slide his dusty old hat down, covering the worry lines on his forehead and obscuring the doubt in his eyes. Suddenly a thought comes to me. I remember the way that Gabriel had stood on a different outcropping and looked down upon Sunny and me that day. How most likely it had been him raining rocks down on Maca and me when we had hiked the arroyo. Maybe, I consider, he is watching us right now.

"You know," I turn excitedly to this surly man, "it does seem like he's acting like a lone wolf. Maybe a lonely one, but wilder than you and me at the moment. But he's also lived like a sociable human being for most of his life. So, what I'm getting at," I say getting more excited by the moment, "is that maybe the boy is nearby and just watching us, this very minute. Cautious like a wolf but curious like a human." I look around slowly hoping beyond hope to prove my point. To hear a twig crackle or see a shadow move through the trees, is all I would need not to lose my own hope.

"That very thought has occurred to me. But again, if he's not choosing to show himself, we're chasing a ghost and he's got the advantage."

I stay quiet and finish my sandwich. I feel a contrariness rise in me like steam in a teapot. When I'm done with my lunch, I pack up all my litter and walk to the edge of the overhang with deliberate steps. When I get to the edge, I cup my hands around my mouth, and with the loudest, calmest voice I can find in me, I begin to call for Gabriel. I holler in every direction but avoid letting my eyes fall on the spot where Charlie still sits on the log.

"Gabriel," I yell, "Sofia has sent us with a message for you." I turn. "Please, Gabriel, let us talk to you." When I finally stop because my voice is hoarse and my throat is on fire, I continue to stand on the overhang, scanning as far as my eye can see. But I detect nothing. I remain there until I hear the rustle of Charlie moving about and packing the horses back up. By the time I get back over there, he is quietly sitting on his horse with Cody's reins in his hands. The lunch area is spotless as if we had never been there. I take the reins and walk Cody over to the log and use it to get my foot in the stirrup and a little extra lift.

IV

The path begins to tilt down in a deep pitch that lurches me forward in the saddle, and I find myself feeling precariously unbalanced. My feet swing backwards in the stirrups and the saddle horn is poking me in the chest. Charlie looks back at me.

"Try sitting up a little straighter in the saddle, Martha. You know, like you're really pissed off at me and are getting ready to stand up in those stirrups to hurl a rock my way."

I give him a look but do as he says, and the correction puts me back in control. I do feel pissed off at the pessimistic cocky old goat. And probably if I had a rock, albeit a small but irritating one, I would chuck it at him. I see him chuckle before he turns back around.

Twice as we continue down the hillside, Charlie pulls up and reins us in. The first time, he gets off his big black horse and, on hands and knees, studies the path in front of us. He doesn't say anything, just remounts and moves on. I wish I could get stubborn enough to not break down and ask what he saw, but that is not the way my brain behaves.

"So, what did you see back there?" I finally ask.

"Just a little more evidence that your boy and his dog have used this trail. Footprints, some old urine and not quite dog scat.

"What do you mean not quite?" I'm feeling irritated with his riddles.

He makes me wait. "Okay. What I'm seein' in the tracks they're leavin', looks suspiciously like coyote scat. I don't know. But there is the chance they're just using the same path and the two signs are not related at all."

I try to stay calm and speak in a chummy tone, '*try*' being a dubious word since calm is not what I'm feeling. "Why do you make me fish for the answers to what you're doing and thinking? Aren't we trying for teamwork here?"

"I think I made it pretty clear; I just don't want you to get your hopes up. You got your heart set on something pretty ambitious and the more I get a sense of this character, the more I'm convinced that his cloaking skills are damn admirable."

The second time he pauses is when a gusty wind sings through the tops of the ponderosas using the needles to whisper and sigh. We both cover our faces while the dust and debris swirls in miniature cyclones around us. The bright sun momentarily hides behind a cloud. When it's over, he turns in the saddle and looks back up the sweep of hillside that we have just come down, inspecting the small sliver of horizon that is still visible.

"Might be something movin' in. A little afternoon shower. You remembered to bring some rain gear, right?"

I nod, not caring too much whether he sees it or not. I've been paying a lot more attention to the trail, trying to see on my own what the man has been seeing and maybe even what he's missed. It's this close attention of mine that pays off. As the trail levels off and Arroyo Coyote becomes intermittently visible through the trees, Charlie picks up the pace a bit, but I hold Cody back so I can continue studying the trail signs and other forest secrets around us. On my own, I have noticed several piles of the scat that he referred to and because I too know coyote sign, I have to agree with Charlie that it is more coyote than dog. I have seen small mounds of deer pellets and looking higher into the trees we pass, I have seen evidence of some creature, maybe a porcupine, chewing bark off the high branches of the ponderosas. I've spotted two cottontails and several flickers that I am pretty sure the man never even noticed. It's when a flash of white catches my eye, and he is several paces ahead of me, that I know I scored. I call out his name and he immediately doubles back.

"You okay?" he asks as he brings his horse around so close that our knees touch.

"Great," I say. "But look over there." I point to a round white rock resting on the forest floor. "It's one of Gabriel's. I'm sure of it."

Charlie dismounts and hands me the reins to his horse. I watch carefully as he squats down and dislodges the chalky white skull rock. Charlie trades me the thing for the reins of his horse, then stands back a step, stroking his long beard, and watching me intently. This one has no face drawn on it. It is smoother than the other two and where he might have drawn a pair of eyes on it, instead are two rounded sockets that have been carefully scooped out.

Awkwardly, I dismount with the rock cradled in one arm.

"What are you doing?" Charlie asks, taking Cody's reins when I offer them.

"I'm just going to put it back where we found it. You know he has his reasons; some part of his reality depends on the validation these rocks provide in his world. I don't want him to think that we came here with the intention of taking that away from him or to strongarm him away from his refuge. The system of beliefs that he has built around them is as strong as any belief we have that he needs our help." I walk off back towards the dip in the soft dirt the rock has left.

"Well, that's why we brought you along," he says rather loudly and gruffly. "I'm not sure I deciphered a word you just said, but I'm sure what you're sayin' is the gospel as shrinks know it. And I know, I got nothin'.

Suddenly I notice that he's watching me hobble back with great intensity.

"Hey," he says sternly, "are those snake bites actin' up? I don't think I noticed you lookin' quite this lame earlier."

"Thanks for your concern," I bite back just a little too sarcastically. "I'm just a little saddle sore." But as I say it and continue to walk back, I'm worried that he might be right, because it's more my calf aching than my thighs. Charlie helps me mount back up onto Cody, then hops easily onto his horse.

"I forgot to ask you what your horse's name is?" I say as we resume our course.

He chuckles and without looking back, says, "Gonzo."

Once down in the arroyo, I realize that we are in a section that I haven't been in before. It's wider and flatter than the portion that I'm familiar with. It seems like the thought hits us both at the same time that we've been traveling for a time without the sunshine. The breeze is also becoming cooler, turning into a gusty wind. I see Charlie inspect the sky and evaluate the cloud cover.

"I don't know, these summer storms are unpredictable. This could just blow right out of here without a ruckus at all. Or..." he looks back at me and smiles devilishly.

"What do you say we take another little break?" I suggest.

"Fine by me." He slows Gonzo to a stop in an area where a drainage ditch t-bones our arroyo. A large tree has fallen across the smaller arroyo, and it is to a branch from that tree, that he wraps his horse's reins, then lowers himself onto the log, where he promptly pulls off one of his boots. From my vantage point on my horse's back, I see that his foot appears to be a little deformed, a crooked healing from his accident perhaps. He rubs it vigorously without looking up at me.

I dismount and tie Cody to a different branch and limp off down the arroyo a few paces before I start calling out Gabriel's name again. I urge him to join us so that I can give him the message from Sofia. In the distance, I hear the soft rumbling purr of a thunderstorm. I turn to Charlie. "Seems really far off, don't you think?"

"Hard to say, down here," he answers while pulling his sock and boot back on. He takes a couple of bottles of water out of his saddlebag and sits back down. I turn back to the arroyo and try to lure Gabriel in with my best therapeutic sweet talk. When I peek back at Charlie, he is sipping his water and watching me closely. Self-consciously, I walk a little further down the arroyo. The wind is blowing hard enough now that I feel like my voice is not carrying very far. But it does not drown out Charlie's voice and the sound of something tumbling down the hill behind us. "Son of a bitch!" he yells.

I turn just in time to see the rock land just slightly to the left of Charlie, but very close to Cody who reacts with a dancing backstep. Luckily, I had secured the reins tight enough to hold him. By the time I reach the log, Charlie has things back under control and I pick up the rock. It looks very much like the same one that was on the boulder.

"This is great!" I say excitedly. "I think he must have heard me." I pat Cody on the neck, to add a little more reassurance to the now nervous horse. "He's got to be up there somewhere close." Another rumble of thunder punctuates my enthusiasm.

"Well, we best be on our way, then. This most peculiar boy will undoubtedly be leading us on a wild goose chase till he gets tired of the game." Charlie hands me a bottle of water. "Bottoms up, missy. No point in dryin' out. And here," he pulls a cellophaned square out of his pocket that looks like a homemade brownie. "Put this in your saddlebag for later. It was one of Camila's favorite treats. She made sure I knew exactly how to make them on my own before she passed." He smiles but there is still pain reflected in his faded blue eyes. Not only can I see it in his face, but there's a bitter weight to it that makes me suddenly sad for him. I make a conscious effort to soften my sharp edges.

"Thanks," I say sincerely. "And thanks for being so patient with me. You're truly being more helpful than I'm giving you credit for," I add.

Charlie Walker, I realize, is not so much crusty and cantankerous, as he is cautious and mistrustful. He seems quite set on denying himself hope and possibility. But what he is superb at is tracking and understanding the behavior and movements of a stray renegade, whether that be a boy or a cow. He picks up Gabriel's trail easily and we move back up the hillside that we came down from the east, but now we're heading up it to the west. The sky continues to darken, and the wind drowns out any attempt I make to call out Gabriel's name, so I finally surrender to riding quietly, watching the trail sign along the way, and studying the backside of the cowboy and his horse. Charlie's straight spine and strong shoulders belie the severe injuries that he sustained in the rodeo accident. Despite my frustration with the man, it is reassuring to observe the sure competence he exudes. My mind wanders. Before starting back on the trail, I had wrapped the rock in my jacket and tied it to my saddle. I reach back to make sure it's secure and not bouncing painfully on Cody's hip. That is when, I could swear, I see the boy materialize like a ghost between the trees behind us, slinking elusively like a tangled-hair predator taking the measure of his prey. But when I turn completely in the saddle to confirm what I have only glimpsed, he has vanished.

I suppress the urge to yell his name. Instead, I close my eyes and form an image of Sofia, then a picture of Sofia with her arms wrapped around her brother. I try to imagine young Sofia and Gabriel, with their mother, crossing the desert like stealthy, shrewd refugees. I want so badly for him to sense a connection to me. How can I make him trust me? How can I reach a boy who communicates more willingly with rocks than humans? I reach back and put my hand on the rock wrapped in my jacket and trace the groove of one of the sockets. And that's when I feel myself in a freefall, effortlessly drifting through the layers that separate one lifetime from another, and I know we will meet.

There is a soft enchanted feel to the air, yet magic sparks and crackles. Here it is night, a moonless black night. The stars burn with foolish abandon, ignoring the fact that they too live finite lives, yet they cover the heavens in a shimmering cobweb. In the distance, animals cry out in voices that continually oscillate between haunting and horrifying. Though I do not know this, I sense the damp coolness that comes just after a storm. My position is fixed and try as I might, I cannot travel in this world. I am only eyes on watch, a disembodied essence buried in a boulder, personified, anchored and ossified. I feel the weight of the ages scouring away at my carapace, unhurriedly eroding the distinction between me and all other life that crawls upon the back of this earth.

She sits cross-legged, a few feet from where my fundament meets the loamy peat. In her lap lies a flute, silent and still. On her face is the transfixion of one in a deep trance. When her eyes clear and she reaches her small palm to my face, her fingers caress my petrified skin. I can feel her power as it burrows through the impenetrable me. So thoroughly can she excavate into my rockbound spirit. She is of such a way, that in the mere cycle of a breath, this sorceress has wandered purposefully through my lifetimes and found the marrow of my human soul. Here she lingers and stirs in the brew of me, provoking such a feeling of delight that I have never known. When she leaves me, the emptiness is unbearable. But she knows this. And she knows the remedy.

The one who lifts the flute to her lips, appears one last time in front of me. From the spirit of her instrument, a song races with the wind in the trees. The crooning whispers conjure the passage of time in living images from a child's picture book. Exquisite notes that flip through the pages of the rapture of a cosmos that still breathes. The beasts of the land hold their tongues and the nighttide swells celestial. It is a serenade at once ethereal and carnal, wonderous and fevered. Before my rock-bound soul, I see those who have gone before and those who choose to come again. And at the tip of this expanding root that feeds this tree of life is a seed buried in the stars. Rain falls upon me like tears from my own soul. I am washed and I am transformed.

V

Thunder cracks like the shattering of a great boulder, then rumbles its way down the canyon. I know now that it is an otherworldly power that has transformed me. I know that I am allowed for this moment to master the art of communicating with Gabriel. And I know he is near.

Moisture that has been collecting in dark clouds above us reaches a deep purple state of saturation, and surrenders. Windblown sheets of rain are loosened upon the mountain. Without my poncho, I am instantly drenched and shiver involuntarily as the temperature plummets in the wake of the storm. Ahead of me, I see Charlie waiting for me. He too, seems to have given up on the idea of retrieving his rain gear from the saddlebags. Through the veils of rain, he looks like the gray silhouette of a man-ghost upon a shapeless beast.

Without warning, another bolt of lightning rips the sky open in a pale jagged fissure, and as I fumble frantically with the reins, still another lacerates the air among the ponderosas on my right. While I shield my eyes against the blinding light, a deafening explosion splinters a nearby tree igniting a plume of spark and flame. I watch the incineration of large branches that lift and scatter as if they were the charred bones of giant birds in flight. Peeking out between splayed fingers, I glimpse the dismembered trunk flaring and sizzling as torrents of rain hammer at the doomed flames. All of this takes so few seconds, and those are the precious seconds that Cody needs to make up his equine mind that the only prudent response left to him is to stampede wildly into the forest. No amount of reining can change his mind, and as I glance sideways at the rain-blurred trunks passing so closely that my knees bang painfully against them, I try to grab the saddlehorn and fold forward to create a streamlined profile of horse and rider, two who will not be torn apart.

It seems like we have been recklessly bolting through the trees for an eternity, imprisoned by a storm that shackles the two of us to blindness and terror. A hopeful moment emerges. Cody seems to regain his senses and sees the wisdom in slowing down. What his foolish brain is really thinking is that changing his course and charging straight up a slick, rock-strewn hill, at a death-defying angle with little to no visibility, is the path to safety. In one powerful leap over a downed tree, the horse continues his own frenzied path up the hill, while I am not only unseated but rise into the air vertically with swimming arms and legs. I land hard on my ass but can't pause to assess the damages as the slope of the hill rolls me like a pill bug over rocks and between trees. All I can do is ball up tighter and cover my head the best I can.

I feel myself suddenly stopped by a thing, a thing firm enough to halt my downward tumble, but not so hard that I'm shattered by it. It takes so long to finally suck in a breath and gain a sense of my bearings that just raising myself to hands and knees becomes the challenge. My vision continues to spin and the food in my stomach is ready to eject, but when the hand of God reaches down to me from the rain-soaked heavens, I see it and I grab it with the desperation and hysteria of a drowning woman. Shock and disbelief are added to my already traumatized body and mind as I look up into eyes that look so damn much like those of the angel, Sofia. Shining with the burnished brown of a tiger's eye gem, those fathomless eyes fringed with dark lashes are at once merciful and exquisitely feral.

Gabriel holds my grasp only long enough to pull me to my feet, then signals a command to follow him. Every bone and muscle in my body cries out as I hobble dizzily after the sinewy boy who slinks through the trees with the grace of an animal. When he gets too far ahead, he slows. When I stop to catch my breath, he stops, and it is in this erratic fitful manner that he leads me through the storm-wild forest to a limestone shelf that juts out over a large area of dry real estate. I drag my broken self under the ledge and collapse in a soggy heap at the rear, as far from the still-raging storm as I can get. In this, I too, feel my animal roots, but more akin to a frightened, soggy, mud-plastered rat.

While I am discovering the gash on my temple, the multitude of abrasions on my skin and the tears in my clothing, Gabriel stands just outside the protection of the cave and places two fingers in his mouth. In that time-honored way, he sends forth a whistle so shrill and loud I want to cover my ears. One is all it takes. A medium-sized, coyote-looking, dog, hurls its sodden self at his feet. Also at his feet, a bundle that the creature sniffs then shuns with disinterest. It is my jacket and by the skull-shaped lump it makes, I figure the rock is also there.

In a moment of sheer flashback panic, I shudder at the predicament I find myself in. Gabriel looks back at me, his face the impenetrable archetype of animal-like detachment. It serves only to make me feel more isolated and increasingly vulnerable to re-experiencing the terror of being kidnapped. Whimpering, I crawl forward towards my jacket, the only thing that is familiar to me, but I am met by a toothy growl from the canine at his feet.

"Basta!" he commands and turns away from me. The dog sulks at his feet but stops, and I proceed on hands and knees toward my jacket. I pull the whole thing, rock and all, back to the rear of the cave, and with shaky fingers untie the knot. The jacket is mud-caked and wet but no matter, I put it on. The rock, I roll abruptly back towards the entrance. In this moment I feel almost as trapped as I felt in the ruin with two rattlesnakes as my companions.

The furious winds taper, and the storm begins to move off to assert its frenzy elsewhere. The rain simmers to a mist, the thunder returning to an impotent grumbling.

Gabriel ducks down and moves towards me. When he is a few feet away, he sits cross-legged in front of me. He has brought the rock with him and places it between us. The young man with Sofia's gentle face, speaks.

"Tell me, por favor, what does my sister say?" His voice is like a hushed lullaby lilting along the hills of his Mexican inflections. His coyote-dog comes and lays behind him.

I nod toward the animal. "What's his name?"

"He did not come with a name. This one was abandoned by his pack for his injuries. A wound to his abdomen was full of poison. I made him well and he made me his pack. Is my sister okay?"

I want to answer him, but suddenly I am fixated on the dog. "Is he a... full coyote? He seems so obedient." I shift my eyes from the animal to the young man. His face, unlike his sister's, seems so emotionless. He returns the conversation to what he wants to know.

"Sofia?" he asks.

"She's worried about you," I say through chattering teeth. He looks at me passively, then crawls back to the front of the shelf. "¡Venga!" he commands the dog. When Gabriel is standing upright, he looks back at me. There is a subtle shift in his features, a softening of his mouth, the flicker of empathy in his eyes. "Come with me," he says softly. The bigger part of me wants only to curl up in the safety of this shelter and rest, but I will myself to scoot forward, because I cannot lose this boy, not now that I have finally found him.

Grim Enlightenment From the Dealer of Delusion

I

We move gradually higher. The trees thin out a bit and the rock outcroppings become more numerous. Above us, the sky has been swept clean, reborn into a brilliant blue. Still, off in the distance, I hear the unruly rumblings of the storm as it presses on toward the flatter desert lands. Gabriel has been carrying the chalky skull rock and as before, he waits when I get too far behind. Twice he has helped me over trunks that lie like decaying dinosaurs in our path. I have not laid eyes upon his coyote-dog since we left the shelter.

Suddenly Gabriel stops and I pull up just behind him. "What's the matter?" I ask as he tilts his head one way, then the other. He uses his hands to pull his thick black hair back into a ponytail, releasing it abruptly into a chaotic black halo around his head. Without answering, the young man moves forward. "What is it?" I ask again, but as I follow, and he widens the gap between us, I see that we are entering a clearing festooned with tall grasses and wildflowers that are drying in the breeze. There, a well-lived-in clearing with a small tent, large fire pit, ropes strung across trees like clotheslines, pots and pans strewn about, and a variety of other items one might need when on an extended camping trip, are scattered all about. “Is this where you are staying?” I puff out as I catch up with him. Leaning down and bracing my arms on my thighs, I catch my breath.

“I live here.” he states matter of factly. Moving quickly around the camp, he gathers up several of the chalk rocks from different places and brings them all to reside near the fire pit, along with the one that he has carried up the mountain. “Come. Siéntese, por favor.” He offers me a seat on a low flat stump that has also been placed near the firepit. I slump down gratefully, and with a shiver, try to loosen the fabric of my wet clothes that are sticking uncomfortably to my skin.

“Gabriel,” I say firmly, as I lower myself onto the stump, “Sofia wants you to come and see her. She misses you.” I watch him closely as I say this and am rewarded when a tiny wince that narrows his eyes just enough to let me know that he regrets causing his sister discomfort. It relieves me to see a sliver of human emotion there upon his face.

He gathers dry wood from under a small tarp and brings it to the pit. After gathering rainwater from all of the containers and pots that are lying about and pouring it all into one large container, Gabriel fills a pot and brings it over to the pit. Kneeling next to me, he arranges twigs and small sticks and lights them with a cigarette lighter from his pocket. While he is still bent over his chore, he finally speaks. “I miss Sofia. Did she send you here to find me?”

“Yes,” I answer excitedly, “Yes, she did, Gabriel. I met her at Los Pinos when I visited there. Later she came to see me and told me about you and how she has been so worried because she hasn’t seen you for such a long time. That man that was with me, he’s a friend of mine. He came to help me find you, for Sofia.”

Gabriel raises himself to his feet. Without answering me, he walks away to retrieve some larger pieces of wood and brings them to the fire. Because I still feel chilled, I move my sitting stump closer to the crackling blaze. The smell of the burning wood has a way of soothing me and it improves my perspective just to stare into it. "Gabriel," I say, "I have to find my friend, Mr. Walker. *He's* probably really worried about *me.*" I shift my gaze to the sky, and though it is still bright when I look back at the trees around us, I can tell by the shadows that the sun is dropping. "It must be getting late." I add.

Gabriel looks up at me after balancing the pot of water on top of a small wire grill he has stabilized between two rocks. "We can talk. I will make you tea and food, then we can go down the mountain." He pulls a baggie of dried plant leaves out of his pocket and sprinkles, what I'm guessing are some kind of herbs, into the water. When he sees me staring at the leaves curiously, he responds, "A tea to warm you and calm your disorderly spirit. Sofia grows and dries the plants."

I chuckle to myself at that assessment of my spirit. Disorderly just about nails it.

I sniff the steam from the pot as it begins to boil. I can smell chamomile and the stinky sock smell of valerian root. I position my nose over the growing steam from the pot as the boy slips back into the camp. Out of the corner of my eye, I see his coyote slinking around the perimeter. Turning fully around, I consider this young man, as he uncovers a stash of hoarded canned goods, jars and baggies of unidentifiable content. There are a few large plastic containers that at a glance, look like bags of flour and other bagged dry goods. The white chalky skulls that remain at the fire pit beside me stare blankly into the flames. I count them. There are seven assembled near me, including the hollow-eyed one that traveled up the mountain with us. To my surprise, I find myself staring into the drawn-on face of the one from my house that ended up at Charlie's, or at least one that is eerily identical to it.

I turn back towards Gabriel.

"Can I help you with anything?" My offer is met only with a deep warning growl from his pet. I watch Gabriel re-cover his cache and retrieve two tin cups from a large plastic box near the tent. All that he has gathered gets deposited into an oversized canvas bag and he makes his way back to the firepit.

Using an old rag, he drags the boiling pot off the flames, pours the contents into the tin cups, and then hands the fullest to me with the rag wrapped around its handle. "Drink up," he says blandly. He sets his on the ground next to him, adds another powder to the liquid and leaves it to cool while he pulls another stump close to the fire pit.

I cannot drink the steaming brew but rather linger on the scent still trying to identify the mingled fragrances.

"Will you eat meat?" Gabriel's voice startles me from my daze. "Sofia doesn't eat meat anymore."

I begin with a stutter. "I... well, I... what kind?" I finally sputter out, picturing some kind of moldy rotting bologna.

"Well-killed and well-kept deer meat. I'll make a stew."

"That sounds rather delicious," I say with a sudden and genuine hunger. A sandwich can only get you so far.

"Do you feel well enough to cut up the onions and potatoes?" he asks, pulling those two items from the canvas bag at his feet. I nod and he answers, "But continue to drink your tea until it is gone and then we will start."

We sit quietly for a time, me studying the flames, and Gabriel taking sips of his tea and shuffling through the things in his bag. At one point he gets up and repositions one of the mute white rocks from its lone position opposite from me and gives it a new perch between the two of us. I look down at it trying to appear casual and disinterested, but shudder just a little as I look into that drawn-on face. I sip my tea.

"There is passionflower and skullcap grown by Sophia in the tea. How do you feel?" he asks after a long but easy silence.

"Much better. Thank you, Gabriel, for taking such good care of me." I do feel warming and a borderline cheerfulness spreading like the late afternoon sun through my body.

"Also, a teaspoon of sativa." he remarks indifferently.

"You mean like marijuana?" I ask, only mildly taken aback, because I'm not feeling particularly overreactive to anything at this moment.

"Yes."

"I see. Do you mind if I ask why you put that in my tea? And what did you put in your tea after it boiled?" I try to smile trustingly at the beautiful boy sitting next to me.

"A small amount of salvia divinorum," he replies flatly. Gabriel stares at the fire, holding his cup gently, only taking a small sip now and then.

"What is that?" I ask. I feel calm and warm, pleasantly curious.

"It's a plant in the family of sage. It's used to assist in communicating with difficult spirits."

"You are planning on communicating with a difficult spirit?" I turn towards the young man with a silly grin on my face. "I do that all the time without salvia."

"What you say is true, but you have cut off communication with one who wishes to reach you. She has insisted on my help and taken away my power to refuse."

Like a sharp clap of unexpected thunder, all the sunshine of the moment evaporates, and I look down at the rock sitting between us. "Gabriel," I demand, "What are you talking about? Who are you talking about?" I turn on my sitting stump so that I am facing him full-on, but he doesn't meet my eyes. Instead, he stares intently into the flames of the fire.

After many uncountable minutes pass by, I suddenly rouse from having some kind of waking dream while waiting for his answer. He says, "It's time to prepare the stew." Rising from his cross-legged seat in one graceful motion, Gabriel fetches a pot of water and places it on the fire. He pulls a large hunting knife from the sheath on his hip and hands it to me. Potatoes and onions?"

I jerk with surprise as one onion and two potatoes appear on my lap. "I need to know what you're talking about, Gabriel," I persist, but am no longer sure what I am asking. The knife feels heavy and solid in my hand and as if it knows what to do, I begin to peel a potato.

"We'll talk, but you are hungry, and the stew must cook." He produces another knife and begins to shred a chunk of meat into the pot.

When I look up from my work, I see the coyote sitting a few feet from the fire pit. Gabriel throws him a piece of the meat, then turns back to me. "You can put the pieces right into the pot." When he is done with the meat, he reaches back into a canvas bag and pulls out sprigs of dried plants that he crushes between his fingers and sprinkles into the concoction. I watch him carefully, remembering Sofia's story of survival and make sure that I do not see any beetles or spiders going into our meal. So far there are none. Suddenly, he tilts his head and sniffs the breeze like a wild animal sensing something. I look to see if the coyote is reacting, and he is not.

"Is it the spirit?" I ask as I watch him closely.

"No." he shakes his head and walks back towards the camp.

I stand too. My body is stiff and though I know the ache is there, it is like a distant message that hasn't quite reached my brain yet. The coyote gives me the eye and a slow rumbling growl, but this time I look back and use the word I heard Gabriel use. "Basta, coyote!" I am astonished by how firm and forceful the words leave my lips. He slinks off without further comment. Finished with the task of adding the vegetables to the stew, I take a few steps toward Gabriel, who seems to be chatting with himself and possibly, I fear, spirits. "Gabriel," I shout a little too loudly. His head jerks up from whatever he is kneeling and doing. "Sorry, I just wanted to see if it's safe for me to go use the lady's room over there." I point towards a thick stand of trees that will give me some privacy. He stands up and gives a clipped whistle to the coyote, who trots eagerly over to the young man.

"That is a good spot," he says with a nod and turns back to his task.

It feels remarkable to amble among these tall trees and breathe deeply of the rain-scoured mountain air. The scents of the forest are pungent with that deep musty smell of damp soil and the perfume of wet bark and pinecones. I walk a little deeper, savoring the sight of the slanted sunlight dappling the needle-covered soil. Rays of light filtering through the trees illuminate swarms of gnats that look like delicate gray shape-shifting clouds. Finding the perfect spot, I take care of business. A visceral sense of belonging sends me into a slow circular twirl that turns my world into a 360-degree view. A feeling of untroubled solitude that has eluded me for so long suddenly anchors me to this spot for a moment. No wonder the boy lives here. An odd flutey bird call lures me deeper into the trees and I spy the biggish songstress flit from tree branch to tree branch, chattering a series of loud complicated sounds. His curved bill is striking and suddenly I want only to befriend this brown fellow. That is until I see the coyote dog slithering through the trees with his eye trained on me. His path leads him to a spot several yards in front of me, at which point he lays down, without taking his eyes off of me. Fortunately, he is quickly joined by his young master.

"It's time for you to return," Gabriel says softly, then follows with an even gentler comment, "It's very easy to get disoriented out here." His voice takes on a hint of kindness that I haven't sensed until now.

"I know," I say with one long sniff of the air, "but I was enjoying the way the sun creates the spectacle of lights and shadows, and the smells from the rain are exquisite. Did you hear that bird? It was like a flute serenade." I see him looking at me curiously. "Okay," I concede, "I guess more time passed than I realized. How late is it getting to be?"

"The sun is close to setting and the stew is ready to eat." He turns abruptly and gives a short sharp whistle.

I find myself chronicling all this in my head with the voice of a news reporter. *How did this lost Santa Fe therapist, a domestic coyote and a feral mountain boy end up stranded on the top of a mountain? And who is this spirit who wishes to communicate with Dr. Hooper? Stay tuned.* I smile at the backside of the boy as I follow him with humble obedience back to the camp. He does not take us the same way out that I took in. Instead, he leads us to a place where a monstrous ponderosa rises from the bare rocky earth. "Grandfather pine," he remarks as he gathers pinon nuts from beneath the behemoth tree.

When we get back into the open meadow, I see that Gabriel was right, the sun is dropping below the horizon in a blaze of glory that inflames the leftover rain clouds with a florid crimson. The sight of sunset is a stark reminder of the reality I haven't yet dealt with. I am far from home with darkness approaching quickly. I have no idea what happened to my horse or to Charlie, but I can guess that the man is terribly worried about both of us. And suddenly I am worried that Cody may be hurt. What if he broke a leg running up the mountain like some kind of spook-crazed creature? This is all my fault, and it sucks the air out of me. I start to pace.

"Here's your bowl. Be careful, the stew is very hot."

Like a small child, I am instantly sidetracked from my frenetic thoughts by the soft composure of his voice. I accept the bowl and go sit on my stump. Twilight descends.

"Why do you want to live up here all by yourself, Gabriel?" He has been busy up until this moment reawakening the fire and nurturing it into a blaze that can chase shadows from around us. I stopped asking him to take me down the mountain. Even if he freely offered at this moment, I would no longer accept. The darkness that now surrounds us is ripe with night noises and phantoms that I catch glimpses of from the corner of my eye. The fire has become my life force, and the small circle of light around it, my sanctuary.

"Here, in this forest," he says without looking at me, "I am not broken."

"I don't think you're broken. Sofia doesn't think you are broken."

"There is no place for me among all of those people. Inside of me, there will always be the voices."

As if to reinforce the command that this phenomenon has over him, he tips his head and turns away from me. Is he receiving some kind of communication from one of those at this very moment?

"Gabriel," I call him back gently. "There are ways to calm those voices down. I know that they are an important part of you, but it might be that they are keeping you from doing the work that you should be doing among real people."

"She is ready for you," he says as if he has heard nothing I have said.

"You're not listening to me," I respond before actually hearing the words that he has just spoken to me. "Who is ready? What are you talking about, Gabriel?"

"Please," he begs. It is the most emotion I have heard from him. Fear. It sounds like fear. "She will not leave me alone. You have to listen to me and then listen to her."

I turn to look at him, his face is pale even in the blushing firelight. Deep within his eyes, there is a ferocity, a recklessness that scares me.

"Gabriel!" I demand, "Please look at me and tell me what's going on."

And though he tips his face towards me, his eyes are hooded by his lids and the crescent of his eye that is still visible is blank and unfocused. In his hand, he holds the white rock, the skull with the drawn-on face. For just a split second, I fear that he is going to strike me with that rock, but he doesn't. He gently places it on my lap and grabs my hand. His hand is feverishly hot. With it, he guides my hand to the top of the skull-rock.

"You keep it there," he commands in a whisper voice.

In a growing state of panic, I look around wildly, hoping foolishly that some kind of help is lurking just outside the ring of fire. The only thing that is immediately visible is the yellowish-green of the coyote's eyes reflecting the firelight like some kind of banshee. He takes a stance of rigid vigilance. I can only guess at what he senses, and it cannot be a sense of all-is-well. I keep my hand on the skull.

II

"You are drawn to things metaphysical, are you not?"

I look around to see how Gabriel has changed his voice. It is a voice full of nightshade and moonlight. They are words that travel such a great distance, disembodied and floating in a black soup that is thick and frightening. I reach out with trembling hands into a blindness that is so complete that I raise my fingers to my eyeballs to make sure that they are really there.

"It is that singularity, to which, I, incautiously find myself drawn, intrigued by a man who is at once so banal yet astonishingly skilled in the thaumaturgical sciences." The voice seems to hover in front of my blind eyes.

I feel the minute ebb and flow of air as something moves past me. A draught so gossamer as to resemble the brush of the silken web of a spider. Therein, the relief, an acquittal of sorts from this sentence of darkness that I have been suffering. A gentle scintillating glister emerges, guiding me through the black moments. As the materialization of tracings and silhouettes comes into order, that which grants me my orientation, also bestows upon me a sense of destiny and design.

"I beg your pardon?" They are words that are born from my tongue, but I did not shape them voluntarily, methinks.

"May I be so bold as to call you William, Master Turnbull?"

In my waning confusion and the lifting of darkness, I can only think to answer, "Most assuredly, Madam. Howbeit, my lady, by what appellation shall I name thee?"

"Madam," she purrs. "My sweet graceless alchemist, just as you have been schooled. But in light of such a serendipitous occasion," the witch continues to vamp with her opioid tone, "Sabine also resonates well, strikingly as the name passes between your full lips. Nevertheless, tis, but for your tongue only. And only whilst we dwell here in this inconspicuous lodging of mine, do I dare offer you up this name."

"Sabine." I tremble imperceptibly, rolling the syllables slowly over my tongue. "Sabine de Paris," I say with a stroke of my beard and a gaze around the room. Upon the table in front of me, I find myself staring hungrily at a manuscript that holds ciphers and symbols that I hope to liberate in the grand design of everlasting life and fortunes unfathomable, a finale or will it be a folly, beyond

my imagination. As I know it now, standing here in the presence of this sorceress, I am willing to go to any lengths to procure my ends. By any means, it will be here that the diviner of black arts will expedite the workings of the alchemist for his pièce de résistance. I place my fingers tenderly on the open page and stroke the words scribed so carefully onto the yellowing vellum. "Dear God!" I close my eyes and moan with an excitement akin to rapture.

She moves in behind me, like the black widow she is, and closes her hand over mine, my hand that greedily traces the symbol. "It will, as I have promised you, all be ours," Her whispered breath is heated, bringing hunger and ambition to my ear. I turn to face her. She stands only a few finger-breadths shorter than I, a tall woman, severe in carriage and yet darkly arousing. She has shed layers of her black outer garments and as I place my fingers on her waspish middle, I can feel the heat of her flesh beneath. She cannot, however, dispel the cloak of depravity that hangs about her like a plague upon her mortal landscape. She is elementally malignant, and yet, I am loath to admit that I will swallow her malignancy whole, in the name of consummating the apogee of my alchemical magical quest. Twill be my greatest triumph, that to which I aspire and let it be done in the company of my beloved Percy Devereaux and my cherished young lamb, Rufus.

She leads me to the bed chamber, one partitioned from the workroom and one that astonishes by the number of gossamer tapestries suspended like webs of ambush, tinctured with the deep colors of blood and pitch. Here a man could disappear into the folds and be lost to his own soul, or, as in my case, to an unsound mind. Behind a cockled pinch of bloodshot drapery, the large black bird roosts, still as death in its iron cage. That is, save for the chilling spectacle of its luminescent eye that follows Sabine's hand as it presses feverishly against my chest. Long thin fingers brush against the rough spun fabric of my smock until they find the small buttons to release. First that garment, then my breeches, which fall to the floor like a spiritless carcass. Our careen towards the pallet of fine down, is the dance of the devil. As one, we writhe in our passion, groping amidst the cobwebs of drapery until we find ourselves well-bedded.

I am consumed. The fires of lustful carnality crush down upon my frail self. I surrender, invite willingly, the inferno of wicked erotica, the delirium of flesh. It is here, in the throes of this seduction, that I discover leverage and superiority. Sabine, the most powerful sorceress, abandons her domination to the biddings of my depravity, my lust that wishes not only for her body but for control of her conjurer's mind. Somewhere in a sensibility that is not altogether mine, I know that there is a price that will be exacted for my actions.

The moon has risen exposing a slender spillage of pale light through a small gash in the wall that serves as a window. My body feels despoiled and doomed to shame, but my mind is alive and euphoric as I move unhindered about the workroom under the burning eyes of my harlot lover. Her manner is, in all ways, solicitous and agreeable as we provoke the spirit of iron with a sulfuric compound releasing the vapors of hell which we guard against by wrapping rags about our noses and mouths. The crucibles are alive with the incarnating and fixing domination of iron. We move among the moon and stars and no obstacle seems too great with the witch's raw materials, apparatus, and abstruse powers of the black arts. In the end, the light, flush with the amber surprise of sunrise, seeps through the tapered window, and I am convinced that I have forged the essence of the alchemical compounds that will be the meridian upon which my venture into wealth and immortality lie.

My body and mind are humming with triumph, and I find my lust once again awash against the shores of this dark woman, she who I have allowed to purloin the stone of my righteousness. We couple like creatures of the dark, once again lost among the muddling shrouds that hide us from the scrupulous world outside this lair. When she leaves the bed, it is with the bidding that I remain secluded whilst she procures sustenance for the two of us and accommodations for my voyage back to my village. While she is away, I fill my pouches with the missing elements of my paltry workshop. Deep in the back of one of her cobwebby wardrobes, I find a small pendant on a silver chain. Pressed and molded into the large disc are the symbols of the alchemical marriage, the embodiment of the potent union of duality. There a man and a woman stand naked, each with a penetrating eye gazing fiercely at each other, he with the face of the sun and she with the face of the moon whence a human head would be. Both don the crowns of a king and queen. She, overplated in mutable copper is coupled with he, who glows with cool shimmering silver. Behind the union is the triangular motif for fire, that which is bred in the womb of the earth. I slip the piece over my head and cover it securely against my chest.

Delving deeper into the texts upon the benches, I deceivingly think to tear out several pages, but with a start, hear the heavy clop of a shod animal outside the window. Quickly, I stow my pouches just out of sight and drop onto the small unstable chair at the back of the room. Arms crossed hiding my damned heart, I nod as she enters the room.

"Paris does seem to be putrefying from its bowels outward," she cautions as she discards her rain cloak. "They are calling it the Black Pestilence. It was most difficult to secure just the very few items I sought, as doors are being barred and windows boarded."

"I've heard tell. It would seem that a miasmic wind doth carry the pestilence to us. It is prudent that I leave soon and continue our work in my own village which I hope remains happily unscathed."

"Yes, you must. In preparation, I have secured two beasts, one to bear your bones and the other to carry our apparatuses. I will follow as soon as I can."

"You will?" I try vigilantly to remove the vexation from my tone. "The village is small and meddlesome. An arrival such as yours will cause quite a pother." I rise slowly from the chair and prepare two lamps for lighting, whereas the skies seem to be gathering a storm and the room has suddenly gone dim. My sorceress clears a bench and upon it places her salvage. There she prepares wine-dipped toast, a crock of olive oil, cheese and dried fish. A large flagon of ale rests between two drinking cups. I stand to pour and fill both. "à ta santé." We raise our cups and empty them glibly. I pour again, and we partake of the victuals.

"I will not enter your village as if to display my queerness," she says, "but neither will I cower as if I be a defenseless lamb. You will find my presence prerequisite to your success, Monsieur Turnbull. Do not think to betray me. That would be a very bad notion to entertain, mon amour, and you do not yet have a wit of my true powers." We drain another cup, but in an instant, the witch blazes me with a look that strikes as if searing the very flesh from my bones. I swallow the lump in my throat and approach her.

"There is no treachery planned, mon chéri." I place my fingers gently upon her suddenly pinched face. "We work together, and we will keep the maelstroms of my village at bay." Just as I finish this half-truth, we both turn to the window as a crier passes.

He calls out in public exposé, "The Great Pestilence is upon us. Wash yourself of Wickedness. God has turned his fury upon us. A blight upon our lands..." The voice drifts off but not before we hear a lusty rap upon the wooden door, the thud of a prognostication being hammered upon our door.

"It is time to ready you for your journey," she whispers with an urgency that out-distances any emotion I have yet seen in her eyes nor heard from her voice.

I try again, this time circling her small waist with my forearm while trying to draw her close in an embrace of reassurance. "All will be well, and we will forge ahead with our plans." I pull her fiercely closer and can feel surrender decant into her small frame as she pushes back against me. The tryst lasts only seconds as another crier graces the path beyond our door.

"Be you a sinner, purge thyself and remove thyself from the masses. Those without sin, cover your ears, seal thy mouth and nose, do not breathe of the miasmic winds that drop this blight upon the innocent and the guilty alike." Again, the crier's voice fades into the distance.

I pull away and we both begin to prepare equipment and chemistries, tools, and to my surprise, even the ensorcelled manuscripts, for transport. The morning has turned to the damp drizzle of early afternoon by the time we have finally finished. I don a heavy traveling cloak and she, a lighter one to accompany me out into the lane where the horses stomp wetly in the gathering puddles. They have become restless.

In this dark moment of our farewell, I stand before her, ready and eager to take my leave of this bleak and diseased city. Like a predatory cat she moves closer, and the muddling fog settles upon us and a misty brume curling like a viper about the two of us. The witch's hand finds its way through the tunnels of my heavy garb, slips its way beneath the fabric of my breeches, and squirms until it has found my manhood. Grasping it firmly in her warm hand, she reaches up to kiss me. I rise disgracefully to the feel of her touch and release a gasp.

She holds me this way until my vision turns blurry and I want to swoon like a frail sickly child. I try to sharpen my aspect, to pull away from her bedevilment, but I am fastened to this moment with a lock as strong as time. A shapeshifter, methinks, as her form reconstitutes right under my nose. Unquestionably the witch grows taller, her thick black locks turning to dust around her skull and a flush like a spilled chalice of wine spreads across her features. Unbeknownst to me until this very moment, I too am being reassembled.

And that hand is still down my pants as I look up into his cold eyes. My muscles spasm and I try to wrench away from him, pulling his claw out of my pants and holding it away from my body. Mr. Misterioso. The Phantom of the Opera. My reincarnating nemesis who will hunt me through life and death just for sport. Dear God, what horrors lay ahead of me!

"Now do you remember?" he cackles. "The promises and the deceptions? Can you recall the way you bartered your body and soul to me? Was it worth it, you charlatan, you whore?" He moves back towards me, menacingly, breathing heavily. "Maybe it was fortuitous just so I would have some kind of plaything, a diversion as we slither down this path to eternal hell. Together." He grabs my wrists and holds them together as if clamping them in the devil's own handcuffs, then pulls me against his chest. "I loved you!" he hisses.

As he says these revolting words, he pushes me away and I collapse in front of him, a submission, I can tell, that titillates him even further. I rally and lift my chin so that I can look him directly in the eyes. "I will not travel that road with you," I whisper fiercely. The shudder that rumbles through my body does not clear the chaos that has become the eternal thunderhead in my stormy soul. "That is no longer who I am. Don't you know how the soul can evolve?" I seethe. "You loiter in the past at the cost of your own soul, you monster!" I feel my hair squalling around my face like a fractious halo and have the mundane thought that I have lost my hair clip. It's what makes me look around and realize that I am not in the woods. There is no tree, no sunset sky, just a vast nothingness that surrounds the two of us. Suddenly he kneels in front of me.

"You know that you are mine for the taking. You have no recourse, no magic, no strength that will ever rival my own. You surrendered that opportunity long ago." He reaches the long gangly fingers of one wine-stained hand towards my face, locks his gaze on mine and continues. "Oh yes, mon cherie, I do know all about the transfiguration of a soul. Mine grows more tenacious and gruesome with each passing lifetime. Mine has become exceedingly creative and more cold-blooded as I have toyed with you and so many others through the ages. Believe me, I have learned some frightful ways to exact pain and suffering. Would you like to see?" He leans his body into mine and I swear I can smell the noxious odor of burnt sulfur on his hot breath.

"I will put an end to you," I pant. "I will find a way to stop your quest for revenge and this wicked obsession for cruelty." But he is slowly pushing me to the ground, one hand pressing against my chest while the other remains clamped upon my neck. Suddenly, his black-cloaked body is on top of mine, and I am being driven into the ground and can no longer take even one small shallow breath. His fiendish face hesitates above mine, his fetid breath finding its way into my brain like a nightmare, his hand finding its way back under my clothing.

"I struggle for one last breath, then suddenly feel nothing. See nothing. Hear nothing. I am, at this moment, oddly grateful for the death that is descending upon me. A peculiar peace settles around me.

III

My eyes resist opening. I can only take feeble sips of air as my chest is being crushed by an unexplainable weight. When I feel like I can work the muscles of one arm, I curl that one arm clumsily to the top of my body. It takes a minute, but the realization comes instantly when it comes. I am being smothered by the dead weight of a body on top of mine. With the strength that horror can lend to a situation like this, I push against the weight as if I have channeled the strength of a pro wrestler and fling the body off of me. The thump it makes as it hits the dirt a few feet away is a sickening sound. With my newfound brawn, I jump to my feet and stare with utter confusion into the blackness of night. There are stars above, but no moon. There are the pulsating embers of a fire that seem to be flickering in weary surrender to the oppression of darkness. A few feet away, like a pool of negative light, is the dark hump of the body that I have just heaved to the side.

Where am I? Who am I? And how is it that I have come to be standing here at all? The numbing mystery of it all forestalls the terror of reality from sinking in. The truth of my circumstances and the recall of what I just experienced commences. The witch, the dark diseased city of Paris, my own disgusting lechery, Mr. Misterioso, the storm, my horse, a coyote, Charlie Walker, the boy. The boy. Panic rises. Where is he? Where is Gabriel? I stare, momentarily paralyzed at the shadowy unmoving body that lies in a heap off to my side. With a terrifying ferocity, up from behind the body creeps the snarling phantom of a coyote. It stations itself over the body. I hear a weak sob tremble its way through me. I try to remember the command I had given to this coyote earlier today, but my brain is a kettle filled with smoke and little substance.

Slowly, taking a few cautious steps, I attempt to circle around the two, but the coyote propels forward like an arrow with bristled hackles. It issues another chilling growl. Collapsing right where I am, I cover my face with my arms and try to think, try to remember, but mostly try to calm the pounding of my heart which I fear could burst any minute.

"Basta!" the word finally jumps from my mouth, and I rise commandingly to my feet. The creature responds and slinks back behind the shadowy prominence.

I kneel down and feel for a pulse along Gabriel's neck. When I feel the strong cadence of the blood pulsing through his artery, I am encouraged. I brush the curls back from his forehead and methodically begin feeling for bleeding or bumps on his head and neck. There is a slight fluttering of his eyelashes and a weak moan as I examine the back of his head where I finger a swelling the size of a tennis ball. Pulling my hand away I can feel the slime of blood. Gently, I probe each limb but feel nothing out of the ordinary. The bump, the blood and the coldness of his skin remain my worst findings.

Turning to the fire, I toss twigs and leaves on the embers until I see a small flame, then rebuild it quickly with the branches that lay neatly stacked beside the pit. Gabriel's face looks sickeningly pale in the flickering light. Stumbling along and falling to my knees time after time, I work my way blindly back to his tent. Once there, I find his sleeping bag, a flashlight, which I immediately flick on, and a warm jacket for myself. The path back to the fire is much easier with the light. Gently, so as not to cause any further harm, I roll him onto the bag and wrap him into the cocoon of it. Grabbing a large wad of the fabric I slowly and gently pull him closer to the fire. A whispered sigh escapes through his pale lips and for just a moment his eyes open and something resembling a smile passes across his face as he tries to focus on my face. Then he is gone, back into his stupor.

Laying down next to Gabriel, I keep one hand on his chest so that I can feel the steady rise and fall. In these moments, while fear reigns and sleep is not an option, I comb my memory in an attempt to recreate all that happened in this world and all that happened in that world. It's a sickeningly intimidating task, but along the way I finally grasp that the two-headed monster, Madame/Misterioso, was, with his/her menacing sorcery, able to take over the body and spirit of this poor innocent boy, the one that I almost killed by bashing his head on a rock. "I'm so, so sorry I whisper in his ear and let my tears fall freely upon his face. In a state of tortured exhaustion, I am gradually pulled unwillingly into sleep. My sleep world is as tormented as my waking reality. Abominable images of human evil, symbols of revolting acts, death and pestilence, betrayal and vileness. I hear myself cry out in horror with each fugitive nightmare. The struggle to wake myself is tenacious but unsuccessful. Thankfully I finally sink deeply into a dreamless state. Bolting upright, I am nothing if I am not the full scale of confusion. There is still darkness. There is still a warm body under the palm of my hand and there is, once again, the slow seep of reality filtering into my brain. When I am more alert, I decide it is way better to stay awake and spend the rest of the dark hours conjuring up a plan to seek help for the wounded boy.

Figuring out how to boil the water on the fire and finding some of that tea in Gabriel's pocket, I set about to spend a wakeful, watchful night. The tea once again is calming and I am only slightly startled by the hoo-hoo, hoo-hoo of a great horned owl in a nearby tree. Far off in the distance the ruckus of a pack of coyotes stirs the quiet, but Gabriel's coyote, while listening intently, makes no move to answer back nor move from his vigilant station next to the boy. Through the trunks of the trees that bristle like towering porcupine quills behind us, the ghostly moon inches higher and higher headed for the expanse of the obsidian sky. As the tea warms me, I hug my knees to my chest and vacillate between the idea of leaving Gabriel on the mountain while I find help or cell phone service, or devising a method to construct some kind of litter to drag him down the hill with me.

It's just as the moon journeys to the crest of the ponderosas, that the coyote becomes markedly alert, scanning the darkness with the ears and eyes of an aroused predator. In response, I feel a creeping sense of dread eroding the hard-fought-for calm that I have finally achieved. I check Gabriel, who appears to be breathing regularly, and clicking the flashlight on, I go in search of something that can be used as a weapon. Meanwhile, I hear a low and hostile growl coming from the coyote who has moved back on top of Gabriel. I search in and out of the tent, and finally, lean up against a stump, I see an ax used for splitting wood. Grabbing the tool, I quickly return to the fire and build it up to the heights of a homecoming night bonfire. It explodes into ferocious flames that send smoke and sparks shooting into the moon-washed night.

The snap of a branch sends the coyote into such a state that he brandishes each growl with a showing of tooth and gum. Abandoning his spring-loaded posturing, he begins to creep silently towards the sound, though he deliberately stops at the edge of light provided by the bonfire. I position myself close to Gabriel, stand with ax in hand, and ready myself for whatever evil lurks just beyond my scope. Beneath me, Gabriel, suddenly and astonishingly, rolls over and tries to sit up. Propped on his hands, he looks around in confusion yet remains completely silent. There is the sound of more and larger branches cracking, giving way to the thump of footsteps on the bare wet dirt. Just as I am sure my heart is about to fail and Gabriel is looking up at me with large glassy eyes that emit a bewilderment that I can't attend to at this moment, a huge form steps out of the trees. The coyote whines and I raise the ax over my head, an illusion that is bigger and braver than I could ever feel at this moment.

"Martha?" I hear my name spoken in a deep and cautious timbre that drifts across the flames like smoke from the fire. I take a step forward and see a man, a large bear of a man holding the reins of two familiar horses in one hand while shading his eyes against the sudden brightness of my bonfire, with the other. The ax falls carelessly from my hands, and I use the last of my adrenaline-fueled strength to stumble over to the man before collapsing in his arms. Deliverance is the only word that whimpers through my brain.

By the light of the moon, we three warm ourselves around the campfire. Gabriel still hasn't spoken a word, but I take note of the way he keeps glancing at Charlie Walker. There is a hint of wariness mixed with curiosity in his expression as Charlie keeps up a steady banter of quiet conversation.

"Son," he says, "I know you're the one who's been dipping into my larder, but I can see by your camp here," he makes an expansive gesture with his arm, "that those things might a seemed to you like necessities at the time. And now I'm just feelin' beholdin' to you for taking such good care of my friend, Martha, here. Might say those goodies were a prepayment for your services. You can't imagine how I felt when I watched that pony of hers take off like a bat outta' hell. She and that damn horse got clean away from me, while my own vinegary beast cooked up his own brand of storm tomfoolery."

IV

"Where in the world did you find Cody?" I ask as I push my hands deeply into the pockets of Gabriel's jacket and shiver with a sense of the deep night chill.

"That damn walnut-brained horse," he chuckles, "I'm guessing from the tracks I followed in the mud, he dumped you, climbed up the hill a few hundred feet, found hisself a nice lightning-prone clearing, and set up housekeeping in the rain. I should'a never let you get that far away from me in a storm like that. There's just no such thing as horse-sense when it comes to booming acts of nature, you know?"

I look at the man, recognizing now, how deep the rivers of unselfishness and kindness run through him. "How did you find this place?" I ask softly.

"Tracking ...till I lost your tracks. Then I lost the light of day, so I figured if I rested and waited till the moon came up, I'd just move on instinct. That and the hint of smoke that me and the horses were gettin' whiffs of on the breeze. You and the boy did right building that fire nice and high. Led me right to you in the end." He strokes his long beard and his eyes glitter in the light of the fire. "Our boy over there okay?" he asks with a nod toward Gabriel. Gabriel answers for himself with one stiff nod back.

I say, "He had a fall and he's got quite a bump and a laceration on the back of his head." Needless to say, I say nothing about the trauma Mr. Misterioso might have inflicted upon the poor boy's soul. "He was unconscious until right before you showed up. I was trying to scheme up ways to get him off this mountain, so you can imagine the relief I'm feeling right now." No sooner do the words leave my lips, then I also begin to shiver uncontrollably and the tears of stored-up shock start to rain down and hit the dust.

The big man hoists himself up from the dirt next to me and wanders over to where the horses are tied up. I feel so embarrassed crying in front of him and am sure I have flustered him. I work hard at breathing in calm and swiping away the tears. When he returns, he is carrying one of those big leather ranch coats. He exhales a grunt as he sits back down, closer to me this time, and wraps the coat around me.

"You know, missy, you also got a pretty good laceration on the side of your face." He takes a finger and very lightly traces the path of the cut. I feel the scrape of his rough flesh on the dried blood. Shaking his head, he gently pulls me closer into the reassurance of his warmth and strength. Through my stifled sobs and the shivering I can't seem to stifle, I see Gabriel watching us. Very slowly he re-bundles himself into the sleeping bag and lays down, curled like a kidney bean around the curved stones of the campfire pit.

"I'm not sure we should let him fall asleep," I say through my chattering teeth. That's about the last thing I remember because somehow wrapped up like a baby, listening to Charlie's heartbeat and warmed by the soothing crackle of the fire, I fall into a deep and dreamless sleep.

I awaken not because of any sound or smell that reaches my senses through the fog of sleep, not because I can hear the deep chatter of Charlie's voice and smell the satisfying odor of food being cooked on a campfire. No, I awaken because of a terrible sense of foreboding, a sense that some inherent part of me is gone. It is a strange hollowness that is carving its way through my insides, an unexplainable sadness that delays my participation in the present.

"Ya' mean you never drink coffee? Who on this god-forsaken planet doesn't drink coffee?"

"I have tea." I hear Gabriel answer, in what I have come to know as his normal bland tone. I smile to myself wondering what concoction he will brew up for the big man.

"Well, make it a strong one, son. By the way, where's your salt and pepper? I'd like to season these eggs up a bit. Nothin' worse than tasteless scrambled eggs made from powder. Where'd you get these things anyway? Or should I not ask?"

I open my eyes and stretch out one cramped limb at a time. The ache is intense and the cut on the side of my face is burning and itching at the same time.

"Hey, look Gabe, sleeping beauty has awoken. Might as well brew up some tea for her highness too." I finally get into a position where I can see the two of them. Charlie is moving about the food bins picking this and that out. Gabriel is fetching water from one of the containers, and beside me, in a frying pan, is the sizzle and aroma of some kind of meat cooking. It would seem that the break of day has not quite broken. Besides the light of the fire there is only the half-light that begins to wash over things, right before sunrise. Charlie has taken ownership of the flashlight, but Gabriel moves about easily.

It takes a few more minutes for me to get on my feet, but when I do, I limp slowly over towards Charlie. "Can I help with anything?" I ask. My voice rasps with the harshness of a lifetime smoker.

"Naw, we got it under control, right son?" he says with a Santa Claus smile.

Gabriel nods and goes about the business of brewing up some tea.

The horses are peacefully grazing in the trees behind camp. The sky is rousing and brightening with each passing second. Like a cleansing, a sweet-tempered breeze ruffles my unrestrained hair. It is not hard in this moment to warehouse the evils of the night and deflect that recent feeling of sorrow, if only for just now. For at this moment, I wish only to revel in this odd drama of camaraderie. Charlie, Gabriel, and I awkwardly navigating an unimaginable sequence of unknowable events. "We three odd ducks," I mumble, smile and hobble back over to the fire.

During the early morning hours, the sun was a welcome comforter taking the chill from the mountain air, but by midday, its hot brilliance cooks us with a fierceness characteristic of these southwest mountains. We work our way across a high treeless meadow. Without even a breeze, I find myself shedding one layer of clothing after another until I am down to my t-shirt and jeans. Cody is making up for past transgressions by picking his way carefully and steadily along the trail with no input from me. I have spent the morning distractedly watching the two men in front of me. Charlie made the decision to have Gabriel ride with him after witnessing the young man suddenly collapsing and almost tumbling into the firepit; this just after we had shared a delicious breakfast of snake meat and eggs. Luckily, I wasn't informed as to the nature of the meat until I had already eaten it. Before being illuminated as to the source of our breakfast sausage, I had been going on and on about its exquisite flavor.

"It's rattlesnake," Gabriel mumbled, then swooned and hit the dirt. It took only seconds for Charlie to revive him, but there was no arguing with the big man about our transportation arrangements up and down and around this mountainside.

In the hours that have passed, the miles that we have meandered through meadow and woods, I have seen Gabriel slump listlessly in the saddle, positioned strategically in front of Charlie, three times. Each time, Charlie's big arms gently encircle the boy and keep him upright while he mutters some kind of encouragement into his ear. It takes a few minutes, but each time Gabriel bounces back. Twice I have heard them engage in lengthy conversations that I have to say, I am very envious of, and find myself altogether surprised by, Gabriel's chattiness. Could it be another symptom of his concussion?

We stop several times to quench our thirst and snack on some dried meat that Gabriel offered to bring along. I do not question its persuasion, just chew and appreciate its salty tanginess. Somehow, I maintain my emotional equilibrium and ward off any dark memories or thoughts or apprehensions. I am content to be a part of this trio: the loner, the social misfit, and the maverick. This, I think, is a brainteaser, because which one of us is which. I chew on this for a while.

"Heads up, compadres, we're getting pretty close to the old ranch." Charlie seems just as fresh and hardy as when we started hours ago. I feel exhausted and pretty cranky. Every muscle in my body has turned into a separate ill-fated calamity. Cody picks up the pace following suit with Charlie's horse, and it turns into a trot that serves only to increase my distress with each bouncing step. When I see the shine of the propanel roof of the barn, I not only feel the deep relief of homecoming but feel the cell phone in my pocket begin to ping with a store of undelivered messages and calls.

"Civilization!" I shout out happily to the men in front of me.

"Hey Woman, don't be insulting my years of building up the life of a recluse with that terrible word." Charlie laughs turning backward in the saddle, just to present a ludicrous grimace to me in a candidly good-natured moment.

I return his volley. "Don't delude yourself," I retort with visions of the last twenty-four hours still fresh in my mind, "that running water, electricity and cell service are not attributes of a primitive life. I feel like we are returning to urban sophistication."

Charlie shrugs and says something to Gabriel who is now sitting up stiffly in the saddle in front of him. With a gentle kick, I see him urge his horse into a brisk canter. Cody gets the message before I do, and in what feels like a few anxious beats of my heart, his vigorous canter delivers us home. Just as I left it, my dusty little car is still parked in the drive and the welcoming sight of real buildings couldn't be more reassuring. The horses move quickly towards the barn with the promise of real hay, stopping just short of the closed barn doors. We are greeted with whinnies from the back corrals. I wait as Charlie carefully helps Gabriel slide from the saddle and then pauses to make certain that the boy can manage on his own two feet.

I'm not sure I can get off my tall steed on my own. My legs are beginning to feel like gumby limbs and I'm also pretty sure I'm not feeling my ass. Charlie assesses my situation with a look of thorough amusement before strolling over to give me the same assistance that was offered to Gabriel.

“Why don’t you take Gabe over to the house and dig up some refreshment while I get these beasts settled? It’s unlocked and there’s plenty of soda in the fridge.” He takes Cody’s reins and gives him a gentle pat on the neck. “There’s some chips and salsa, some sandwich meat, whatever suits your fancy.”

I hobble over to Gabriel and ask, “How are you feeling? Are you dizzy? Is your head hurting?” I put my hand on his arm. He neither acknowledges it nor does he try to brush it off.

“Just my butt.” he answers matter-of-factly.

“Well let’s go on in and get you fixed up and in a chair in case that dizziness comes back.” Now I slip my arm under his elbow and guide him towards the house. I hear Charlie muttering to the horses as he creaks open the barn door.

Suddenly I hear his booming voice call to me. “Hey, Martha, would you mind putting on a pot of coffee while you're in and about? Much as I’m obliged to Gabe’s efforts with that tea, it’s a little like drinkin’ donkey piss for an old perennial coffee drinker like myself.”

“Will do, boss.” I answer playfully and turn back to give him a little salute.

Once in the cool shadiness of Charlie’s cabin, Gabriel wants nothing but to lie down on the sofa. I find a pillow for the boy and cover him with a light blanket that is folded on the sofa back. I smooth the hair off his forehead with that motherly impulse to nurture and comfort the young and the ill. “You going to be okay? Do you need anything else?” I ask.

He looks at me with those deep glassy doe eyes and mumbles, “I’m okay,” then curls up like a fetus and closes his eyes.

I fetch the coffee out of the cupboard and start the pot to brew. The smell is otherworldly and downright homey. I putter around finding the mugs and pouring up some cream in the little pitcher I find. I pull a loaf of what looks like banana bread out of the refrigerator and after slicing it up and going back for some butter, I finally sink into one of the chairs at the kitchen table. I pull my cell out to start checking messages and as I start to scroll, I become increasingly alarmed by the number of voicemails and texts that have been left by Graciela, Diego and John. My heart is beating just a little too fast as I listen to the first voicemail from Graciela.

"Amiga, this is really important. Call me." I hit the button to hear her next one. "Honey, you gotta call me. It's about your mom." Now I'm starting to get alarmed. Next one. "Martha, please don't panic. Just call me back or meet me over at the hospital." I drop the phone and it clatters to the floor. I hear Gabriel moan softly at the noise it makes.

After quickly checking on him, I bolt out the door and run towards the barn. Charlie is carefully brushing the foamy sweat off of Cody's back. "Charlie," I huff. "I've got to go. Something's going on with my mother. I think she might be in the hospital." Charlie looks up at me with a concern that shadows his usually bright blue eyes.

"Do you want me to drive you to the hospital? I can put these guys up in a hot second and be ready."

I try really hard to calm my voice so he trusts that I'll be fine on my own. "Thanks," I say, "but I'll be fine. If you wouldn't mind keeping an eye on Gabriel, that would be better. If he seems like he's having more symptoms of a concussion, you know, like seeming confused or you can't wake him up, that sort of stuff, then, if you wouldn't mind, take him to the emergency room." I feel my panic rising again. "I better go. My friend's been trying to reach me since last night." I say this as I'm backing out the barn door.

"Don't worry, Martha. Everything's going to be alright."

"Thanks for everything." I say.

"Hey Martha. Just really quick. Do you have Gabe's sister's number?"

His practicality startles me out of my mad dash. "Let me find it. It's on my phone. I have a pen in my car. Can you come with me and I'll write it down?"

We take care of business and suddenly I find myself flying down the dirt road, praying that I don't run into any oncoming cars on something this narrow.

V

When I get to the first red stoplight in town, I decide to listen to the last message, because I'm not sure where I should go. It's from Graciela. *"Marta, I don't know where in the hell you are but when you get this message just come to your house."* The light changes and I move with the traffic, I move with a glimmer of hope in my heart that maybe, whatever the crisis might have been, maybe, everyone is okay and back at home again.

As I pull up to the house, all seems quiet. Almost as if no one is around at all. But someone is around because Graci's car is parked in front of my mom's car. Walking up the sidewalk, I feel like the wayward teenager coming home after a night of partying with full acceptance of the fact that there will be hell to pay. The door is unlocked so I just walk in and am immediately greeted by Maca's friskiness. Her tail thrashes madly, welcoming me back. When I look up from rollicking with my girl, I see Graciela standing like a faded apparition in a beam of dusty sunlight from the window. Her hands are tucked in her jeans pockets, her shoulders noticeably slumped, and her pale face is unreadable. She makes no effort to come closer, to smile, or to welcome me home. I tip my head in mute confusion.

"Graci, what's wrong? Tell me." Still, she does not move, and poised there, she looks like an image in a faded photograph. I'm afraid to ask again, to set one foot on the path towards her. Afraid that if I don't stay in this moment of limbo, suspended from reality, from knowledge, from truth, my heart will surely break, and I will clearly be shattered by the weight of revelation.

Slowly she steps towards me and already my tears are brimming, fear is icing my veins. When she reaches me, I think oddly that it might have taken her seconds, yet maybe years to reach me. Her arms gently enfold me, and she walks me to the sofa, sitting me down and arranging my limp self like a child's doll.

"She's gone, corazon. Your mom has passed away."

The tears don't come. They too begin to freeze. I look at the pain in Graci's eyes and let that be mine because I continue to feel nothing. I think for a moment that she must be mistaken because I just saw my mother, had dinner with her, and dropped my dog off with her. I am sure Graci must be confused.

"I'm so sorry. I tried so hard to get a hold of you. She had a stroke and there was nothing they could do for her." She lifts my chin so that our eyes meet. "Do you understand what I'm saying to you?"

Just meaningless words, Graci, that batter against the closed passages to my brain. Suddenly she sits back on the sofa and pulls me into her arms, cradles me and tucks my head under her chin. Her embrace is firm. It holds my atoms together. It stops me from just breaking apart and scattering like so many fine grains of human frailty.

We stay like this as the light in the room gradually drains away. Maca lays at my feet without stirring. There is a thick silence that surrounds us, muffling and detaching us from the real world. We are an island surrounded by grief that has not yet washed ashore. Once, I turn my head to look at the mask hanging on the wall, then settle back against Graci and close my eyes. In the dim room, I hear my voice, low and hushed, asking where Diego is.

“He’s with Señor Rivera. They too cling to each other with their sadness. He’s a fine man who will take good care of the boy.” She takes a deep breath and I feel her chest rise and fall beneath me. I hear her heartbeat in the rhythm of endurance. The room sinks into a shadowy darkness, but we remain deserters from our own existence, content to simply fade like the furniture around us, into the night. At some other point, I ask if John knows.

“He knows. He’s on his way down from Denver,” she whispers and shifts her weight on the sofa. “He expects to be here after midnight. Maybe you should try to lay down and get some sleep, pobrecita.”

I know it takes an immeasurable morsel of time for me to digest what she has just said and to retrieve my voice which seems to have wandered off into the night, but Graci is untroubled by this fact and waits. “No, Graci, not yet. I want her to come and say goodbye to me.” I look up at her, though I cannot really see her face. “Do you think she will come?”

“Maybe, Marta. Who knows the way of souls? But we can stay right here, just as we are. We’ll wait.”

At another distant point, I don’t know when, I must have fallen into a deep sleep. Now as I open my eyes, I sense that I am lying down. The room is still steeped in blackness.

You're awake?” her words hang above me like reassuring stars in the night. I realize she is still sitting, and my head is pillowed on her lap. My thoughts again move like slippery minnows in a pond. There is no possessing them for more than a second, which is untroubling in this fugue world that I suddenly find myself living in. In this asylum, I have no thought, no words, no need to remember. I close my eyes.

The voices are muffled, the room awash in a dirty gray half-light. I sit up finding myself alone in the living room. My heart feels crushed, yet for just a few confused seconds, I have no memory of why. The flood of pain starts as a trickle of memory that soon enough turns violently into a storm rage. She did not come to say goodbye. I wasn't there to send her on her journey. I reach for the trash can and retch while gasping and sobbing and shaking uncontrollably. It is John's hands that I feel holding me up. It is his voice that fills my ears with his soothing elixir of words and sounds. His breath smells of coffee. In this world of ruthless lightning bolts, the ones that take as much as they give, I have been granted the boon of people who are strong enough to lift me up and keep me from drowning in my own filth and wretchedness. Gasping and moaning, I throw myself into his arms to find an antidote to my crimes.

Behind Every Shadow

I

It's the details of my to-do list that keep me from turning to stone, that help me to keep moving. With Graci's help, I find a reliable college student willing to fulfill the rest of my housesitting commitment to Cassandra. Goodbye gentle horses, farewell stunning vistas. I move back into my own house with Diego. Though he is more inclined to spend his time at Señor Rivera's, he does seem comforted by my presence, and truth be told, I too, feel less distraught when I am in the old man's company. The task of sorting through my mother's things can only be attempted when Graci is there with me. She doesn't have to be in the room, just nearby. There are so many ghosts. I feel my amiga quietly observing me from time to time as I cull through her belongings and pack box after box to give to shelters and Goodwill. When night comes, I await for her last visit, restless and unsettled in my own bed, the last bed she slept in.

My mother, in the last few years, had insisted that she be cremated when the time came. We used to talk about taking a trip back to the avocado orchard to visit my father's grave and see if it might be possible for my mother to be buried beside him. But in these last years, she was adamant that she would see him soon enough without their decaying dead bodies having to be laid next to each other. A bit grotesque, yet I thought I could see her point. She wanted her ashes to travel with the wind. Unlike most people in New Mexico who become irritable and agitated by the strong relentless spring winds, my mother loved them. There are voices in the wind, she would say. Ancient songs deposited with the ancient soils into the circular currents of the world. How often I have watched her with an ear cocked like a curious puppy, listening. Just soulfully listening. I gave her an unconditional assurance that when the time came, I would honor her wishes. Now she waits for release within a beautiful handmade wooden box that Señor Rivera insisted on carving. In my sorrow, this detail seemed too overwhelming, so I conceded to his offering, his gift to my mother.

Graciela and John have been working on a memorial service for Alice. She had so many friends that I never knew about in Albuquerque. Melanie was the one who made us aware of them and how sad they all were. Since her revelation, my phone and mailbox have been inundated with so many blessings and condolences, that I felt I was compelled to honor my mom's friendships with these people by giving them a way to celebrate her. So, in a week's time, a gathering will be held at a lodge that is situated part way up a mountain road surrounded by trees and sky and hopefully her song amplified in the wind. There, embraced by the comforting arms of evergreens and aspens, we will honor the life of my mother.

Diego and I were the only ones who went to see her body before it was cremated. We needed to grieve her in our own ways. He, to mourn the loss of the one who loved him in a way that probably saved him from a life of unimaginable hardships; and me, I had to find a way to make my conscious mind believe and understand that I would never feel her touch, hear her voice, or feel her mother love again. Graciela and John waited outside the building for us. I know we came out looking more ghostly than we went in.

Diego seems changed, sadder and even less childlike. There is strange clarity in his brown eyes, and he hasn't worn his cap in days. He is worried. In two days, my daughter Olivia and my granddaughter Skyler will arrive from London where they have been living while Olivia has been studying to become an art therapist. The boy won't say, but I'm pretty sure, he is fretting about losing his new status as my kid when my genetic family gets here. I can't seem to find the words that will reassure him, and I see him clinging more and more to Rafael, spending his time with the man and Maca. I catch him staring at me strangely sometimes, but when I ask him if anything is wrong, he just shakes his head and apologizes.

I did register him at one of our local elementary schools, much to his disapproval. "Did you think you were done at the ripe old age of ten, almost eleven?" I had asked when he offered me a sour look.

"Ever heard of homeschooling?" he answered with a scowl aimed at me, his new transgressor and now, parental authority. I also made a dentist appointment for him.

Charlie Walker has called several times. Somehow that whole fiasco now seems like one inexplicable adventure that I made up just to pass the time in my former life. But what is very real is how things unfolded for Gabriel. Charlie did worry about Gabriel's state of mind. He fussed over the boy's ongoing weakness and disconnectedness from the real world, so he took him to see Cheryl, a retired nurse who had helped his wife remain at home during the end stages of her terrible illness. "Cheryl's opinion," Charlie insisted, "is worth all that bloated nonsense that those so-called professionals spout off." It's obvious, he possesses no great love for medical institutions. "Other than a tenderness at the base of his skull, a bit of malnutrition, and "the typical demeanor of one who is on the spectrum", Cheryl pronounced him sound enough to return to Charlie's care.

"Do you know what that means," I ask, "to be on the spectrum?"

"Damn straight, I know. She explained the whole thing to me, not that I give a good goddamn about psychological explanations for why we are what we are. I'm sure people got a feed bin full of 'em for me."

I laugh. "Well, I got nothing for you except a kind and caring man. And I should know since it is kind of my profession." I chuckle again.

"Oh, and by the way," Charlie grumbled, "that damn coyote dog followed us all the way back to my place. Never saw the clever little ghost dog until we got back from Cheryl's, and there he was, layin' on my front porch like he owned the place."

Charlie took Gabriel to see his sister, and the three of them, becoming as thick as thieves, came up with a plan. Charlie insisted that Gabe continue to stay with him until he was feeling better. He offered to get the sister and brother together frequently and Sofia loved the idea. She sent them home with remedies from her stockpile for just about every ailment the two came up with.

"I can use the boy's help around the ranch," Charlie contended. "When he's up to it, of course." "Of course," I had answered, smiling a bit smugly on the other end of the line. Looks like maybe, Charlie finally got a son, and Gabriel, well maybe both he and his sister will find family in this gentle Grizzly Adams of a man. This was a chapter I never would have predicted. His condolences for the loss of my mother were so heartfelt that I lost it and sobbed into the phone. He refused to hang up until I could at least breathe again, all the while quietly saying just the right words in his soft grumbly voice.

Grieving is not a thing that you come to the end of and move on. It has become a living part of me. Like a bloodborne pathogen, it inhabits my body and leaves me feverish and shaky when it so chooses. I am one who must move through the haze of these Alice-less days of late August. She has not come to me. I have not yet said my goodbyes, but in the process of packing up her many things from my house, I did find a letter sealed in its snug little envelope. She had carefully printed my name with a blue pen across the front and left it for me to find. I hold it, sniff it trying to catch her scent, and then clutch it next to my heart. All this on a daily basis, but I cannot find the courage to open it, and so each day I put it back on the dresser next to her picture.

II

The day is unusually cloudy and a little cool for this time of year, particularly here in the mountains. The lodge smells of smoke and cedar, its log construction simple and rustic. A roaring fire has been lit in the large fireplace built of river rock and sweat. Folding chairs have been placed in an informal scattering around the hearth's comforting blaze and crackle, and the number of friends and family who have turned out is both heartwarming and heartbreaking.

Olivia is more beautiful than the day I last saw her, maybe a little too thin, her skin, London-pale and luminous, her hair a long brown cascade pulled back into a high ponytail today which makes her seem younger than her twenty-five years. She grieves her grandmother with silent tears that appear without warning. She too anguishes over the fact that not only did she not get the opportunity to say goodbye, but she also has not seen her grandma in person since last Christmas. Skyler, on the other hand, is a bundle of five-year-old friskiness blended with a playful silliness that cuts through the solemnity of the day like a laser beam. She has even bedazzled the new somber Diego and whisked him off into a magical childish diversion, the kind that has sadly been in short supply for a boy with so much loss to call his own. I watch from the split rail balcony of the lodge as the two race between the trees with Maca at their heels. Skyler picks up a stick and casts spells while Diego twirls in a frenzy of spell-bound dizziness and finally tumbles into a dried pile of pinecones and needles.

While I am watching them play, Sunny appears at my side. I can't help but glance at her abdomen. I notice a small bulge under the fabric of the plain blue dress that drapes gracefully over her slender profile. Her dark blue trench coat hangs open, allowing me this glimpse of either the emerging baby bump or perhaps it is only the one inconsequential flaw I look for on this perfect female body. We all have flaws, right? I don't remember inviting Sunny. That unfriendly notion must be reflected in my eyes when I silently look up at her. She smoothes a wrinkle in the fabric over that bump, then turns fully on to face me.

"I'm so sorry, Martha." Her smile wilts and her eyes seem to well up with tears. "Your mother must have been an exceptional woman to have brought a saint like you into this world."

Feeling flustered, I am about to regurgitate a few stiff words and send her on her way, when I remember that this is a woman who essentially grew up without a mother. Her loss of motherly love came early; when she was just a girl. Guilt makes me think better of what I was about to say; besides her words, most likely just trite funeral remarks made to a person with loss. Instead, I offer her a half smile. Her response is dramatic and predictable. She enfolds me in a sweeping Sunny hug that almost lifts me off my feet. It's awkward and quite embarrassing, so I peek to see if anyone is watching. The air pinches in front of me, quivering in tiny swells. Time or motion or perhaps just some glitch in my brain slows this world down around me or maybe it's my own heart weakening. I find myself melting drowsily into her arms, at once consoled by the strength and buoyed by the love born into that embrace. In every way, I am a child, and it is my papa who offers me these arms to fall into, to soothe me. And here in his arms, I grasp his message, his appeal to release my mother, his firm bidding, as he draws Alice closer to him. I raise my arms and wrap them around him. I feel his heart beating beneath my breast, his warm breath on my cheek.

"Martha. Sunny. We're ready to begin." It's John's voice coming from the door. I can hear the nuance of satisfaction in his voice, and it provokes me to pull away from Sunny, red-faced and suddenly agitated. He smiles. "Graciela wants to be the first to speak. She wants you there. Says she has some humdinger memories she doesn't want you to miss." He takes my hand and grins at Sunny. "I wouldn't want to miss it either. I saved two seats for you ladies, just inside the door."

I allow myself to be led into the room. For just a moment, Sunny grabs my other hand. Her grasp is warm and firm, reassuringly unfaltering, and I return the handhold. We pass by the table that is so beautifully graced with the box that holds all that is left of Alice's earthly body. There is an impressive array of photos scattered singly and in albums and small mementos that her friends were encouraged to bring. Tall beeswax candles flicker against the dim light of the room and a calming fragrance of sandalwood and frankincense smokes from several sticks of incense that Graci created just for the occasion.

Graci, in her black slacks and dark leather coat, steps forward to a place beside the fireplace. Her short thick hair is pushed back from her forehead revealing the two paths of silver that travel from temple backward. She stands tall and undeniable in front of the gathered flock. She, who is my soul friend, looks upon me with an amused challenge in her brown eyes.

She begins. "Alice was one like so many, who was fated to be a single mother. What she probably did not expect was the rearing of a daughter who would provoke such challenging contests of will and giftedness. I first met the two of them in Flagstaff Arizona, where Marta and I attended the same junior high and Alice took a job as the office secretary. I cannot tell Alice's stories without telling Martha's. Their lives are the warp and weft of an intricately dyed fabric woven in the tangled fashion of mothers and daughters. There lies the texture of blood and genes, the colors of wisdom and struggle and the patterns of the heart, just as it should be for mothers and daughters." She takes a moment to look at the faces that are turned to hers. When her penetrating gaze turns to me, my own eyes are red and wet with tears.

John leans into me and wraps an arm around my shoulder as he whispers in my ear, "Graciela is an amazing wordsmith. You are so blessed with her friendship." His voice is rough and emotional, and I gently press my face into his shoulder in acknowledgment of his words and to soak up the tears.

"First, before I regale you all with one of these charming stories, I would like to share with you the Alice that I have grown to know through all these years. Alice has always been a woman of character and strength. Her dedication to helping others extended far beyond her daughter and her daughter's friend. She has always reached out to those around her. In Flagstaff, she was a member of a team of faculty who, on a weekly basis, put together packs of food and supplies that were given to students whose families were challenged just to meet their children's basic needs. In Albuquerque, as many of you know, she visited nursing homes and read to those whose eyesight no longer allowed them to crack the pages of their favorite books. And out of love and her ongoing devotion to children, she just recently brought our young friend Diego into our lives. That is Alice. That and so much more."

Graciela grabs a folding chair from next to the fireplace and settles into it. "Now for the stories."

If anybody can portray the life of my mother, it is Graciela. Graci who has her own amazing gift of seeing people as they truly are. And I am grateful that she has chosen to do this, because I feel certain that I would not have the strength to speak to my mom's importance and the love that I have for her, without completely breaking down. I sit back and listen as Graciela weaves her stories and bewitches every one of the good people gathered here.

When she is done and there is a palpable need for a few moments of quiet reflection, John moves to the front of the room. His guitar is leaning against the wall, and he picks it up and sits in Graci's chair. With his instrument cradled like an infant in his arms, his fingers possessed with musical grace, they strum and pick upon the strings as if directed by angels. The spell that a musician such as John can gently conjure lures those who listen into the deepest chambers of the human heart. The room is his. After John's offering, Alice's gracious friends begin to come forward with their own memories. So deeply and lovingly they honor the departing soul of my mother.

III

I listen, and drift, and remember, as the voices recall my mother. At times I wander into my own memories and linger there in a dreamy state. It's not until an odor of smoke worms its way into my consciousness that I stir and look around the room for the source. It's the smell of cigarette smoke and the unlikeliness that someone would be smoking in this room that sparks my attention. I wonder for a moment if I am imagining it. It only takes a glance to discover the source. The smoke-laced breeze from the open door leads my nose to the balcony where stands a gentleman dressed in a sophisticated suit of mourning. His dark sable-colored overcoat is trim and falls just above the knees of his immaculately pressed trousers. The matching dapper fedora is cocked slightly to the side and, for this reason, I cannot see his face, only the hat and the curlicues of smoke that rise from beneath the brim. I watch as he returns his gloved hand to rest casually on the railing holding a cigarette inserted into a silver old-fashioned cigarette holder. I see the small red glow of the tip and a thin trail of smoke swirled by the breeze. I smile to myself. Perhaps an admirer of Alice's. She did have her charms, even at her age. Suddenly, it's as if he can hear my thoughts and he gently smothers the glowing cherry of the cigarette against the rail and after giving just the tip a pinch, I see the package he pulls from his pocket. Carefully, he removes the barely burned cigarette, leaving it on the rail and deposits the holder in a pocket. Thus begins his slow dramatic pirouette that reveals that this is no bloody gentleman.

No longer do my lips turn upward with my wishful thinking. He finishes his circle facing me fully, momentarily filling the space of the open door with his wretched silhouette. His head cocks to the right as he draws that evil gloved hand that had just held his cigarette to his heart in a gesture of mocking grief. It is the demon himself, in the flesh. My vision wavers and my heart boils. Mr. Misterioso. He achieves such an expression of contemplative sorrow that it precipitates a wave of nausea in me, and I think I might lose it here in this room. The red port wine stain on the left side of his face glows like blood and as he moves his hand from his heart to his hat, he lifts it an inch above his balding claret stained skull. I stand abruptly, and quickly glance at John on my right and Sunny on my left. They are raptly engrossed in the woman who is speaking to Alice's involvement with her mother in a nursing home. I rise from my chair and clumsily excuse myself. John looks up and nods with a smile, but quickly turns his gaze back to the speaker.

The balcony is empty. He is no longer there, but I rush out the door, just the same. My gaze swings right, then left with a sense of horror growing in me by the minute. My god, I wonder, did he have something to do with my mother's death? I lean out over the rail and search for him. The clouds have turned. They are denser, their hue, the deep mauve of a fresh bruise. The wind picks up and blows the hem of my dress, wickedly baring my thighs. It is when I look up from securing this mischief that he reveals himself below me. With a tortured grimace on his face, he steps from behind the trunk of a tree. Removing his hat and holding it to his chest, the beast glowers at me, his cold orb eyes burning needles of dry ice into my chest.

I ignite like a match put to dry pine needles, and throw a raging glare back at him. For an eternity our eyes are locked, and I cannot, do not want to, turn away. In that unbearable coupling, the flickering frames from the film of our many lives together flash through my brain, a series of fantastical movie clips, the accounting of so many lives lived in our eternal struggle between good and evil. I see it with a clarity that I have never before witnessed, the scars that we have inflicted on each other, the bloodshed in the name of our souls. I see the paths we have chosen, forever intertwined in the ferocity of metamorphosing. The clashing of choices clangs in my ears like the echo of deadly swords. There is no predestination, there is free will, the swords resound; they are voices forged of metal and fire. I choose good, he commands evil. Battles won and lost and won again. It is in this timeless moment that I choose to recognize the very elemental structure of his soul. But this time, I see his soft spot, his vulnerability, and I bind the knowledge of this Achilles heel into every cell of this earthly body.

He looks away first and I am abruptly emboldened by his withdrawal. I search for and find resolve. It is a vision that will carry me through this lifetime. I hope. For I am no longer afraid.

What I am now, is dogged in my belief that I can vanquish his poison, and should I stay relentless in my courage, I pray I will be capable of protecting those around me.

Turning from the sorcerer demon, I leave Misterioso before he can have the satisfaction of walking away from me. John is standing in the doorway. His expression defies definition but likely holds a mixture of fear for me, bewilderment and fascination. I smile and reach up to kiss his cheek.

"I think it's my turn to speak about Alice," I say. Slipping past him, I walk with a new resolve, back into the room.

The Letter

To my baby, my girl, the amazing woman who is my daughter:

There are so many thoughts that I want to share with you. You have found this letter. I have moved on. There are things that I will be able to explain to you and maybe some that I will have no words for. You know better than I that words are merely tools of the brain and mouth, but the language of the soul is spoken without words. As I have always done with you my sweetpea, I will do my best. As you have for me, please be patient.

You have been my greatest teacher, daughter. In the beginning, because of you, I secretly began a quest. That which you simply seemed to experience as glimpses into past lives, became for me, the choice of a path that would lead to a lifetime of searching for understanding. At first I simply wanted to know what my adolescent daughter was afflicted with. I searched for answers. Unbeknownst to you, there were doctors, psychologists, psychiatrists, fortune tellers, palm readers, psychics, a minister and a priest. Their theories and their advice varied and all gave me food for thought and reasons to believe, but none satisfied the hunger to keep plumbing the depths of the unknown. An obsession I kept from you for fear you would interpret it as evidence that your mother thought there was something wrong with you. You never did know, did you?

The loss of your Daddy, when you and I were both so young and unprepared for a life on our own, was part of the catalyst that created a determination in me to do everything I could to protect you and at the same time, nurture your wild little self. I hoped that you would never suffer, but learned, often from you, that hardships are what grow our spirit. Then as your only parent, I wished at least to fortify you with the deftness it would take to navigate the pain and insults that life would inevitably bring to one as gifted as yourself. I know I was over-protective and fretful. At times I felt inadequate and depressed, and I was sure that I had failed miserably at being the right mother for the miracle that you were and still are. At times I could feel you pushing against me, pulling away from me and this was more terrifying than you could possibly imagine. Or maybe now with your own daughter and granddaughter, you do know what I'm talking about. But the one thing, Martha, that gave me courage and the will to go on, was the knowledge and the faith that there does really exist a recycling of the soul. This was the saving grace that you opened my eyes to. It let me believe that all the years of dreaming and yearning for your daddy were not just that. They were missives from my love that one day, I would be reunited with him. Your daddy, my husband died... but he never left me. And as time passed, his guidance and presence appeared to me every day in every way.

As our time came nearer, there were night visits and days of feeling his constant presence. His voice, his ethereal closeness was ever-present and his ghost, if you will, would find me when I most needed him, when I cried out for his guidance. Sometimes it happened when I merely needed his companionship. He never let me stop believing that I would see him again. He never wavered in his faith that we would be together again. As time went on, my sweet, I knew that he whispered the truth. For your sake and mine, I have spent a lifetime combing through literature and holy books, poetry and essays. I've paged through documents and treatises, all in search of this thing, this afterlife some call reincarnation, transmigration, rebirth. There are so many who believe they understand this progression and write so eloquently about the transformation. Believe me, daughter, the years I spent with my secret studies have definitely not been a waste but in the end, I knew that when the time came it would be your daddy's voice I would trust.

My husband would vanquish my fears and confusion, embrace my soul with peace and the knowledge that I had fulfilled and been filled by the lessons of this life. Sweet Pea, this, he has done. Now it is time, time that loops the wheel back to me, picks me up and delivers me to a new life. You, without really knowing, helped me to understand what I understand. Only now as I write this do I regret that I never shared this part of me with you. You have always been brave and forthright and used what you have to make sense of an incongruous world. You, daughter, have helped so many to do this.

I have never come any closer to knowing why you were given the gifts you have, my daughter. I do not know why I have given the gift of your father's ghost. What I do know is that you have chosen to use them well, to help and to heal. I know that you will find peace and a new place on the wheel by continuing that mission. You have so many left in your world to love and who love you. I beg you, please daughter, do not be sad. I feel joy and confidence in these moments before my journey. And if in my leaving, I can do for you what your father did for me, believe me, my love, I will try. With an eternity of love for you, I whisper goodbye and leave you with the lines from a poem you composed in your teen years. Imagine as you read it, how I have cherished it and saved it all this time, my sweet, whose love of poetry has never escaped me. Be strong, Sweet Pea.

Your Mother in this life and...

Is it but one life we are granted?
I had wondered, but now know not.
Is there but one path to panacea?
That by no means seems the plot.
Is this my soul recycled and reborn?
If such is the way, why have I forgot?
Is it my destiny to see but not be?
Will I forever live blind of my own?

Thank you for reading the second book in the Hooper's Junction series.

Your support is greatly appreciated!

Don't forget to leave a review of the book wherever you picked it up.

For more information about Hooper's Junction and other book releases go to HoopersJunction.com

Or get in direct contact with me by email at kkcrews@hoopersjunction.com

Made in the USA
Middletown, DE
17 August 2024